PRESUMPTION
OF GUILT

PRESUMPTION OF GUILT

LELIA KELLY

Kensington Books
http://www.kensingtonbooks.com

KENSINGTON BOOKS are published by

Kensington Publishing Corp.
850 Third Avenue
New York, NY 10022

Library of Congress Card Catalog Number: 97-073753
ISBN 1-57566-249-3

First Kensington Hardcover Printing: February, 1998
10 9 8 7 6 5 4 3 2 1

Printed in the United States of America

For my Parents

ACKNOWLEDGMENTS

Many good wishes came my way as I wrote this book, accompanied often by hard labor—proofreading, editing, and cheerleading. Special thanks are owed to Kay Kidde and Laura Langlie, who saw great potential where I was timid, and to John Scognamiglio of Kensington, who is a pleasure to work with. All the friends who believed deserve thanks, too: Paul Amador, Jan Butsch, Katherine Charapko, Russell Galen, David Hancock, Cindy Hockenhull, Kathy Jones, Kae Jonsons, Lex Kelso, Jack and Anne Koo, Susan Lipsitch, Jill Parsons, Dave Stern, Deb Strek, Carmel Tuths, Chris Westbrook, and Dr. Martin York and his staff. I owe Cameron and Grantland for making me smile every day, and my family for not questioning my decision to give up a "real" job to write books.

1

You've just been found "not guilty" of a felony, even though everyone in the city thinks you did it. What are you going to do next? Laura Chastain watched as Alex Hunicutt Jr. whooped, and turned around to high-five his buddies, the testosterone-poisoning cases who had hulked in the gallery throughout the three weeks of his trial, so identical in form and function that they had merged, in Laura's mind, into one bull-necked, multilegged, living, breathing sperm bank. She glanced at the jurors, filing out of the room, looking back over their shoulders, already second-guessing, regretting, and formulating the excuses they would make to the television cameras. *The prosecution didn't make its case . . . we would have liked to send him away for some time . . . there was reasonable doubt. . . .* It was a new American ritual: the miscarriage of justice and its televised aftermath. Laura shoved her papers back into her case and snapped it shut, wanting to get out of the courtroom as quickly as she could. With luck, she might avoid the cameras. She knew a back way out of the building, and, with the jurors as a diversionary sop to the media, she might manage to sneak down the hallway unnoticed . . .

"Nice job, Counselor." Her hopes of getting away without recrimination were shattered; she turned and faced Amos Kowalski, the head of the Atlanta Police Department's sex-crimes squad. "I especially liked the part where you talked about what she was wearing. You know, I never knew the words *three-inch heels* could sound so . . . dirty."

His eyes traveled down to her own shoes; she had to stop herself from telling him that their heels were no more than two inches high, if that, and that she was only wearing them, anyway, to appear more imposing to the jury, that it was different, it was *business*. But she didn't; she picked up her briefcase, shouldered her purse, and looked him squarely in the eye. "Gee, I'd really love to stay and discuss the semiotics of female footwear with you, Lieutenant, but I've got to be going."

"Why? Got an axe-murderer you need to spring? Did the cops forget to get a search warrant to look in the refrigerator for body parts?"

Laura felt herself growing angry, and she knew she was about to say something she would regret, but that didn't stop her from saying it, anyway. "You know, Kowalski, for a guy who didn't do his job, you're pretty quick to jump on me. Has it occurred to you that if you hadn't tried to make this into a media circus, if you had settled quietly and quickly when I offered to, you might not look like such an almighty gooberhead right now?"

"Gooberhead? Strong language, Counselor. But you're pretty good at name-calling. Why didn't you just go ahead and call Cheri Moore a slut? Would that have saved some time?"

Laura's eyes narrowed. "Face it, Lieutenant: You lost. You decided to try to make a show trial out of a nothing case. I don't know what you were trying to accomplish—are you bucking for a promotion or something? Did you think it might look good on your résumé to send the son of a prominent local businessman to jail? Well, deal with it; you made a mistake. You tried to paint a champagne-swilling, cocaine-snorting opportunist as a rape victim. All I did was point out that she said 'yes' to pretty much everything until the clock struck midnight, when she apparently turned back into a virgin. Juries aren't stupid, you know; they heard her story and his. They bought his. Get *over* it."

"I'm already over it, believe me. Are you, though? I'm just curious about how you plan to justify this to yourself when you hear that Hunicutt's been arrested again. Because he will be, you know; he's done this before and he'll do it again. But what if the next girl ends up with more than just a few bruises? How will you feel then?"

"You know something, Kowalski? Your naïveté shocks me. For a cop, I mean—you're acting as if this is the first time anyone ever held a woman accountable for her actions. Find the clue bus and flag it down: It's always been this way. And you know something else? There's nothing wrong with it. It is not an infringement of a girl's human rights to tell her that, when she's out with a man she doesn't know, maybe she shouldn't suck down a quart of booze, and then hoover in a bunch of coke, because she might just lose control of the situation. It's the advice my grandmother and mother gave me, and if I ever have a daughter, it's what I'll tell her." She waved her hand toward the empty jury box. "Every one of the members of that jury was wondering from day one *why* Cheri Moore went home with a man she only met in a bar that night—after, of course, she let him buy her enough drinks to float the Navy. Not to mention the illegal drug usage, which you tried so hard to keep out of testimony, Lieutenant. My client—" she glanced at the still-celebrating Alex "—was my best evidence. There wasn't a parent on the jury who would want their daughter hanging around a man like that. They would expect her to have more *sense*. They expected the same of Cheri Moore."

"So at least you admit you were defending a little thug. And what about his behavior?"

"Alex has a transactional mind," Laura answered. "If he gives something—like a line of coke—he wants something in return. In this case, it was sex. Why are you holding him to a higher standard than Cheri Moore, anyway? You think men have the control chromosomes that we lil' girls lack?"

"Don't be ridiculous," he said, dismissing her sarcasm with a wave of his hand. "But any man worth a damn knows that a woman's not consenting if he has to put his hands around her neck to get her to stop screaming."

It was true that the photos taken of the girl on the night of the attack—the *alleged* attack—had shown a red ring around her neck. Laura had managed to get the jury past it, by focusing on the larger issue of the "victim"'s behavior, but when she had first seen the police file, her instinct had been to plead it out. Alex might even have done a little time for assault, if Kowalski had just listened to her all those months ago. But no, Kowalski and the district attorney had insisted on a felony rape charge. And who knows? Hunicutt might even have learned a lesson in jail—maybe there would not be the "next time" that Kowalski predicted, and that Laura, too, knew was as depressingly inevitable as the next Eagles reunion tour. So why hadn't he just smelled the dadburned coffee back then, last summer, when all this could have been avoided? What had he expected her to do— roll over, and let the son of her firm's biggest client go to the slammer? Say, "Gee, Kowalski, I guess you're right—let's send this boy to *jail,* where he belongs." Then maybe she could have gotten into that exciting career in telephone sales she had always wanted. Who needs to make partner at the best law firm in Atlanta, anyway? She wanted to swing out her foot, in its high-heeled pump, and kick Kowalski sharply in the shin. More sexual violence, but he was *asking* for it, after all. Her mouth twitched involuntarily; Laura had a strong sense of the ridiculous, and the idea of getting into a slap-fight with Kowalski—who towered over her—tickled her.

"What? You think this is funny?" he asked, annoyed.

"No, it's not that. Look, I'm tired, you're tired—let's talk about this some other time, okay?" She smiled, in an effort to end the conversation on a pleasant note, and stuck out her hand. He refused to shake it.

"I don't think I have anything to discuss with you, Ms. Chastain. Have a nice day." He turned on his heel and left, leaving Laura, hand still outstretched, to gape after him. Her hand was instantly seized, though, in a muscle-bound grip.

Alex Hunicutt Jr. was one of those huge blond guys who spend far too much time in the gym, and far too little lifting books and newspapers. Some women might find all that muscle tissue attractive, but Laura was not among them. She preferred men who could capture dinner in the frozen-food aisle, not kill it with their bare hands. Under ordinary circumstances, Alex would have been unemployable, but Alexander Hunicutt Sr., a local construction-development magnate, had hired his offspring as soon as that young man had managed to squeak out a degree in management from a third-rate institution of higher learning. Little Alex bore the impressive title "Vice President of Operations," a vaguely defined post which allowed him a nice office, a company car, and lots of time in the company fitness center, the design of which was one of Alex's few concrete accomplishments. He was probably just something else to grin and bear at Hunicutt Construction, a place, she gathered, where working conditions were stalaglike at the best of times. She withdrew her hand from its fleshy prison, and accepted Alex's accolades.

"God, Laura, you're great. I mean, you were just *great.* Man, I was nervous, though, weren't you? I mean, when that jury came back in, they weren't smiling, or looking at me, or anything. I thought if they were going to find me innocent they were supposed to make eye contact with me."

Laura looked at her client—her *former* client, now, thank God—and shook her head. "In the first place, Alex, they found you 'not guilty.' There's a world of difference between being 'not guilty' and being innocent. And they didn't look at you because they were ashamed of what they were about to do. If they could have, trust me, they would have sent you to jail for the maximum sentence possible. *They didn't like you,* okay? This was not a vindication for you. But they listened to the judge's instructions, thank God, and they didn't get swayed by emotions."

Alex looked wounded, his petulant mouth turning down at the corners. Laura had hurt his feelings. Good, she thought. Let him run to his daddy and tell him she was mean to him. "Look, Alex, I have to get back to the office. I suggest you go straight home. Do *not* say anything to those reporters, do you hear me?" He nodded, still clearly unhappy.

She sighed. "You better come with me; I know a way out. Is one of your buddies going to give you a ride home?" Odd, she thought, that his father wasn't here to perform that office. Odd, in fact, that he hadn't showed his face at all during the trial, although he had called Laura every night for what he referred to as a "debriefing" on the day's events. Alex's mother was dead, and he was an only child, so Laura had expected more of a show of support from the old man. He'd pay her bill, though; maybe that passed for affection chez Hunicutt.

She led Alex to the back of the courtroom and opened the door; to her relief, the hallway was almost deserted, and the few people in it didn't seem terribly interested in talking to her. She held the door for Alex and his adherents, who tried to squeeze through at once, in a single, steroidal mass. She shook her head; they were lucky to have been born rich, these guys—they certainly weren't going to make it in the world by dint of their animal cunning. They finally managed to get into the hall, and she steered them, buffalolike, toward the exit. They had almost made it when she heard someone calling Alex's name.

She turned and saw Sally Rivers, the sassy investigative reporter for Channel Two's evening news, racing toward them with her camera and soundmen in tow. Her hair looked *fabulous*. "Oh, no," Laura said. "Alex, shut up. Let me talk. And don't smile." She turned to his friends. "That goes for you, too. *Stop smiling.*" She might as well have been talking to Mount Rushmore, which the four young men who surrounded her resembled.

"Ms. Chastain, can I talk to you for a minute?" Sally Rivers clattered toward them down the marble hall in her ridiculous little shoes.

"We have no comment," Laura said.

Sally took that as a "Yes", and the cameraman began filming. "We're here with a Channel Two *exclusive*—Alex Hunicutt and his attorney are leaving the courthouse after Hunicutt was found not guilty of raping Cheri Moore. Alex, how do you feel right now?"

Laura took a step back and ground her heel into Alex's foot. "Owww," he said.

"We have no comment," Laura added.

Sally persisted. "Does this mean that you'll be returning to work for your father, Alex?"

"He has no comment," Laura said. Alex didn't make a peep.

"What about you, Ms. Chastain? As a woman, what do you think about the Georgia Women's Defense League protest going on outside the courthouse right now?"

Laura hadn't been aware that there was a protest, but her heart sank at the news. She answered Sally's questions, though, with a tinge of sarcasm. "As an *attorney,* all I know is that a jury of twelve people just found my client not guilty of the charges against him. If anyone has a problem with that, I suggest they take it up with the jury."

Sally furrowed her brow in an expression of deep, deep concern. "But don't the protesters have a point, Ms. Chastain? Shouldn't you, as a woman, be discouraging this sort of blame-the-victim defense?"

Laura felt anger rising in her. Surely the protesters could have found a better poster child than Cheri Moore. She wondered if they were aware of Cheri's pending civil suit, running to the millions of dollars, against Alex. This whole thing had been about money, and nothing but, since Alex flashed his bankroll in that bar and Cheri ran panting to his side.

Laura looked at Sally levelly, and answered her in a calm voice. "Everyone is entitled to an opinion, and everyone is guaranteed the right to express that opinion. In this case, though, only twelve opinions counted."

With that Laura turned, and began walking toward the exit, Alex and his phalanx with her. She instructed one of the more alert-looking ones to get his car, and to bring it back to pick up Alex. She ordered him home, but she knew without asking that he would be hitting every bar in Buckhead within hours. Suddenly very tired, she trudged to her own car.

She started back toward midtown, to the office, but she changed her mind before she got there, and turned toward home. There, she opened a bottle of wine, and drew a hot bath. She let the answering machine pick up on her calls: The office wanted to know if she would be coming back in. Her mother wanted to know when she would be coming for Christmas. Then, a hissing anonymous woman threatened to destroy her for having defended Alex Hunicutt Jr. Laura wondered why it was that activists lacked any sense of irony—this one apparently felt that threatening a woman was the most effective way to combat violence against women. *Thank God that I don't have to take myself that seriously,* she thought. She returned the calls to the office, and her mother; then she ordered a pizza, and ate it, glazed and passive, in front of the television.

At eleven, she switched to Channel Two; Alex's acquittal was the top story of the day. After a lead-in from the studio, they flashed to Sally Rivers reporting from the courthouse. In a few seconds, Laura saw her own image appear on the screen. She leaned in closer. Do I really look like that, she asked herself, so *severe?* She looked petite, anyway, surrounded by Alex's mountainous pals, and nothing she said was in the least indiscreet. It was all very lawyerly, in fact, which she hoped the partners of Prendergrast and Crawley would note if they were watching. Television appearances were frowned upon at the firm; in fact, P&C usually turned aside sensational cases—unless, of course, a valued client was involved. Laura thought they should unbend a little; it's not as if they had to pursue the tabloid cases, but some controversy, some publicity, might actually be good.

She turned off the television when they switched to coverage of the kidnapping and rape of a young girl. Now that, Laura thought, is what rape is. She hoped Kowalski would forget his vendetta against Alex in light of this new case—heck, she hoped everyone would forget Alex. She felt guilty for being grateful that a child's rape could benefit her, but at least she could tell them tomorrow at the office that something else would soon replace the Hunicutt case as Atlanta's cause célèbre, and Prendergrast and Crawley could go on its way, as it had for seventy-five years, undisturbed by reality.

WTLK: All talk, all the time. We know what's on your mind—and we want everyone else to know it, too. You're listening to the Scott Ressler show, and we're talking about those craaaazy feminists. We have a caller on line one—Dave from Austell, are you there?

Hey, man. Am I on?

You are, my friend. What's on your mind?

You're the greatest, man. I listen to you all the time. You rule, man. . . .

(Laughter) You don't get out of Austell much, do you, Dave? Do you have a comment, or do you just want to hump my leg?

Yeah, man, I want to say . . . you know . . . that trial, that Hunicutt guy . . . man, he didn't rape nobody.

That's not what the cops thought, Dave.

The cops don't stand for nothin' no more. It's all politics, man . . . you know, they just wanted to nail a rich guy. These girls, you know . . . the way they dress, and act, and all . . . then they yell rape when you don't ask 'em to marry you.

But here's the thing that gets to me, Dave: The cop who testified was a man, but the lawyer who got Hunicutt off was a woman. What kind of screwed-up thing is that, when a woman is the only one who'll stand up to these feminists, these "all intercourse is rape" dykes? Thanks for your call, Dave. By the way, Sidekick Mel, did you see the eleven o'clock news? Did you see that girl?

I watched it with you, o great one.

Of course you did. We do everything together, don't we? Did you get a load of that lady lawyer, the one who defended the kid? Whoa, now there's one I could rape (laughter). . . .

2

The following morning, Laura fought her way to the office through the notorious Atlanta traffic. As she lived in-town, she could avoid the interstate, although, when she slowed to a near stop each morning on Peachtree Road in Buckhead, she wondered if she wouldn't be better off on its eight jammed lanes. She could, theoretically, take the MARTA train; she lived within walking distance of a station, and the offices were built practically on top of another station—it would seem ideal. But the catch was that nothing else she needed access to—the Fulton County Courthouse, the State Supreme Court, clients' offices—were located close enough to a train stop to allow her to do her job effectively without a car. That was Atlanta, though; its growth had occurred late enough to allow planners to benefit from the lessons of older cities, but they hadn't. Atlanta, Laura believed, actually *aspired* to be Los Angeles.

Prendergrast and Crawley had its offices in a new, elaborately postmodern office tower in midtown. The offices were one of the firm's few concessions to the late twentieth century; in almost every other respect, the partners insisted on distinctly premodern amenities—coffee in china cups with saucers, and no trousers on the female employees. Computers had been grudgingly recognized as superior to typewriters and carbon paper, but speaker phones were strictly forbidden. All that was fine with Laura; she actually liked the idea that P&C was a little island of graciousness in a graceless world. More substantial issues—like the partners' continued refusal to seek out criminal casework—were more burdensome to her. She knew that, if she were serious about pursuing criminal practice, she would probably have to leave the firm—not a decision she wanted to face, after putting in more than five years as an associate. Too bad she hadn't known, when she joined, that she would discover her talent for getting lawbreakers acquitted.

Laura had planned, while in law school, to become a corporate litigator; criminal law, although interesting to her academically, had seemed sleazy. Criminal practitioners either defended scum, or prosecuted scum for subsistence wages. Corporate was a much sounder career path, she thought—but that was before her boss had referred one of the firm's corporate clients, booked for a DUI, to her. Laura had loved the trip to night court, and had started asking for those assignments when they arose. Her boss, a litigator with no time for nonsense, happily acceded to her demands. It was always made clear, however, that Prendergrast & Crawley did *not* solicit criminal cases. Still, every so often, an executive finds himself in the wrong seat of a police cruiser, and maybe P&C was the only law firm he knew. Laura had strict instructions to settle cases, or, if they were more complex, to refer them to another firm after handling the initial crisis. She did as she was told, until one client presented her with such a fat, sweet violation of his Fourth Amendment rights that she begged to be allowed to take it all the way. She won, and once her nose was under the tent, she had convinced the firm to allow her to take a few more. Alex had been her fifth successful defense. His had been only her third jury trial, however, and she had been a nervous wreck.

It's good to win, she thought; better, because she needed the victory as ammunition in a discussion she planned to have with her boss this week. She wanted the firm to set up a criminal practice, and she wanted his support.

Laura made her way into her office, a small one, although bigger than those allocated to some of the newer associates. She kept it neat, not because she was especially tidy, but because she knew that if she relaxed her vigilance even for a day, if she failed to return even a few files to the file room when she was finished with them, she would soon be living under waterfalls and cascades of paper. Lawyers put everything on paper, and they keep the paper forever. Only the strong survived; all others would eventually lose a piece of paper that was actually critical to a case.

The design of the office was not conducive to paper storage; there were almost no drawers or filing cabinets in the tiny room. Some clever designer had sold the firm on an expensive "modular" furniture design, which consisted of a wall of sketchy shelving, from which projected a "desk," which Laura compared to an ironing board. Basically a long plank, it was supported on one end by the wall unit, and on the other by a single leg. It had no drawers, and very little surface space—and it had the additional disadvantage of being open underneath, forcing the women of the firm to sit modestly at all times. Or maybe that was the point.

She settled in with a cup of coffee and began sorting through her in-box. The trial had lasted longer than expected, and she had been hard-pressed to keep abreast of her other responsibilities—not that anyone had bothered to ask if she needed help. She performed a quick triage on the mound of paper, and turned her attention to the most urgent matters. A noise made her look up, in time to see a large flower arrangement with legs enter the room. "Good Lord!" she said, getting to her feet. "Here, let me help you with that."

She made a move to help the secretary with the flowers, and was waved off. Cecelia, the secretary Laura shared with several other associates, heaved the flowers onto the corner of the desk. She was a tall, strong woman, in her late thirties, who tended not to bond with her charges; she had seen too many of them burn out and leave, shattered by the work. With Laura, she was more relaxed; Laura looked like one who could last into partnership, which meant that Cecelia could step up as well. Laura knew very little about her, other than that she was divorced, and the sole support of two young children. She was just as happy to have a secretary who didn't demand friendship with her employer; those inevitably led to disaster, Laura had observed.

Cecelia panted with mock exertion. "Thanks, I've got it. Just tell me what you did to deserve these—did you win the Kentucky Derby?"

Laura laughed. "I haven't done anything that I know of. Let's see who they're from; maybe it's a mistake." She fished among the fragrant jungle for a card; her excitement and pleasure were quickly extinguished when she saw the signature on the card. "They're from Mr. Hunicutt—thanking me for getting Alex off."

"Oh, well. They're pretty, anyway."

"Maybe in a hotel lobby, or on the altar at St. Peter's, but don't you think they're a little excessive?"

"Yes, but you know Mr. Hunicutt; he thinks bigger means better. Now, as long as I have your attention, let me catch you up on a couple of things. First, Mr. Scarborough wants to know if you've sold your tickets to the Yule Log yet."

James Scarborough was the firm's managing partner, a fussy little man; the Yule Log was his baby, an annual Christmas fund-raiser. It used to be an all-male event, and Laura, for one, wished it still was. Just her luck to have joined the firm the year the almighty Yule Log went coed. Laura sat down, heavily, and threw her hands up. "No, of course not—I don't know anyone who's willing to pay two hundred dollars to go to a party! Why can't we just have a bake sale or something? No one wants to get dressed up and go to a party with a bunch of lawyers."

"Be that as it may," Cecelia said, sternly, "he'll want to know that you've at least tried. And Libby wants to know if you've received the psychologist's report on Stuart Maulding."

"Yes, I got it, and I sent a copy to Libby two days ago. She's lost it, of course; here—take her another one." She handed Cecelia a copy of the report, and the cover memo she had carefully drafted; she always wrote "C.Y.A." memos to Libby—when you work for someone that disorganized, you'd better Cover Your Ass. Libby Arnold was the firm's "family practice" specialist; she helped rich people divorce each other and fight over their children—like poor Stuart Maulding, a kindergartner who had seen more psychiatrists than clowns in his sad, short life. Libby was one of two partners Laura reported to; family law was not one of Laura's areas of interest or expertise, but there were no other associates who could put up with Libby's work habits, or who were as comfortable in a courtroom as Laura—and Libby's cases did require numerous court appearances. Laura had agreed to work with her only because she knew that all the court time would be a benefit to her career—and it had been, she had to admit. "Anything else?" Laura asked.

"Nope," Cecelia said. "That's it."

"Great. I have a lot to catch up on. Take messages for me, okay? I'm going to plow through as much of this garbage as I can before lunch."

"Will do." Cecelia left, closing the door behind her, and Laura turned to the brief she was preparing for her other boss, Tom Bailey. Bailey was the firm's chief litigator, and his cases were far more interesting than Libby's. He defended corporations against lawsuits of all kinds, and acted as plaintiff's counsel, when it suited him— he only took cases he found intriguing. Hunicutt and Company was a client of Tom's; Alexander Hunicutt Sr. turned to him for advice on everything, and when his son got hauled in on rape charges, Tom had thrown the case to a grateful Laura. Laura had joined P&C for the opportunity of working with Bailey, in fact; some of his cases had set precedents which were taught in law schools. He had made a guest appearance as a lecturer in her second year, and Laura had been chosen to escort him around the campus. When his visit ended, Bailey had casually given her his card and invited her to look him up when she was ready to talk about jobs. No more encouragement had been needed; Laura had arranged an interview with Prendergrast and Crawley as soon as she decently could. She worked for Tom the summer before her third year; when the three months were up, it was a foregone conclusion that she would be invited to join the firm as an associate. She hadn't been disappointed in her choice—at least, not until she had fallen unexpectedly in love with penal law. If she talked to anyone about her growing unhappiness with the firm's lack of criminal practice, it would be Tom, but it wasn't that easy. Laura knew he would be disappointed that she was thinking about leaving; he had done so much for her over the years . . . she quashed the guilt and got to work.

Two hours later, she was immersed in the brief, when a tap at the door broke her concentration. She looked up, annoyed, and saw Cecelia peering around the corner of the door. "Laura? There's a man here to see you. He won't tell me what it's about."

"Did he give a name?"

"Jeff Williams." That was familiar; Laura tried to remember where she had heard the name . . . good Lord, he was a cop, on the sex-crimes squad, one of Lieutenant Kowalski's guys. He had been only peripherally involved in Alex's case; she remembered seeing his name on some reports. She had never bothered to subpoena him, and the prosecution hadn't called him as a witness either. It had been Kowalski's case all the way, as far as she could tell.

"Send him in," she said. He probably just wanted to give her more of what she had gotten from his lieutenant in the courthouse the previous afternoon. Fine; let him rant a little. She straightened the papers on her desk, and in a moment, Cecelia ushered him in. Laura had never met Detective Williams, so she was surprised at the size of the man who entered her office. Jeff Williams was big, linebacker-big, and like a linebacker, he looked as quick as he was strong. She guessed that he was about her age; he had a pleasantly average-looking face, under a head of thinning brown hair, but, as she stood to introduce herself, she noticed something in the set of his mouth that told her that this was a man who took himself seriously. She extended a hand; it was swallowed up by his.

"Detective Williams? I'm Laura Chastain. How can I help you?"

"I think I need a lawyer."

Direct enough; abrupt, even, and certainly not what she had

expected. She indicated a chair. "Really? Why don't you have a seat and tell me about it? Would you like a cup of coffee, a glass of water?" He shook his head. "So why do you think you need an attorney—and why me?"

He sat down, and looked at her levelly. "I saw you on television last night, after you got that little prick off, and Kowalski was bitching about you all through the trial, so I know you're good. I need good." His accent was generic Midwestern; another transplant. Laura, who hailed from Nashville, had almost stopped expecting people to speak with the accent of the region.

"I take it you're in some kind of trouble," she commented.

He laughed. "Didn't you see the paper this morning?"

"I was running kind of late today, so I just had a chance to glance at it. Hang on a second." She walked to the door, called to Cecelia to take messages, closed the door, and returned to her desk. "Go ahead."

He took a deep breath. "A suspect died in police custody late last night. In *my* custody. I think they're going to try to pin it on me."

"Tell me everything," Laura said, pulling a pad from a drawer and preparing to take notes. "Every detail."

"Okay. You heard about the little girl who was raped yesterday afternoon, right? That twelve-year-old?" Laura nodded; this was the very case she had hoped would distract Atlanta from Alex. It was beginning to distract her, at least. Williams went on. "Some guy grabbed her when she was walking home from school, took her to a vacant house, and raped and sodomized her. It was on the news last night."

"I saw the report; it was horrible. Go on."

"Well, we got the guy. He is—was—a punk from the girl's neighborhood. He had no real criminal record—one marijuana possession bust, slapping a girlfriend around once, but no sexual assault record. Anyway, the girl knew him, because he was apparently in the habit of hanging around the schoolyard when classes let out. She picked his mug shot out of a photo lineup, so we got a warrant for his sorry ass. I made the arrest, and I put him in an interrogation room. He wasn't gonna talk without a lawyer, so I left him in there, handcuffed to the table, you know what I mean? And I go off to wait for the public defender to get there so I can question the asshole. When the lawyer finally does come, he goes into the interrogation room and comes out yelling that his client's dead. And sure enough, he is.

Strangled. With a nightstick, maybe; there was a mark across his neck."

"What time did all this happen?"

"I brought the guy in about eleven last night, and processed him . . . the lawyer musta got there some time after midnight."

"Who had access to the interrogation room?"

He laughed, a touch hysterical. "Everyone. The fucking room wasn't locked from the outside—the asshole was handcuffed to the table, which was bolted to the floor. I was worried about him getting out, not about keeping cops out of the room."

"How long was he alone in there?"

"Maybe a half hour. Maybe more. I don't know. I went back to the squad room, talked to Kowalski, got the guy's rap sheet—it took a while for the lawyer to get there. We didn't do anything wrong with the arrest. You can ask the uniforms who went out with me as backups; everything was by the fucking book all the way." His voice grew louder, and he leaned forward in his chair and tapped a finger on her desk to emphasize his point.

"Calm down," Laura ordered him. "I'm not saying you did it, but why would they be so quick to suspect you, if so many other people had access to the room?"

He shrugged. "Fuck me if I know. I think they're going to say that I was enraged, or something, and that I killed him because I hated child molesters. Which I do, of course, but not enough to throttle them with a nightstick."

"Were you enraged last night, with this suspect? Did you say or do anything that might make people think you had it in for him?"

"No way. I was *happy;* ask any of 'em who were there. It was the sweetest arrest I ever made—we get the report of the rape from a neighbor of the girl's at about four. While she was in the emergency room—before we even talked to her, or anything—my partner and I headed down to where he grabbed her. Between five and seven, I talked to a couple of kids who were out playing, asked them if they had seen a man hanging around when they left school. Oh, sure, they say; Corey was there—everybody knows Corey. Turns out the guy's a regular at the schoolyard, likes to look at all the little girls. There are several complaints about him in the files from teachers and parents at the school; the cops ran him off the playground a bunch of times. We show the girl his picture, and she says he's the one. So we get a warrant, and by ten o'clock last night, I'm heading down to his place to arrest him. It was like shooting fish in a barrel. You ask anybody—I was as happy as I could be, not *enraged*. That's a bunch of crap."

"Detective, I need you to be honest with me. You haven't retained me yet, but this conversation is privileged. If you killed this man, if you went a little bit nuts, and got rough, I think I can make a jury understand. He was a rapist, and a child molester; juries hate those guys. But it's going to be awfully hard to convince that same jury that person or persons unknown sneaked into an interrogation room and popped a street hood for some mysterious reason. Do you hear what I'm saying? If you did it, tell me now, and put it in my hands. I'll do my best for you either way."

Williams exploded in a series of blasphemies and obscenities. Laura had met a lot of cops, and she knew that they were prone to colorful language, but she had never met anyone to equal Jeff Williams. She would confidently back him in a scatology contest against a whole team of sailors. The upshot of Williams's outburst was that he hadn't laid a finger on the dead man, and that Laura could take her attorney-client privilege and shove it someplace painful. If his outrage was an act, it was a good one. Laura managed to calm him down, finally, and assure him that she believed him. "Where's the investigation now?" she asked, grateful to move the discussion onto a less emotional topic.

"Internal Affairs is crawling all over our squad room, and the chief is having a press conference at noon. I'm suspended with pay pending the outcome of the investigation, so I'm going home, I guess. But I thought I should stop in here and talk to you first."

"Have you talked to the investigators?"

"Of course. I told the Internal Affairs guys exactly what I told you—that I left the sonofabitch alone to wait for his fucking lawyer. Next time I saw him, he was dead."

Laura sighed. "You should have called me first. Don't say another word to anyone."

"Does that mean you're gonna help me, Ms. Chastain?"

"We'll see, but first, there are a couple of things I need to tell you. First, I'm expensive. I'm not a partner here, and I can't take pro bono cases without partner approval—and I doubt they'd approve this one. Can you pay?"

"I got money. I got some money I inherited. I'll pay anything." He sounded panicked.

"Okay, we'll worry about that later. Second thing—don't talk to another soul. No cops, no reporters. Got it? You only talk to me from here on out. If I can't take your case, I'll find someone who will."

"Okay."

"Now tell me, Jeff, what do you think happened to the guy, if you didn't kill him?"

There was a long silence before he answered. "I dunno. Somebody must have gotten in there and offed him."

"Why?"

"How should I know? He was just another piece of urban shit. Goddamn it, he was a rapist. Whoever did it did us all a favor, that's all I know."

It was time for Laura to broach another serious topic. "Jeff, if this comes down to your being charged, I'll need to know what they can throw at us, so please don't take offense at what I'm about to ask you. Have you ever gotten rough with a suspect before? Ever been brought up on disciplinary charges, that kind of thing? You have to be honest with me."

He hesitated. "No. Well, maybe a time or two, but everyone does, Miss Chastain. You would too, if you saw what we did. . . ."

"But is there anything in your file that could be used to paint you as a brutal cop?"

"No. Once, a suspect filed a complaint that I slapped him around, but it was dismissed after the investigation."

"Very good. Next question: The girl who was raped is black. Can I assume that the suspect was, too?"

"You can assume that, yeah."

"Okay, now, tell me the truth: Can they play the race card? If I take your case, am I going to hear a list of the racial epithets you use when you're alone with your pals?"

"No. No way. Look, I've got no problem with the black people in this city—most of 'em are as honest as you or me. I've had black partners, worked with black cops and crime victims for years. I'm not a fucking racist." Williams was indignant.

"Okay. You understand why I have to ask." Laura put her pen down, sat back in her chair, and looked at Williams. "I'm interested in your case. I want to do some checking on my own, and I need to clear this with the firm. Give me your address and a phone number where you can be reached later today. And get together some financial information for me; we need to demonstrate your ability to pay."

He recited his address and phone, and gave her a cellular phone and beeper numbers as well. "I moonlight a little as a security consultant—

glorified watchman stuff—so I carry a phone and a beeper. But I'll be at home the rest of the day; can't go to work, and the press is on my ass already. I'll be waiting to hear from you."

"Fine. Just remember, 'no comment' is all you can say to anyone. If Internal Affairs comes back after you, tell them you want me there."

"Okay." He rose, relief on his face. "Thanks, Ms. Chastain."

"Call me Laura. We can't be formal if we're going to be working together."

"Thanks. I knew you were the right one; anybody who pisses Kowalski off as bad as you did has to be a good lawyer."

She laughed. "The lieutenant doesn't like to lose, I don't think."

A bitter cloud passed over Williams's face. "No, he doesn't. He sure as hell doesn't."

Laura let the remark pass, and escorted him to the door, with a further admonition not to say anything to anyone. She escorted him to the elevator, and accepted his effusive thanks, and tolerated a crushing handshake. She stood there for a moment, lost in thought as the elevator doors closed.

3

Back at her desk, Laura took out her copy of the morning newspaper. The story of the girl's rape—which had probably been the original lead—was buried in the story of Corey Taylor's arrest and death. That meant that outrage over the original crime would be muffled by the debate over the new one—police brutality trumps the ordinary brutality of the criminal in a state obsessed with the rights of the individual. There was a picture of Corey Taylor beside the story; it was a mug shot, showing a petulant young man staring defiantly at the camera in the manner of suspects everywhere.

Laura knew that she wanted to take the case. It would be a big step for her, her first independent bit of business. It wasn't, however, the sort of thing that the firm would like to be involved with—it promised to bring even more cameras, even more controversy, than the case of Alex Hunicutt Jr. But she wanted it; it would be *hers*—not Tom's, not Libby's. She could use it as an opportunity to turn criminal law into something the firm did on its own merit, not just an outgrowth of the corporate and family-law business. There were a lot of rich people in this town who crossed onto the wrong side of the law these days, people who could afford P&C's rates. She could get them those clients, with a little judicious publicity. It was time to have that talk with Tom Bailey.

She pushed back her chair and headed for Tom's office. His secretary's desk was vacant, but the door to his office was ajar. Laura approached, and craned her neck to see if her boss was free. He wasn't; she could hear his voice in conversation on the phone. She started to back away from the door, but he had spotted her, and waved for her to come in. She slipped in quietly, and perched on the edge of one of the leather chairs.

Tom had one of the biggest and nicest offices on the floor, despite the fact that, technically speaking, he was a junior partner. He was in his early forties, much younger than most of the crustaceans at the firm; he had made partner after he had landed the Hunicutt account at the precocious age of twenty-eight. He was a legend in legal circles; his retention by a client was enough to drive the opposition to the bargaining table, making his appearances in court rare and highly anticipated events. In the courtroom, Laura had often smiled to herself at the curled lip, and the theatrical shrug in the jury's direction, implying a "we-know-they're-trying-to-fool-us" complicity with those people who couldn't have had less in common with his custom-shirted, Bentley-driving self. Tom was, in fact, a very rich man, scion of one of those complicated, many-branched Southern families that had petered out, too refined to reproduce, making him heir to several eccentric and crotchety old people who had dutifully passed on and left him with big chunks of Atlanta's real estate, banking, and mercantile empires. The money he made as a partner of P&C must have seemed paltry, which left Laura to conclude that the man worked because he loved the law—or maybe he just loved getting on people's nerves.

Laura waited patiently for him to finish his conversation, looking around his office for distraction while he finished. She had spent so many hours in there that she knew without looking exactly where the diplomas—B.A., Harvard; J. D., Yale—were hung, and she could recite from memory the items on the desktop, which was always clean and neat. But there was not one personal item in the entire room; no photos, no mementos of friends or lovers. Tom Bailey, cipher. She watched as he made notes in his quick, neat handwriting on the pad in front of him, and tried to look at him objectively. Five years of working with him had stripped away her early hero-worship, although familiarity had bred anything but contempt. His appearance had hardly changed since they first met; that might be the same titanium-white shirt, and tastefully patterned tie, he had worn at her interview. His dark hair was beginning to show gray in places, but it looked good on him, making his blue eyes look darker.

Tom was handsome, in a conventional, conservative way. To Laura, though, his attractiveness was more based in his self-possession, a quality that made him the center of attention wherever he stood. It wasn't his size; his height was just average, and he was more lean than muscular. Women swooned over him, in any case; half the female associates at the firm were struck dumb in his presence. The combination of looks, brains, and money was pretty potent, unless, as Laura pointed out to her lovesick colleagues, you had to put up with his temper and his perfectionism. She liked to make him seem worse than he was; secretly, she enjoyed her exclusive, privileged relationship with the star of the firm.

Finally, he hung up the phone, and sighed. *"Deliver us, Dear Spirit, from the tantrums of our telephones . . ."* Tom was probably the only attorney in Atlanta who could quote W. H. Auden.

Laura grinned, and finished the quotation: *". . . and the whispers of our secretaries, conspiring against Man."*

"Don't let Cecelia hear you accuse her of conspiracy. So, what brings you in here—are you celebrating your victory yesterday?"

"You mean Alex? Thank God that's over."

"I saw you on television; you looked very serious. Who were those . . . *large* men with you and Alex?"

"Alex's frat brothers, his bodyguard from the Nation of Crisco. He'd meet a better class of person in prison."

"Someday, he'll get the chance—unless you're willing to defend him next time, too."

Laura shrugged. "If you want me to, I will. Under protest, though; he's disgusting."

"I couldn't agree more. Which is why I agreed to join you for dinner tonight."

"What?" Her head jerked up.

"That was Alexander Hunicutt on the phone; he and Alex wanted to take you out, to thank you. I thought you might not want to go alone, so I invited myself along."

"Thanks, but I would have preferred you to decline for both of us, Tom."

"It's just a couple of hours, and Alexander wasn't going to take 'no' for an answer. We might as well grin and bear it. Seven-thirty tonight. You'll have time to go home and change."

"What's the matter with what I'm wearing now?" Laura asked, indignant.

Tom threw up his hands and laughed. "Nothing. But we're going to Provenza, so I just thought you might want to change. Believe me, I think you look just fine all the time."

Provenza was a high-end restaurant; most of the women there would be dressed up, loaded for bear, in fact. Laura was wearing a plain dark suit, nice, but drab. Maybe she should consider changing, but into what? She stopped herself; she hadn't come here to talk about her wardrobe. "Tom, I need to talk to you about something. I have a new case, and I really want to take it."

He raised his dark eyebrows. "Gracious, Grasshopper." He called her that from time to time, in reference to the master-disciple relationship from the hoary TV show "Kung Fu." A little private joke between them. "How did this happen? Are you advertising?"

"In a manner of speaking. It was my TV debut last night that did it." She launched into the details of the case, sparse though they were.

His expression didn't change as she related the facts to him, but when she finished, he frowned. "I don't know. Police brutality—you know what the press can do with that."

"But he claims that he didn't do it," Laura pointed out. "I'll try to construct a defense based on the presence of another killer."

"Ah, the innocence defense! That's an old horse that doesn't get out of the barn much these days. So what's your angle on it? Is he the unfortunate victim of circumstantial evidence? Or has he been framed—is this a conspiracy I see before me?"

She grimaced. "Don't be disingenuous; you know I'm not going to try and cook up some wacky conspiracy theory. Williams says that someone else did it, and there are plenty of people who could have, if everything he says about the setup at the police station is true. But I don't necessarily buy his story; I told him that, if he killed the guy in a moment of rage, he stands a good chance with a jury. In fact, I could probably bargain it down to manslaughter two with the district attorney right now; I've got to believe that neither the district attorney nor the cops want a trial. But he says that he wants exoneration. Fine. I promised to try for it, but there's always the fallback of pleading guilty to a lesser charge."

"And how do you plan to exonerate him?" Laura thought she saw a slight twitching at the corners of Tom's mouth, but she ignored it.

"I'll hire Kenny Newton to look into the dead guy's background, and find out who might have wanted him out of the way." Newton was a private investigator, a former cop, who Laura had used with great success in the Hunicutt case. It was he who produced the witnesses to Cheri Moore's cocaine and alcohol use on the night of the alleged rape. Kenny knew cops, and he could get inside the Police Department's investigation.

Bailey leaned back in his chair. "Do you believe this Detective Williams is innocent? Did you look into his eyes, into his *soul*, Grasshopper?"

Laura shrugged. "My eyesight isn't that good. But he says he's innocent, and he has no reason to lie to me; he knows all about privilege. I'll take his word for it, but I'll back it with some real evidence before we get to court. Otherwise, I'll try for a deal."

Tom nodded. "A plea would be preferable to a trial; try to get him on the path of least resistance."

"Exactly. I need time to conduct an investigation, and to build the best strategy. I've asked Williams about his record on brutality. There may be a couple of incidents that the district attorney can drag up, but there's hardly a cop out there who hasn't slugged a suspect from time to time. I'm pretty sure that the prosecution won't play the race card, at least. I wouldn't take it if I thought there were a risk that the firm might be depicted as a defender of racist cops."

"Racist cops are entitled to the best defense they can afford, too," Tom said, with a smile. "Speaking of which, can Williams—afford us, I mean?"

"He says so; I'm going to look at his financials before I take the case. If he can't, I'll find him someone less pricey. I'm not looking to do this pro bono. Look, Tom, I know P&C thinks criminal work is tacky, but it's what I want to do—and this is a great case, any way you look at it. I need to know if you'll back me, and let me take it, and some others after it. Otherwise, I might have to start looking around for a firm that has a real criminal practice."

Tom's expression changed suddenly; Laura was afraid for a moment that he might lose his infamous temper, but he didn't. He seemed to be struggling with something, though, and it took him a moment to speak. When he did, he sounded serious. "Leaving Prendergrast and Crawley? I had no idea you were thinking along those lines."

"Neither did I, until recently, but the few criminal things I've done—even Alex—have been the most fun I've had since I passed the bar. If I stick around here, though, it's going to be just the occasional possession charge, or assault, when one of our corporate or trust clients puts a foot wrong. Like Alex—rich people whose money gets them into trouble once in a while."

"I see. You want to deal with full-time lawbreakers, not these motley amateurs?"

"I might not put it exactly that way, but, yes, I suppose so. There are tons of white-collar criminals who can afford us; why should they have to look in the yellow pages for a lawyer? And just in the past year, three pro athletes were arrested in town on criminal charges—they can all pay our rates. I can get that business, Tom, you know I can."

"I believe you; that's not the problem. It's a question of what the other partners will think—do they want professional athletes on their client list? As you said yourself, they might think it's tacky."

"You and I both know that the bigger firms are taking business from us every day, Tom; we're dinosaurs. The day of the small boutique firm is over. I knew it when I joined; if it weren't for you, I would have gone someplace else to start. And now ... well, I'd hate not working with you, but if I'm going to work these ridiculous hours, I might as well be happy."

He nodded. "I hear you. Don't do anything in haste, Laura; you know I'll back you as far as I can. Let me put out some feelers."

"Thanks, Tom. I didn't come in here to deliver an ultimatum, but I thought you needed to know how I'm feeling."

"I appreciate that. Of course, if you took on a criminal caseload on your own, I might have to find another associate to help me."

"Understood. I've learned a lot from you, Tom, and I'm grateful, but I feel like I have this ... *calling* for criminal law."

He nodded. "I understand. My only concern is that we keep you here, at P&C. I don't want to face you in a courtroom someday, Grasshopper. You know all my tricks."

Laura smiled. "I'd beat you fair and square, no tricks. So, what about Jeff Williams—can I tell him I'm his lawyer?"

There was a pause, during which Tom looked at the ceiling. Laura waited without speaking. Finally, he looked back at her, sat forward in his chair, and waved a hand in her direction. "Okay, Perry Mason, amaze me. Go forth and free this man from the shackles of injustice."

"Well, he hasn't been arrested yet, so there aren't any shackles to speak of, but I'll do you proud."

"I'm sure you will. Oh, by the way, have you run this past Libby?"

"No. I thought, I mean, if you okayed it, I thought she would ..." Laura's reply trailed off. What she meant was that she thought that Tom's support would outweigh Libby's inevitable disapproval.

"I see; I was the easier mark. That's alright, Grasshopper; you know I'm a sucker for those big eyes of yours. You can leave Libby and the rest of 'em to me. You just worry about your client."

Her client. "Thanks, Tom." She rose and left his office hurriedly, before he could change his mind. Back in her office, flushed with excitement, she picked up the phone.

4

"Yell-oh."

Laura smiled when Kenny Newton answered the phone in his customary way; Kenny was one of her favorite people. He was a big man—a former college football player, in fact—and, given his past as a cop and his present work as a private investigator, he should have been a tough guy, a loner. Far from it; Kenny was genial to the point of goofiness, and he was quick to whip out pictures of his wife and kids at the slightest provocation. Despite his lack of resemblance to Sam Spade, however, Kenny was good at his job; in fact, it might have been his cornpone demeanor that allowed him to accomplish as much as he did. People liked talking to Kenny; they told him all kinds of things. They had told him all about Cheri Moore, and now Laura was hoping that someone would tell him something about the dead rape suspect that would get Jeff Williams off the hook.

"Hey, Kenny, it's Laura."

"Counselor! Saw you on the TV last night. I said to myself, 'Dang! She shore is purty—for a lawyer.'" Kenny liked to dial up the redneck accent from time to time; sometimes talking to him was like watching an episode of "Hee Haw". "We got that bad boy off, I see. I'm not so sure we done good there, Laura."

"Me neither, Kenny, me neither. The courts will get another crack at him, though, one of these days. In the meantime, you and I have something new to work on. How's your schedule?"

"Pretty good. I gotta catch a coupla folks in flagrante, but that ain't hard. What you need, sugar?"

"Have you been following this rape case—the little girl who was kidnapped yesterday?"

"Sure have. Justice was swift and sure this time, anyway—cops got the guy, and didn't even bother with the trial."

"Well, see, that's what everyone is going to think. But you and I know different."

"We do?" He sounded skeptical already.

"Yes, indeed. See, the cop who arrested the suspect says he didn't kill him. I'm going to represent him."

"Naw! You got you another innocent client, then. You ever meet any guilty people, Chastain?"

"Certainly not. Now listen while I give you all the deets." She ran down the story for Kenny, including some additional details she had culled from the newspaper report. Little was known about the dead suspect, other than his name—Corey Taylor—and his age, twenty-six. He had lived with the grandmother who had raised him, and had not held a job at the time of his death. Laura was sure that there would be reporters crawling all over Corey's family and friends by now; she wanted Kenny to get down there as quickly as possible, before everyone got sick of telling their stories. "I need for you to find out if Corey was involved in something that might have gotten him killed. He had a marijuana bust—maybe it was a drug thing. Jeff Williams says he has no idea, but he thinks someone on the force must have gotten to him while he was alone in that interrogation room."

"Dang! I'd like to get me some of the mushrooms Williams orders on his pizzas. Sure you don't want me to try to find the shooter on the grassy knoll while we're at it?"

"Just take a shot at it, Ken. I have faith in your ability to work miracles."

"Good, 'cause that's what it's going to take. How can I get in touch with Williams? I want to get his story firsthand."

"He's at home, suspended with pay pending outcome of the investigation." Laura gave Kenny Jeff's home number and address. "Did you know him when you were on the force?"

"Naw. He's gotta be at least ten years younger than me; if he was on the force, he was still in uniform when I left."

"He's on Kowalski's squad," she said. Kowalski was a pal of Kenny's. "Does Amos like Williams?"

"Please. You think Amos talks about that kind of thing with me? We're guys, Laura; we talk about sports and hooters. However, I happen to be seeing him this evening, and I'll ask him about Williams. Not that he'll say anything with an investigation underway. You know Amos: Mr. By-the-Book."

"Oh, I know. So you'll get started right away?"

"Just as soon as I can get ahold of Detective Williams. Maybe I'll take a drive over to his place and check him out in person, see if I think he's full of crap or not."

"I would appreciate it. And since you're going anyway, could you pick up his bank statements? He says he can afford us, but the managing partner will need to see some proof."

"He sure can't afford you on a cop's salary. Hell, he can't afford me, either."

"He inherited some money, but I don't want to take everything he has. If it looks to you like it's going to be easier to throw him on the mercy of the court, just say the word, and we'll try to bargain this down. I'm not interested in fighting windmills."

"Gotcha, boss. I'll get back to you later in the day. Okay if I stop by the office?"

"Of course; any time. You can see the flowers Pa Hunicutt sent me, in gratitude for saving Alex from cavity searches."

"Flowers? He sent me a bottle of Scotch."

"Damn! I hate being a girl—I'd much rather get booze than flowers."

"Really? Good to know; I'll tell Kowalski that if he wants to win your heart, he should skip the roses and go for the Vat 69." Kenny had a dream that Laura and Kowalski would get together; like all happily married people, he hated to see his friends still single. Laura and Kowalski seemed like a natural match to him—they were both smart, and driven. Laura didn't have the heart to tell him that they had driven straight into each other the previous day, at Alex's trial. Let him dream.

Laura laughed. "See you later, Kenny." She hung up, happy to know that the best man was on the case. She could concentrate on other things for a while, like what she was going to wear to Provenza that evening. Had Tom meant that she *should* change, or had he just assumed she would want to? She could use a new outfit, anyway; she decided to take a long lunch hour and go shopping. Heck, she had earned it, and as soon as the Williams case started up in earnest, she knew there would be no time for leisurely lunch-and-shopping expeditions.

Laura told Cecelia she'd be gone for a couple of hours, and headed out. She took her aging car from the garage beneath the building, and drove out into the rainy afternoon, to her favorite boutique in Virginia-Highland. With the holidays approaching, the store was a vast wasteland of velvet party frocks, but Laura's eyes lit on a suit that was perfect for dinner with a client. It was black, with beading on the collar and cuffs of the fitted jacket. Black wasn't exactly a departure for her; Laura had very cautious taste in clothing, gravitating to neutral colors. Her jewelry was equally conservative—no dangling earrings—and her nails, though always perfectly manicured, never bore any shade but the most transparent shell pink. Laura ascribed her low-key style to her job, but an astute observer might note that, like many young women, her clothing reflected someone not yet sure of herself, more guided by convention than by her convictions.

She looked at her reflection in the dressing room mirror. She saw a well-groomed young woman of medium height, indistinguishable at first glance from thousands of other similarly well-groomed young women. On closer inspection, however, an observer might notice her wavy dark hair, tamed by a good haircut, and her brown eyes, lightened by gold flecks. She was justifiably proud of her perfect complexion; she was unable to tan, and had always avoided exposure to the sun, preferring an arresting pallor to a cycle of burning and peeling. She eyed the suit critically, wondering if it clung a little too suggestively to her curves. She had been allocated slightly more material than she cared for in the bust and rear departments, and she certainly didn't want to buy anything that exaggerated those areas. She pirouetted, admiring the perfect fit, and overcame her doubts. She bought it, despite her alarm at the price tag, and stopped off for lunch at Murphy's.

When she returned to the office, trouble was lurking: Cecelia told her, with an expressive eye-roll, that Libby was looking for her. Laura put down her bags, and headed for Libby's office; a cloud of perfume and the clank of big jewelry told her, while she was still a few doors away, that the second of her bosses was in. She tapped on the door and stuck her head in. "Libby? You wanted to see me?" She walked in, and looked for a place to take a seat; she moved a few files off one of the chairs while Libby watched impatiently.

Libby Arnold was not an organized attorney; her office swam in paper. She couldn't keep a secretary. No one was up to the job of finding everything she lost—or up to taking the blame for it, as Libby would never admit that her own bad habits were the problem. Her credentials—both academic and social—were impeccable. Her law degree came from the University of Virginia, and her Daddy had been a judge. Laura knew from old photos the firm kept on display that Libby had, in her early days there, been a beauty, a cool WASP goddess. Her looks were faded now; the blond hair was suffering from too much coloring, and, like many women slipping into middle age, she made the error of clinging to the lipstick shade of her youth. Libby also tended to wear brightly colored suits, in an ostentatious display of femininity. Sadly, she wore them with no sense of style, and ended up looking like a frumpy First Lady. Today, she was in pink, which clashed with her chipped coral manicure. A cigarette butt smoldered in an ashtray on the desk. Laura rarely saw her take a puff, but the lit cigarette was as much a fixture in Libby's milieu as was her outsize jewelry and too-high heels.

Laura braced herself as Libby's eyes narrowed. "Yes, I did want to see you. Tom Bailey tells me you're taking a new case. I don't think it's appropriate for you to have your own caseload, and I told him so. I didn't even think you should have had the Hunicutt case."

"I'm sorry you feel that way, Libby." There was nothing else to say. With Tom's approval, it was a done deal. Libby could vent, but that was about all she could do.

"What about *my* caseload? It's fine for Tom, but I don't have four associates at *my* beck and call." Her voice was ragged with petulance.

"I know, Libby," Laura sighed. "I've got your calendar covered, and if anything else comes up, I'm sure I can handle it. My case is going to start slowly—I'm sure it'll be a little while before I have any real work to do for Detective Williams's defense."

"Let me remind you that my clients are this firm's bread and butter. You may think it's glamorous to take these high-profile cases, but they're not what pays the bills around here."

Oh, I know, Laura wanted to say. *I know that keeping a custody case alive lets you run up your billable hours, Libby, so you can look good at bonus-time—never mind the poor little kid in the middle.* Instead, she rose. "If that's all you wanted, I should be getting back to my office. I'm expecting some calls."

"Fine. Just so you know where I stand. And I'm taking this to James Scarborough; Tom's behavior will be discussed at the next partners' meeting." Laura nodded and left without comment; she was more than sure that Tom's behavior was a topic at *every* partners' meeting, although he did seem to take particular delight in baiting Libby.

Poor Libby. Laura and the other female associates laughed about her, but they did appreciate that when she joined the firm twenty-five years earlier, things hadn't been so easy for a woman. Not that they were now, of course, but for years, Libby had been the *only* female attorney at P&C, excluded from the dinners, the golf games, the hunting trips—even, until five years earlier, the Yule Log, the firm's most important client entertainment. No wonder she was bitter. Poor, *poor* Libby; Laura could picture her discussion with Tom. To salve her conscience, she returned to her office and worked diligently, for an hour or two, on a motion in one of Libby's cases. She sent an E-mail to Libby, giving her an update on the rest of the still-outstanding cases as well. She felt better for it. At four, Cecelia buzzed; Kenny Newton had arrived. "Send him in," Laura said, clearing her desk. He bounded into the office, smiling broadly.

"Hey, sugar. How's my favorite crusader for justice?" He crossed the room, kissed her on the cheek, and flopped into a chair. Kenny was big, over six-three, with bright brown eyes and an all-embracing smile. In his late thirties, his light brown hair was thinning a little, and, as some big men do, he was getting a little soft—but he was still formidable-looking. Laura had worked with him for a couple of years now, and she could honestly say that she would trust him with her life.

"Fine, thanks," Laura said. "But I'll be even better if you tell me you found out something real evil about Corey Taylor."

"Not going to be that easy, I'm afraid. I do have a couple of tidbits, though. Here goes: Corey Taylor, twenty-six, lived with his grandmother—you know all that—who raised him from a pup. Mother deceased when he was about three, of injuries sustained at the end of a boyfriend's fist. Father's whereabouts unknown. Spotty record of employment; seems to have lived off Grandma since he dropped out of high school. Three arrests: One for marijuana possession; he got probation. One assault; beat up a girlfriend—for that, he did three months, with a year's probation. One drunk and disorderly, resisting arrest, about six months ago—did thirty days, with another year of probation."

"No history of sexual assault?"

"Well, sexual violence, if you count smacking the girlfriend around. I need to talk to her; I got a name and a current address on her. He did have a reputation for hanging around the schoolyard; that's how the cops got him so quickly yesterday—the kids who left school with the girl he raped saw him there. He must have liked young girls, and finally acted out a fantasy yesterday."

"Or maybe the rape was just incidental—maybe he was doing something else at the school."

"Drugs, you're thinking. It's possible, but no one mentions Corey's name in the same sentence with drugs. He seems to have been a moderate user of weed, no more."

"Child porn, then," Laura ventured.

"Wouldn't that make nice headlines?" Kenny grinned at her. "But I just don't think it's the case. He seemed—according to the kids I talked to—just to stand and stare at the little girls. They used to tease him."

"Uh-oh. Why didn't the school administrators do something about it?"

"They called the cops a few times, but it obviously did no good. But let me get to the good part: Corey had a brother. A half-brother, really; he was a few years older than Corey. Name was Tony Harrell. Their mother seems to have slid downhill over time: she was married to Harrell's father, but he was killed in a car wreck. After that, she seems to have taken up with a series of men, culminating in the one who killed her. I got all this from Granny, by the way, and she's not talking to the press, so you won't be hearing all this on the news."

"You wizard! How did you manage?"

"Easy. She's a church lady, and when I was in uniform, I worked on a break-in down there at her church. She remembered me. She reminded me about Tony; I knew him, too, slightly."

"Really? How?"

Kenny paused for effect. "Tony was a cop."

Laura sat back, weighing the possibilities. Corey had a connection to the Police Department, and he had been killed—presumably—by a cop. Could he have known something about someone, through his brother?

Kenny was watching her, a smile playing on his lips. "Aren't you gonna ask me why I said *was* a cop?"

"He quit the force?"

"Nope. Dead. Dead end."

Laura tossed a wad of paper at him. "You got me all excited!"

"Well, I got pretty excited too, but then Granny told me Tony's tragic story: he was the light of her life, her good boy. He was working his way up in the Department, just got married, then, boom! One cold winter night, his furnace malfunctions and kills him and his new bride. She cried when she told me, and I'll be durned if I didn't get a little misty, too. That left her with Corey, her bad boy, who's been nothing but trouble since. Tony used to be able to help out with him, but he's been gone five years—and all of Corey's arrests have come since then."

"That," Laura said, "is the saddest story I've heard in a while. But it gets us nowhere, doesn't it?"

"Oh, nowhere-point-two, maybe. I've got a couple more people to talk to, but I wanted to report in. I need to check Tony Harrell out with some cops, and find out who he ran with when he was in the department. If we're right, someone there still has a tie to Tony—and to his brother. And there's a man I'm supposed to have a chat with tomorrow, who they say knows the dirt on Corey, guy by the name of 'Smoothhead.' I'm looking forward to that. And there's the girlfriend. In the meantime, here are Jeff's bank statements for the past year—he says can you make copies of them and send him back the originals? While you're at it, make copies for me; my accountant will want them, and who knows? There may be something interesting in there."

"No problem," Laura said, opening the most recent bank statement and pulling it out. It was a Cash Management Account statement from Merrill Lynch. Laura flipped directly to the ending balance; Jeff Williams owned a nice nest egg, a couple hundred thousand dollars, conservatively invested. "He can afford me, but not forever. You better come up with something quick."

"We'll see what Mr. Smoothhead has to say tomorrow."

Laura put down the bank statement, and looked at Kenny. "So tell me what you think of our client."

"Jeff? Hard to say. He's a wild man today, that's for sure; the reporters are camped all over his lawn, driving him crazy. He smokes too much."

"But do you think he's being honest with us?"

Kenny shrugged. "I'm not a mind reader. All I know is that the guy is one determined sonofabitch; he's not going to do any time for Corey Taylor."

"Did you talk to Amos yet?"

"Of course not. I'm going to wait until the moment is right, tonight; he might open up a little, under the influence of a beer or two. Care to join us?"

"Can't. The boss is making me have dinner with Alex and his daddy. You're on your own with Kowalski—get him drunk and pump him for details."

Kenny chuckled. "Fat chance. The guy has a hollow leg. You'll have to do your own espionage—sleep with him, and he'll spill his guts."

"Fatter chance. He hates me, especially after the Hunicutt thing. Better leave my name out of it, in fact."

Kenny rose, shaking his head. "Amos doesn't hate you; he thinks you're pretty. Said so to me just this morning."

Laura blushed, flattered, and hastily changed the subject. "One more thing on Williams: I called the district attorney's office. That dweeb, Davis Shelton, is handling the case; he wouldn't say anything other than that they're 'looking at the evidence, with a view to preparing an indictment by the end of the week.'" She imitated Shelton's tight-lipped yuppie drawl. "Think he talks like that all the time?"

"Oh, yeah; that man doesn't have a spontaneous bone in his body. Speaking of which, if you change your mind, Amos and I will be at Manuel's. And I'll call you as soon as I hook up with ol' Smoothhead tomorrow."

"Thanks, Kenny, you light up my life." He left, blowing her a kiss.

5

After the initial excitement of taking on her new case, Laura relapsed back into her routine. The case she was working on for Tom—a Hunicutt subsidiary was being sued for various environmental-law infractions—required much research, and she wanted it out of the way before the Williams case gained momentum. She didn't want any distractions, not even one of Tom's cases, although she would never stint on her industriousness where he was concerned. She spent most of the afternoon and early evening in the library, and on Lexis, the powerful legal database, looking for relevant case citations for her brief. When she found what she needed, she headed back to her office. As she crossed the lobby, just before seven, she glanced out the floor-to-ceiling windows. Despite the rain, and some low-lying fog, the view, of tall buildings, bare-branched trees, and light-streaked highways, was impressive; she stopped to enjoy it for a moment.

Laura was ambivalent about Atlanta; she wasn't a native—few residents were—and she was as often aggravated by the city's boisterous, preening self-promotion as she was charmed by its unexpected graces. Atlanta seemed as ambivalent about itself: Was it Southern, or part of some larger, free-floating mall culture that superseded regional identity? The latter view seemed to prevail, although Southernness forced its way from time to time into the picture, like a crazy cousin at a Delta wedding. It was perhaps inevitable; the South is one of those places, like Bosnia and Ireland, where history sits on your shoulder and talks about itself, loud and incessant. Atlanta plugged its ears, hummed a happy tune to drown out the irritating voice, and threw up skyscrapers, all to no avail: It was built on the blood-soaked soil of the Confederacy, and there was no forgetting.

Laura didn't blame the place for embracing the future at the expense of its "heritage"; Atlanta wasn't an old city to begin with, and history had been more or less forced upon it. Before the Civil War, Atlanta had been a scrappy parvenu among older, more gracious cities, like Savannah and Charleston; it wasn't even the capital of Georgia when the war broke out. So it hardly seemed fair that Atlanta (née Marthasville), scorned as an upstart by the agrarian aristocracy, had become the embodiment of the Old South for so much of the world—all because it had the misfortune to be burned, first by Sherman, then by Hollywood. It was the second, fictional burning that had done the most damage, leaving the city hobbled by hoopskirts, its hands tied by Mammy's bandanna. Tourists came to town and wandered the streets, looking for some relic of The Book, or The Movie, but the city rigorously denied them the gratification. There were no monuments, no shrines, other than the derelict apartment building where Peggy Mitchell had written her book, but every time they tried to restore it—Yankees, always, raising the funding—someone burned it down. It was impossible not to enjoy the irony.

Laura, who hailed from Nashville (itself a schismatic city: spangled Nudie suits versus tan riding breeches), sympathized with Atlanta's desire to get shed of the unpleasant past, although she drew the line at out-and-out revisionism. There was an ongoing argument in her own family; Laura was exasperated at her father's and brothers' membership in the Sons of the Confederacy—how could they defend that flag? How could she not? they asked in reply, enumerating the Chastain dead and maimed. She would have to face it again, in a few weeks, when she returned home for Christmas. They would sit down for their annual dinner, in fact, beneath a genuine Southern icon: a tattered, water-spotted, elaborately framed print of *The Burial of Latane*, pronounced "Latanay".

The *Burial*, a fixture in a certain sort of Southern home, represented everything Laura found wonderful and annoying about the South: a sentimental lithograph dating from the post-War era, it portrayed a group of womenfolk, and one lone male slave, burying a gallant Confederate officer. It was every Southern myth rolled into one— the beauty of the Lost Cause, the patriarchal view of slavery, and the valor of the women. Of course, what Laura saw was the *absence* of the men who had started the war, and who went on to lose it— making them the only Americans, pre-Vietnam, to taste the sting of defeat. Try getting the Sons of the Confederacy to admit that; they could argue, bland-faced, that Lee was the superior general. But he *lost*, Laura said—and the winners get to write the history. Southerners, however, consider history to be their exclusive province; nowhere else are events of the past century discussed as if they had been featured on *Nightline* the previous evening. These however, were sentiments Laura voiced only at home; they were not likely to advance her career at the firm, which was itself encrusted with Old South ties, down to a partner descended from General Stuart himself.

She looked at her watch; it was time to stop daydreaming and get ready for dinner with the Hunicutts, those unreconstructed good ol' boys. Provenza was just downstairs, in the lobby, which meant that Laura could wait until the last moment to prepare herself for her ordeal. Reluctantly, she headed for the ladies room, washed her face, and reapplied her minimal makeup. She changed into the new suit, and evaluated herself critically before ripping off the price tags, making it irrevocably hers. She wavered for a moment. The skirt, a slim column that reached to the middle of her calves, clung to her curves; the short cut of the jacket didn't hide anything. Laura had been told, by several boyfriends and many construction workers, that her butt was one of her best features, and she didn't mind showing it off a bit, but to the Hunicutts? Pearls before swine; caviar to the general. At least Tom would see it. She blushed, and wondered where *that* thought came from. She looked at her watch; Tom would be waiting for her. She dashed back to her office, and met Tom standing in the doorway.

"Gracious," he said, taking in her altered appearance.

"What the heck; I don't get out all that much," she said, by way of explanation for the outfit. "I clean up pretty good, though, don't I?" She grinned, broadening her Southern accent.

"You do indeed," he answered.

She took her coat and briefcase, and they boarded an elevator to the lobby. They were early, but the maître d' and his crew recognized Tom, and flapped around them in an obsequious minuet, taking their coats, and ushering them to a secluded table to await the Hunicutts. Offered a drink, Laura asked for a seltzer with lime. Tom ordered scotch. She would have a glass of wine with dinner, but she had learned long ago that it was best not to drink at corporate dinners; it only made her sleepy.

"This will all be over in a few hours," Tom said. "Then you can have your life back."

"I don't mind, although I'd rather be home watching TV," Laura said. She looked at him; he was relaxed and smiling. She saw an opportunity to bring up something. "Tom, I wish you wouldn't provoke Libby."

"But it's fun."

"Yes, but I'm the one who suffers."

He pretended to be apologetic. "Then I'll stop, right away."

"No, you won't. I'll be back in her office next week, listening to her blow steam about some other move you've made, using me as your pawn."

He might have replied, but they were interrupted by the advent of the Hunicutts; they stood to greet their approaching host. Alexander Hunicutt Sr. was in his late fifties, silver-haired and iron-chinned, with a booming voice. He accepted the homage of the waiter escorting him without ever acknowledging his presence, extending his hand to Tom long before he reached the table. "Bailey," he said, by way of greeting. They shook hands, and he turned to Laura. "And Ms. Chastain. How can I thank you for the fine job you did? We owe you a great deal of gratitude. Alex . . ." He looked around, suddenly aware that his son wasn't following in his wake. "Where did he go?"

"He stepped into the men's room, sir," the waiter said.

Hunicutt frowned, as if he disapproved of Alex's weakness in responding to the call of nature. On the other hand, Laura thought, chances were pretty good that Alex wasn't in the men's room for any of the usual reasons. Pa Hunicutt must have known that by now.

Tom took up the slack. "Have a seat, Alexander, and tell the man what you want."

"What are you having? Scotch? Bring me the same. Well, Bailey, I have to tell you that your girl might just get all my business one of these days, if you don't watch your back."

"That would be fine with me," Tom said. "It's why I hired her: so I can put my feet up on my desk and do nothing."

"She's sharp, that's for sure."

Laura was about to object being discussed in the third person, when Alex made his debut at the table, sniffling lightly and flicking at the tip of his nose with his finger. Laura glanced at Tom, to see if he had noticed; he met her eyes evenly.

"Sit down, for Chrissake," his father growled. "Bailey, I want you to tell me what I have to do at this deposition next week." After his greeting to her, Hunicutt hadn't acknowledged Laura's presence again; all his conversation was directed to Tom. Tom, to his credit, tried to draw Laura into the discussion; Hunicutt would listen to her comments politely, and then turn back to Tom.

Despite his captain-of-industry facade, Laura could see that Hunicutt relied on Tom's judgment almost absolutely. And why not? Tom was brilliant, and, maybe even more crucial from Hunicutt's perspective, Tom was the real thing—a gentleman, a patrician, in contrast to Hunicutt, the arriviste. Every detail of Tom's appearance, from his careless haircut to the dull-gold antique watch he wore, said "old money." Hunicutt, on the other hand, was too highly groomed; the monogram on his cuff thrust itself too insistently onto the attention of the onlooker, and his watch screamed "Rolex." Tom was everything that Hunicutt, in short, wanted to be. Looking at them together, Laura reflected on the peculiar relationship that a client sometimes has with his lawyer—the lawyer is a hireling, yes, but in this case, better-bred, better-educated, and smarter than his employer.

Laura, resigned to being excluded from the conversation, tried to start several small conversations with Alex, but all her efforts were useless. Mostly, Alex stared straight ahead, focused on the middle distance, before excusing himself and scurrying to the men's room, returning agitated and grinning.

At last, Hunicutt Senior called for the check, by snapping his fingers in the air. Tom cringed, but said nothing. They managed to get through the closing ceremonies; Laura was forced to allow Alex to plant a kiss on her cheek. He and his father were whisked into their waiting car, while Tom and Laura made the more plebeian trek to the garage.

"It's over, Grasshopper," Tom said, soothingly. Laura nodded. Her feet were killing her, and her head was pounding. Her car and Tom's were among the few left in the garage at this hour, and, although they were parked in sight of each other, he escorted her to hers. "It gets better," he offered, as she unlocked the door.

"It can't get worse," she said, not in the mood to banter. "I'll talk to you tomorrow. Oh, I'll be late; I think I'll go over to Jeff Williams's first thing tomorrow."

"Who's Jeff Williams?"

"My new client; the cop, remember?"

Tom nodded. "Right. I forgot. Well, drive safely."

She nodded, and closed the door, locked it, and turned the key. Nothing. She tried again. She checked the headlights; they were in the on position. She put her head on the steering wheel. Stupid, stupid girl; it had been raining when she went out this afternoon, and she hadn't switched them off. Her ancient car didn't have any of those new fail-safe systems to cover for human error. She heard tapping on the window, and looked up and saw Tom still standing there. She rolled down the window.

"Dead battery?" She nodded. He frowned. "I would jump-start

you, but I left my cables in my other car. Do you have a set?" She shook her head. "Come on; I'll drive you home."

"It's out of your way," she protested. "I'll call a cab."

"Don't be ridiculous. Come on." He opened the door and held out his hand; she took it, and he pulled her up. They walked to his car, the magnificent black Bentley, one of the few displays of wealth he allowed himself. He held the passenger door for her, and she settled into the leather seat. He got in, and started the engine; they glided out of the garage and onto Peachtree Street, rain-glazed and nearly deserted at this hour. He turned on the wipers; their soft thwocking, and the hiss of the tires, were the only sounds for a while. When they stopped at a light, he looked at her. "I know you hate that part of the job. You'd never volunteer to spend time with people like the Hunicutts."

She nodded. "It's worse than I thought, Tom. His father takes no responsibility for Alex. I'm going to be right back in court again, defending that little punk. Kowalski was right."

"Who's Kowalski?"

"The lieutenant who heads the sex-crimes squad. He thinks I'm a soul-dead yuppie who defends the guilty."

"You're not. You have a good mind and a better heart."

"Thanks for the vote." She was quiet for a minute, and then she laughed. "You know, it just occurred to me that Jeff Williams is on Kowalski's squad; he's going to start to hate the sight of me. I'm sure he thinks Jeff is guilty—so, once again, Amos Kowalski gets to act morally superior to me."

"That's one of the consequences of defending criminals, Laura; you'd better be prepared for it."

"I am. Just thinking about the look on Kowalski's face when I get Jeff off is compensation for being scorned now. I'll tell you something, Tom; after Alex, I really *need* an innocent client. I want to hear the gavel swing down, and the judge dismiss all charges—not just on a technicality, not just because he's 'not guilty,' but because he's *innocent.*"

"And you're convinced that he is?"

"I want to believe he is, yes. Why would he lie to me? Even Alex told me the truth—his version anyway, which was enough for me to figure out what really happened that night. Ugh, just thinking about Alex and that girl makes my skin crawl; they deserved each other, in a really sick way. But what did I do to deserve Alex?"

Tom laughed, then turned serious. "You don't have to defend Alex again, or anyone else whose case you don't like."

Laura looked at his profile. "How can I avoid it? Won't Hunicutt take his football and go home?"

Tom shrugged. "If he wants to move his business away from the firm at this point, let him. He'd be a fool; we know more about Hunicutt and Company than he does. It would take him years to rebuild the resources he has with us."

"I can't expect you to take that risk just because I'm squeamish about a little cocaine-snorting waste of genetic material."

"Why not? Soon—maybe sooner than you think—you'll be a partner, and I see no reason why you can't pick and choose your clients the way the rest of us do." He glanced at her face, and saw her surprise. "Oh, don't act like you don't know; it's a shoo-in. There's no other associate on your level. And I'm backing you." He said that without false modesty, just a statement of fact: If Tom Bailey wanted her to be a partner, she would be. "I've been thinking about our conversation this morning, and I'm going to suggest that you be put in charge of building a criminal practice for the firm—maybe even hiring a couple of associates to work under you. I see no need to cling to the fiction that you're just a hired hand. We can't afford to lose you, Laura; it's time the firm woke up to reality."

It was true; Laura knew that she would make partner. All the associates knew where they stood. Some of them were relieved to know that they were off the partner track; they were the ones who left at five, and had lives. Some of the unchosen associates, however, continued to work frenetically, even though they and everyone else knew that it was over. Like snake bodies severed from their heads, slithering around without a destination. Laura wouldn't have stuck around if she couldn't have made partner; what would be the point? To have Tom confirm it openly, though, was a surprise. She tried to think of something to say in reply, but couldn't, so they rode on in silence.

They were getting close to her town house, just off Peachtree in Brookhaven. They had passed Tom's neighborhood already; he lived in Buckhead, in one of the baronial mansions on Valley Road. Someone had once pointed out the house to her, although it wasn't visible from the street except as a fragment of a roofline, or a reflection of light from an upstairs window. Funny that they had never been inside each other's houses, after all these years. She showed him where to turn off Peachtree; when they turned into the driveway of her complex, she leaned across him to aim her clicker at the infrared eye of the security gate.

"Quite the secured compound you have here," he murmured.

"It convinced my mother that I'm safe living on my own." She pointed him to her unit, and he pulled into the miniature driveway. "Would you like to come in?" she asked, not sure why.

"Okay," he said.

They walked up the short front stair, and she unlocked the door. The town house wasn't big; it had a living room, dining room, and kitchen on the first floor, plus a small den she used as an office. There was a deck off the kitchen, and a half-bath. There were two bedrooms, and a full bath, upstairs. Laura hadn't spent a lot of time decorating, but she had painted the walls of the living room a warm gold, which set off the striped damask couch, and the collection of small, battered Oriental rugs she had strewn on the hardwood floor. An old blanket chest served as a coffee table, surrounded by an assortment of odd chairs, many bought for a few dollars at flea markets, and upholstered in the dark colors of jewels. Tom's eye, though, lit on a strange object which stood opposite the sofa, between two windows. "Gracious," he said.

"I didn't have anywhere else to put it," Laura said. Okay, having a big leather saddle in your living room might be suggestive of . . . something, but it was, after all, one of the few really beautiful—and expensive—things she owned, even though she rarely used it for its intended purpose these days. So, she kept it in the living room, stirrups and all, oiled and glowing, resting on a blanket stand she had picked up at a tag sale.

Tom crossed the room to look at it more closely. "I think it's lovely. Unusual as furniture, but lovely in itself. Do you ride?"

She shrugged. "When do I have time? I *used* to ride."

"We'll have to go together one of these weekends; I know a place in the mountains where they keep some pretty good horses."

"I'd like that," she said. Did he mean it, or was he groping for conversation, feeling as awkward as she was? No, Tom was never awkward. "Would you like coffee, or something?" she asked.

He was standing a few feet away from her, in the center of the room; she had taken his coat and hung it, with hers, in the hall closet. His hands were in his pockets, and he was smiling. "No," he answered. "I don't want coffee."

And then she knew what he knew, why she had asked him in,

and why he had accepted. She took a few steps, and stood in front of him, not touching him yet, but looking at him.

I am going to sleep with my boss, she told herself; after five years of absolutely nothing between us, we are going to be lovers. He smiled at her, and she stepped into his arms. When he kissed her, she tasted scotch, and cigars—very male, and surprisingly pleasant. She slipped her arms around him, under his suit-jacket; she could feel his leanness beneath the crisp cotton of his shirt. It felt perfectly natural to kiss him, despite all the years they had spent together without so much as making meaningful eye contact. It was as if, when he talked of her as a partner, an equal, he had slipped some invisible tether that was holding them down, tying them together as boss and subordinate. When the tether loosed, their friendship, with all its respect, affection—and desire—had floated free. *But it must have been there always,* she marveled; *how have we kept this secret from ourselves for five years?*

She rested her head on his chest, and listened to his heartbeat, and his quiet breathing. He unbuttoned the bottom buttons of her jacket, and slipped his hand underneath it, where it rested, warm and surprisingly soft, on her rib cage, just under her breast. They stood like that for a time, until she stepped backward, and gave him her hand; she led him upstairs.

(Music) Scooooott Ressler!

Welcome back, folks. Give us a call, and let us know what's on your mind—those of you that have one, anyway. We've heard from enough stupid people for one night. Ed from Norcross, you're on.

Hey, Scott. How're you doing?

Pretty good for a man surrounded by idiots. You're not an idiot, are you, Ed?

I hope not. I wanna talk about this cop, the one who killed the guy. . . .

Okay, I think you mean the cop who ALLEGEDLY killed a suspect.

Whatever. I mean, who can blame the cops? They try and do their job, but those judges won't convict anyone. This guy who got killed, he raped a little girl. . . .

ALLEGEDLY raped a little girl, Ed. We wouldn't want to violate anyone's civil rights, would we?

Aw, man, you know he did it. But he probably never would have done any jail time—some psychologist would have talked about his childhood, and all that crap. . . .

Exactly. So who can blame a cop, who's trying to do his job as best he can, with the limited resources available to him, if he goes a little nuts and squeezes a little too hard on some scumbag's neck? Thanks for your call, Ed. That's what we're talking about tonight, folks:

Why the courts won't let the cops do their jobs. I don't want to hear a lot of crap about police brutality—I think we need more brutal cops. Am I right, Sidekick Mel?

Very much so, Scott. . . .

6

Jeff Williams knew more variant usages of the word *fuck* than Laura had thought possible. So far, in the half hour she had spent with him, he had used it as a verb, of course, but also as a noun, and an adjective, in its participle and gerund forms. He had compounded it with other words to form interesting new nouns, *head* and *wad* being two of her favorites. The man was a fucking dictionary.

Jeff was beside himself with rage and anxiety; Laura regretted her decision to come out to see him this morning, but he was her client, after all, and she thought he could use the support, not to mention that she wanted to go over his story as many times as possible, in the hopes of shaking out some new detail which would help them. She should have gone straight to the office, closed the door, and told Cecelia to take messages. She needed time to think. But she hadn't. After Tom left, she had rolled out of bed, in a manic frenzy, and showered. She called the garage and told them where they could find her dead car, then she called a taxi, and directed it to take her to Williams's house. There, she had been greeted by a sleepy contingent of journalists, waiting for something to happen. She was, apparently, their long-awaited news event; they had surged forward in a mass, bristling with microphones and cameras. She managed to get away from them, and into Jeff's house, where he had immediately begun this extended, obscene rant. Her hopes of a productive meeting were fading; she had thought that if they were to go, one by one, through the members of his squad who were on duty that night, they could maybe place someone who didn't belong there near the interrogation room. But Jeff wasn't interested in talking about anything but effin' this and effin' that.

She drew a breath, and interrupted him. "Jeff, listen to me. You have to calm down. This is your life right now, and you're just going to have to deal with it for a while. In the meantime, pacing around and yelling is not getting you anywhere."

He stopped pacing long enough to light his fifth cigarette. "Fuck that. I want those vultures off my fucking lawn."

"Fine; call the cops and have them send someone out to do crowd control."

"Fuck the cops; I don't want their help."

"Then you're going to have to put up with the human yard furniture for a while. Look, if this isn't going to be productive, I can go. I have things to do back at the office." *Like see Tom,* she thought; what would that be like, seeing him for the first time after last night? She scolded herself for thinking about him again; this was not the time to get all doe-eyed about a new lover. "Answer my question, Jeff: Who from sex-crimes was on duty night before last?"

Jeff sighed, and flopped onto the couch, resigned. "Me. Eleanor Haines, my partner, of course; she went to call the district attorney when we brought the asshole in, so she was on the phone most of the time we were booking the sorry-assed little shit. Mark Little; he's another detective."

"Where was he?"

"Little? Probably in the can. He has digestive problems. His partner would know—Bruce Stevens; you ask him. But this is no good; it was a uniform that did this, not a detective."

"What makes you say that?"

"I saw the mark on his neck; had to be done with a nightstick. Detectives don't carry nightsticks." Jeff took a pull on the cigarette, and looked at her earnestly; he was clinging to the nightstick theory as the single piece of exculpatory evidence they would need.

Laura sighed. "Detectives must have access to nightsticks, Jeff— you're in a police station, for pity's sake. There must be a few lying around."

"Nope. They're checked out to cops, just like the guns. They're *weapons.* And I don't have one, see what I mean? How could I have killed a guy with a nightstick if I don't even have one?" He leaned forward and thumped a huge fist on his knee as he spoke, to emphasize his point.

Laura didn't know how to convince him that the medical examiner was unlikely to state with certainty that a nightstick had been the murder weapon. Something *like* a nightstick, perhaps, but there would be no absolutes in this case. She was surprised at Jeff's naïveté, in fact, and she wondered if the earnestness she saw in his face was really the heavy concentration of the not-so-bright. She had seen that look before, on the faces of the slow kids at school, on clerks at the Qwik Mart, on other clients' faces as she tried to waken them to their options. Jeff was not *getting* it. She sighed. "Who else was on duty?"

"That was pretty much it. That time of night, on a weeknight, there's usually only one detective team, no lieutenant. The rest of them were there because it was a big case. Kowalski's always there for the big cases, the ones that get a lot of press."

"Kowalski was there?"

"Yeah, he was honchoing the investigation from his desk. We were doing the work, you know—we were the ones who questioned the kids from the school, and who ID'd Corey Taylor as the bad guy. But Kowalski had to be there, too, you know, just to *be there*. He was supposed to have the night off, after that Hunicutt thing, but he came back to the squad room, all pissed off. At *you*," Jeff said, laughing at the memory.

"You're saying Kowalski didn't have to be there?"

"Nope."

"Do you get along with the lieutenant?"

Jeff averted his eyes, and shrugged. "Kowalski's okay, I guess. I mean, I don't have a personal relationship with him. He's real by-the-book, not much for hanging around with us. Distant. But he was on me like stink on shit on this case; he came in while we were booking Taylor, watched the whole thing, and he even came into the interrogation room with me. He does that on big cases—any time he might get his picture on the news."

Jeff sounded bitter; Laura could tell that there was a problem between him and Kowalski, but he wasn't going to say what it was. Maybe Kenny could help. "Did Kowalski say anything to Taylor?"

"No. Not a word; just watched."

"What about you? Did he talk to you, or Haines?"

"Yeah. Told me, anyway, to make it clean. He said he didn't want any problems with this one."

"Why would he have said that? Had there been problems in the past with your arrests?"

"No," Jeff said, beginning to get agitated again. "I already told you that—that's not my style."

"Take it easy; I just want to know why Kowalski made a remark like that. Is that the kind of thing he'd say on every arrest?"

"No. He doesn't usually get that involved. Except in situations like your Hunicutt case; he was all over that one, too."

Laura thought back to the afternoon when the police had come for Alex. They notified her in advance that Alex would be arrested, so she had been able to negotiate an orderly surrender. The rich *are* different; they get a polite phone call before the cops come. She had been allowed to stay with Alex through most of the booking process, and the questioning, of course, until they had taken him to the holding cell to await his quick, prearranged arraignment. Kowalski had been there, from soup to nuts; he had done all the talking, and had questioned Alex. There was another detective there, a black woman—that must have been Jeff's partner, Haines.

It hadn't struck her as significant at the time; she had assumed that Alex was getting the kid-glove treatment because of his last name, but now she wondered. Could Kowalski have known something about Corey Taylor that made him special, too—like, that Taylor's brother had been a cop? Laura tried to remember when Taylor's brother died; it had been five years ago, she thought. Kowalski hadn't arrived in Atlanta until two years after that, so there was no way he could have known Tony Harrell. Scratch that theory, then.

She looked at her notes again; there was something else she wanted to ask Jeff. Oh, yes. "Why was Taylor left alone? Shouldn't someone have been with him?"

"Yeah, someone should have been. In fact, he should have been returned to the holding pen, but it's on another floor, and it was too much of a pain in the ass. His lawyer would have gotten there as soon as we'd checked him in, so, what the hell, we left him in interrogation."

"So you didn't follow proper procedure?"

"Nope," he said, with a shrug.

"I take it that proper procedure is more honored in the breach than the observance." He looked puzzled; Shakespeare might have been beyond his reach. "I mean, did you normally ignore procedure, when it would be inconvenient?"

"All the time. If we followed every rule, we'd never get anything done."

"Why leave him alone in the interrogation room? Couldn't you have had someone stay with him?"

"No, 'cause you'd have to take *two* cops in there to do it. See, you leave him with one, and the guy gets hurt, there's no one to say what happened. So you always do everything in twos, and we just didn't have the manpower that night."

"So Kowalski was aware that Taylor was in there alone, and that it was a breach of procedure?" Laura made a few notes; this could help them.

"I guess so. Yeah, he knew—I told him that the guy was lawyering up, and that I'd left him alone to stew."

Interesting. Laura was on the point of following up with another question about Kowalski's behavior, when her beeper went off, causing her to jump nearly out of her skin. She hated the damn thing, but James Scarborough, the managing partner, insisted that all the attorneys at P&C carry them, so they would never be out of touch. It made Laura feel like a bike messenger, but she acceded to the policy, and went along. Tom didn't, of course; he had tossed his in a desk drawer, and said no more on the matter, although he carried a cellular phone—turned off, of course, so that its ringing wouldn't disturb him.

She dredged the shrieking beeper from her briefcase, and checked the number. She felt a little disappointed to see that it wasn't Tom calling. It was Kenny.

"Can I use your phone?" she asked Jeff.

"Yeah. It's still off the hook; they were going to break my answering machine, they were calling so much, so I just took it off."

Laura punched in the number of Kenny's car phone; he picked up after one ring. "Kenny? Laura. You beeped?"

"Sure did. Where are you? I think I may have something."

"What?" she asked.

"No, I want to tell you in person. Where are you?"

"At Jeff's. Can you come here?"

"I'm on 85 North right now; I'll be there in about ten minutes. Sit tight." He hung up.

Laura turned back to Jeff. "That was Kenny Newton—he thinks he may be onto something. He's on his way."

They killed ten minutes talking about the reporters on the lawn; Jeff returned to his toccata-and-fugue on the f-word. Laura's mind drifted, to Tom, and the night. It hadn't been awkward, as her other "first times" had been; she and Tom knew each other well, better than most new lovers. They made love the way old friends would, with more warmth than passion. No talking, either; having made the decision, neither was inclined to discuss or analyze it. They had made each other no promises, had not lied and said "I love you." Tom said nothing at all, in fact, beyond his muffled cry of "Sweetheart" as he climaxed. They hadn't done a postmortem, thank God, and she was especially grateful that he hadn't asked her the question, that very anxious male postcoital query: "*Did you . . . ?*" In fact, she hadn't, which wasn't important. Try telling that to a man, though; the question makes liars of too many women where honesty should be the law. But they had to talk sometime; this morning they had hidden under cover of appointments, and busyness. They would have to meet, soon, in their new roles. Laura wondered how it was going to feel.

A fluttering of the media flock told them that Kenny had arrived; he pushed through the cameras and the hairdos without a word, and bounded onto Jeff's doorstep. Laura opened the door. "Well?" she said.

"I bring you greetings from Smoothhead," he said, stepping inside and acknowledging Jeff with a nod.

"Who *is* this Smoothhead, anyway?" Laura asked.

"A guy—a bald guy. He's more or less the mayor of his little stretch of Pryor Road, down by the Carver Homes. If there's anything that goes on down there, Smoothhead is going to know about it."

Jeff snorted. "A drug dealer, is what you're saying."

Kenny shook his head. "No, I don't think so. I think Smoothhead draws his power from the sheer force of his personality. All things come to him, in time; he's sort of like Buddha, know what I mean?"

"No," Laura said. "But *you're* being a little too Zen here for me. Start over, but this time have it make sense."

"Gawd, you're cranky. Somebody give you decaf by mistake this morning, Counselor?" Kenny grinned; he knew something, and he was going to give it up in his own way, in his own sweet time. Laura walked back to the living room and sat down to wait him out. Kenny took off his coat, and asked Jeff for a cup of coffee.

"Only got instant, and creamer from a jar," Jeff muttered. "I can't get out of the house to the fucking grocery store."

"I'll pick up some things for you," Kenny promised, "but get me some coffee now; I was up half the night. The baby's sick," he added, more for Laura's benefit that Jeff's. Jeff muttered something, but went to the kitchen to get the coffee. "How's he holding up?" Kenny asked, when their client was out of earshot.

"Pretty fucking well," Laura said. Kenny looked startled; Laura almost never cursed. "Sorry; I've been with him too long. He could use some vocabulary-building. I was trying to get a feel for who was at the police station that night—who might have had access to Taylor."

Kenny nodded, "That's going to be real important. I've sniffed around; I tried to talk to Eleanor Haines, but she gave me the party line. One thing, though: She admits that Jeff handled the arrest by the book, and that he was relaxed and happy—not like a man who was about to pop off and kill a guy. The uniforms who went as backups on the arrest say the same thing; all in a day's work for our boy, no sign that he was about to go crazy and kill someone—if that's what the theory on this case is. But that's all I'm going to get, outside of a courtroom; they've been told not to talk to me. And Amos is even tighter-lipped than usual. You gotta put the whole bunch of them on the stand; when the charges are filed, you'll need to subpoena the department time sheets for the night, and the visitor sign-in sheet. That should give you a picture of everyone who was in the building. If I have to, I'll check each and every person who was there, until we hit pay dirt."

"So it sounds as if you think Jeff is telling the truth."

"Yep. Although, naturally, I've got nothing to back it up. But I always was one of those cops who went on instinct."

Jeff came back in, and handed Kenny a mug. "So what does this Smoothhead have to say?" he asked.

Kenny took a sip of the coffee and wrinkled his nose. "Man, you make lousy coffee. Let me back up. I was referred to Smoothhead by a neighbor of Corey's; he lived with his grandmother, you remember. I talked to all the neighbors yesterday, after I talked to the grandmother. One of them told me that, if Corey was up to anything illegal, no one in the building would know about it—Corey kept to himself. But Smoothhead, who spends his days and nights sitting outside his building, watching the neighborhood, would know if there was something up. So, this morning, I head down to see if I could hook up with him. Smoothhead is a character," he said, shaking his head. "About fifty, I guess; he's in a wheelchair—paralyzed from the waist down in Vietnam. But, man, what a talker. After an hour or so, I get him off 'Nam, off the Atlanta Police Department—which he hates, by the way; it was a big mistake to tell him I was a former cop— and onto Corey. After a lecture on men who like little girls, and what all this TV is doing to our society, I got the dirt."

"Which is . . . ?" Jeff asked, impatient.

Kenny looked at him, and laughed. "Hey, I had to sit through over an hour before I got the nugget. Be grateful for the Kenny

Newton Condensed Version. Corey Taylor," he paused for effect, "was selling guns."

Laura was momentarily speechless; Jeff, never lacking for le mot juste, said, "Fuck!"

Kenny laughed. "I had to tell you in person; it was too good to tell over the phone."

Laura shook her head, "Yes, but Kenny, *guns?* He was a street punk—or that's what you told me. Isn't it kind of hard to get illegal handguns?"

Jeff answered for Kenny. "It sure is—even in Georgia, which has no gun control laws to speak of. You're saying that asshole was getting guns from someone?"

Kenny nodded. "But don't ask me who; Smoothhead says he doesn't know where they came from. I figure, though, that Corey was the conduit for someone who might have had difficulty making connections in the projects."

"A white person, you mean?" Jeff asked.

"Exactly."

Laura frowned. "It's good, but as a motive for getting him killed inside a police station—I don't know."

Kenny shrugged. "It all goes to his bad character, anyway, and I have a feeling that if we follow this thing up, we'll find somebody at the other end who had a good reason to want Corey not to talk."

"You mean a *cop* with a good reason to shut him up," Laura amended.

Kenny looked troubled. "I'm afraid it has to be a cop. Look, this thing is going to get a lot more complicated before we get to the bottom of it. I say we take it one step at a time."

"So what's our next step?" Jeff asked, impatient.

"Smoothhead is going to try to find one of Corey's guns for us. If we can get our hands on it, we might be able to figure out where it came from. I hope."

Laura knew that she should have been delighted, but she could only see a murky mess in front of her. Stolen guns? Illegally imported guns? And who in the Police Department knew all about it?

7

They were still sitting there, a few minutes later, each contemplating the possibilities, when Laura's beeper screeched into life. "Dammit," she said, peering at the message window. Probably nothing—Libby had lost another brief, no doubt. But it wasn't; it was Davis Shelton, the assistant district attorney who was handling Jeff's case. The message was tagged *urgent*. "I better call him," she said. "Don't say a word till I get back." She went into the kitchen to make the call. Davis picked up right away. "Davis? It's Laura Chastain. What's up?"

"You're officially Jeff Williams's attorney of record, am I right?"

"One hundred percent."

"We want a meeting with you and your client. Now, right away." Davis's tone was peremptory; he had a deal for them.

"Want to give me the deal over the phone, so we can talk it over in the car?"

"There's no deal," he said. Davis was a poor negotiator. Of course there was a deal; otherwise, there would be no meeting. Laura was sure of one thing: If she were horse-trading with Shelton, he'd ride home on a chihuahua. There were folks in the district attorney's office who were sharper; it was good luck to have drawn ol' Davis, although it did mean putting up with him, the humorless little troll.

Laura tut-tutted. "Davis, you disappoint me. You want us to drive through all that lunchtime traffic, and there's no deal for us? Will you be serving sandwiches, at least? We need an incentive to come see you."

"Just get down here. Otherwise, your client is going to be under the damn jail by tonight."

"Now I'm scared. You're going to arrest my client, a cop with a spotless record, and put him 'under the damn jail' for the murder of a no-good, child-raping punk? On what evidence?"

"You know as well as I do that there's no one else who could have killed Taylor."

"On the contrary, Dave—" he hated to be called Dave "—*anyone* could have killed Taylor. Maybe you should be looking for someone with, oh, what do they call those things . . . a *motive?*"

"Are you coming, or do I send out the guys with the warrant?" She'd had enough fun. "Yes, we'll get there as soon as we can. Put the sandwiches out; I'll see you in a half hour or so." She hung up.

Kenny and Jeff looked up at her anxiously when she returned. "Boys, we have to go downtown. Kenny, are you free? My car died last night, so I came here in a taxi. I think you should drive us. We can talk about Smoothhead in the car."

"No problem."

"Jeff, change. You need to put on a suit." He was wearing jeans and a Hooters T-shirt. He looked like a thug. He nodded, surprisingly docile, and went back to his bedroom.

When they were alone, Kenny raised an eyebrow. "Davis wants to deal?"

"Of course. Put yourself in his shoes: He's got a political hot potato. The Police Department doesn't need a brutality scandal, so they want to punish someone, right away. But the dead guy wasn't exactly a solid citizen. They know that no jury is going to convict Jeff of murder, unless they make it a racial issue—and how can they do that? How can they paint Taylor as a victim, when he raped a little child—a *black* child? No, this town won't stand for it; we're not L.A. The best thing for all concerned—and you can bet that this has been decided at the *highest* level—is to make it go away fast, and put someone in jail, *without* a trial. I'm holding that card, anyway: I can take this to a jury, and to court of public opinion—if I have to."

"Would you take a deal?"

She shrugged. "A good enough deal, yes, although it would be tough sale with Jeff. And I doubt that we'll get their best offer on the table today, anyway. There's no need for us to plead it out so soon; I think we should take our time. How good is Smoothhead's story, anyway?"

"Not good enough yet."

She sighed. "Damn. I'm not in the mood for a poker game. Give

Davis this: He's hitting us at the right time—purely by accident, of course. Who knows? Tomorrow, we might just blow this thing wide open. Today, we have nothing."

Jeff came back, in a suit, knotting a hideous tie. Laura surveyed him critically, and decided that he would do. They headed out the door. The sight of Jeff set off the media, and they descended on them like pigeons on corn nuts. Kenny put his arm around Laura's shoulders, and led her through the crowd. She didn't attempt to say anything at all to them, not even "no comment." They were nearing the curb, where Kenny's car waited, when Sally Rivers popped up in front of Laura. "Ms. Chastain! Laura!" she called out, presuming on their previous acquaintance. "Will you be defending Detective Williams?" Laura feinted left, then right, but Sally was determined. Short of hitting her, Laura didn't know how to get past her.

"No comment," she said.

"Can't you at least tell us if you're representing him?"

"Detective Williams hasn't been charged with anything. You'll have to excuse us now."

Sally stood her petite ground; Laura wondered why more reporters weren't assaulted by their quarry. She was getting annoyed enough to take a swing at the little munchkin herself. Sally thrust her mike back into Laura's face. "Is it true that Corey Taylor was involved in child pornography?"

Laura had to laugh, which startled Sally, allowing them to sidestep her. They got to the car with no further questions, and pulled away from the curb, filmed and photoed all the way. "See, I told you kiddie porn was going to make good headlines," Kenny said, looking back at the media mob in his rearview mirror.

"I'm glad they're picking up on that, instead of some other angle. The worse they make Taylor look, the better for us," Laura said, grimly. "Now, tell us more about Smoothhead. How does he know Corey was selling guns?"

"Smoothhead is very antigun; he has no respect for the kids who carry them. He's old-school, so to speak, a real disciplinarian. He knows about the guns, and Corey, because the son of one of his friends bought one off Corey last year. When the father and Smoothhead found out, they went nuts, and reamed the kid out."

"What happened to the gun?" Jeff asked. "Do they still have it?"

"No, unfortunately. And they didn't do the sensible thing, either—they should have taken it to the cops, but the only thing Smoothhead hates more than gun-toting punks are gun-toting cops. He says the cops don't respond to crime in the projects, that they want all the folks down there to kill each other. Says it's genocide."

"That doesn't make any sense," Laura said. "The chief, and almost half the department, are black."

Kenny chuckled. "Hey, take it up with Smoothhead—it's his theory. Anyway, they took the gun out of town, and dropped it in Lake Lanier."

"Shit," Jeff said. "They'll never find it. People have drowned in that lake whose bodies never turn up."

It was true, Laura knew, Lanier was a man-made lake, but it was so deep, and cold, in parts, that people had been known to drown from the shock of hitting a cold spot—and their bodies were never found, carried far away by the currents, and snagged on debris at the bottom. They would never find a gun dropped there a year ago. Hopeless.

"I know," Kenny said, "but it's not the only gun Corey sold. Smoothhead is making inquiries; he's going to try to find someone who still has a Corey Taylor Special, and get them to talk to us. It's a long shot: First, Smoothhead has to find this theoretical person, and then he has to talk him into letting us have the gun."

"There must be some other way. Who did Corey hang with? He had to be selling the guns for someone," Laura said. She refused to believe that a street hood could originate and run a gun-selling operation all by himself; Corey had never, according to everyone Kenny spoke to, shown any initiative.

"Corey was a loner," Kenny said. "Remember, he wasn't just any punk—he was a child molester. And you know those guys; they don't form relationships with adults. I still have to talk to the girlfriend; she's our best hope, but she's moved on somewhere,and I'm having some trouble finding her. I'll get her, though. In the meantime, I'm betting on Smoothhead."

They had been zipping south on I-85 to downtown. Kenny steered the car onto the exit ramp, and headed them toward the district attorney's offices on Pryor Street, across from the Fulton County courthouse.

Jeff, who had been brooding in the backseat, spoke up. "What's this meeting about, do you think?"

"A plea bargain," Laura said. "You're a problem, and they want you to go away."

"So what's their offer going to be?" he asked, fiddling with the knot in his tie like a man who rarely wore one.

"Assuming they're going with the theory that you killed Corey Taylor because you hate child-raping scum, I think they'll offer us voluntary manslaughter."

"There's no mandatory sentence on that, is there?" he asked, frowning.

"No. One to twenty, unless it's your third felony."

"So what kind of sentence do you think we're looking at?"

She thought for a moment, and shrugged. "I would guess closer to twenty years than to one. They have to balance Corey's despicableness against the specter of police brutality—it'll be a tough call for the DA. Let's just wait and see what they have to say."

They were nearing the Justice Center on Pryor Street; Kenny pulled up in front of the building, a relatively new, glass-cathedral affair, and dropped them off. He went to find a parking space while Laura and Jeff went inside. Once in the building, Jeff's demeanor changed; where he had been belligerent, he became nervous. Laura assumed that it was dawning on him that this was real trouble. She felt for him; as a cop, he knew how the system worked. He must have felt, suddenly, like an outsider. The assistant district attorneys, who had been on his side in the past, would now be adversaries. His fellow officers, and his lieutenant, weren't standing by him, either. Laura felt his loneliness, and sympathized. She patted his arm comfortingly in the elevator. "We're making progress, Jeff. You can get through this."

He looked straight ahead and nodded; Laura assumed that he didn't want her to see his face. The elevator doors opened, and she announced their arrival to the receptionist, who escorted them to a conference room to await Davis Shelton. They waited, and waited. Kenny joined them, and they waited some more. Jeff began to sweat and curse Davis Shelton. "That little shit. I always hated him, the little cheesedick. He blew a case of mine, you know that? Dealt a rape down to assault, and the guy got probation. Wasn't two weeks before he was climbing through another window with a stocking over his face—raped another lady. Cheesedick."

"Calm down, Jeff," Laura said. "This isn't doing any good. Let me do the talking." The door opened, and Davis entered. Laura had to try not to laugh; he tried hard to compensate, but Davis was a weenie-boy, and there was no hiding it. His scanty blond hair waved wildly with static in the dry office-building air, and he had a big soup stain on his tie. "Hello, Davis," Laura said.

"Laura," he nodded. He acknowledged Jeff with a curt nod, and pointed to Kenny. "Who's he?"

"My investigator," Laura said, with no further explanation.

"I didn't say anything about investigators coming to this meeting," Shelton huffed. "I want him to leave."

"Don't get your knickers in a twist," Laura said. "This meeting is off-the-record anyway."

"He's not covered by privilege," Davis pointed out.

"No, but he is covered by the fact that if he's indiscreet, he loses his meal ticket with P&C," Laura said. "He stays."

Davis didn't try to negotiate the point further. "Meredith is joining us."

Now, that put a new face on things. Meredith Gaffney was Davis's boss, and she was not a weenie-boy or a cheesedick; she was tough, and smart. Laura frowned, and did some quick calculus; she could have buffaloed Davis indefinitely, but with Meredith there Laura needed a new strategy. She needed to show Meredith that, if it came down to a court battle, she had something in her arsenal other than Corey Taylor's bad character. Meredith was smart enough to concede that. There was no way she could go with Smoothhead's scanty hearsay at this point—there was no proof that Corey had been selling guns, and, even if there were, there was nothing to connect his arms dealing to his death. Her mind raced; she could hear Meredith approaching.

Meredith entered the room as she always did, noisily, calling orders over her shoulder to the secretaries and assistants who followed in her wake. Her deep, hoarse voice was well-known in the halls of Georgia justice. There was no one better at her job than Meredith. Laura, although she wasn't especially eager to see her today, usually enjoyed their encounters. She liked working with the best.

"Laura!" Meredith said, extending her hand. "Congratulations on Hunicutt, I let Amos talk me into that one. He's a real Savonarola sometimes; he can preach me into seeing things his way. Win some, lose some; we'll see little Alex again some day, I'm sure. Kenny!" She crossed the room and gave Kenny a kiss on the cheek; they were old pals. "Still on the dark side, I see."

"Gotta make a living, Mer—another mouth to feed, you know."

"I heard about the baby. Gimme," she said, holding out her hand for the inevitable picture.

Davis frowned; this was not the way he liked things to go, but then again, he was not one-tenth as good at the job as Meredith. *He should be taking notes,* Laura thought. *Meredith has a relationship with me, and with Kenny, a relationship that will survive any individual case. We see each other over and over, the same players. Sure, the basis of the system is adversarial, but that doesn't mean we have to take it personally. He should notice, too, that Meredith has not said a word to Jeff, not even made eye contact, although she knows him as well as she knows us.* Jeff had noticed; he was pale, and sweating, fully cognizant at last of his new status as a defendant.

Meredith cooed over the picture of Kenny's new daughter, handed the picture back to Kenny, and snapped into business mode. "Laura, you have a problem. Your client—" she never looked at Jeff "—killed a suspect in police custody. It appears that the victim was guilty of a heinous crime, but that's no justification for murder. Of course, I see extenuating circumstances in Detective Williams's case— maybe he's been under job stress, and couldn't handle another child molester. It's feasible that a man doing a tough job, like his, could break down. We think a jury would be sympathetic."

What Meredith was saying was that she knew Corey Taylor would make a repellent picture for a jury. It was time for Laura to show hers. "I'm sure a jury would be very sympathetic, if in fact Detective Williams had suffered a breakdown. So far, though, no one's provided any evidence that he did. So you have no motive, no witnesses, no forensic evidence that points to my client—and you know as well as I do that anyone in that building had access to that interrogation room."

"But no one had a compelling reason to go in there but Detective Williams. No one, in fact, saw Corey Taylor alive after your client put him in that room. I believe he was dead when Detective Williams left him in there, Laura."

"I'm glad you have a strong belief system, Meredith; it helps in a job like this. But, unfortunately, I have a belief, too, which is that my client is absolutely innocent. Someone else killed Corey Taylor."

Meredith threw back her head and laughed, a throaty, hearty laugh that ended in a resounding snort. "That's good, Laura—and I suppose Internal Affairs is covering for someone?"

Laura shrugged. "Buy it or not, Meredith, but your theory cuts two ways. There might have been a cop in that building who had had it up to here with child molesters. In fact, anyone on the sex- crimes squad could fit that description."

Meredith wasn't laughing now. "Get serious, Laura; you're not going to try and hang this on another detective on his squad."

She shrugged again. "As far as I know, no one has stepped forward to characterize my client as distraught, or even unduly stressed by the case. On the contrary, he appears to have done a really soul-satisfying job: The child was attacked on her way home from school, and he had the suspect in custody before midnight. He tells me he felt good—happy, even—to have done such a good job. Maybe someone else on the squad was having a tougher day, though." Laura felt Kenny, sitting to her left, stiffen, wondering if she was really going to go there. Was she? Until she had started talking, she hadn't known, herself. But why had Kowalski been there, on a night he should have been off duty—a night after he had suffered a humiliating defeat in court, in a high-profile case?

Meredith leaned forward. "Give me a break. You're not seriously suggesting Amos did this?"

"Did I name any names? There were any number of squad members there that night. All I'm doing is pointing out that, in the eyes of a jury, each one of them had as much opportunity as Detective Williams, *and* the same motive you're attributing to him. You don't have a case, Meredith. So let's cut to the chase: What's your deal?"

Meredith sat back; she was angry at Laura's sneak attack. Laura didn't have time to feel bad, though, for Meredith, for Kowalski, or even for Kenny. She had a job to do, and it was easier to negotiate with an angry person than someone in control of her emotions. Meredith's reply was curt. "Voluntary manslaughter. He serves ten to twelve in a state facility."

That meant Reidsville, the infamous state prison, straight out of a Broderick Crawford movie. A cop would survive about a day there. Laura shook her head, vehemently. "Involuntary manslaughter, unlawful—five to seven at a minimum security facility." Jeff sat up straight, and started to say something; he hadn't authorized Laura to make that offer, and he wanted to protest that he wasn't going to do time for Corey Taylor. Laura silenced him with a blazing look. It was posturing, not a real offer; Meredith wasn't going to take the deal—not now, anyway. Jeff, and Kenny, had to understand that she was buying them time, a day, maybe more, to turn something up. If Amos got a little mud splashed on him, that was too bad. It was working; they had to see that it had worked.

Meredith stood up. "Well, I guess this meeting is over. You'll be hearing from us again, Laura. Kenny, all the best to the family."

All shook hands, and Meredith and Davis walked out. Laura

gathered up her things; Kenny and Jeff both started to talk. "Not here," Laura said, cutting off both of them.

They left, and rode together in the elevator in thick silence. Once outside, both men let loose. Kenny won the right to yell at her first. "Godammit, Laura, what was that—dragging Amos in? You would seriously take that in front of a jury?"

"Did you see a jury in that room? No, I would not, but can't you see that it knocked the legs out from under Meredith?"

"I can see it pissed her off. She's a good lady, Laura; why'd you have to go and do something like that? You know how close she and Amos are. Dammit, you know how close he and I are, too."

"Get your emotions out of the way, Kenny. We had nothing going into that meeting, and I had to think of something. And it worked, didn't it? She's afraid that we'll actually drag Amos—or another detective—into this, and *that's* a can of worms she'd rather keep closed. Call it tossing a virgin in the volcano—and Kowalski is the virgin. I think we won a round, guys."

It was Jeff's turn. "You call that winning? You offered to send me to jail, for fuck's sake. You know what happens to cops who go to jail? Plus which, I did not kill the little turd, and I'm not doing a day for a crime I didn't commit. You stupid *bitch.*" He towered over her, menacing, his fists clenched.

Kenny, calmer now, stepped in. "Back off, Williams, she's right. She's better at this than we are. Although," he glared at her, "I hope to God we can back up all our big talk, because if we have to take this pile of shit to court, God knows what the outcome will be. And I won't let Amos be slandered in public, Laura—I mean that."

"I understand," she said, stroking his arm. "It just came out. I could have beaten off Davis with a Tinkertoy, but with Meredith there, I needed a bigger stick."

Kenny shook his head. "I wouldn't want to be you, Laura."

"Then thank God you're not. Look, I need to get back to the office, and Jeff needs to get home before the media gets a whiff of where we are. And you have a date with Smoothhead, I believe."

Kenny nodded. "I'm parked over here; I can take you to your office, and Jeff home. Your car situation okay now?"

"I guess so; I called the garage. If it's not, I'll get a ride home." Like last night, she thought. Suddenly, she was eager to see Tom; she wanted to throw herself on his chest, and be told that she had done the right thing.

They got in the car, Laura in front with Kenny, and Jeff sullenly alone in the backseat. Kenny pulled out of the garage and maneuvered through the tangled one-way streets back to Peachtree. They were silent for a few blocks, until Kenny spoke. "So what's next?"

"I wish I knew," Laura said."Technically, the ball is always in their court—they could go for an arrest—" Jeff's head jerked up at that "—or they could make us another offer. On the other hand, if we get enough new evidence, I can take it to them—and the press— and hope they drop their investigation of Jeff, and go after whoever Corey was dealing with in the department."

"So we wait," Kenny said.

She nodded. "Yep. And they can take as much time as they want to. But if they *do* charge Jeff, it'll be a bluff. They've got no forensic evidence, no witnesses we can't impeach—and we know they don't want this to drag out into a trial."

But I don't either, she said to herself, *not with what we have— a skimpy story about Corey selling guns, and the even skimpier theory about another cop on the squad sneaking in to kill Corey for reasons unknown.* Would either be sufficient to create reasonable doubt in a jury's mind? She wouldn't want to bet on it. She glanced in the mirror, and saw that Jeff was brooding out the window, his face angry and shadowed. He was not, perhaps, the world's most lovable client, but she wouldn't want to throw even him in front of a jury on such a slim chance. They had to get more information on Corey's sideline, or they would have to bargain Jeff's freedom with Meredith Gaffney. He wouldn't like it, but he'd like Reidsville a hell of a lot less.

They reached midtown, and Kenny dropped her across the street from P&C's offices. She said good-bye to both of them, admonishing Jeff to keep his temper and not to talk to anyone. She hurried upstairs, glad to leave the tense atmosphere inside the truck. She wouldn't admit it to Tom, but she was a little worried. There were other things to say to Tom, anyway.

8

There was a stack of messages waiting, mostly unimportant, although Cheri Moore's attorney had called to notify Laura that he would not be pursuing her civil suit against Alex Hunicutt. And why should he, Laura thought. He took it on a contingency, and the settlement they'd get—with no criminal conviction—wouldn't be worth his time. Ah, justice; smells like money. She crumpled the message in her fist and tossed it away, disgusted. She should call the Hunicutts and let them know, but she wasn't in the mood to hear them crow.

She flipped through the remaining pink "While You Were Out" slips, looking for anything urgent—anything from Tom. There was nothing. Libby, however, was up in arms about something; it looked as if she had called about five times. With a sigh, Laura picked up a pad and pencil, and trudged to Libby's office. Boss Number Two was in a snit, just as she expected, about nothing. She claimed that she had needed Laura's notes from a meeting the previous week. Why she couldn't take her own notes, Laura didn't know, in addition to which it had been an extremely unimportant meeting. This was another game of Tom vs. Libby badminton, with Laura as the shuttle-cock. She felt a surge of annoyance at both of them—big babies.

When she escaped Libby's clutches, she realized that it was well past lunchtime, and she was hungry. She ran down to the deli in the lobby, and picked up a sandwich to eat at her desk while making notes of the meeting at the district attorney's office for Jeff's file. She strained all the time to hear Tom's voice in the hall, and she jumped when the phone rang, hoping it would be him. At three o'clock, she gave up on subtlety, and decided to go to his office with the trumped-up excuses of informing him about Cheri's dropped lawsuit, and updating him on the Williams case. His office was empty, and his secretary was away from her desk. Laura hesitated; she could leave a note, or come back later and hope to catch him in. As she was trying to decide, his secretary, the redoubtable Frances, returned with a stack of photocopies perilously balanced in her arms. Laura reached out and took some of them from her, and followed her into Tom's office, where they stacked them neatly on a table.

"Thanks," Frances said. "I thought I could make it, but I almost lost it. I'd hate to have dropped this—it would take half a day to get the pages back in order."

"No problem. So where is Tom, anyway?"

"Oh, that's right—you've been out. Tom was called to New York. There's some big case that's going to be argued in Georgia, apparently, and they want him to handle it. A nice sexual-discrimination suit." Frances had been with Tom since he was an associate; had she not been an extremely stylish and self-possessed woman, only a few years older than Tom, Laura would have described her relationship with Tom as "motherly." *Protective* was perhaps a better word; Tom had a lot of demands on his time, and Frances made sure that time was used efficiently. She was now fussing over the pile of papers, her back to Laura, luckily, so she could not see the disappointed expression that crossed the associate's face.

Laura struggled for an appropriate remark. "That's great. Will he be gone long?"

Frances shrugged. "Who can tell? I left his return flight open, but I booked the hotel for two nights. He said he'd try to call in. Do you need to speak to him? He's in a conference room at Starling and Hawkins this afternoon, and he's staying at the St. Regis; I can give you the numbers."

"No . . . I mean, it was no big deal. I'll see him when he gets back."

She returned to her office, unaccountably depressed. She sat at her desk, picking at the remains of her sandwich, and staring into space. After a while, she roused herself from her stupor, and put in a call to Alexander Hunicutt Sr.—no point in mooning over Tom all afternoon; that would gratify him too much, for one thing. "Please hold," Hunicutt's secretary said.

"Hunicutt," he barked, after a moment.

"It's Laura Chastain, Mr. Hunicutt. I have good news: Cheri Moore is dropping her suit against Alex."

He chuckled. "I suspected she would. We had a talk with that attorney of hers."

Laura stiffened. "You settled? Mr. Hunicutt, I don't think you should have done that without talking to Tom or me."

"Pfft," he said, dismissing her scruples. "Didn't settle a damn thing; that little slut didn't get a nickel from me. We just convinced that ambulance chaser of hers that he'd be better off dropping the whole thing."

Laura blanched, something she had never done before. It was interesting; she could actually *feel* the color bleeding from her face, and her stomach folded in on itself like a catcher's mitt. "You *bribed* him, Mr. Hunicutt?"

"Who said anything about a bribe? We just had a talk. If I threw a little business his way, put him on retainer, well, that's not a bribe."

"Yes, it is. You could be charged with a felony, and he could be disbarred. Mr. Hunicutt, if you don't mind my saying so, that was an extremely stupid thing to do."

"But who's going to find out, Laura? You're not going to say anything—hell, you can't. Anything I say to you is privileged. I could confess to murder and you couldn't do a damn thing about it—unless you wanted to get disbarred yourself."

"That's beside the point, Mr. Hunicutt. It's a matter of ethics. And how do you know this man won't say something to someone? You've created a pretty big liability for yourself, as I see it."

"He won't talk, and risk getting disbarred. I know lawyers, Laura, and, if you'll pardon my saying so, you guys are so afraid of losing your licenses that you wouldn't turn in Hitler if he confessed six million murders to you. Thanks for your call, though, darlin', and tell Tom I need to talk to him."

Laura swallowed the angry response that she was about to make. "Tom is out of town for a day or two. Would you like me to have him call you?"

"No, it'll keep. You be good, now." He hung up.

That bastard. That stupid, arrogant *bastard*. She slammed her fist on the desk. She would love the whole thing to blow up in his face, love to see him go down on this one. The *bastard*. She was on the point of buzzing Tom's secretary, and getting his number in New York, when Cecelia appeared at her door.

"This must be your week," she said, and Laura noticed that she was holding another floral arrangement, which she handed to Laura. It was small, and rounded, with tiny white rosebuds, and little purple somethings in it, fringed with a lace collar and tied with a satin ribbon, like a Victorian nosegay. Next to Hunicutt's massive arrangement, it was tiny—and perfect.

"Mercy," Laura said, "they're beautiful." She fished for the card, but she had known at a glance who they were from. The card was discreetly unsigned: *I'll call you tonight.*

"So who are they from?" Cecelia asked. "Not a client, I bet, not with that blush on you."

Laura laughed. "No, they're from a man."

"I didn't know you were seeing anyone. Is this new?"

"No, it's been going on a while."

Cece crossed her arms. "Laura, I answer your phone, and I can't remember taking any calls from a new man. I think I know who sent those."

Laura looked up, startled. She didn't want to lie to her secretary, but it really wasn't any of her business. "You'll just have to take my word on this, Cece. They're from a friend."

"Look, most of the people around here are too busy to notice what you're wearing, let alone who you're dating. Not me, though; I see how a certain partner looks at you. He's been crazy about you since the day he hired you. And *you'd* be crazy if you didn't return the favor."

Laura was even more startled; how could her secretary have seen something that had escaped her own attention? She remained silent, not wanting to admit anything to Cecelia, although she trusted the secretary's discretion almost as much as she did her own, and Tom's.

Cece waited a moment, then shrugged. "Well, whoever he is, he has good taste—in flowers and in girls."

"Thank you," Laura said, returning to her seat with the arrangement cradled in her arms as Cecelia returned to her desk. She looked at her watch: almost four. She would sit by the phone all night waiting for his call. She had a lot to tell him—Hunicutt's outrageous behavior, the meeting with Meredith, Smoothhead—but nothing seemed half as important as telling him how much she loved the flowers, and how much she missed him.

She was staring off into space again, but her reverie was interrupted by the phone. She frowned at it; she didn't want to talk to anyone. She'd let Cecelia take a message. In a minute, though, Cecelia appeared at her door. "Laura? It's Jeff Williams. The police are at his place with a warrant."

"Search warrant?"

She shook her head. "No; they're arresting him. He's being charged with felony murder."

Laura jumped to her feet. "Those jerks! Murder two! They're out of their minds. I'm going to make them sorry they messed around this time." As she talked, she was putting on her coat, and stuffing papers in her case. "Are they taking him downtown now, or should I go out there?"

"He wants you to meet them downtown."

"You bet I will; will I ever. This is out of control! Five o'clock in the afternoon . . . they're playing hardball, Cecelia. They want him to spend the night in jail. God, I'm furious." She hustled out the door, no longer the least bit dreamy.

Cecelia stood in the doorway of her office, and called after her. "Will you be back in the office today?"

"No. This is going to take a while," Laura hollered over her shoulder, from halfway down the hall.

"Don't you want to take your flowers, so you can enjoy them at home?"

"Forget it," Laura said. "I've got to kick some district attorney butt; I don't have time for flowers." And she meant it.

This was an outrage, playing games like this. Meredith knew very well what a night in jail meant to a cop; this was a deliberate humiliation, and it was aimed at her, not Jeff. If Meredith wanted to get back at her for her threats against Kowalski, well, she could have picked a fairer fight. Putting Jeff in jail for a night—for felony murder, of all the stupid, overreaching charges—even Kowalski wouldn't countenance this. Or would he? Was there something going on in that squad room she didn't know about? The cops had been too quiet on this one. Damn! Why hadn't she headed down there this morning and talked to Kowalski, and to Jeff's partner? Laura had a bad feeling, suddenly; she was missing too many pieces. Did Meredith Gaffney know something that she didn't? Her palms began to sweat. *I should have taken the offer, or at least made a realistic counteroffer. Now Jeff's going to jail, and it's your fault, Chastain.*

She was in her car, heading downtown, before she began to calm herself even a little. One step at a time, she told herself; damage control is what Jeff needs, not a lot of second-guessing. Stay the course. The warrant is out there; she needed to get the best outcome possible for Jeff: a bail hearing tonight, or tomorrow morning at the latest. It was a felony charge—that meant a Superior Court judge would have to conduct the bail hearing. But they should get bail; Jeff had been under investigation for forty-eight hours without showing the slightest tendency to flee. Damn the timing, though.

She pulled into an overcrowded parking lot near the Fulton County Justice Center, and flashed her pass at the attendant. He waved her through, but she had to park in the farthest corner. She practically jogged to the building. Please, let me be here before him, she said. She needn't have worried; she waited, pacing and planning, for fifteen minutes before a flurry of activity alerted her that they had arrived. She went outside, and saw that someone had tipped off the press, presumably the district attorney's office. Meredith was going to pay for this—if she felt this media zoo was just compensation for the potshots Laura had taken at Saint Amos, she hadn't seen anything yet. *I'll show her media frenzy*, Laura thought grimly, as she pushed her way through a crowd of cops and reporters. She wanted to be the first person Jeff saw when he got out of that squad car.

He was handcuffed, a sweatshirt draped over his wrists to hide the cuffs, and he looked like a baffled, defeated prizefighter, eager to get back in the ring despite the blood blurring his vision. Laura elbowed an Internal Affairs officer out of the way, and took Jeff's arm. "We're okay," she said to him, raising her voice to be heard over the hubbub of shouted questions and orders barked by the cops.

They managed to get into the building, and Laura saw Meredith for the first time, standing to one side with Davis Shelton. She glared at her, but said nothing. Jeff had been booked, fingerprinted, and photographed. Laura had a chance only to declare that she was his attorney before they took him to a holding cell. Finally, she was ushered into a room where Jeff, stripped of personal possessions, awaited her.

"You didn't see this coming, did you?" he asked, bitterly.

She shook her head. "No. I didn't think they'd go ahead with what they have. They're bluffing, Jeff; they'll make us another offer, I'm sure; they just want us to know they mean business."

"Can you get me out of here?" His eyes were pleading.

"I don't know. It's obviously part of their strategy, arresting you late in the afternoon. I'm going to try for a hearing tonight, and I'll stay here as long as I have to, but we might as well resign ourselves to the fact that you may be spending the night in jail. I'll make sure you're isolated from the general population, though; Meredith won't want that on her head, I'm sure."

He laughed, hollow and exhausted. "Think so? That bitch would love to see me with a coupla black eyes."

"She's not a bitch; she's just very, very tough. And good at her job. But so am I, Jeff, so am I. We're going to get through this. They're just trying to shake you up, get you into a frame of mind to plead."

"I won't. They can keep me in here until the trial, but I will not plead guilty to killing that piece of shit."

He lifted his head, defiant, as he spoke, and Laura, touched by his crude courage, put her hand on his shoulder and gave it a squeeze. "Atta boy. Let's get it over with, now; sooner you get in line, the better chance you have of getting your bail tonight." He nodded, and Laura called for the guard to let her out. She turned and gave Jeff the thumbs-up as she left him; he returned her salute, wanly.

In the hallway, she saw Meredith and Davis. She stalked up to them, and, ignoring Davis, turned her wrath on Meredith. "What's your game, Meredith?"

"Game? Just doing my job, Laura."

"Bull; you didn't need to move on this tonight, and you know it. Where's your decency? We could have arranged a surrender. You want him to spend the night in jail; you think it'll soften him up for a plea. You don't know him, Meredith; he won't go for it. But you do know me, and, so help me God, I'll raise questions on the public record that'll curl your hair. In fact, I might just have a little press conference right here, tonight, since you've already gathered the sharks. Want me to use Kowalski as chum?"

"You wouldn't."

"Try me." She looked Meredith directly in the eye, defiant. "Guess calling the news hounds wasn't such a great idea after all, huh?"

"We didn't," Meredith said.

"Come on—you expect me to believe that they're here as a result of their keen journalistic instincts? This is an ambush."

"The Police Department must have alerted the press, Laura; I swear to you it wasn't us."

"Whoever—I could care less. But I'm going to walk out there right now and give them Kowalski, unless you get Jeff out of here by ten o'clock tonight." It was nearly seven.

"I can't guarantee that, Laura," Meredith said. "Be reasonable. And you can't go out there with some concocted tale."

"Can't I? You have," Laura replied. Amos Kowalski chose that moment to amble down the corridor toward them. "Why don't you ask him what he thinks, Meredith?"

"Ask me what?" Kowalski said, stopping to join them. His suit jacket was off, and his shirtsleeves were rolled up on his forearms. He was a big guy, almost as big as Jeff, but wirier. Not the kind of guy to play around with.

Meredith rolled her eyes. "Laura has a theory—a crackpot theory—that someone other than Williams, on your squad, killed Corey Taylor. She thinks it's you, in fact, and she's willing to take that speculation to the press."

Laura watched Kowalski's face; she didn't know him well. Despite Kenny's fondness for him, she thought that he was a cold guy, too self-controlled by far. Distant, as Jeff said. Laura wondered if he had a temper. How was he going to react?

He laughed. He threw back his head, and laughed. Laura felt her own lips twitching in sympathy, but Meredith was not amused. "It's not funny, Amos. She's acting irresponsibly. Can't you see the implications—that the cops are scapegoating one of their own to cover a brutality scandal at the top?"

"Of course I see, and my hat's off to her. If she steps out there with that story, the department's going to be putting out the fire for months—and Jeff Williams's trial will be a circus. Face it, Meredith, you're going to have to give the lady what she wants."

"Get us into a courtroom, now," Laura said.

"I'll get a gag order," Meredith said. "I'll fix it so you can't talk to the press."

"When? In the next five minutes? I don't think so," Laura said. Then, in a conciliatory tone, "You've made your point. Just don't make Jeff spend the night in jail, Meredith, and I'll keep a lid on my wilder theories. For tonight, anyway."

Meredith looked at Amos for a moment; he shrugged, and she sighed. "Okay; I'll move it up. But the offer of man one is off the table, Laura. We're not negotiating anymore."

"Fine. Let's just get this over with, so we can get ready for a trial."

The two women looked at each other for a long moment. At last, Meredith smiled and stuck out her hand. "I should have remembered you've been learning at Tom Bailey's knee. See you in the courtroom." She left, towing Davis in her wake.

Laura turned to Kowalski, still standing beside her with the remnants of a smile on his face. "Sorry to drag you in, Lieutenant. I was looking at a volcano, and you were the only virgin handy."

"No sweat; you did what you had to. Meredith would have done the same, in your place. But, Chastain, I want you to know something: I didn't kill Corey Taylor."

"I never seriously said you did."

"Your client wants you to think I did, though."

She shrugged. "He's not the one who pointed to you; that was all me. Kenny had a bird about it." She looked up at him. "Internal Affairs rushed to the conclusion that it was Williams too quickly. I think you're going to be surprised when the whole story comes out, Kowalski."

"If Jeff Williams is innocent, I will be surprised," Kowalski said.

"What makes you so sure he's guilty?" Laura asked.

He shook his head. "Save it for your cross-examination, Counselor." He looked down at her, then reached out to push aside a stray lock of hair that had wandered onto her cheek. She was startled at his touch. "Be careful, Laura. I don't want to see you get burned."

"Don't worry about me," she said, but he was spooking her. Once again, she had the queasy feeling that everybody else knew more than she did—it was like coming in midway through a play, without a program: Who were all these characters? "I have to go; I've got a client to bail out." She walked away, but she could feel his eyes on her until she turned the corner.

Three hours later, Jeff was a free man, pending a preliminary hearing scheduled for the following week. Laura had moved that the case be dismissed on the grounds that the prosecution had no evidence; the judge deferred consideration of her motion until he could hear both sides argue the matter more fully. It was a goal to strive toward, at least, but Jeff didn't seem to think it meant anything; his world had been shattered by the humiliation of the arrest. Laura drove him home in silence, looking sidelong at his immobile profile from time to time. She stopped at the curb in front of his neat ranch house. "Try to sleep, Jeff. At least it's all out in the open now; first thing in the morning, I'm going to subpoena the Police Department for time records, sign-in sheets, Taylor's arrest record—everything they've got. And Smoothhead's going to come through with one of Corey's guns. It's going to turn out okay."

He nodded. "Kowalski was in the courtroom."

"Yes. I talked to him before the hearing."

"He thinks I did it, doesn't he?"

She couldn't lie to him. "Yes. He does."

"Laura, I been a cop for ten years; it's my life. And I'm good; ask anybody. But Kowalski's never liked me. I don't know what I did to piss him off, but he's been up my rear for the past three years, ever since he got here."

"When it's over, you can request a transfer off his squad."

Jeff nodded. "I'm gonna do that. Thanks, Laura; I'm glad you're my lawyer."

"Get some sleep," she said, patting his hand. She watched him walk up the path to his front door before she drove away. It was after ten, and she was exhausted and hungry—not to mention that she had probably missed Tom's call. She stopped and picked up a salad at the grocery store, and headed home. The answering machine was blinking like a buoy: four messages from Tom, the last one sounding concerned. She jotted down the number he left, and dialed it on the cordless phone while she put the salad on a plate and poured a glass of wine. "Conference room," a male voice answered.

"I'm looking for Tom Bailey. Is he there?"

"Yeah; lemme get him. Bailey! Call for you!"

There was a pause before she heard Tom's voice. "Bailey," he said, and she melted.

"It's me."

"Laura! Where have you been?"

"Bailing out my client."

"They arrested him?"

"Oh, yeah, we've had a big day."

"What's the charge?"

"Tom, I'm tired. I don't want to talk about the case. I want to talk about the flowers, and you, and how much I miss you."

His voice softened. "I miss you, too. It was just bad timing, Laura; I didn't want to leave so soon after. . . ."

"I know. I understand. Are you having a fabulous time in New York?"

"No. I haven't been out of this building since I got here. And I doubt I will. But I am looking out the window; I can see the Chrysler Building, and the Empire State. They're all lit up."

"I bet it's beautiful."

"I would rather be looking at you, sweetheart. They're calling me back now; I have to go."

"Call me tomorrow; I do have business to catch you up on."

"I will. Sweet dreams."

"You, too." She hung up, and wiped away a tear. He better come home soon; she was tired of fighting the world alone.

WTLK: Twenty-four hours: All talk, all yours. It's the Scott Ressler show—honk if you're listening!

I tell you folks, sometimes I think they do this stuff to get on my nerves. Just because you got a white cop who kills a black suspect, do you have a racial incident? How about we just say a cop killed a child molester, and leave it at that? Race has nothing to do with this case, folks, nothing at all. This is pure and simple a case of a cop who'd had it up to here with liberal judges and psychologists. We have a caller on the line. Derek from Atlanta, you're on.

Hey, man. How you been?

Pretty good. What's on your mind?

You're talking about this Taylor case. I respect what you're saying, man; nobody wants to defend a child molester. But as usual, the press is buying the police story. If you knew the real story, you'd feel different.

I bet you're going to tell me the real story, aren't you?

You're not going to hear this on the news, man, but Corey Taylor didn't rape that girl.

No? Why'd she say he did, then?

She's a kid, man; you know she's gotta be scared. The cops told her what to do. But ask anybody in the neighborhood, and they'll tell you she was seen leaving school with a white man. . . .

That is without a doubt the biggest crock of doo I've heard all night. You're saying the cops framed Taylor, then killed him?

Things like this happen all the time. . . .

Goodnight, Derek. (flatulence sound effect). Sorry about that caller, friends; we don't need that kind of irresponsible talk. . . .

9

"Ms. Chastain! Ms. Chastain!" To Laura's horror, the press was not only waiting for her, they had been clever enough to figure that she would be entering the building through the parking garage. They rushed toward her as she got out of the car, dragging equipment as they came. She stood frozen for a moment, unsure what she should do. Her instinct was to get back in the car and run away, tires shrieking, or to put her head down and muscle through them as she had done the previous day. It occurred to her, however, that she could make them go away peacefully, and take some control over the publicity of Jeff's case, if she made a simple statement to them. She stood, and waited for them to reach her.

Sally Rivers was in the lead, despite having the highest heels in the crowd. She was so absurdly petite, even with the heels, that Laura wondered how she managed not to be knocked down and trampled by the journalistic throng. She thrust her microphone at Laura, and shouted her question louder than all the others combined. "Will you be using an insanity defense?"

Laura shut the door of her car, and looked down at her. "Hello, Sally." That would make the others angry, she knew, messing up their feed by talking to only one of them, but Laura knew that she might need an ally in the media as this thing dragged out. She was making friends with Sally. "Who said anything about insanity? We entered a not guilty plea, and we'll take that to a trial."

"But," Sally, said, artfully throwing an elbow at a blond guy who Laura recognized as someone named Brad, "isn't the evidence against your client overwhelming?"

Laura laughed. "Who have you been talking to? There's no evidence at all. But you'll know more after the preliminary hearing next week. Until then, I hope that there's no rush to judgment in the media."

Brad managed to oust Sally from her spot, and, his brow artistically furrowed for the benefit of his cameraman, asked a Tough Question. Brad had aspirations for the big-time, Laura could see; he was probably the kind of little doink who watched *60 Minutes* on Sunday night instead of *The Simpsons*. "Was the murder of Corey Taylor racially motivated, Ms. Chastain?"

"You'd have to ask the murderer that, but I don't know where you can find him—or her. You'll have to excuse me now; I'm late for a meeting." She waded purposefully into them, and, at least partially satisfied, they stood aside and let her pass.

That went well, she thought; she had managed to say exactly nothing. She hoped, fervently, that the partners of Prendergrast and Crawley would see it that way when they saw her on the six o'clock news. She prayed, too, that all the old trilobites had gotten safely inside without being assaulted by the jackals; she didn't want to think about what James Scarborough would do if the partners were disturbed by reporters on their way into work. With or without Tom's backing, that might be the end of her independent caseload, and a criminal practice at the firm.

For the next few hours, Laura worked like an insect, drafting subpoenas of everyone and everything she could think of. She was going to drag every member of the sex-crimes squad up on the stand at that hearing, so help her, *including* Kowalski. And she was going to get a list of everyone else who had been in the building, and at least threaten to subpoena them as well. She also requested Jeff's personnel files; if Kowalski wasn't going to talk to Kenny, they would just have to find out what he thought of Detective Williams some other way. The file, of course, was not Jeff's property, and Laura didn't expect the police to volunteer to give it to her, but one way or another, she was going to get her point across to the judge: There were a lot of people who could have throttled Corey Taylor, any number of them with better motives than Jeff Williams.

After lunch, her morning's work off in word processing, she felt a need to be up and doing. She grabbed the phone and called Kenny. "Hey, Ken—you talked to all the cops on the sex-crimes squad, didn't you?"

"Yup. All of 'em said the same thing; they think Jeff did it, but they won't say why."

"What about his partner—Haines? Can't she say more about Jeff's state of mind?"

"Sure, probably—on the stand. I know Ellie; I like her a lot, and I think she likes me, but she wasn't talking."

"Why, Kenny? Because Kowalski has told them not to?"

"Could be. Whatever the reason, though, I got nothing from any of them."

"What if I called her?"

"Laura, sweetie, if she ain't gonna talk to me, who she knows and loves, she sure as heck ain't gonna talk to you."

"Says you. Maybe I can . . . bond with her, or something. Maybe it's a girl thing. Think I should give her a call?"

"Knock yourself out. But Eleanor's tough, and professional—I don't think you're going to get her giggling and talking about boys on a short acquaintance, Laura."

"Who says I want to? Gimme her number."

Kenny was right about Eleanor Haines's professionalism. After making it through the voice mail system, and getting the actual Detective Haines on the phone, Laura found herself at a conversational loss. "Detective Haines? My name is Laura Chastain. I represent . . ."

"I know who your client is," Haines said.

"Well, I though maybe you and I could get together and talk. . . ."

"I don't see why," the detective said, still chilly.

"Strictly off the record," Laura said. "Jeff Williams is your partner, and I thought maybe you could give me some insight into the workings of the squad."

"You mean, I could tell you why we think Jeff killed Corey Taylor."

"Yes, if that's what you want to do, fine," Laura answered, frustrated. "All I'm asking for is a few minutes of your time."

"Under the circumstances, I don't think it's appropriate for us to talk."

"Oh, come on—Jeff hasn't been charged, and I told you, it's off the record. I couldn't possibly use anything you say in court!"

There was a pause on the other end of the line. "I'll have to get this okayed," Haines said.

"That's fine; I understand," Laura said, knowing full well who would be doing the okaying. "Ask Lieutenant Kowalski; you can call me back."

Haines did call back, in about an hour, to tell Laura that she could meet her that afternoon. She named a diner close by police headquarters. Laura knew the place; it was where all the cops went to work on their ulcers with bad food and toxic coffee. Kenny loved it. Laura wrinkled her nose, but agreed to meet Haines there. "How will we recognize each other?" Laura asked.

"Oh, I'll know you—I've seen you on television," Haines answered. Laura thought she detected a note of scorn in that remark, but she let it pass. She put her head down and worked until it was time to leave for the meeting, and ended up rushing, afraid she was going to be late.

She needn't have worried; once in the diner, she stood inside the doorway, and looked around for anyone who might be a black female sex-crimes detective, but saw only uniformed officers and the occasional slumming member of the brass. Laura took a booth, and ordered a cup of tea; she'd had the coffee here once, and that had been enough. The waitress brought her a metal pot of hottish water, and a bag of supermarket-brand tea; Laura dunked the bag while watching the doorway for Haines's arrival. At three-fifteen, an attractive, well-dressed black woman, unmistakably a cop in her bearing, entered and looked around until she spotted Laura. She walked across the diner, and took a seat in the booth.

"Sorry to keep you waiting," Haines said. "I got hung up."

"No problem. Do you want to order something? It's on me."

"Tea for me, too."

Laura called the waitress, who was obviously thrilled to have two such big spenders on her shift; she sloshed hot water as a sign of her contempt. "So, you want me to spill my guts about Jeff," Haines said, as her tea brewed.

"I wouldn't put it exactly that way, but I am curious as to why Jeff was elected guilty by consensus in the department."

"Elected? He was charged because he did it."

"Come on, Detective Haines; you'd hardly call what happened in this case an investigation. You were on the Taylor arrest, too—were you questioned as a suspect? Did Internal Affairs ask you about your state of mind, want you to account for the time Corey was alone in the interrogation room?"

"Of course. And I answered all the questions to their satisfaction. Look, we sit on an open floor. There aren't a lot of us. It's not hard to keep track of who is where for a half hour or so, and we were *all* present and accounted for—Jeff, too. But that's not surprising; Corey Taylor was dead when Jeff left him in that room."

"Why weren't you in the interrogation room with Jeff? Should a cop ever be alone with a suspect?"

"No. It's against procedure."

"So why did you bust procedure and leave Jeff alone with Taylor? Why was Taylor left alone for more than a half hour?"

"Look, it happens, Ms. Chastain. It won't again, believe me; we've all had disciplinary notes put in our files—Amos, too. But Corey Taylor wanted a lawyer, so Jeff said he'd take him to a room where he could wait. It would have taken an hour to check him into holding, for God's sake—we do this all the time. I said okay, and let Jeff take him away, while I sat down to do the paperwork—which I always do, by the way, because Jeff hates paperwork." There was an unmistakable note of anger in her voice.

"You don't like Jeff, do you?"

"That's irrelevant; he was my partner. Despite what you see on the TV shows, we don't all love each other."

"But you *really* don't like him—why? Is he a bad cop? Doesn't do his job?"

"No—on the contrary, Jeff is a very good cop. Good instincts, levelheaded. He's competent. If you ask him, of course, he'll give you some crap about how he's intuitive, and I'm analytical—that was his excuse for dumping the paperwork and the follow-up on me, anyway. It's garbage; my instincts are as good as his, *plus* I get the paperwork done."

"This is a lot of hostility, just because a guy was a little lazy on his follow-up. It sounds like the fallout between you and Jeff might have been . . . *personal.*"

"Don't even go there; I'm engaged, to a very fine man. I wouldn't touch Williams with a barge pole, anyway—he's a slob. Would *you* date him?"

"That's beside the point."

"Exactly. So don't go tagging me with that. Look, I don't know what you want me to say, but I'm not hiding anything, and neither is Amos. Jeff killed Taylor, and if I were you, I would be making a deal."

Laura frowned. "Detective, you know there's no case against Jeff. Why should I do what Meredith and Amos want, and send my client quietly away to jail? You say you're not hiding any cards; well, neither am I. Any one of you could have killed Taylor, and we all know how loyal cops are to each other. If you suspected that one of your other colleagues had tippy-toed in there and wrung Corey's useless neck, would you speak up? It's very convenient that the most unpopular guy on the squad was alone with the suspect for a few minutes, isn't it? I think someone else was, too, maybe someone more popular."

"Oh, yes, Amos told me that you think he did it."

Laura threw up her arms in frustration. "All I've said is that he *could* have, not that he did. But you at least acknowledge that he could have, don't you? Can you honestly tell me you can account for Kowalski's whereabouts during that half hour or so?"

"Of course not. But why would Amos have done it?"

"Why is Jeff supposed to have done it, Detective? Will someone just tell me that?" Laura thumped the flat of her palm on the Formica tabletop to emphasize her point.

Haines was silent for a long minute. "Cops know character, and Amos Kowalski has one of the best characters I've ever seen. Jeff Williams has one of the worst. I know what I know, Ms. Chastain, and that is that Jeff did it. I'll say that in any number of courtrooms, and nothing you can do will change my mind. You don't know Amos Kowalski. . . ."

"But I do; I've sparred with him before. He's smart, and quick—and decent. He had also just lost a case that was very important to him, only hours before Taylor turned up dead."

"Hunicutt? You think that got to Amos? Crap. I took Cheri Moore's complaint; I followed the case closely. Amos knew it was a long shot, but he also knows a rape when he sees it. Sure, he wanted to make a point, but he also wanted to get a dangerous man off the streets."

"Then why didn't he take the deal we offered last summer?"

"Three months in a country-club prison, and a year of probation? He would have carried that on his conscience forever; he preferred losing honorably to taking a deal he thought was bad."

"Was it his decision to make, Detective? Was it the best thing for Cheri Moore, or even for Alex?" What had Meredith called Kowalski—Savonarola? A man burning with righteousness. "Who died and made Amos king?"

"Look, I didn't come here to talk about my boss; I came here to talk about the Taylor case, and I've told you all I'm going to about Jeff. You can subpoena me, and I'll say the same thing—we all will. Jeff did it. You may think it's just speculation, that we haven't shown motive, or even opportunity, but if a jury hears seven of Jeff's fellow detectives call him a killer, it's going to carry some weight. I have to get back to work now." She stood, and prepared to leave.

Laura stood, and shook Haines's hand. "Thanks for coming, and tell Amos I said hi."

Haines left, with a curt nod, and Laura settled the check. The conversation gave her food for thought, at least; there was some kind of *cult* around Kowalski that Laura just didn't get. He was a nice guy, and smart, but his more heroic qualities eluded her. And yet, people she respected—Kenny, Meredith, and even Eleanor Haines—would crawl through shattered glass for the guy. Go figure, she shrugged. But there are people who buy tickets to Charlie Sheen movies, too; everyone has a following. One thing she had gleaned, however: The prosecution's case was still based entirely upon one factor—Jeff's access to Corey Taylor, and to the interrogation room. Laura was pleased by that; she knew that she could demonstrate that anyone with a badge could have gone into that room, at any time. Knowing, too, that there had been a violation of procedure—one that did not reflect well on Lieutenant Kowalski—also weighed in their favor. Who, Laura wondered, could have seen the entrance to the interrogation room? Everyone? No one?

Back in her car, Laura took out a small notebook and flipped to a blank page: *Get Jeff to draw diagram of squad room, marking positions of interrogation room and all officers present at time of killing.* She had the distinct feeling that wagons were being circled by the sex-crimes squad, and she wondered why. Was it to damn Jeff, or to protect someone else? And, if protection was the goal, who could inspire that kind of loyalty?

10

Word Processing had delivered a crisp stack of subpoena requests for Laura when she returned; she signed them, and told Cece to get them to Meredith and the judge before close of business. There was a sheaf of messages, too, including several requests for interviews from various media outlets. Laura flipped through them; they ran the gamut of print, television, and radio. Even the producer of the Scott Ressler show, Atlanta's on-air bile duct, had called. She sifted them, and kept only Sally Rivers's message, which included a beeper number. It might come in handy.

Laura cleared her desk, satisfied that she had done a decent day's work; she began to think that she might even get home at a normal hour. In a cheerful frame of mind, she called Jeff, just to pep him up.

"How are you holding up?" she asked, with genuine concern.

"How do you think?" he snarled. "I still can't get out because of all the damn reporters, and daytime television sucks."

Laura felt genuinely sorry for him; Jeff may not have had the sunniest disposition to begin with, but the strain of the last few days would have made anyone surly. "Kenny said he was going to try to stop by today," she said, hoping that would cheer him up.

"Yeah, he did. He brought me some stuff from the grocery store, and a carton of cigarettes. He's okay."

"He is," Laura agreed, silently blessing Kenny. "Well, I don't have much to tell you, but I did talk with your partner this afternoon."

"Oh? What did she have to say?" Jeff asked, with a snort of laughter.

"She doesn't think too much of you," Laura said, seeing no point in pretending otherwise. "She thinks you killed Corey Taylor—but she doesn't offer a good reason why. By the way, could you draw me a little diagram of the setup of the squad room, and the position of the interrogation room where you left Taylor?"

"Sure. But if you want to know if anyone could see the entrance to the room, the answer is no. It opened off a hallway, just outside the squad room. And I'll tell you something else—you get to the rest rooms by going down that hall."

"So any number of officers might have walked past that room, and no one would have questioned why they were going that way."

"Exactly. And who knows how many cops had to take a leak that night? Might have been someone from another floor, even—there's a stairway that opens into the hall."

Laura was delighted by what she heard. "Jeff, this is great. It puts everything in a new light. We're not just looking at cops on your squad—it could be anyone who was in the building that night. You sit tight, and try not to go crazy, okay? I think we're finally getting somewhere."

As a reward for being nice to Jeff, Laura got a call from Tom almost as soon as she replaced the receiver. Her heart pounded when she heard his familiar voice, but she kept the conversation strictly to business—not hard, since there was so much of it. Tom promised to call Hunicutt and lecture him on the perils of bribing officers of the court, and he listened with a chuckle to her story of the showdown with Meredith. He wished her luck with Smoothhead, and promised to return in time for dinner on Friday night. "I told them I couldn't stay the weekend. They whined about it, but I was firm. You know lawyers: If someone doesn't stop them, they'll work around the clock."

"And why not? They're getting paid," Laura said. "But they're going to let you go?"

"They can't stop me. I may have to come back next week, but I'm taking the weekend off." He said that with meaning.

"What time do you think you'll be back tomorrow? Will you come into the office?"

"Probably not. I'll call you and give you a better guess tomorrow. You can make a dinner reservation somewhere."

"Why don't you just come to my place? I'm a decent cook, when the spirit moves me. We can stay in."

"I'll come straight from the airport. I have to go now, Grasshopper; take care."

"You, too."

After getting off the phone, she took some time to think about what she would cook, and to jot down a shopping list. She could get some of the work done tonight, so she wouldn't have to hurry tomorrow. She put some thought into it; she wanted to impress him with her talents as a domestic goddess, but she didn't want to make dinner too fancy—that would defeat the let's-stay-at-home intention. She was considering her meager wine cellar, and wondering what she should add to it, when the phone rang again. This time, it was Kenny, destroying her plans for a quiet evening of cooking and cleaning at home. "We have an appointment with Smoothhead at seven sharp; I'll pick you up at your office at six-thirty."

"Can't he do it earlier?" Laura protested. "I was looking forward to a nice night at home."

"Hey, Smoothhead calls the shots. And believe me, he's enjoying this. It plays right into his conspiracy-theory outlook, except this time he gets to be the conspirator. I believe he wants to meet under cover of darkness."

"Kenny, level with me: Is this guy a nut?"

"Sugar, he's as crazy as a half-drunk Mississippi novelist—but that doesn't mean that he can't help us. He says he has a gun for us. By the way—how much cash you got on you?"

"I don't know; maybe forty or fifty dollars."

"Well, run to the bank before it closes, shug; you need about four hundred, I figure."

"What for?"

"Baby, tonight you're buying your first illegal handgun."

Some time later, Laura tried not to be nervous about heading into the worst part of town, at night, with nearly five hundred dollars in cash on her. Kenny was with her, after all, and not only was he a big guy, he had a gun. She shifted in the seat of his truck, and fiddled with the radio, which was blaring country music. Laura hated country music.

"You're not uptight about this, are you?" he asked.

"Yes. How do you know we're not being set up?"

"Smoothhead's not the type. He's on fire for justice; he wants to win one against the Man."

"Aren't *you* the Man? Not to mention Jeff, and me, too."

"Under other circumstances, maybe, but what Smoothhead would like is to make the cops look like donkeys."

"Even if that means exonerating a white cop?"

"Do me a favor, and don't point that out. I don't think we have any need to go and interject rationality onto our dealings with Smoothhead."

They traveled in silence for a few minutes, or as much silence as Clint Black and the twanging DJ permitted them. "So what else have you been up to?"

Kenny sighed. "Digging into Tony Harrell's background, trying to find out who his buddies were when he was on the force. A lot of time has gone by, and the department's changed a lot. For one thing, it's about thirty percent bigger—everyone's new. Hell, I don't know any of them anymore, after seven years off the force."

"But you must have been able to find out who his partner was," she said. "They must keep records of that."

"That was a piece of cake. Only problem is that he retired three months *before* Tony died—to a farm in Alabama. I called him up; he remembered me, and he was happy to talk. According to him, Tony was a saint—never broke a rule, never even bent one. A by-the-book cop. He and Tony became partners when Tony was just a rookie, but they hit it off despite the age difference. The man *cried* when he talked about him."

"Are any of his other friends still on the force?"

"A couple, and I've talked to them too. Same story everywhere: Tony Harrell was the perfect cop, and his death was a tragedy."

"Who was his partner after the other guy retired?"

"He didn't have a regular one—he rode with a couple of rookies in the last months of his life. No one remembers who they were, but I'm a-workin' on it."

Another silence. "I saw Kowalski last night," Laura volunteered.

Kenny nodded. "He told me. Said you almost made Meredith calve."

"Well, what could I do? She called the press down there, and paraded Jeff through all that—I had to fight back. Kowalski didn't seem too upset."

"He wasn't. Thought it was right spunky of you, in fact."

"Did he tell you that he warned me off?"

"About what?"

"Said he 'didn't want me to get burned.' What do you think he meant?"

Kenny shrugged. "Who can say? Amos is very tight-lipped about this with me. We talk about sports, and hooters, even more so than usual these days."

"How do you know Amos so well, anyway? He wasn't on the force when you were."

"No, we met through a mutual friend. Amos didn't know anyone when he came to town, and he got more or less frozen out by the guys on his squad for a while. See, he was brought in to clean up a mess. Sex-crimes had blown a couple of cases, had charges dismissed and evidence thrown out, that kind of thing. The former lieutenant was sloppy, but beloved. That wasn't good enough for Charlie Sisson; he tossed him out right away when he was made chief, and brought Amos in from Chicago."

Laura nodded. Charlie Sisson was Atlanta's controversial chief of police, a volatile fireplug of a man. He had come from Chicago to be head of Public Affairs for the Atlanta Police Department, after holding the same post in Chicago. While at Public Affairs, he had thrust himself into the spotlight at every opportunity, becoming enormously popular with the public, who cottoned immediately to his no-nonsense law-and-order line. He was less popular, rumor had it, with the City Council. Still, the mayor had managed to get him appointed chief when that fell vacant, and there was no denying that major crime in the city was down since he had taken over. It made sense that he would have brought in some of his protégés from Chicago, but it hadn't occurred to Laura that Kowalski was one of them.

Kenny continued his story. "Anyway, Amos wasn't instantly accepted when he took over the job. There are a lot of guys who don't like Sisson, and they see Amos as his boy."

"That's ridiculous; Sisson's done a great job. Why wouldn't he be liked?" Laura asked.

Kenny shrugged. "He's an outsider—that's enough. And he has a reputation for interfering with operations."

"So what if he does interfere—how much can that affect the average officer? Most of them probably never see the chief, except on television."

"Don't be so sure; he's pretty active, and takes a personal interest in the big cases. He was a beat cop and a detective for a lot of years himself, and, according to Amos, he was pretty darn good. Amos respects Sisson. They're not friends, exactly, but a lot of the guys assume they are. Makes Amos kind of a teacher's pet. But I think most of the guys on his squad are with him now."

"So how did you and Amos get to be such buds, anyway?"

"When he first got here, he was a little bit lonely, to tell you the truth. I met him through another lieutenant, old pal of mine from Narcotics, who had taken a shine to him. The three of us went out one night, and Amos and I liked each other. There's a lot to like there, Laura. You should spend some time with him. He's not just some dumb cop—he actually reads books, just like you."

Laura changed the subject quickly. "Jeff Williams says Amos doesn't like him."

"He may not. There's no rule that says the boss has to love every-body on his squad."

"Do you think Amos may have jumped to a conclusion on this one—just assumed that Jeff did it, because he's not especially fond of him?"

"Could be. Amos isn't perfect, even though he thinks he is. I'll tell you one thing, though; Amos is convinced Williams is guilty."

"Oh, I know; he told me so right out. So did Haines, and so would the rest of them, I'll bet. What do you think Amos will say when we spring Smoothhead on them next week at the hearing?"

"I think *he'll* calve."

Laura laughed. They were getting close to Smoothhead's territory now, turning off the expressway and heading for the projects. Public housing in Atlanta had never sunk to the depths it had in other cities; it had instead declined to a uniformly depressing level shortly after being built, and stayed that way, teetering on the edge of despair, but never quite toppling over. They approached from Pryor Road, past a community center and a large, impressive church, an architec-tural oxymoron among the squat cinder-block convenience stores on either side of it. They turned left at a tiny, round public library building that looked stubbornly cheerful and out of place on the bare grounds. Across the street, on private property, rose a few derelict apartment buildings, home to those who could not qualify for public-housing assistance. They were as squalid as any suburban nightmare could imagine; Laura shuddered at the sight of them. Then, they reached the projects themselves, and Kenny steered toward Smooth-head's building.

It was a cold night, but Smoothhead and his court were outdoors, huddled around a fire made of scrap lumber in a old barrel. It was the kind of gathering Laura had seen before, driven past in a locked car, the shadows of men hugging themselves against the cold, passing bottles sheathed in paper bags, and telling lies—a variation on the sports-and-hooters theme Kenny and Kowalski pursued in more comfortable, expensive surroundings. She could make out one seated figure, in a wheelchair. "Smoothhead?" she asked Kenny. "The man," Kenny said. "Ready? I'll introduce you, and then let Smoothhead go at his own pace. He'll want to lecture you for a while; just listen, and don't, for the love of God, try and rush him. This is his show." Laura nodded. "Bundle up, sugar; you're going to be outside for a while." They pulled on gloves, put on hats, climbed out of the truck, and crossed the ground to the bonfire. The men fell silent at their approach; Kenny nodded and howdied as he passed them, leading Laura to Smoothhead's throne. "Hey, Smoothhead; how's it going? This is the lady I was telling you about, Laura Chastain. Laura, this is Smoothhead."

Laura extended her hand. "Nice to meet you, Mr. . . . Smoothhead." He took her hand in a spring-loaded grip, and held it for a long minute. Smoothhead wasn't a big guy; if he stood, he probably wouldn't have been much taller than Laura, maybe five-eight or so. But sitting in his wheelchair, he looked huge, with a chest like a Volkswagen and arms like industrial piping. And his head was, in fact, smooth; not shaven bald, but absolutely devoid of hair. He didn't even have eyebrows. What did they call it, when someone lost all body hair? *Alopecia.* Laura had once read a story in a magazine about a girl who had lost all of her hair after a terrible auto accident; the condition could apparently be brought on by trauma. She thought of Smoothhead in Vietnam; did he have hair when he went over there? He had gone there with a pair of working legs; what else had he left in that swampy green hell?

Smoothhead was looking her over, too, narrowing his eyes, and taking her in, from her black felt hat, and her voluminous black coat, to her pump-shod feet. Her toes were getting cold already. There was silence, then Smoothhead spoke. "So this is the lady lawyer. A *lady* lawyer. A lawyer will take the poor man's money, to get him the justice that God gives for free. I ask you, is that right?" A murmuring of "uh-uh", and "no, sir" rose from the assembly. "And should a *lady,* a woman, the vessel God has chosen for the bearing of little children, be taking money from the poor man for justice?" The crowd indicated that it thought not. "But hold on a minute," Smoothhead said, raising an arm to quell the ripple of disapproval he had stirred. "This lady is fighting for a man who has been wronged by the police. No *man* stepped forward to help him. This man, falsely accused, must rely on a *woman* to get him some justice."

Laura didn't dare meet Kenny's eyes, for fear of laughing, because it wasn't funny, really, it wasn't. Smoothhead was a street preacher, a man of great authority among his flock, and it would not do to smirk or chuckle here, in his church. He continued, as Laura felt sure he would do for some time to come. "What are we to make of this situation? A man is dead, a bad man—" a few amens from the congregation—"and the police are quick to accuse another man of his death. But was not the man's death just? Was this not a man who raped our daughter?"

The volume of assent rose; child molestation is probably as prevalent in the African American community as it is anywhere else, but the ideal of manhood there is much narrower; a child molester is, if possible, more of a pariah then he would be in the suburbs, where he might be pitied as "sick." Here, in the projects, Corey Taylor was worse than merely ill; he was not a man. "Was this not a man who sold guns, the white man's guns, to our sons, so they could kill each other?" More agreement. "We should rejoice at the death of this devil! We should be happy, and say 'Hallelujah!' But instead, the police are quick to punish his killer. Oh, they were quick. How long have some of you waited for justice from the police? When you have been robbed, and beaten, have the police arrested your tormenter in a *day?*" Vehement "no, sirs" all around. "But when this devil is killed, when this devil *who was a friend to the policeman,* is killed, justice is swift. They accuse one of their own, a good policeman, the policeman who arrested this devil in a day. The policeman who gave us *our* justice! And where is his justice?" Dramatic pause. "This lady will get it for him!. She has come here to ask for our help in getting justice for the man who helped us by taking this devil away, and I say, we should come to her assistance!"

It made sense, in a way, the canonization of Jeff Williams; Smoothhead was right that most crimes in the projects went unsolved, and, even when they were, justice was bartered and diluted, with little satisfaction for the victims. That Jeff had arrested Taylor within hours of his crime was in itself a unique event, and there was probably little regret in this community that Corey had not lived long enough to bargain his way into a light sentence. Still, Smoothhead was blurring the issue quite a bit; he didn't seem to care whether or not Jeff had actually killed Taylor. If anything, he believed that Jeff *had* done it. So much for that reporter this morning, handsome Brad, who had been so eager to play the race card—she could show him a group of black people who applauded the death of one of their own, even at the hands of a white cop. It just goes to show, Laura thought, that if you stay in this business long enough, you will see the line between right and wrong, good and bad, shimmy around like the San Andreas Fault. A philosopher, of course, would be dizzied by Smoothhead's argument, and Laura wasn't following it all that well herself, but she knew one thing: He was inclined to help her, and Jeff Williams. She wished that he would do it, already; her toes were really cold now, and beginning to go a little numb. She wished she had changed into something warmer; she wished she were at home.

Smoothhead continued for another fifteen minutes, however, before he showed signs of coming to a conclusion. Kenny slipped a hand onto the small of Laura's back, and kept it there, comforting and reassuring; she felt a surge of warmth, and gratitude for his presence. Kenny was her friend, and a good one. She hoped he would have time for a beer, and maybe some dinner, when this was over; she wanted to thank him, and, finally, get the giggles out of her system.

At length, Smoothhead cut to the chase: he was ready to produce a kid who had bought a gun off of Corey. He called out his name. "Antrus! Antrus Caldwell!" A middle-aged man, wearing an army fatigue jacket, led a sullen-looking preteen from the crowd, and propelled him to Smoothhead's side. "This is Antrus Caldwell, and his grandfather, James Caldwell. Tell this lady where you got your gun, Antrus."

The kid mumbled something, and Smoothhead clouted him on the shoulder to improve his diction. Laura winced; that was no way to treat a child, even one who had bought an illegal handgun. Antrus, however, straightened up and spoke directly, defiantly, to Laura. "I bought a gun. From Corey."

"When?" Laura asked him.

"Last week," he said. How heartening to know, Laura thought, that one of Corey's last acts on this earth had been to sell a deadly weapon to a child. She was beginning to agree with the Neanderthal law-and-order faction, that whoever had throttled the life out of Corey Taylor had done society a big favor. "Why did you buy a gun, Antrus?" she asked, gently.

"I needed it to take to school so nobody would mess with me. I got tired of them buggin' on me all the time. It's a good gun."

"I understand," she said. "Did Corey come to you, and offer to sell you the gun?"

"No, man, everybody know Corey got guns," he said, scornful

of her ignorance. "I asked him last summer could I buy one from him. He told me I'd have to wait."

"Why did you have to wait?"

" 'Cause he didn't have no guns. Told me I'd have to wait until Christmas, 'cause that's when Santa bring him his guns. So I did, and I got me a gun. It's my gun," he said, raising his chin. "I bought it with my own money."

"I understand," Laura said. "But you realize that Corey probably stole that gun from somebody else, and that you could be in a lot of trouble for having it, don't you?"

"Don't care. I can't go to school without no gun. Don't nobody be buggin' on me when I have my gun."

Laura almost felt sorry for the child; he seemed genuinely terrified of the prospect of going out unarmed. Still, he was lucky not to have hurt himself, or someone else, with it. There's nothing more dangerous than a teenage boy, pumped full of hormones and utterly lacking in patience, having a gun. Antrus would be better off without his piece in the long run. "Can I see the gun, Antrus?"

"I have it," his grandfather said, producing a handgun from the pocket of his jacket. "I never knew the boy had it until yesterday; you best believe I whipped him good when I found it. He's a good boy, Miss, makes good grades. He doesn't need this kind of trouble. He lives with his grandmother and me, and we try to keep him away from the troublemakers."

"I know you do," Laura said. "We'll make sure there are no charges against him, and we'll pay him for the gun."

"No, ma'am; he'll give it to you."

"Please, let us pay him—let him buy something else with the money. A bicycle, books, whatever." *Let's give him back his childhood,* was what she wanted to say. The grandfather nodded, grateful and relieved. Laura had no idea what the gun was worth, but whatever they paid him for it would probably put a few Christmas presents under the tree. Where had the kid gotten the money in the first place, she wondered, although she really didn't want to know.

Antrus's grandfather handed her the gun, an ugly, snub-nosed revolver; Laura took it as if it were a piece of raw liver. He smiled at her reaction . "It's not loaded, Miss."

Kenny stepped forward. "What is it?"

"Real antique," Mr. Caldwell said. "Smith & Wesson, .38. Can't say the last time it was fired—don't know if it even works. Antrus says he never shot it."

Kenny glanced up at Caldwell, and smiled. "You know your guns. Army?" Caldwell nodded. Kenny peered more closely at the weapon in the uneven light of the fire. "I'd say it's about thirty years old, probably stolen from somebody's house—right out of the dresser drawer where they kept it for protection. How much you pay for this bad boy, Antrus?"

Antrus muttered something. "Speak up, boy," Mr. Caldwell said, whacking him on the shoulder Smoothhead hadn't already gotten.

"Hundred dollars," he said.

"Where'd you get a hundred dollars, boy?" his outraged grandfather demanded.

"Earned it," Antrus said, avoiding Mr. Caldwell's gaze.

"The hell you did—your mama gave you that money, didn't she?" He looked at Laura. "His mama runs with a bad crowd; my wife and I had to take in her children. Every so often she comes around with some new boyfriend, gives the children money. He knows he's not supposed to take anything from her." Antrus snuffled, and looked at the ground.

"Well, why don't I give you the money, Mr. Caldwell?" Laura said. "That way, you can make sure Antrus spends it on better toys this time around." She took her wallet from her purse. "Let's say two hundred—to thank you for your trouble." He started to demur, but she pressed the money into his hand. "You're helping us a great deal, Mr. Caldwell; I want you to know how much we appreciate your assistance." He nodded, and thanked her gruffly. "We may need to have Antrus testify at a pretrial hearing next week, but he won't get in any trouble because of it, I promise you. How can we get in touch with you if we need him?"

The grandfather gave her his phone number at the auto repair shop where he worked. Antrus was one lucky little boy, Laura thought, to have this man on his side. She then turned to Smoothhead. "And you, too, sir; I'm very grateful for your help. We're going to try to get to the bottom of this whole mess, and find out where Corey was getting these guns."

Smoothhead accepted her homage with a gracious speech. They stood around a little longer, to be polite; Kenny finally brought the meeting to a close by putting an arm around Laura. "Gentlemen, it's been a pleasure, but I want to get this lady home before she freezes to death. Smoothhead, thanks; I'll be talking to you." Handshakes all around, and Laura tottered back to Kenny's truck on nearly frozen feet. "You were beautiful, Laura, just perfect," he said, when they were safely inside. Kenny started the truck, and turned on the interior light. He peered at the gun, and jotted down its serial number on a pad he pulled from the center console. Then he grabbed his cell phone and dialed.

"What are you doing?" she asked.

He held up a hand, indicating that he needed silence. She obliged, and listened to his half of a conversation. "Amos? Hey, buddy, it's me. I need a favor. . . . What have I done for you lately? Why, I've brightened your life in a thousand little ways, not to mention I paid your bar tab the other night and lost twenty bucks to you at pool. . . . No, just run down a serial number on a gun for me. . . . Aw, c'mon, all you have to do is call one of your lackeys in the squad room. It'll take you five seconds. . . . Okay, I'm in the truck. Call me back." He put the truck in gear, and pulled out of the parking space. "He's bitching about it, but he'll call me back. You hungry?"

"I sure am. I'll buy you dinner, if you've got the time."

"Cindy's gonna kill me, but I've already missed dinner at home. Let's get Mexican."

"I'm game." They steered back to the interstate, and headed toward town. They were just past the stadium when the phone rang. Kenny picked up. "Yell-oh. Oh, it's you, Kowalski; I told you it wouldn't take you a minute with all that technology you boys got at your disposal. . . . No, I'm not gonna tell you that; where I got the gun isn't important. Just tell me if it's stolen, and from who. . . . Well, screw you, too, Kowalski." There was an interlude during which epithets were exchanged. It was a good thing Laura knew they were friends; otherwise, the conversation would have sounded like a quarrel. "We're on our way to get some dinner; you can meet us at El Azteca. . . . Oh, all right, you girly-man; we'll go to Murphy's, but I'm warning you: Chastain had her heart set on a burrito. She ain't going to be happy about having to eat goat cheese." He hung up, and barked a laugh. "We hit some kinda nerve, Laura. He's incredibly pissed off. We're going to meet him at Murphy's; it's close to his house, and he wants to walk."

"What do you think it is?"

Kenny shrugged. "Gun must have turned up as stolen, but I figure it's also one that was used in some kinda crime. It could mean Corey was involved in something bigger—armed robbery or something. Who knows?"

"I'm not real comfortable going to Amos on this, Ken," Laura said. "He has a vested interest in seeing Jeff convicted."

"Amos won't deny the truth, even if it's not in his best interest," Kenny replied. "He's the most honest person I've ever known. You can trust him, Laura. I do."

That had to be good enough, because there was no one Laura trusted more than Kenny. She looked sideways at him, his big frame going soft around the midsection, parting company with his hair. A guy like Kenny was what every woman needed. Not that Tom was a bad deal, she hastily added to herself; his complexity was as satisfying, in its way, as Kenny's straightforward good-guy-ness. Thinking of Tom brought on a pang, and she turned her eyes and looked out the window into the night. They were getting close to Virginia-Highland; Laura was surprised that Kowalski lived there. She would have put him in a more suburban setting, but then, she didn't know him all that well. Kenny managed to find a parking space not too far from the restaurant, and they hurried to get inside. They told the hostess they were meeting a man; she immediately escorted them to a table where Kowalski sat glowering over a beer.

"What took you so long?" he grumbled. "Give it to me."

Kenny sat down, and grinned at his friend. "Not so fast, slick. Tell me what you know."

"Give me the gun first."

Laura spoke up. "We can't give you the gun, Kowalski; it's important to my case. I'll enter it as evidence, but until then, I keep it in my custody. Or Kenny's," she amended, not really wanting to take on the care of a handgun. "But the court will have it next week."

"So why does this lil' ol' gun have your jock in such a big ol' knot, anyway?" Kenny asked, folding his arms and looking at Kowalski with a twinkle in his eye. "It's stolen, right?"

"Not exactly," Kowalski said. "That gun doesn't exist, technically."

"It's a counterfeit serial number?" Kenny asked, leaning forward.

"No, that's the original number. But that gun has been destroyed—according to official records, that is."

"I don't get it," Laura said. "How do you mean, destroyed?"

"I mean, its former owner turned it in, with all his registration papers, and it was sent to a scrap yard to be melted into scrap metal."

"Turned it in?" Kenny asked. "Who the hell to?"

Kowalski looked very unhappy. "The Atlanta Police Department."

11

"Holy smokes," Kenny said. "Holy *smokes.*"

"You can say that again," Kowalski said, pulling on his beer. He looked miserable, Laura thought, troubled and ill at ease. "You two have opened some huge can of worms, but I'm not quite sure what kind of worms they are."

Laura thought she did. "Cop worms, Kowalski, that's what they are. Someone in the department took a gun that was supposed to have been destroyed, and gave it to Corey Taylor, who sold it to a twelve-year-old. I'd say there's a little problem Internal Affairs overlooked in their haste to get Jeff Williams behind bars."

Kenny was still puzzling it out. "So where did this gun come from—was it evidence that was supposed to have been destroyed?"

Kowalski shook his head. "It's worse than that. I mean, every once in a while, something disappears from the property room, little bits of evidence, et cetera, maybe even the occasional gun. If that were the case, I'd say, 'Oh, it's just a coincidence—this gun got loose, and ended up with Corey Taylor.' Coincidence, but explainable. But this gun was never entered as evidence anywhere; it was never used in a crime, not reported as stolen. The cops only had temporary possession of it."

"I am not following," Laura said, impatient. "Just spit it out, Kowalski."

He looked annoyed. "I'm trying. But it's so weird. See, about five years ago, the department started a program, a public relations thing: Toys for Guns. The idea was to get people to turn in guns, and get toys in exchange—you know, to get people to voluntarily take weapons off the street."

"I remember reading about it," Laura said. "Some businessmen underwrote it, the mayor was involved—it happens around Christmas, right?"

"Exactly," Kowalski said. "It's been run for the past five years, at Christmas. All in the spirit of giving—you know the drill. I never paid it any attention; they always asked me to get volunteers from my squad to man the collection points, but I thought it was utterly bogus and self-congratulatory—not to mention useless. Christ, it's not as if the bad guys were going to turn in Desert Eagles to get a Tickle Me Elmo doll. Anyway, this serial number you gave me came back as having been registered to a Mr. Jim Hanks, of Angelo Road. It also showed as having been turned in to the police two weeks ago, in the Toys for Guns drive. I called Jim to check it out. He got real agitated with me; said he had turned it in, and he had his receipt, if I didn't believe him, and he was going to have a few words to say to his city councilman. I told him that it was a mistake; that I had misread the serial number, and I was sorry to have disturbed him."

"You're a smoothie, Amos," Kenny said. "Thinking on your feet, all the time."

"Shut up. Anyway, if the gun you have really is Jim Hanks's, I can tell you one thing about it—it's a piece of crap, at least thirty years old. Jim probably hadn't fired the thing since 1969; he figured he'd get rid of it, and get a little something for the grandkids in the bargain."

Kenny nodded. "I bet most of the guns turned in were like this one." He produced the gun from his pocket, after checking around to make sure that no diners at neighboring tables would be alarmed by it.

Kowalski looked at it, and nodded. "Right. Dad's old revolver, kept in the nightstand in case the Communists invaded, and he had to defend the homestead. Old service automatics, the .22 rifle that was never used for anything but shooting tin cans off fences. The real arsenal stayed out there in the hands of the bad guys."

"So," Laura said, "this gun was scheduled to be turned into a hunk of scrap, but it missed its date with the smelter. How?"

"I wish to hell I knew," Kowalski said, "but like I said, I was never involved with the program. Public Affairs set it up, cops manned the collection stations. I'm guessing the guns were logged in, then sent to the scrap yard. There must be some kind of receipts for them, so someone at the scrap yard must have been involved, too. It's a mess."

"How many guns are we talking about?" Laura asked. "Ten? Fifty? A thousand?"

"I have no idea," Kowalski said. "When they asked for volunteers, I took one step backwards. I have enough real work to do without playing Santa's little armaments elf."

"What are we going to do?" Kenny asked.

Kowalski looked uncomfortable. "There's not a lot I can do; the pressure's on to wrap up this case. The pooh-bahs want this swept under the rug, before it turns into some kind of brutality scandal."

"And Jeff Williams was the sweepee," Laura said. "Never mind the truth."

That sparked anger from Kowalski. "Hey, there's no proof that Williams didn't kill that kid. I'd still bet my badge that he did, in fact, and that all this is nothing but smoke and mirrors—a coincidence, no more or less. Corey Taylor was bad news. He raped a kid; why shouldn't he have been selling guns to them, too?"

"Did you know that his brother was a cop, Amos?" Kenny asked.

"It came up, but the brother's record was clean as a whistle. Hell, it was cleaner. Guy was a model cop, plus which he's been dead five years. And he didn't have anyone close to him left in the department. If he had been running a scam with his little brother, there was no one left to keep it up after his death. We looked at it, Kenny, but it's nothing—another coincidence."

"There are too many coincidences for my taste in this case," Laura said.

"I have a suggestion," Kowalski said. "And you didn't get this from me; I want nothing to do with any of this. But you should talk to someone in Public Affairs about the Toys for Guns program—find out who runs it, and how it works. I'll do what checking I can behind the scenes, but I don't want anyone to know I'm talking to you two clowns."

"Clowns?" Kenny said. "I beg your pardon, but I think us clowns just busted your case wide open."

"And," Kowalski said, lobbing a roll from the basket on the table at his friend, "you just bought an illegal handgun. I could arrest you two morons right now—in fact, I should, just for being so freaking stupid. How much did you pay for that piece of crap, anyway?"

"Two hundred," Laura said.

Kowalski laughed. "Not only did you break the law, you got screwed. Nice going, Sherlock and Watson—or is that Boris and Natasha?"

"Hey, I let her do the negotiating," Kenny protested. "She over-paid, but it was her money."

"I wanted that kid to have a decent Christmas," Laura said, in her own defense. "I got the feeling that things were a little tight at home."

"Aww, a lawyer with a heart," Kowalski said. "I'm all choked up."

Laura lobbed a roll at him, and soon they had put talk of the gun behind them, and were enjoying dinner. Kowalski was surprisingly relaxed, and funny, when he wasn't being a cop. He looked nice tonight, in jeans, with a flannel shirt unbuttoned over a T-shirt. Pretty eyes . . . Laura stopped herself. Another five minutes and she'd be one of his disciples, too. The guy had something, that was for sure.

They ordered one dessert, and split it among the three of them. If they hadn't been there to talk about death, and guns, it would have been merely a great evening, picturesque enough for a beer ad: three attractive, youngish people, laughing and talking. At nine-thirty, Kenny looked at his watch. "Oh, boy, am I gonna be in trouble. C'mon, Laura, I'll take you back to your car."

Kowalski waved him off. "No, just run along, Ken. I'll get her home. I want to have a little chat with her anyway."

Kenny nodded, and left, tossing a twenty on the table to cover his share of dinner. Laura stuffed it back into his pocket, and he kissed her on the cheek before hurrying back to his truck, and home to his patient and understanding family. Kowalski asked for more coffee, and pulled a cigarette out of his shirt pocket.

"I think this is the no-smoking section," Laura pointed out.

"It's okay; I don't smoke anymore. I just like to hold a butt once in a while."

"You used to smoke? I wouldn't have guessed. You look like a clean-livin' guy, Kowalski."

"Hey, your body can be a temple—mine's more of a Vegas wedding chapel. But I don't want to talk to you about health and hygiene."

"You want to talk about Jeff, but let me stop you by saying I don't think we should. I don't think we can, in fact, without compro-mising both our positions."

"All I want to say is be careful. I told you the same thing last night, Laura, but this gun thing throws a new light on the matter. I don't know what is going on, but that makes me worry all the more. I just don't want to see you hurt."

"Tell me one thing, then: Was Jeff involved in the Toys for Guns program?"

He shook his head. "No. At least, not since I've headed the squad— that's three years. Jeff never volunteers for anything. Look, there's nothing specific, but I have a bad feeling about this. I can't get my arms around it, can't make the pieces fit. I am sure that Williams is guilty, but all the rest . . . call it cop's instinct, Laura; there's more here than meets our eye. Be careful."

"I am careful, and I have Kenny to take care of me."

"That you do, and there's no one better. You're a nice girl, Laura, despite your despicable clientele. Maybe, when all this is over, you'll let me buy you dinner."

"I'd like that, Amos." She looked at him, trying to determine if his intentions were romantic. Was he responding to Kenny's importuning, or was he genuinely interested? Or, she thought, remembering that much of Kowalski's behavior on the night of Corey Taylor's death was unexplained at best, was this something else entirely? She looked at him closely, but his face was giving no clues. "I am seeing someone, but I'd like to be friends."

"Figures. Well, I can always use another friend." He averted his eyes as he replied; maybe he was romantically interested in her, and what had passed between them was no more than an ordinary rejection of a polite advance. But his very inscrutability raised questions. He didn't act like an ordinary guy, interested in an ordinary girl. Of course, their circumstances—they were, technically, on opposite sides of a criminal case—made that difficult. Still, she couldn't shake the feeling that Kowalski wanted something more from her than dinner, and she was wary of giving away too much.

The check chose that moment to arrive, and they wrestled for it. Laura was insistent. "I promised to buy dinner for Kenny, and I feel like I owe you, too. Let me."

"Okay, so long as you promise me to charge it to Jeff Williams's defense, as an incidental expense."

She laughed. "Done. Look, I can take a cab back to my car."

"I'll drive you." She paid, and they walked back to Kowalski's place. They didn't go in; his car, a black Jeep, was parked in the drive. They didn't talk much during the brief trip to midtown, but he leaned over and kissed her on the cheek when she got out. "Take care, Counselor," he said, smiling.

She smiled back at him from the doorway of the Jeep. "Thanks; I will." He waited until he saw that her car started, and followed her out of the garage. She waved to him as they went in opposite directions.

She got home in time for the eleven o'clock news, and flipped on Channel Two. She wondered if they'd still be running the clip of her from the garage this morning—that seemed like an age ago. She had to wait; the story, since Jeff's dramatic arrest, had dropped in importance, and followed a house fire and a big accident on the Perimeter. Then Sally Rivers popped up at the news desk, to update breathlessly waiting Atlanta on the case of the killer cop. They ran the clip of Laura—she made a note to wear darker lipstick when she thought she might be caught on-camera—and then flashed to Sally, standing in front of Police Headquarters later in the day. "Sources have told Channel Two News that Jeff Williams's file contains several reprimands, and that the detective was, in fact, on disciplinary probation at the time of his arrest. . . ."

Laura sat upright and howled in outrage. Where the hell were they getting that? She didn't even have access to Jeff's personnel file yet. And if that was true, why hadn't he told her? She didn't know who she was more incensed at: Jeff, for not telling her what he must have known she would find eventually, or Meredith, for leaking this little tidbit to the press. She zeroed in on Jeff, and called him at home. His answering machine picked up. "It's me, Jeff, Laura Chastain. Pick up—I know you're there."

She waited, and called out again; after a moment, he answered. "Hey, Laura. What's up?"

"What's up? I just saw the eleven o'clock news, that's what's up. Why didn't you tell me you were on probation?"

"Huh? How'd they get that?"

"I assume the District Attorney leaked it; it's all part of their campaign to put you under pressure to bargain. And I have to say, Jeff, they scored one this time. Why didn't you tell me about this?"

"It's got nothing to do with the case, I swear. It's just fucking Kowalski—I told you he hates me. He's always on my case about something. The probation is nothing; I was late with some paperwork, and he used it as an excuse to jump all over me. He wants me off his squad. I was there before he was, and he's threatened by me."

"So why not tell me, if it was just a personality conflict?"

"Like I said, it's got fuck to do with the case. I didn't think it was important."

"Well, it just became important. You just lost a round in the court of public opinion—everyone who saw that story, every potential juror out there watching the news, or reading a newspaper—is now going to think that you had roughed up suspects before. If we get in front of a jury, I'm going to have to talk a blue streak to undo this damage."

"God, I'm sorry Laura, but I really didn't think it would matter. I wish this whole thing was over."

Laura softened. "It will be, soon. Kenny and I have some good news for you, by the way." She told him about the gun, leaving out Kowalski's involvement. "Any of this mean anything to you?"

"Uh-uh. I never volunteer for those stupid things. Public relations is useless."

At least he and Kowalski agreed on one thing, anyway, Laura thought. "I guess I'll have to make an appointment with someone down there tomorrow, and try to get a handle on how the exchange program worked, and see who might have been monkeying with the receipts."

"Good luck; they always put the burnouts in Public Affairs. It's great, though, what you and Newton are doing. I don't know how to thank you."

"Wait until I get you out of this, then you worry about that. Get some sleep now."

"You too," he said.

Laura couldn't sleep, though; she was too busy fuming about Meredith's underhanded move. If she wants to play hardball, Laura thought, she'd better be wearing a cup. Two can play this game.

SCOOOOOOOOOOTTT RESSLER!!!!

Welcome back, one and all, on another perfect December night, to the show that tells you what Atlanta is really thinking. Give us a call. Red from Marietta—if that's your real name—you're on. Go ahead. (Pause) Red? You with us?

Hello? Scott?

You got me. What's up in Marietta, Red? Why do they call you that, anyway—you got red hair, or are you one of those dadburned Communists?

Used to have red hair, Scott, but I ain't got none at all now. Listen, I want to talk to you about this cop. You see the news? Now they're saying he was on probation, or something.

Yes, I saw it. They didn't say why, but I guess he must have been tough with suspects in the past. What's your comment?

Well, what I want to know is how come the cops aren't sticking up for him? How come no one's come out and said they thought he done the right thing?

Probably because they're not allowed to talk to the press, Red—I've called some of my contacts down at police headquarters, and they tell me the lid's screwed on this one tighter than Liz Taylor's face. Something's up, though, you just know it is.

I think this guy's a whatchacallit—you know, when you blame a guy for something . . .

A scapegoat? You could be right, my friend. But did you get a load *of who's defending him? That's right, folks; it's our friend from the Alex Hunicutt trial. I want to get that gal on the show—what's her name, Sidekick Mel?*

Uhh, lemme see—Laura Chastain.

Well, get Laura on the show, Mel—it's time you earned all that money I pay you.

I'm trying; she won't return my calls.

Mel, NO women return your calls. (laughter) Maybe you shouldn't have asked her what she was wearing. . . .

12

"My name is Laura Chastain. I'd like to arrange a meeting with someone on your staff to discuss the Toys for Guns program."

The flack on the other end of the phone line, the third one she had been transferred to so far, hesitated. "I think you should go through the district attorney's office with your request."

"Why? Got a problem talking to a citizen about a public relations program? And since when does the district attorney run the Police Department?"

More hesitation. "Can I put you on hold?"

He didn't wait for a reply; Laura fumed and drank coffee while she waited for them to confer—probably calling Meredith Gaffney, the wimps. Fine; if she had to add this to her yard-long list of subpoenas, if she had to drag all this out on the witness stand, she would do it. If the judge would let her, that is; she would have to demonstrate relevance, which shouldn't be too hard. She needed to go back downtown, and get formal affidavits from Antrus and his grandfather . . . she drummed her fingers impatiently. How long were they planning to keep her on hold?

After five or so minutes, the flack came back. "I'm going to transfer you. Please hold."

He shot her into space before she could protest, but the phone was answered after two short rings, by an authoritative baritone voice. "Ms. Chastain? May I ask what your request relates to?"

"To whom am I speaking?" Laura asked, irritated.

"Charles Sisson."

My, my, Laura thought, setting down her coffee cup, and straightening in her chair. The chief of police, taking a personal interest in a case. Of course, Laura recalled, he had been head of Public Affairs before he was made chief; he was a man who knew the power of publicity. His frequent appearances at press conferences during the crises that faced the city served a dual purpose: to provide information to the public, of course, but also to impress on them his role in important events. The mayor who appointed him had been shrewd enough to see the value of a top cop who could spin his own stories, although Sisson's popularity with the voters reportedly gave the mayor cause for concern—there were rumors that Sisson had his eye on his boss's job. It made sense that Sisson would be following the Williams case closely; it carried a huge potential for bad publicity. It might even have been Sisson behind Meredith's hasty offer of a plea. So why was he coming out from behind the curtain now, in response to Laura's innocuous questions about a seemingly unrelated PR program? Laura decided to play chicken with him.

"Good morning, Chief Sisson. I think you know what this is about."

"I'm sorry, but I don't. Of course, I know who you are—and who your client is—but I can't imagine why you're requesting a meeting with Public Affairs on a topic that has absolutely nothing to do with your case."

Laura took a moment to think; if Kenny was right, Kowalski would not have told his puppet-masters about their meeting last night, or about the gun. Laura didn't want to get Kowalski into trouble. To avoid answering the question, she took a full-on blowhard approach. "Look, Chief, I've been very patient, and very discreet, while the district attorney and the Police Department have tried to conduct a referendum on my client in the media. I'm tired of leaks and innuendo."

"We've haven't given anything to the press, Ms. Chastain."

"Save it, Chief; I got that line from Meredith Gaffney, too. So where *does* Sally Rivers get access to confidential personnel files—files that I can't even get without a subpoena? If you want to slug this out on-camera, I can call a press conference right now and make all of you look like donkeys. Ask Meredith, if you don't believe me. I can also bide my time, and subpoena you and the head of Public Affairs for appearance at the pretrial hearing next week. I'll turn that hearing into a circus that won't soon be forgotten. Play it however you like."

The chief clucked his tongue. "There's no need to make threats. What if I say yes? Before I can give you access to my people, I need to know *why* you want to ask questions about the Toys for Guns program." He was polite, but insistent.

"No, you don't. Look, you can set up an informal, friendly meeting today, or you can take your chances at the hearing. No skin off my nose. But I have most of today free; it would be a mighty good time for me to invite a few reporters up to my office. Some of them might be interested in knowing that the Police Department arrested Jeff Williams before any witnesses were interviewed. They might be *very* interested in learning how Corey Taylor made his living."

Long silence. "I'll arrange a meeting, but a city attorney will be present. He'll make the call on which questions are answered."

"Fine. But I want to talk to someone who knows the nuts and bolts of the gun-exchange program—don't send me one of your big boys if he can't answer detailed questions."

"I'll let you talk to Jennifer Fraser; she's coordinated the program for the past two years."

"That sounds good. I'll be in my office, waiting for a call from your people. It's been a pleasure talking to you, Chief Sisson."

The chief hung up without returning the pleasantry. Laura could just picture the activity down at headquarters; they were no doubt placing the call to Meredith right now, and ordering the Internal Affairs officers out to question Corey Taylor's friends and associates. Fine; let them. Laura had an idea of the reception they would get from Smoothhead. Cece buzzed through. "Kenny's on the line," she announced.

"I'll take it," Laura said. "Yo, Kenny."

"Mornin', sugar. I saw the paper, so I can guess what kind of mood you're in."

"Huh? Oh, the personnel file. No, I'm over that; I reamed Jeff out good last night for not telling us he was on probation, and I'm filing a motion to suppress anything in his file. Jeff says it's a mountain out of a molehill; he was behind on his paperwork and Amos came down hard on him for it. I think I can do damage control at the hearing once I have access to the files and can put Amos on the stand. But wait'll I tell you who I just talked to."

Kenny hooted when Laura related the story. "You're making them *uncomfortable,* sugar. They're sitting down there right this minute, scratching their heads and trying to figure out how the two things fit together."

"They'll figure it out eventually, and I don't care if they do. If they have some inkling of the kind of hell I can raise at the hearing, so much the better. So what are you up to today?"

"I got a nice, early start this morning, and I have good news—

I found Corey's girlfriend. Ex-girlfriend, I should say. Miss Carla Riggins."

"Really? Where'd you find her?"

"She moves around a lot—the address I had was two moves old. She's not exactly a productive member of society; I caught her coming home from work early this morning. The baby gave me an early start today, anyway, so I figured, what the hell—I'd cruise down to Glen Iris and check the action."

"She's a hooker?"

"Yep. Sad, really. She's very young. Told me she's nineteen, but I would guess it's more like seventeen, and looks even younger." Kenny sounded pained; his oldest daughter was eight, and he was daddy-to-the-world.

"Which explains Corey's attraction to her."

"Exactly. And when they were dating, she would have been a young-looking fifteen, and he in his twenties." He snorted in disgust.

"What did she have to say?" Laura took out a pad, and started making notes.

"Not a lot that was coherent; she didn't even know that Corey was dead. Not a big one for watching the news, or reading a newspaper, this girl. She wasn't all broken up when I told her, though. She says that Corey was nice to her at first, bought her stuff, gave her money. She slept with him—he wasn't even her first, poor kid—and everything went fine as long as she stayed pretty much in the little-girl mode. They first had trouble when she took some of his money and got her nails done—got those, whaddaya call 'em? Extensions. He went nuts; I guess it ruined the illusion for him of her being a kid."

"So he beat her up?"

"Several times. There was an incident over a red dress she bought, something about the girls she was starting to hang with—he didn't take kindly to any independent action on her part. He finally went too far, and sent her to the emergency room. That's when the cops arrested him."

"So did she know anything about his selling guns?"

"Not about the guns, specifically, but she said that Corey told her that he was set for life, that he had a connection with someone who was going to take care of him forever."

"That sounds like blackmail to me," Laura said, drumming her pen against the pad, growing excited.

"To me, too. He flashed money around, talking big about knowing things."

"Any idea what he knew?"

"No. She thinks it had something to do with his brother being a cop. He talked about Tony Harrell all the time; she says that he alternated between idolizing his brother and calling him a chump, for doing things the hard way."

"How long had the brother been dead when this girl knew Corey?"

"A year or two at most."

"So it's possible that he could have uncovered whatever scam it was that Tony was into—the guns thing, I'm guessing—and muscled in."

"That's what I'm thinking," Kenny said. "But it's not much to go on."

"Maybe my meeting today will shed some light. What about the girl—what kind of witness is she going to be?"

He laughed. " 'Bout as credible as a congressman, I'm afraid. And it's just hearsay. You can always put her up there, for what it's worth, but Meredith isn't going to run from the courtroom with her tail between her legs at the sight of Carla."

"Does she ever? It's mounting up, though, Kenny; I can feel something happening here. I just wish I knew *what*."

"You'll figure it out, if I know you. Now, I need to take the rest of the day to catch some folks with their pants down; I've been neglecting my other cases. You know how to get me if you need me, though. I'll just be settin' in the truck with my camera, eatin' doughnuts, so I'd appreciate the diversion."

"Okay. I'll call you after the meeting with the PR pukes. Happy hunting, and be careful out there, Snoop."

Cece rang through again to say the Police Department Public Affairs officer, Jennifer Fraser, was on the line; she could meet Laura at eleven, at her offices. Laura confirmed the meeting, and began to prepare a list of questions. They were all innocuous on the surface, except, of course, her request for a list of all the cops who had been involved in the program since its inception. She expected to be denied on that one, but she might as well ask now, and subpoena later. She went for a refill of her coffee cup, and when she returned, Cece was holding a call for her. "It's Meredith Gaffney. I thought you would want to talk to her."

"I sure do. Thanks." She hurried back to her desk, and picked up the blinking line. "Hello, Meredith."

"Hello, Laura. What the hell are you up to?"

"Me? Why, just defending my client, that's all—something he seems to be more in need of than ever."

"What's this about the Toys for Guns program? Are you trying to create some kind of diversion?"

"I have legitimate questions, which I would like to have answered in a professional manner. My reasons for asking them, however, I don't feel compelled to tell you or anyone. On the other hand, I will tell the ladies and gentlemen of the press if there's one more leak out of your office."

"That didn't come from us, Laura, I swear. I was as upset as you about those personnel records being revealed."

"Somehow, I doubt that. Where else could they be getting that kind of crap, Meredith?"

"It has to be coming from the cops. I spoke to Charlie Sisson about it. . . ."

"And he swore it wasn't them. There sure is a lot of poltergeist activity surrounding this case, isn't there? Just let me put you on notice: If you leak one more time, I'm taking everything I know, and some stuff I don't, right out there to the cameras. Get it under control, Meredith."

"I will. There will be no more leaks. But that's not why I called you. I want to make another offer—a final offer. Williams pleads to man two, and serves two to three at a minimum security prison. It's the best he's going to do, Laura."

It was a good offer, an *outstanding* offer. Two days earlier, it's what she had told Kenny she would be willing to take. Considering the severity of the crime—murder of a defenseless man—and the political overtones, it was a helluva deal. She knew Jeff wouldn't take it, but as his attorney she would feel obligated to tell him that this was a very attractive bird in his hand. "I'll have to take it to my client."

"I understand. It's on the table until five o'clock this afternoon. And I repeat: It's final. Take it today, or take it to court."

"I hear you. Well, thanks for the call. I'm off to Public Affairs now—I'm sure you'll get the details of my questions in a couple of hours. I could save you the trouble, and fax you my notes now, but I know you like a challenge."

"Laura, how old are you?" Meredith asked.

"Thirty. Why do you ask?"

"Because, if you're this much of a pain in the ass at thirty, I'm retiring before you get to forty."

Laura laughed. "I'll take that as a compliment."

"It was meant as one. I'll let you go forth and stir up trouble now."

"I'll call you before five."

She glanced at her watch; she would just have time to call Jeff before leaving for her meeting at Police Headquarters. She dialed his number, and listened to his terse answering machine announcement: "Leave a message."

"Jeff, It's Laura. Pick up, please." She waited a moment, then spoke again. "Okay, I have to leave to get downtown, but I want you to know that there's a new plea offer on the table." She described it. "It's a good offer, Jeff, and I think you should seriously consider it. We have nothing to go on, not really. I know you don't want to plead guilty, but there's a good chance that we're running full-speed up a dead-end street, chasing Corey Taylor's ghost. If we come up empty, without another credible motive or suspect, a jury could easily convict you of more serious charges—and you could do some hard time. We have until five o'clock to consider the offer; I'll call you as soon as I get back to the office. Don't get all bent out of shape," she added, knowing what his reaction would be, "just think about it. Talk to you later."

She hung up. She would have preferred to talk to him in person, give him a few more of the pros and cons, but he must have been in the shower. Bad timing. But bad timing seemed to be a hallmark of this case; every time she thought she had a grip on it, something unexpected and unwelcome arose. Those leaks from Jeff's file, for instance—who really was behind them? Certainly, everyone on the prosecution team had a motive for making Jeff Williams look bad (and Laura look naive), but she trusted Meredith Gaffney—she *had* to trust Meredith, or she might as well pack in her faith in the whole system. So it had to be someone in the Police Department, and that could mean anyone, all the way up to the chief. Sisson would certainly know who to call, if he wanted to do a little judicious leaking—but why create a second scandal in his own department? She already had a cop suspected of killing a suspect in custody; it would hardly be a public relations coup to unleash a sexual harassment brouhaha on top of that. That left the possibility of someone acting as a free agent, someone with a special grudge against Jeff Williams. Eleanor Haines? No, she wouldn't have access to his personnel file. There was one cop who did, though: the inscrutable Lieutenant Kowalski, the guy who knew everything about Laura's defense strategy.

For the first time since she had taken the case, Laura was inclined to agree with Libby Arnold, her nemesis at P&C—she might, just might, be in over her head.

13

The Public Affairs Division of the Atlanta Police Department had its offices at City Hall East, a white elephant of a former retail building located to the north and, as the name implied, east of the original neo-Gothic wonder that was City Hall. Laura had never seen the building before, but she liked it, a yellowish block, carved with art deco motifs. Whether it was an appropriate venue for the conduct of city business was another matter; it was certainly inconveniently located.

Once inside, she asked for Jennifer Fraser; she was asked to sign in, given a visitor badge, and sent upstairs, to another reception area. There, she was asked to wait. After about ten minutes, a secretary approached, and told her they were "ready for her." *Ready for me?* Laura thought. *What do they expect? A full-frontal assault?*

She was ushered into a small conference room, where two people waited. The city attorney was easy to identify, by his frazzled expression and bulging briefcase. Jennifer Fraser, to Laura's surprise, was wearing the uniform of a patrol officer, down to the gun and cuffs. She had expected civilian clothes, although she couldn't say why. Fraser was a tall, thin woman, probably in her late twenties, although a perpetual frown had prematurely creased her brow into an accordion of wrinkles. She had dark hair, which could have used shampooing; it was pulled back into a careless ponytail, and, when she extended her hand in greeting, Laura noticed that her nails were ragged and chewed. Something Jeff had said popped into her head: "They put the burnouts in Public Affairs." Laura had doubted him at the time—surely a burnout would be the last person the department would want dealing with sensitive matters, as they surely did in Public Affairs. She had to admit, though, that Jennifer Fraser was the textbook picture of a burnout. Laura wondered what had happened to cut short her career as a working officer—had the male officers been rough on her? Or had she gotten too much reality, and run from it?

"Hello, Ms. Chastain," Fraser said. "I'm Jennifer Fraser, and this is Mike Brannon. Would you care for a cup of coffee?" Mike Brannon said nothing at all, barely shook her hand.

Laura declined the coffee. "This shouldn't take long. I've prepared some questions, so why don't we just get down to it?" Jennifer gestured to an empty chair, and Laura sat down and pulled a pad, with her list of questions written on it, from her briefcase. "I understand that you've been coordinating the program for the past couple of years, Officer Fraser." Jennifer nodded in response. "How long has the program been running?"

"Five years."

"Who originated the idea?"

She shrugged. "I wasn't involved then, but I think that there were a number of similar programs in other cities started up at the time. Someone in the department, or in the community, must have decided it seemed like a good idea."

"How does it work? Tell me what's involved in setting it up."

She sighed, and chewed a thumbnail. "Well, I get started about July, when I get in touch with potential sponsors, and ask them if they'd like to support the program again. This year, fewer said yes, so I think it may be our last year. Anyway, I get the cost of the program underwritten. The chief and some of the city councilmen help, too, you know—twisting arms for donations and all that."

"What sort of costs need to be underwritten?"

"The cost of the toys, for one thing; that's the biggest single item. We buy most of them, although we also approach retailers, and ask them to donate nonviolent toys. But there are overhead costs, too: setting up the collection points, and the transportation and disposal of the weapons."

That, of course, was of particular interest to Laura, but she decided to circle around and come back to it later. "And what happens after you've got the funding in place?"

"Then, I arrange for the collection sites. I try to set up five to ten, conveniently located at places where folks are likely to be running errands on weekends anyway. We get permission from the property owners to set up the sites."

"And then?" Laura prompted.

Fraser shrugged. "We get volunteers—all cops, weapons-certified —to man the collection points. Oh, and there's the publicity. We put ads in the papers and get the local radio and TV stations to run PSAs publicizing the program. We also put up signs giving detailed information in public places—grocery stores, dry cleaners, you know the drill. And I try to get the newspapers and TV stations to run stories on the program, but that's gotten harder the last couple of years."

"Old news?" Laura said, sympathetically.

Fraser nodded. "Public response is way down, too," she said glumly. "We've just completed this year's program, and fewer weapons than ever were turned in. We expanded the program to collect those realistic-looking toy guns, too—you might remember last summer, when that kid was wounded by a cop who thought he had a gun, but it turned out to be a toy. We got almost none of those."

Laura nodded, sympathetically. "What kind of weapons are turned in, usually?"

She shrugged. "Older things—small-caliber handguns, hunting rifles, and shotguns. Not the kind of things that you see used in major crimes, but it was never meant as a *crime-prevention* program," she said, leaning forward and showing the first sign of animation yet. "I mean, just getting old guns out of homes, where they could cause an accident, or be stolen for use in a serious crime, is good, don't you think?"

"Of course," Laura said. "I question the need for anyone to keep a weapon in their home—it's very unlikely to be used for self-defense, isn't it?"

"Exactly. Almost never happens. What does happen, though, is that kids play with 'em, and get hurt, or killed. Or it's there when someone is thinking about suicide."

"And it becomes a self-fulfilling prophecy," Laura finished, sympathetically. "If there's a gun at hand, it's likely to be used."

"Exactly," Fraser nodded. "But we probably won't run the program next year; the response was too low, and the publicity value has really diminished."

"How many guns were collected, in previous years and this year?" Laura asked.

"We can't answer that," Mike Brannon said. So, he did have vocal chords.

"Why on earth not?" Laura asked. "Isn't that something you publicize?"

"In previous years, yes," Jennifer said, glancing at Brannon. "It's a matter of public record. But this year, we thought it was best to keep quiet about the drop-off in response. It could be misinterpreted."

"I see," Laura said, although she really didn't. "Well, if it's a matter of public record, I suppose I can find the figures on my own. Tell me more about what happens to the weapons once they're collected. How are they secured at the collection sites, for instance?"

Fraser glanced at the attorney, making sure it was okay to answer that one. He nodded, but made a note of Laura's question. "We transport receptacles for them to each site."

"What kind of receptacles?" Laura asked.

"Basically, sturdy wooden cases—with locks, of course. Safes would be ideal, but that's impractical—they would have to be large enough to accommodate the rifles and shotguns, and big safes are just too heavy. So we keep all the collected weapons in a locked box, and there's an armed, on-duty patrolman there to guard it."

"Plus the volunteers," Laura prompted.

"Yes," she said. "Usually, two volunteers, plus the duty officer, plus someone from Public Affairs, like me—all of us armed. So there's virtually no threat of the weapons being hijacked, if that's what you were wondering about."

She hadn't been, but she wondered why Fraser had brought it up. Could it be that the fail-safe had failed, and that someone had gotten away with a box full of guns—someone like Corey Taylor? That would be something that the cops would want to keep a lid on, but it would seem impossible to keep something like that a secret from the press. "So you collect the weapons, and put them in a box. What happens next?"

"An armored police vehicle picks them up, and transports them to a scrap yard, where they're destroyed."

"How do you guarantee that they are destroyed?"

"We keep a manifest of weapons collected at each site, signed by the volunteers who actually log in the weapons, and countersigned by the armored patrol that picks them up—they're required to check the manifest against the weapons actually on hand, and certify it."

"And what about the scrap yard?"

"Another countersignature is required there, verifying that the weapons on the manifest were all turned in and destroyed. Bug-proof."

Not exactly, Laura thought; a creative criminal could divert the weapons in a couple of ways she could think of. She decided to test her theories. "Really? What's to stop someone from hijacking a load of guns, plus its manifest, on the way to the scrap yard—that way, all the weapons that show up are certified as destroyed, but not necessarily all the guns that are turned in?"

Fraser smiled and shook her head. "We thought of that; a separate copy of the manifest goes to the scrap yard."

"What if someone at the scrap yard were suborned, bribed to countersign for guns that never made it to him?"

"Why would anyone do that? I'm telling you, Ms. Chastain, most of the guns turned in are hardly worth the trouble of stealing. I remember last year, we got—I swear—somebody's old World War I sidearm. It was so rusted it couldn't have been fired, not in a million years. What's your angle on this, anyway? Are you saying that these guns aren't being destroyed?" She was defensive, almost hostile.

"I'm not saying anything. I'm just here, as a citizen, to ask a few questions, which I'm almost finished doing. Except for one—can I get a list of all the cops who've volunteered for the program, from its inception through this year?"

"No," Mike Brannon said.

"Why not? I can subpoena it," Laura said.

"You can," he said. "But until the court orders us to release that list, we would consider it a violation of the privacy of the officers who volunteered for the program. If you don't have any more questions, I think we should end this meeting."

"Fine," Laura said. "We'll subpoena the department for the list." She couldn't think of any more questions to ask—none that Brannon would allow Fraser to answer, anyway—so she started to wrap things up, replacing her notes in her briefcase. "Thank you for your time; you've been very helpful."

Fraser was about to answer when the door opened and Charles Sisson walked in. Laura had seen him on television many times, and had spotted him across the room at social functions—the chief had even been the honoree at Prendergrast & Crawley's annual Yule Log the previous year—but she had never been in such close quarters with him. She felt a powerful urge to jump to her feet and salute. Maybe it was the uniform. As chief, Sisson had his choice of uniform or plainclothes, but he always wore the full-dress blues in public. *Full Metal Jacket*, Laura thought. It was smart; Sisson was a short man, and the blue suit, its double-breasted tunic blazing with brass, gave him instant authority. The uniform was clearly custom-made, the jacket elongated just enough to give the illusion of more height, and the trousers uncuffed, to avoid emphasis on the shortness of the wearer's legs.

Sisson looked at Laura, and nodded. Laura suppressed the urge to pat her hair into place. "Ms. Chastain? Have my people been helpful?"

"Yes, thank you, Chief. We were just finishing."

"Did you get everything you needed?" Sisson looked at Jennifer Fraser, who avoided his gaze, as he spoke.

Laura shook her head. "Not quite. I'd like a list of all the officers who participated in the exchange program, but Mr. Brannon says I can't have it."

"It's a privacy issue, Chief," Brannon interjected.

Privacy, my ass, Laura thought. "No, it is—or should be—a matter of public record."

Sisson looked at Brannon, and then back at Laura. He smiled, a short official smile. "I'm not a lawyer, so I'm afraid I'll have to take Mr. Brannon's advice. If he says you can't have it, well, I guess you can't."

"Oh, I can get it. I'll go to Judge Root; he'll give me a subpoena, after I explain the relevance to my client's case."

Sisson smiled his camera smile again. "If you tell me why it's relevant, maybe we could release the information to you without a subpoena," he said.

Fat chance, Laura thought; *he won't give me anything without a court order, and I'm not letting him play me for a fool.* She shrugged. "It's probably better that we deal with this matter through the courts. I've taken up enough of your time for one day, anyway." She picked up her briefcase. "Officer Fraser, thank you for your time; you've been helpful." She shook Fraser's hand, and smiled; the officer had jumped like a spooked squirrel when Sisson had entered the room, and Laura sympathized. Laura nodded curtly to Brannon, and turned to speak to Sisson.

The chief shook Laura's hand, and held it just a second too long. "Take care, Ms. Chastain."

"Thanks, I will," Laura said. She had to sidestep him to get to the door; everything was a damn power play for the man. After she left the room, she noticed that Sisson remained, closing the door. *Probably going to interrogate those two. Better them than me,* she thought; she recalled what Kenny had said about line officers resenting the chief's involvement in their cases. A man for details, she thought.

At least it explained Officer Fraser's skittish, bedraggled appearance—working for a man like Sisson might do that to you.

Charles Sisson was still on Laura's mind when she left the building, heading for the parking lot, but her thoughts were interrupted by someone shouting her name. "Chastain! Hold up a minute!"

She turned and saw Amos Kowalski coming her way; she waited for him to catch up to her. "Hello, Lieutenant."

He smiled as he approached her. "Hello. What brings you down here?"

"Why, I've just had a meeting with your Public Affairs people—the woman who was in charge of the Toys for Guns program, in fact."

"Was it helpful?"

"Not entirely." She ran down the highlights for him. "I can think of at least a couple of ways that weapons could have been shanghaied before they were tossed into the smelter, can't you?"

He nodded. "But it makes the most sense, to me, for the weapons to have been taken from the scrap yard, where whoever was doing it would have the pick of the litter, so to speak. If they hijacked a load, they might get some salable stuff, along with a bunch of worthless crap."

She nodded. "Of course, that means that someone at the recycling yard would have to be involved."

He shrugged. "People will do the most amazing things for a couple hundred dollars. It's the pettiness of most larceny that's depressing, Laura; if you'd been a cop as long as I have, you would begin to appreciate how low the price for a conscience is."

"Trust me, I have some inkling. I guess I'm going to have to subpoena for a list of all the cops who were involved, and have Kenny go over it. It has to have been someone who was involved with Tony Harrell, who would have known Corey. Looks like a lot of work to me."

"It will be. Good luck."

"While I have you here, Kowalski, I have a bone to pick with you—Meredith swears she's not leaking to the press, and the cops tell me it's not them. It appears to be someone acting on his own initiative, slipping the press little tidbits about Jeff."

"And you think it's me?"

She shrugged. "You're convinced that Jeff is guilty; you make no bones about that. And you've had access to everything that's been put out there—the timing of his arrest, the contents of his personnel file."

He shook his head. "It wasn't me, Chastain, but I don't expect you to take my word for that. I never deal with the press; wouldn't know how to go about leaking a thing."

"Get real, Kowalski; you can dial a phone—that's all it takes. But I'm putting you on warning, same as I did Meredith and your Public Affairs people: One more leak, and I start doing some plumbing of my own. Got it?"

He smiled. "Heard and understood—not that I can do anything about it. To change the subject, I understand Meredith put another offer on the table."

"Yes," she said, tersely. Even if ethics permitted, she would not discuss the district attorney's offer with Kowalski. "By the way, I met your boss this morning."

"My boss?" He looked puzzled.

"Chief Sisson." His eyebrows shot up. Gratified at his surprise, she continued. "Yes, it seems my questions about the gun exchange hit a raw nerve somewhere upstairs. I imagine that you're going to catch a few questions when you get back into your office."

He glanced back at the building, suddenly seeming reluctant to go in. "Yikes. I had a meeting uptown this morning, so I'm just now getting in. Maybe I should come up with some excuse to stay out a little longer."

"That's one hard-driving man you work for, Amos—how do you do it?"

"Oh, he not's bad, once you get to know him. We go way back; I knew him before he could leap tall buildings, and I don't let him forget it."

Laura shook her head. "He's got a tough job, but he could be a little less military, don't you think? And he didn't seem to care for me too much; you better not be seen talking to me, if you're interested in furthering your career."

"Then I'll begin to shun you immediately. Take care, Chastain— and I mean that. You're digging up some bones someone would prefer stay buried. Here," he reached into his pocket, and took out a business card and a pen; he scribbled something on the card, and handed it to her. "This is my card, with my home number on it. Call me anytime if things start getting hairy."

She took the card, glanced at it, and put it in the pocket of her coat. "Thanks. And have a nice day, you hear?"

"Fat chance, with you stirring the shit. My best to Kenny."

They parted company, and she hurried to her car. Stuck at a traffic light, drumming her fingers on the steering wheel, she ran over the meeting with Jennifer Fraser in her mind, and made a sound between a snort of contempt and a laugh. *I'm not even a criminal,* she thought, *and I could think up half a dozen ways to liberate a few guns from that dopey program. Simply failing to sign them in—palming them under the table—would be the simplest, although it wouldn't net a significant number of weapons. If I had an ally at the scrap yard, that would be the easiest way—I could look over all the weapons, and take my pick—all I would need to do is to get whoever was in charge at the smelter to say they had been destroyed. Could Corey Taylor have done that, though? No—but he didn't have to, did he? He was just the conduit to the street. No, it had to be a cop involved in the organization of the exchange program.* A sense of relief dawned with the thought: Kowalski had never been involved with the program. His position in every other aspect of the case was ambiguous; he certainly had as much opportunity to kill Corey Taylor as anyone on his squad, but unless Laura was seriously going to paint him as deranged by the loss of the Hunicutt case, he had no real motive. She felt buoyed by the realization; she didn't *want* Amos Kowalski to be a bad guy. She was almost cheerful as she returned to the office.

She stopped off in the lobby of the office building and picked up a salad before returning to her desk. Cecelia handed over her messages; three were from Jeff Williams. "And Tom Bailey called; he wants you to know that his flight gets in at seven. He says he'll call you when he lands."

That put a smile on Laura's face, a smile Cecelia noted only with the arch of an eyebrow as she returned to her own desk. A seven o'clock landing would put Tom at her place sometime after eight; she decided to leave the office at four, to give herself plenty of time to get everything ready for him.

In the meantime, through, her first order of business was to call Jeff. His answering machine picked up, and she identified herself. He came on the line immediately, obviously aggrieved. "Where have you been?" he huffed. "I called three times."

"I told you I had a meeting, with Public Affairs. I take it you got my message about Meredith's offer."

"Yes, and that bitch can suck my . . ."

Laura interrupted him before he could finish the thought. "Don't give me any of that crap. There's an offer on the table, and you are to consider it as a rational human being. *Never* use that kind of language around me, Jeff. Attorney-client or not, you show some respect."

"Sorry," he said, meekly. "It just made me mad, is all. I already told you though: I'm not pleading guilty to killing that pervert. I didn't do it, and I'm not doing time for it. So she can—*respectfully*— take her plea bargain and cram it."

"Jeff, I have to tell you that this is not a bad deal. Look at it this way: So far, we have nothing but a bunch of wild-goose speculation about Corey Taylor *maybe* having a buddy at the Police Department, who was supplying him with guns. It amounts to a potential alternative motive for his death, but it depends on an unproved conspiracy theory. To tell you the truth, if I were to go in front of a jury today, I'm not sure I would even bring it up. I'd probably try to implicate one of the other cops on your squad who had equal access to Taylor— especially your partner, or Kowalski."

"So do it. Hell, maybe it was Kowalski. Maybe all the rest of this *is* just a bunch of crap—Kowalski had plenty of time to stroll into that room and choke the guy to death."

"But we would still be taking a huge chance. You can settle this today, and put it behind you. You would serve some time, sure, but at a minimum-security prison, where your personal safety wouldn't be an issue. That's a big benefit, Jeff. Think about it."

"No," was his only reply.

"Okay," she said. "I'll let Meredith know. I'm leaving here at four this afternoon, and I'll put off calling her until just before I leave. Call me if you change your mind."

"I won't."

Laura hung up, dissatisfied with the conversation. For one thing, Jeff's crude remark about Meredith didn't sit well with her. Of course, Jeff was taking all this much more personally then she was—as he should—but the remark had made him seem like a bully. She thought about Kowalski; maybe his problem with Jeff was based on Jeff's style. Kowalski would never use such a gratuitous vulgarity, she was sure.

She wished that Jeff had taken the deal; she wasn't looking forward to going into a hearing with what skimpy evidence she had. If she didn't have more to go on by the end of the week, in fact, bringing up the guns wouldn't make sense—the prosecution might even manage to get the whole line of questioning suppressed as irrelevant, anyway.

Nor did she relish her other alternative, dragging Amos Kowalski's name through the mud to confuse the issue.

She leaned back in her chair and tried to clear her head; maybe she had the answer right in front of her. How would Corey Taylor, an undistinguished punk, have gotten himself on the receiving end of guns taken from the cops? Through his brother, of course; the sainted Tony Harrell must have seen the opportunity to hijack a few street-quality weapons, and make a little extra dough at Christmastime—cops were notoriously ill-paid, after all. Tony must have set the thing up with someone in the department, but he died before he could make it an annual event. He must have told Corey, though, and Corey must have known enough to muscle in on the action. Whoever was pirating the weapons gave them to Corey, who sold them, presumably splitting the proceeds with his partner on the force. But this had been a bad year for the guns, not many turned in, and Corey had gone and gotten himself arrested. His partner must have been afraid that Corey was going to give him up in exchange for leniency on the rape charge. It all made sense, but the mysterious cop was a missing link. Who had known Tony Harrell well enough to run the scam with him?

Laura scribbled notes all over a piece of paper, then crumpled it up in frustration. What a mess; thank God she had the weekend to try to sort out some of it.

14

People who work together usually talk about work; work is one-third of most lives, and, especially for people who happen to like their jobs, uppermost in the mind much of the time. Laura had been afraid that she and Tom, as lovers, were going to be an extension of themselves at work—she asking for his advice on this, he outlining his strategy for that. She needn't have worried. For one thing, the physical attraction they had so carelessly unleashed threatened to cut off all conversation of any kind; the slightest touch could set them off. For another, when they weren't acting like hormone-soaked teen-agers, they returned to their usual style of conversation, which allowed for differences of opinion. The fact that they were arguing, on a Saturday night, in an expensive restaurant, made little difference.

"That's bogus, and you know it," she said. They had just come from seeing a movie, the story of a group of lowlifes who killed each other, and innocent bystanders, with all the creativity a film student could muster, or steal from Asian imports. She knew, of course, that the violence was meant to be *ironic,* that each bullet hole and gout of blood was surrounded by little quotation marks, but she wasn't buying any of it. "Do you think those boneheaded guys sitting behind us were appreciating the *irony* of that man's head being cut off by a chain saw, Tom?" she asked. "They just thought it was *cool.*"

"But isn't that the point?" he said. "To show death in its most baroque form, to demonstrate that we have become so pervaded by violence as to make it almost meaningless?"

"No, absolutely not," she argued, "because most of the guys who make those movies—and almost all of the people in that audience—have no experience of *real* violence. For them, it *is* just a metaphor. For the victims, and their families, and the cops, though, it's anything but ironic. I don't care what the critics say; I say it's just cheap thrills, a chance to make a buck."

"But, Laura," he said, gently, "popular culture follows society; it doesn't lead. Movies, and books, and television reflect—in a pale, distorted way—what's going on in the real world. If a movie disgusts you, you should look around and ask yourself where the inspiration for it came from."

She shook her head, vigorously. "You can't believe that, Tom; you've had some experience with criminals. You know that evil isn't heroic; it's pedestrian and whiny. It's not twenty feet tall on a movie screen—it's sniveling in a jail cell, yelling for its lawyer and talking about how abused it was as a child. You can't argue both sides of *every* question; there has to be a core of belief that you never abandon. I know you stand for something, Tom, so please stop being a devil's advocate when you're not in the courtroom."

She hadn't meant to speak with such passion, and she was afraid she might have offended him. She waited for his reply, and saw a strange look pass over his face. He took her hand, and kissed it. "I'm sorry; you're right. I should lose my own ironic detachment more often, Laura; it's a bad habit. And I agree with you—it was a disgusting movie, unredeemable crap." He looked at her, and chuckled. "I am red, I am gold, I am green, I am blue; I will always be me, I will always be new," he quoted.

"Who's that?" she asked, thinking it sounded familiar.

"Delmore Schwartz, "I Am Cherry Alive." You reminded me of it, just now. The grown-ups do tend to forget what they once knew was true," he added, a little sadly.

"I'm a grown-up, too," she said. "Don't overplay the age difference, Grandpa." There were thirteen years between them, but Laura hardly counted the decade-plus gap. There was too much common ground.

"Sorry. Let me take care of the check, and then you can help me with my walker. What do you want to do now?"

It was only nine o'clock, early enough for them to go to a club, or a café, but neither alternative appealed to Laura. She reached across the table and took his hand. "I'm ready to call it a night," she said, with meaning.

"My God, woman, you're going to exhaust me. I'm not nineteen anymore."

"You started it," she said.

He smiled as he signed the check. "Let's go back to my house, if you don't mind. I need to check on things there." They had spent Friday night at Laura's; Tom hadn't been to his own place since returning from New York.

"Sure," she said.

Tom's house wasn't as large as she had feared it might be, although it was every bit as elegant. Of course, she hadn't expected empty pizza boxes, and neon beer signs on the wall. It wasn't fussy; it looked inhabited, the antiques come by honestly—through inheritance—rather than assembled by a decorator at top prices. Laura looked around the living room while Tom went for a bottle of wine; people paid thousands of dollars to fall short of the slightly frayed, aristocratic look Tom's house achieved effortlessly.

He returned, and saw her looking at an old photo. "My Aunt Bessie," he said, identifying its subject.

"What's she holding?" Laura asked, squinting at the sepia-toned picture. Aunt Bessie was elegantly dressed, but she appeared to be holding some kind of animal. A dog sat at her feet, looking worshipfully up at her.

"A dead possum," he answered, handing Laura a glass. "Don't ask me why; the explanation is lost in the mists of time. But I like the picture anyway; it was taken around the turn of the century."

"You look like the kind of man who comes from a long line of possum-killing women."

"I am. And I expect all the women in my life to know how to deal with marsupials."

"You like yours stewed or fried?" she answered.

"Stuffed and mounted," he said. He steered her to a sofa, and pulled her down into his arms. "You're beautiful."

"So are you. Are we going to tell them about us—at work?"

"It's none of their business what we do in our spare time," he replied, taking her wineglass from her hand. "I've never told them anything about my personal life, and I'm not about to start now. Not that there was anything to tell, until now."

He kissed her; she closed her eyes. "Remember, you're not nineteen anymore," she said.

"Shut up," he answered.

When the sun came through the window of his bedroom, many hours later, Laura propped herself on an elbow, and watched him sleep. He looked sweet; you would hardly suspect that this was a man who could tear through the halls of a law firm, demanding the head of some poor associate—hers, more than once. She hoped that he wouldn't ease off on his perfectionist expectations of her, just because they were sleeping together. Work was separate from all this, but it was still important.

She rolled back onto the pillow and stared at the coffered ceiling. Work; she realized, with a guilty jerk, that she had hardly thought about Jeff Williams since leaving the office on Friday. She had relayed his refusal of the plea offer to Meredith, who was full of dire warnings about the consequences, and then Laura had simply filed him away, to be dealt with again on Monday. Now, though, it was out of the mental file, and there was no stopping the wheels in her brain from turning over his problem.

Her mind returned to the gun-pirating. Tony Harrell had everyone fooled; not one single person who had known him had come forward with anything to indicate that he had been crooked. He couldn't have been the perfect cop he was supposed to have been, though; he must have been very, very good at fooling people. Not like his younger brother—Corey Taylor had been transparently a hood, a small-time loser with a weakness for little girls. No one in the world would believe that he was capable of engineering such an elaborate scheme all by himself. No, it all came back to the elusive Officer Harrell, who had left behind no one to speak ill of him—almost no one who could speak of him at all, in fact. Except his grandmother; maybe time had rosied up her glasses a little bit, blurred Tony's sharp edges into an image of perfection over time. Laura would like to talk to her, and see if she might recall something that would lead them to the real Tony Harrell.

Carefully, so as not to wake Tom, she picked up the phone beside the bed, and dialed Kenny's home number. His wife answered. "Hi, Cindy; it's Laura Chastain. I hate to disturb you, but I need to ask Kenny something." She waited while Cindy called him to the phone; she could feel Tom shift in his sleep.

"Laura? What's up?" Kenny sounded cheerful, as always.

"Hey, I didn't wake you, did I?"

"Wake me? Are you joking? I have kids; I haven't slept in on a weekend in eight years. What can I do you for?"

"Something's bugging me, Ken. We're missing a big piece, and I think it's Tony Harrell. Who was this guy, anyway? He can't have been as good as they all claim; he had to be the one who started stealing the guns."

"Yeah, but every hole I drilled came up dry; the man was the best cop ever to wear a uniform—or he has the best postmortem PR agent ever."

"What about the grandmother—do you think, if we talked to her again, she might remember a less beatified Tony?" Tom was awake now; Laura was lying on her stomach, propped on her elbows, whispering into the phone. Tom rolled over to her side of the bed, and began kissing her, up and down her back. It was distracting.

"Maybe," Kenny was saying. "Maybe if you go down there with me, she would open up a little more, you being a fellow woman and all. You okay?"

She had gasped, a little, as Tom's hands wandered. "It's nothing. When can you make it?"

"This afternoon's okay. I can pick you up at one."

Laura bit her lip to keep from moaning. "Make it two. See you later." She hung up.

"Who was that?" Tom asked, between kisses.

"Just Kenny."

"Uh-huh. And you're going to work today, aren't you?"

"Well, it's important—oh, God—and you would, too."

"You're a very dull girl, Laura Chastain."

"Am not," she protested, and set out to prove it.

Shortly before two, Laura was back at her town house, waiting for Kenny. Tom, amused, had dropped her off, and headed into the office to do some work of his own. They promised to meet back at her place at five; she had given him a set of keys, just in case she was running late. She would have felt guilty, if she hadn't known that he was glad of the opportunity to get some work of his own done. Besides, she didn't want them to be one of those couples who were joined at the hip. A little separation was good. Kenny buzzed from the front gate, and Laura ran out to meet him.

"You're looking very rosy and happy," he commented, as he steered his truck back into Peachtree Road traffic.

She fingered the necklace Tom had given her when he returned from New York; it had come in one of those blue Tiffany boxes, and she would have loved it even if it hadn't been perfect, and beautiful, and tasteful—all of which, of course, it was. She hadn't taken it off since he gave it to her Friday night, and doubted she would for a long time to come. "I've managed to get some rest this weekend," she said.

"Oh. That must be it, then."

She glanced at his profile; he was stifling a grin. "Cut that out," she said. "So I'm seeing someone—is that so wrong?"

"Not at all. I don't know why you have to be so mysterious. He must be really something, though, if you can turn down a stud like Kowalski for him."

"He told you that? I thought all you talked about was sports and hooters."

"We were talking about *your* hooters at the time, so it was appropriate in the context."

She punched him in the shoulder. "Believe me, if Amos had asked a month ago, I would have been all over it. It's just bad timing."

"Maybe you'll get tired of this guy before Amos finds someone himself."

"Not likely. Can we change the subject?"

"Sure, but I don't find Tony Harrell and his grandma nearly as intriguing as your sex life."

"Don't you think I'm right, though? Something's up there."

"Possibly. But will we get anything from the grandmother? I doubt it. If she knows anything bad about him, she's put it in her vault. Tony was her good boy; Corey was the bad one. You know how people create their own version of events."

"It's worth a shot, anyway." They were on the expressway now, cruising south to the projects. They turned off just past the impressive new stadium, where the Olympics had been held the previous summer. At first, it had seemed absurd for Atlanta—*Atlanta*—to host the Olympics, but Laura had to admit that the city had done well. For once, its tireless boosterism had paid off. Sure, there had been a few glitches, but for two weeks the city had finally seemed to live up to its own hype. Laura had attended several events herself; the firm, drawing on her record as a former show-jumper, had asked her to escort groups of clients to equestrian events. She had loved every minute of it; even the packed MARTA trains had felt like a party. Now, though, the city had subsided back into itself, and the Olympic cauldron stood forlornly detached from the stadium, which was being modified for baseball. Factions were squabbling over who would maintain it, or if it would be maintained at all. Atlanta had moved on again.

Kenny steered them back into the projects; they looked different today, in the cold winter light. They were at once more barren, and more benign, almost deserted. The bad guys were sleeping in, and the good ones were at church, which was, in the African American community in the south, an all-day affair. "I bet she's still at church," Laura ventured.

"I bet you're right," Kenny said. "She's probably," he speculated, glancing at his watch, "helping clean up after dinner on the grounds. Let's knock on her door, just to make sure." They did; no response. "I know where her church is; let's drive over there and wait for her."

They parked by the curb in front of the Full Holiness Gospel Tabernacle, a neat red-brick building topped with a modest white cross. After a time, a small group of highly dressed parishioners emerged, spanning three generations. The children ran and chased each other, full of pent-up energy, while their parents and grandparents lingered in conversation. All those family-value blowhards should see this, Laura thought; the vein of decency ran deep in this community. If you listened to the slick hucksters on the right, you would think that black neighborhoods were populated solely by dangerous, gun-toting, teen-impregnating thugs. A myth, of course, and like all myth, based on a tiny fragment of truth: It only took a few Corey Taylors to ruin it for everyone.

"There she is," Kenny said, pointing to a lady in a blue coat. He got out of the truck, and Laura followed. "Mrs. Bledsoe! Hello!" Kenny had been nothing less than accurate when he had described Corey's grandmother as a "church lady." Laura was reminded of her own grandmother when she saw the tiny woman, a hat perched on her head and sensible shoes on her feet. She supported herself with a cane, and appeared to be in her late sixties. There was an air of sadness about her. She brightened, however, when she saw Kenny.

"Officer Newton! How do you do? I didn't expect to see you again."

"Let me introduce Laura Chastain; she's the lady lawyer I told you about—the one who's looking into Corey's death."

"Hello, Ms. Chastain. We're very sad about Corey, but he was a bad boy. We weren't surprised when he came to a bad end. We had the funeral yesterday, Officer Newton; it was nice. Brother Allman preached on the parable of the prodigal son. That's what my Corey was, a prodigal. The Lord welcomed him home just the same, I know." She pulled out a hanky, and dabbed at her eyes.

"I'm sorry I missed it, Mrs. Bledsoe," Kenny said, sincerely. "I know how sad you must be, but Laura and I were wondering if you could talk to us a little more about Corey—and Tony."

"I would be pleased to. The house feels mighty empty now, with both my boys gone; it would be nice if you would come back there with me now. It will ease the loneliness."

"I'll give you a ride," Kenny offered.

They returned to the truck, and Laura squeezed into the middle seat, between Kenny and Mrs. Bledsoe. They drove the few blocks to the building where she lived, and followed her inside. Her apartment was modestly, but comfortably, furnished, and probably the tidiest place Laura had ever seen. She and Kenny seated themselves on the sofa at Mrs. Bledsoe's invitation, beneath a pastel picture of Jesus, flanked by photographic portraits of Tony Harrell and Corey Taylor as boys, and a young woman Laura assumed must be their mother.

Mrs. Bledsoe bustled into the kitchen, and returned with a plate of cookies. "I'm boiling water for tea, if you would care for some," she said.

"That would be nice," Laura said. "We hate to disturb you, Mrs. Bledsoe, but there are some things that don't make sense to me. I wondered if you could tell us more about your grandsons. Were they close?"

She got a faraway look in her eyes. "Tony was seven years older than Corey; he worshiped his baby brother from the day he came home from the hospital. He took care of that baby like he was his own. The boys came to live with me before their Mama died, you know; it got so she couldn't care for them properly, and Child Welfare thought it best. Tony was such a help to me; he walked Corey to and from school, and helped get supper on the table. Oh, he was a good boy."

She produced the handkerchief again, and blew her nose. Laura felt a lump rising in her own throat; for this woman to have lost her daughter, and both her grandsons, seemed especially cruel. "And Tony went on to join the police force," she prompted.

"Oh, yes; he graduated from high school, and went to junior college for two years. He was accepted to the police academy, and he graduated at the top of his class. We were so proud of him, Corey and I, when we went to his graduation. He looked so *handsome* in his uniform."

"How long was he on the force?"

"How long? Oh, I believe it was five years. He had just taken the sergeant's exam when he . . . excuse me a moment; let me get the kettle."

She left the room to make tea, and Laura turned to Kenny. "Any advice on how I should ask her if her grandson was on the take?"

"It's your show," Kenny said, throwing up his hands. "You're the highly trained lawyer. Just do what you would do if she were on the stand, Counselor."

"Thanks a bunch." Mrs. Bledsoe returned with mugs of tea. Laura stirred lemon juice into hers, took a sip, and smiled. "When Tony was on the force, did you meet many of his friends?"

"Some of them, yes. His partner was Officer Maddux, a nice man. He spoke at the funeral, although he had retired and moved away by that time. I liked him very much. But Tony didn't socialize much with the other police; he had his girlfriend, Julie. They married, you know, shortly before. . . ." Her voice cracked.

"I'm sorry, Mrs. Bledsoe, to make you think about all this. It must be very hard on you."

"She was such a sweet girl, and she loved him so much. When they came to tell me that both of them were gone, it was the worst day of my life. It was that new house, you know; the furnace was faulty. And Tony was so proud to have bought a house for his wife. 'Granny, you can come live with us,' he would say, but I wanted those children to have their own life together. They didn't need an old woman around. And then . . ." She trailed off, shaking her head sadly.

"How did Corey take it?" Kenny asked.

"Oh, he was angry. He was just twenty then; he had never graduated from school, and Tony was trying to get him a job at the time of his death. They were very close. Corey thought someone had killed Tony; none of us could convince him that it had been an accident."

"Why would he think that, Mrs. Bledsoe?" Laura asked.

"I don't know, but he stormed around for weeks, said he would get even with the ones who did it. I think he just had trouble accepting that his brother was gone."

"Is it possible that he could have known something, maybe about a case Tony was working on?"

"He could have; the boys saw each other nearly every day. I'm sure they told each other everything—things they wouldn't tell their grandmother." She managed a weak smile.

"Mrs. Bledsoe, please don't take this the wrong way," Laura began, cautiously. "But Tony had just gotten married, just bought a house. Those are major financial obligations; is it possible that he could have been tempted, maybe gotten involved in something he shouldn't have? I only say that because Corey thought he might have been murdered," she added hastily.

To her surprise, Mrs. Bledsoe didn't get angry or upset; she smiled. "Let me show you something, child." She got up and went into one of the bedrooms, and came back with a bulging scrapbook. "This is where I keep everything about my boys, from the time they were babies. I want you to look at it, so you can see the kind of man my Tony was."

She handed the unwieldy book to Laura, who dutifully opened it at page one. There was Tony Harrell as a chubby-cheeked baby, propped on pillows and looking past the camera for his mother, and there he was with his mother and father, in a variety of poses—at the beach, in front of the Christmas tree. Then, when he was about three, no more pictures of the father; Tony's first tragedy. School pictures followed, and Little League poses, bat on shoulder, glowering purposefully at the camera as if it were the opposing pitcher. Then, when he was a little older, a joyful young Tony, quite the little man in a suit and bow tie, clutching a chubby replica of himself as an infant—Corey. And so on, the boys separately and together. The pictures were interspersed with newspaper clippings as Tony grew older: Tony winning a citizenship award, Tony chosen to present a plaque to a dignitary who visited his junior high. He appeared as the shortest guy on the basketball team, a bantam among storks, and as an Eagle scout; then, among a list of the graduating class at Carver High, with academic honors. Tony, grown-up and handsome, laughing with a beautiful young woman; Tony in the uniform of a police trainee, then as a newly minted cop, flanked by his grandmother and the pretty girl, Corey standing beside and slightly to the rear of the group. There were no newspaper clippings about Corey, and the pictures of him became sparser as he grew older. In the later pages, he appeared only as an adjunct to his brother, as best man at his wedding and standing in front of Tony's new house, smiling wanly as his brother and sister-in-law embraced him.

There were also mileposts from Tony's law-enforcement career, short newspaper articles tucked between photos. Laura glanced at them; Tony was listed as arresting officer in several crimes notorious enough at the time to have made the newspapers. His grandmother had carefully underlined his name each time it was mentioned, and any quotes from him in their entirety. The longest article, solemnly affixed to one of the last pages, was his obituary and a brief report on his funeral, attended by as many cops as the Full Holiness Gospel

Tabernacle could hold. It was as Kenny had told her: the saddest story he had ever heard.

"I see what you mean, Mrs. Bledsoe; he was an outstanding young man. His death was a tragedy."

As she spoke, Laura glanced again at some of the newspaper articles. One in particular, which featured a picture of a smiling, blond teenage girl, caught her eye. The girl had been found dead in a vacant lot downtown; it was Tony and his partner who had found her body. Laura checked the date, December 12, five years earlier, about ten days before Tony's own death, which gave eerie resonance to the underlined quote from him: "You always hate it when something like this happens. I look at that girl, and think, 'She's somebody's daughter. Somebody loved that girl. . . . ' " Laura read on, and almost choked.

"Officer Harrell and his partner went to the vacant lot, acting on a tip received in an anonymous phone call. When they arrived, they found the body, which had evidently been transported to the lot from another site. There were no signs of violence on the body, although there was evidence of sexual activity. Police sources speculate that the dead woman may have been a prostitute, although that has not been determined. The medical examiner has issued a preliminary finding of death by a heart attack, possibly resulting from drug overdose, although it will be several weeks before a final cause of death can be determined. Officer Harrell and his partner, Officer Jennifer Fraser. . . ."

"Oh, God, Kenny, look at this—look who Tony was riding with when he died."

Kenny scanned the article. "Jennifer Fraser. Don't know her. Who is she?"

"Kenny," Laura said, grabbing his arm in a strangling grip, "she's the Public Affairs officer responsible for coordinating the gun-exchange program."

"Holy fucking smokes!" Kenny said. "Sorry, Mrs. Bledsoe."

Mrs. Bledsoe, however, seemed more confused than offended by Kenny's outburst. "What is it?" she asked.

"Mrs. Bledsoe, do you remember who Tony rode with after his partner retired? A woman, maybe?"

Mrs. Bledsoe's brow creased with the effort of memory. "Yes, there was a young woman; I don't think Tony liked her very much. She came to the funeral, but I don't remember much about her."

Laura frowned. "Do you think Corey knew her?"

"He might have met her, but I don't see why that matters."

"It shouldn't, except that this woman—Officer Fraser—was in a position to steal guns from the police department, and give them to Corey to sell."

Mrs. Bledsoe looked shocked. "Are you saying that my Corey was selling *guns* . . . ?" Her voice trailed off, and Laura instantly regretted causing additional pain to this woman who had already suffered so much.

"Yes, it looks as if he was—but he had an accomplice in the Police Department. We think it's why he was killed."

Kenny, who had a cop's talent for diplomacy, reached out and patted Mrs. Bledsoe's hand. "Corey fell in with some bad people after Tony died, Mrs. Bledsoe. They took advantage of him, I'm afraid. I wish there was something we could have done back then."

Mrs. Bledsoe smiled weakly. "I know you would have if you could have, Officer."

Kenny reassured her. "Corey's at peace now, and we're going to find the person who did this to him."

Mrs. Bledsoe seemed confused. "You mean it's not that officer they're talking about on the news?"

"No," Laura said. "We don't think it was. Someone else was involved in the gun-selling with Corey—possibly this Jennifer Fraser."

Mrs. Bledsoe absorbed what Laura said, and pondered its meaning. She was an intelligent woman, and it didn't take her long to reach an upsetting conclusion. "But if she was involved, you think my Tony was, too." Distress, disbelief, and defensive anger registered successively on her careworn face. "I can tell you right now that he was not."

"There's no evidence that he was, Mrs. Bledsoe," Laura said, quickly. She would rather be a suspect herself than cause pain to this decent woman. "Corey might have *met* Jennifer through Tony, but there's no evidence that he was a participant in their . . . business." She floundered for a word to describe the unholy enterprise that had united—possibly—Jennifer Fraser and the hapless Corey Taylor.

It was time for Kenny, once again, to be tactful. "I don't think Tony knew anything about this, Mrs. Bledsoe. Everything we know about him tells us that he was a good cop—one of the best. Remember, he didn't know Jennifer Fraser for very long, and you said yourself that he didn't much care for her." He looked at his watch and cast a look at Laura, indicating that they had learned as much as they could, and that it was time to go. He rose to his feet, and Laura followed. "Mrs. Bledsoe, you've been very helpful; we really appreciate your letting us look at your scrapbook." Kenny hesitated for a moment, and then added something in a voice Laura had rarely heard him use, serious and almost angry. "Corey may not have been a good boy, but he didn't deserve to die the way he did. We'll get whoever did it, I promise you."

Mrs. Bledsoe followed them to the door. "Thank you, Officer Newton. And Ms. Chastain. Please call me when you know something."

"I will," Kenny promised again.

As they walked to the car, Laura shook her head. "Poor Mrs. Bledsoe. Lord, I hope that Tony Harrell wasn't involved with Fraser! That poor lady has suffered enough."

"It could have been Corey and Fraser all along," he said. "But, my God! Jennifer Fraser? How could *she* have been involved in this all this time without anyone finding out?"

"She's been in a position to cover her tracks," Laura pointed out. Then, growing more excited as the enormity of their discovery dawned, she clutched his arm. "She could have arranged the whole thing with the people at the scrap yard—what a setup! What do we do now?"

"Now, we go to Kowalski," Kenny said, grimly. "He's the only cop I trust after all this."

Laura agreed, wholeheartedly. "Let's go to his place right now."

15

"It makes sense, I suppose." Kowalski frowned, and pulled at his earlobe, something he seemed to do a lot of when he was thinking.

"You *suppose* it makes sense?" she asked, incredulous. "For the love of God, it's the smoking gun—literally! Follow me down the road again, Lieutenant: Tony Harrell needed money to support his new lifestyle. He volunteered to man a table at the exchange program, and he saw how easy it would be to slip a couple of the more attractive weapons under the table, without logging them in. He could maybe get away with a couple every day he volunteered over the three weekends the program ran, that's maybe ten or twelve guns. If they had an average street value of a hundred bucks, there's a nice chunk of change—for someone on a cop's salary."

They were sitting in the living room of Kowalski's comfortable Virginia-Highland bungalow, afternoon sun pouring through the windows. A small black cat was curled up on a sunny spot on the kilim, and, in the silences while Kowalski thought and tugged on his ear, they could hear the animal purring. It was oddly cozy and domestic, considering the topic at hand. Kenny had gone straight to the refrigerator and taken out a bottle of beer; Laura had accepted Kowalski's offer of coffee, and it perfumed the tidy house as it brewed. If Laura hadn't been so excited, the setting would have made her want to curl up and join the cat in his nap.

Kowalski shrugged. "Maybe you are right, but what's Fraser's role in the scam? She was a rookie, who only rode with Harrell for a few weeks—why would he take her into his confidence? The guy had no record of schmoozing with other cops; even his relationship with Maddux, who partnered with him for almost five years, seems to have been all business. Plus which, we don't know that Fraser was involved in the exchange program at all, until the past two years, when she coordinated it. It just doesn't seem as crystal-clear to me as it does to you guys." Kowalski was making sense, although Laura thought he was showing a complete lack of imagination.

"How's about this?" Kenny ventured. "Fraser finds out what Harrell is up to by accident, and asks for a piece of the action. You've ridden in patrol cars, Amos; you know how hard it is to keep a secret from the guy in the next seat. Let's say Corey is selling the guns for his brother—using his extensive contacts on the school playgrounds of Atlanta, on account of his being a pervert. Fraser muscles in on the deal, but Harrell dies after the first year the program is run. When gun season rolls around the next year, Fraser decides she might as well keep on using Harrell's old distribution channels. Then let's say she requests the move to Public Affairs—"

"Nobody *requests* to go to Public Affairs," Kowalski interrupted. "No cop wants to go sit around with his thumb up his tail, talk to reporters, and arrange trips to elementary schools."

"Maybe no tough, hard-boiled cops like you," Laura interjected. "But let's say Fraser didn't especially like busting criminals and getting shot at. Maybe she killed two birds with one stone—got away from a job she wasn't very good at, and put herself in a position to make even more guns disappear. Maybe she decided that ten or fifteen guns under the table wasn't enough; maybe she wanted to get her hands on fifty, or a hundred, so she culls the best guns from the take when they get to the scrap yard—which means that she had to pay a kickback to someone there, of course, but it would be worth her while."

Kowalski stood up, left the room, and came back with Laura's coffee. "Cream only, right? There are too many maybes in your theory, Chastain."

"What, and there aren't in Meredith's? Look, I admit that nothing we've dug up directly exculpates Jeff Williams. What all this does, however, is shatter Meredith's theory of proof—how can she convince a jury that Jeff killed Corey Taylor because he was emotionally disturbed by a child molester, when I can put Corey in the middle of this web of gun-stealing cops? What we have here is reasonable doubt in the case of *People v. Williams;* it's up to Meredith to make the case against Fraser."

Kenny cut in. "Not to mention that your squad broke about thirty rules of custody that night, Amos—sorry, but it's true. Taylor should never have been left alone, where anyone could get at him. It's going to look like Williams was railroaded because he's unpopular—when it was the whole squad that screwed up."

Kowalski laughed ruefully. "Don't I know it; there's a nice write-up in my file about the whole stinking thing. I can forget seeing my picture on the Employee of the Month plaque for a while."

Kenny laughed. "I'm glad we got onto Fraser, anyway, and that you never touched the gun-exchange program—otherwise, I might have a few questions for you, Amos."

"Oh, thanks for not making me into a suspect—although Chastain here was ready to."

Laura threw up her hands. "Hey, if the girdle fits. . . . but you're with us now, right, Kowalski?"

"Of course, and it does make sense, but you need to get your evidence together. You need proof that Harrell was a volunteer the first year they ran the thing. Without that, you've got nothing. And Fraser, too—was she involved *before* she moved to Public Affairs? And what about her personnel file—did she request the transfer, or was she shunted over there because she was a burnout?"

Laura nodded. "I've already requested a subpoena for the records of who volunteered for the program, and I'll add her personnel file to the list. The judge is going to go nuts, and Meredith's going to challenge all these requests, of course; I'm going to have to show my hand before I get the subpoenas."

"That's okay," Kenny said. "You've asked for the time sheets and the log-in records for the night Corey was killed, haven't you? You need to place Jennifer in the building."

Kowalski paused. "No need for that. She was there."

"Hah!" Laura shouted, waking the cat, who glared at her resentfully, then did a quick face-wash and returned to his snooze. "You saw her?"

"I *met* with her; we were planning to announce the Taylor arrest," he said, grimly. "It was a big deal; the media had been all over the rape since word of it got out that afternoon. But it turned into a press conference to announce Taylor's death."

"Did you hear that, Kenny?" Laura said, triumphant. "I think we have our killer."

"I hear you. You have to admit it looks good, Amos."

"I admit it, okay? I just don't want anyone running off half-cocked. For one thing, you don't want to spook Fraser."

"What, you don't think she'll come after us, do you?" Laura

scoffed. "This isn't Hollywood; women don't run around killing people with ice picks in real life."

"If you're right, she did kill Corey Taylor," Kenny pointed out.

"Pfft," Laura said. "He was chained to a table, a sitting duck. She'd have to catch me first." She was exuberant, laughing.

Kowalski shook his head. "I'm glad you're so confident. But keep it under your hat until you have your ducks in a row, anyway, Chastain. No sense taking chances."

"Of course. But we're all agreed that I take this to Meredith first thing in the morning, right? Maybe I'll just move that the charges be dismissed, and take it to a judge. No sense in letting Jeff twist in the wind while the district attorney tries to play catch-up."

"You're the lawyer," Kowalski said. "And speaking of Jeff, have you told him all this?"

Laura looked at Kenny, feeling guilty. It had crossed her mind that they should let him know, but she found herself putting off calls to Jeff. If she could just have a conversation with him that didn't include ten or twelve variations on that old Anglo-Saxon word. . . . "No, but I'll call him when I get home."

"I'll do it," Kenny said. "I have a higher tolerance for Jeff's style than you do, Laura."

"I'd appreciate it, Ken," she said. "I would, but he's so. . . ."

"Yes, wouldn't it be nice to have a worthier cause than Jeff Williams?" Kowalski said. "Maybe next time you'll get to defend someone you actually like."

"It's not that I dislike Jeff," Laura said. "Okay, if it weren't for this case, I would never have *chosen* to spend time with him; I can do without the crude language, and the macho attitude . . . is that why you have a problem with him, Amos?"

"Those are *among* the reasons," he answered.

"And he doesn't do his paperwork on time, so you put him on probation. But does that make him a bad cop?"

"Paperwork? Is that the reason he gave you for his being on probation?" Kowalski wore a bemused expression on his face.

"Yes. Why? It's not true?"

"Not entirely—like most lies, it has a nugget of fact in it."

Kenny shook his head. "I had a little trouble believing that one, myself. I mean, you're an anal-retentive little weasel, Amos, but you wouldn't discipline a good cop for not crossing all his t's."

"No, I wouldn't. I need a more substantial reason for putting a mark like that in an officer's personnel file."

Laura leaned forward. "Can't you tell us the real reason, Amos? I've subpoenaed the file, anyway, so it's not going to be a secret forever. Plus, there's a good chance the charges will be dropped this week anyway. So you can tell us."

Kowalski shook his head. "No. If you get the file, you can read it for yourself. But up until then, it's confidential. I will tell you one thing: I thought, at first, that the reason for his being on probation was relevant to the charges against him, but, given what you've uncovered, I don't think it is. If it were, I might tell you. As it is, my lips are sealed."

"Fine, be that way," she said. "What time is it, anyway?" She looked at her watch. "Uh-oh; it's already after five. Kenny, we'd better get going."

"Okay. Amos, thanks for letting us run this past you. I'll talk to you tomorrow."

They all rose and moved toward the door; the cat awoke and followed them, twining himself around Laura's ankles. "Yes, thanks. I really appreciate your help, Amos. Well, hello, cat; he seems to like me."

Kowalski shrugged. "He takes a shine to certain people."

"What's his name?" she asked.

"I just call him Cat; he didn't seem to want a name. He showed up a few months ago, looked around, decided he liked the place, and moved in. So I took him to the vet and had his nuts cut off, thinking that might convince him to leave, but he's here for keeps, I'm afraid."

"Then you should give him a name," she said, reaching down to scratch the cat's ears.

"Why should I go to the trouble of giving him a name that he'll never answer to?"

Laura rolled her eyes. "You're such a *guy*, Kowalski. Ready, Kenny?"

"Yep. Later, dude." He and Amos shook hands, and Laura stood on tiptoes and gave him a kiss on the cheek. They drove back uptown, not talking much. Finally, Kenny broke the silence. "Well, it all looks pretty good to me."

"I think so. I can't wait to get Meredith's reaction. I'll call her first thing in the morning, I think, and let her know I'm moving for dismissal on these new grounds."

"Think the judge will go for it?"

"No. But I think it will light a fire under the cops, and that Jennifer Fraser will be in jail by the end of the week."

Kenny frowned. "You know, I hate to think of a woman having done something like that."

"Why? Women can kill—they just don't. Not very often, anyway. Jennifer must have felt really threatened by Corey. It is sad, I admit; I'll be glad when it's over."

"And I can go back to sitting outside hotels with a telephoto lens and a box of doughnuts." They laughed. When they arrived at her house, Kenny dropped her outside the security gate. "Talk to you tomorrow."

Laura hurried inside; Tom's car was parked in front of her unit, and he was in the living room, sprawled on the couch, reading. "I'm sorry; we got caught up." She crossed to where he lay, and sat on top of him, straddling him. She leaned down to kiss him. "Aren't you going to ask where I was?"

"Where were you?"

She told him, and watched his face as the facts came out. At first, he kept the look of detached amusement that he always wore, but as she related her story, it changed to surprise, and then to appreciation. "You're quite the amateur detective."

"Amateur? I am the *queen,* and don't you forget it. Although it was just a coincidence, really, but that's probably how most crimes are solved—a lot of hard work, plus a little luck. Kenny is the greatest."

"I thought I was the greatest," he said.

"Oh, you are, in your own area of specialty."

"Which is . . . ?" he asked.

"This," she said, leaning down, and kissing him, then moving her hands down his body. She smiled down at him as she undressed him; this was the first time she had initiated anything with him, but he didn't seem to mind. He laid back and let her do whatever she wanted; it seemed to dovetail nicely with what he wanted—which was, after all, what eleven out of ten men wanted.

16

Tom left early Monday morning, leaving Laura awake but still sleepy. It was too early to take a shower and get ready for work—not unless she wanted to get into the office by seven, which would be pointless, since she wouldn't be able to get Meredith on the phone until at least eight. So she lay in bed, looking at the ceiling. At six-thirty, she turned on the radio next to her bed, to get the news and the weather. She listened without interest to the traffic report, and groaned when she heard that more rain was expected. Then the announcer ran down "the hour's top stories": A house fire had killed two people the previous night; The state legislature, in its ongoing effort to reimpose the values of the fourteenth century, was scheduled to debate a bill which would require the teaching of creationism in the schools; "And this just in: Sources indicate that Jeff Williams, the Atlanta police detective accused of killing a suspect in custody last week, was on probation and facing suspension on charges of sexual harassment at the time of his arrest. Williams was allegedly accused of harassment by a civilian employee. . . ." He moved on to another story, but Laura was sitting upright in bed, yelling at the radio, so she didn't catch it. Sexual harassment? In the first place, it was, as Amos had said, utterly irrelevant to the case—unless someone wanted Jeff to look like an all-around bad guy. In the second place, once again, Jeff hadn't dealt straight with her—she should not have to get information like this, relevant or not, from her damn radio. Finally, in the third and most important place, what happened to Meredith's and Chief Sisson's promises to stop the leaks?

She picked up the phone, and dialed Jeff's number; she demanded, to the answering machine, that he pick up, which he did, groggily. "H'lo?" he said. "Whassa matter?"

"What's the matter is that you should have told me about the sexual harassment charges. Why do you insist on making me look like an idiot in front of the press, and the district attorney, not to mention the police department?" By which she meant Kowalski, although Jeff didn't need to know that.

"I didn't think it was important. It's bullshit, anyway."

"You don't decide what's important, okay? I do, and if I say I need to know something, dammit, I need to know it."

"Look, I'm sorry. I'll tell you what happened. There's this girl who works in the squad room, like a file clerk, you know, who helps with the paperwork. She's a real pain in the ass, real prissy, and she's always complaining to Amos that she doesn't *appreciate* my language. I told Amos that, if she didn't like rough language, maybe she should go be a secretary at a church or something, but cops are cops. Anyway, it all came to a head one day when she asked me for some reports— some picky shit, as usual—when I was in the middle of a case. I hadn't done the reports, and I told her so, but she kept on yammering about how she needed it, and yah yah yah, she was going to have to talk to Lieutenant Kowalski, so I finally just told her to kiss my ass."

"Did you say 'kiss my ass,' or did you use one of your more colorful expressions?"

"Okay, it might have been a little more graphic. But I swear to God, Laura, if you met this woman, you'd tell her to suck *your . . .*"

"Enough! Jeff, even if I *had* one, I wouldn't always be telling people to suck it. What is your problem? Anyway, it's not as much of a disaster as it could be. Thank God they haven't dug up any brutality incidents, or race-baiting, in your past—neither of which would surprise me at this point. Dammit, why is Meredith still doing this?"

"Hell if I know. Maybe it's not Meredith—maybe it's the cops."

"Chief Sisson says it's not—am I supposed to call him a liar?"

"Well, one of 'em is. But does it really matter now? You're about to go out there and blow the lid off this crap, anyway. Fuck 'em, Laura."

"I suppose you're right. But, Jeff, are there any more surprises in that personnel file of yours?"

"No. I *promise.*"

Jeff's promises were worth exactly nothing to Laura at this point, but she let it go. The sooner she wound this whole thing up, the better. To that end, after she hung up the phone, she did some serious thinking. Jeff was his own worst PR agent: Angry, glowering, crude, and profane, he was likely to create the impression that he was a bully every time he opened his mouth. Eventually, his general character would have become an issue in the trial, if there were to be one, but why was Meredith rushing to the public? She must know that her case, circumstantial and coincidental, was a weak one—weaker than she knew, now that Laura and Kenny had Jennifer Fraser tied in to Corey Taylor. Knowing what she did, Laura could afford to ignore the leaks; by the end of the week everyone would have forgotten about Jeff's record of harassment. On the other hand, Meredith was testing Laura's resolve, and that had implications that went beyond this case. Should she call the bluff, go to the press with leaks of her own, and show Meredith that she was not to be toyed with? She expected to work with the district attorney and the Police Department for many years to come; it certainly wouldn't be good to start off with a reputation as a cream puff, who made idle threats, then backed down.

She hopped out of bed, and ran downstairs to her den-office, where she had left her briefcase. She flipped it open, and shuffled through the papers, looking for one pink slip of paper. When she had it, she dialed the number on it. A pleasant receptionist told her that Sally Rivers was not in, and offered to take a message. "No thanks," Laura said. "I have her beeper number." She dialed that, left her message— tagged "Urgent"—and returned upstairs, to the shower. As she was rinsing the conditioner from her hair, she heard the phone ring; she scrambled from the bathroom, wrapping herself in a robe and trying to contain her dripping hair in a towel. She snatched the phone from its cradle. "Hello?"

"I got a message to call this number. Who is this?"

"Hello, Sally. It's Laura Chastain. Thank you for calling so quickly. . . ."

Laura could almost count the seconds before the phone in her office rang, like timing the interval between the flash of lightning and the rumble of the thunder. Meredith would be getting to her office now, getting the message now, returning the call, and going ballistic just about . . . *now*. She sipped her coffee and sat back, waiting.

At nine-thirty, Cecelia buzzed her. "Meredith Gaffney on the line."

"Thanks. I'll take it. Meredith? Good morning."

"Bite me. I just got a call from Sally Rivers, asking for my comment on a story she's breaking at noon. What the hell are you up to, going to the press with this business about the Toys for Guns program?"

"Oh, Meredith, don't be so shocked. I told you—not once, but twice—that if there were any more leaks, we would retaliate. You took the contents of Jeff's file public, and I had to do something, didn't I? Did you expect me to let my client be tried on talk radio, for God's sake?"

"Laura, I swear to you, we did not leak anything. It must have been the Police Department."

"Cry me a river, Meredith; I gave Sisson the same message I gave you. I'm sure he'll swear up and down it wasn't his people, either. I really don't care who it was at this point; we got our side out there, and it looks, from here, like you've got some fires to put out."

Meredith sounded grim. "That's a fact. Thank God you were discreet, anyway; all Sally Rivers seems to know is that Corey Taylor was selling guns to kids, and that some of those guns may have been diverted from the cops. Wanna give me the rest, or do I have to get the cops to sherlock it out on their own?"

"I'll give you what I have; you're going to be seeing the story in my motion to dismiss this afternoon, anyway."

"Come on, it's not that good, is it?"

"It's better." She gave Meredith the details, leaving out Antrus Caldwell's name for the time being, but pointing to Jennifer Fraser. "There are some gaps, but I think that it pretty well exonerates Jeff. You're on your own when it comes to fleshing out the case against Fraser."

"Not so fast, Miss; there are more than a few holes in your theory—is there anyone who can place Taylor with Fraser? Any record of funds flowing between the two of them?"

"Like I said, that's your job. Corey Taylor's girlfriend knows something; Corey said someone was 'taking care of him.' That sounds like blackmail, or maybe just like a partnership with Fraser—she would need someone to peddle the guns, after all."

"God, it's so complicated. Why are you doing this to me?"

"Nothing personal. If I were you, I'd take a look at Fraser's financial records. Have you ever met her?"

"No. Why?"

"I did, last week. She's a burnout, Meredith. Maybe there's a drug problem in the woodpile. Have fun, anyway; I'm sorry to have to deprive the public of their killer cop–slash–angel of revenge, but the charges against Jeff Williams are not going to stand."

"We'll see about that; I'm not moving for dismissal of the charges against Williams until there's a strong case against Fraser—or some-one else."

"We'll see what Judge Root has to say about that. See you in court," Laura said, with a grin. She hung up, and set about preparing her motion. It was very satisfying, laying out the new evidence for the court's consideration; the holes that Amos and Meredith had pointed to were still there, but the judge would see them through the matching holes in Meredith's case against Jeff. She proofread the document a final time before lunch, and took the finished product back out to Cecelia. "It looks good. Make copies, and call the messenger service—I want this to hit the district attorney and Judge Root in time for them to react to it today."

As she was standing by Cecelia's desk, Tom came thumping down the corridor. "Laura, I can't find Hunicutt's last deposition. You had it last week, I think."

"Yes, but I put it right back in the file, where it belonged, last week. You must have had it since then."

"No, I haven't. Dammit, Laura, I've told you I don't like it when you take pieces of files—check out the whole thing."

"In the first place, Tom, that file takes up two entire drawers now. In the second place," she said, leading him to the filing room, "as you will see, I checked out the deposition last Monday, and returned it Wednesday." She called the file clerk, and asked to see the records, which not only showed that she had returned the document when she said she did, but that one "T. Bailey" had taken it out Thursday morning. "See? You took it out before you got the call to go to New York; you must have been intending to do something on it, but got distracted."

"Oh," he said.

"Oh, indeed," she said. "Now, where could you have put it?" She strode down the hall to his office; he followed meekly. His desk was neat, as always, but his briefcase caught her eye. "You must have taken it to New York. I bet it's still in your briefcase."

"It's not, I'm sure."

"Look in your briefcase, Tom," she commanded.

He did, and sheepishly produced the deposition, which had been sandwiched in another file. "I'm sorry, Grasshopper; I didn't mean to jump on you."

"You never do, but you do, just the same."

He walked over and closed the door of his office. "No, I mean, now that you and I . . . Laura, I shouldn't be thundering around here, biting your head off."

"Why not, Tom? Regardless of our relationship outside of the office, I expect nothing less than complete professionalism when we're in it—which, in your case, means that I expect that you'll continue to jump all over my case and chew me out for minor infractions, real or imaginary. That's how it's always been, Tom—if you change the way you treat me, everyone in the office is going to know we're sleeping together."

He smiled. "You're right. So I take back my apology. Just make sure that, next time I take a document from a file, you put it back. Understood?"

"Right, chief. Anything else?"

"Actually, yes; I do have to go back to New York, on Wednesday afternoon. Hunicutt wants to meet with us before I go. He's all secretive, but he's worried about something. How's Wednesday morning for you?"

She shrugged. "Hard to say. I've just submitted my motion for dismissal; I'm hoping to get a meeting with the judge today, or tomorrow at the latest. If the cops find enough evidence to arrest Fraser, I'm hoping that Meredith will ask for dismissal herself. I have to be available for any meetings or hearings that come up."

"Understood. I'll schedule the meeting for first thing Wednesday morning, and if I have to go without you, I will."

"I don't think Mr. Hunicutt will miss me."

"But I will. Speaking of which, how would you feel about joining me in New York for the weekend?"

She smiled. "I would feel very good about it—provided my workload allows it."

"Well, then, let's just hope this Jennifer Fraser of yours confesses to everything."

"Yes, it would be very convenient for me if she did," Laura agreed.

WTLK: Talking the talk, and walking the walk. Welcome back to the Scott Ressler show. Friends, are you like me? Are you sick of the rain? We could at least get a little snow mixed in with it, for a change, you would think. This is like the flood. Hey, folks, give me a call— we can talk about the weather, we can talk about anything you want. Do we have a caller, Sidekick Mel?

Yes, we do, Scott—Maryann from Lilburn.

Hello, Maryann, what's on your mind?

Hello, Scott. I would like to talk about this policeman who is accused of killing the boy in custody.

Aren't we kind of beating a dead pony here, Maryann? I mean, is there ANYTHING left to say on this subject?

Yes, Scott, I believe there is. For one thing, I would like to know how you feel about the allegation that the police officer was on probation for sexual harassment.

Well, ma'am, you know that story was a Scott Ressler exclusive— we had that before anyone else in town, and I think I made my feelings pretty clear: Girls, if you can't stand the heat, don't go to work in a police station. It takes tough men to do that job, and I think we ought to be down on our knees, thanking them, not complaining every time they use a little rough language.

I agree that their job is difficult, but don't you think that the man's tendency to use abusive language says something about his character?

It says he's a MAN, Maryann, and if you don't like it, you can kiss his. . . . (fade to music: "I'm a Man," by the Spencer Davis Group)

17

By three o'clock Monday afternoon, Laura's motion to dismiss had been received by Meredith, and by Judge Root, in whose court Jeff's case had landed. The press was in full cry, after Sally Rivers's breathless report, on News at Noon, that Corey Taylor had been involved in a conspiracy with someone in the police department—perhaps more than one officer—to pirate and sell guns turned in, in good faith, by the law-abiding citizens of Atlanta. Everything unfolded in accordance with Laura's expectations, down to the call from Judge Root's office, calling her to a meeting in his chambers at four o'clock. Laura drove to the Municipal Courts building, and hurried to the judge's chambers; Jeff was scheduled to meet her there. He hadn't picked up the phone; she'd had to beep him. "Where are you?" she demanded, when he called her back.

"In a bar," he said."Celebrating." She could hear noise in the background that sounded barlike, clinking glass and shouted laughter."Whatever you did this morning was the charm—the reporters disappeared from my lawn like magic. I'm a free man again."

"Well, get yourself freer, and come to Judge Root's office at four. Go easy on the alcohol, Jeff; I want you clean, decent, and sober."

"I'll be there," he promised.

He wasn't, when Laura arrived about ten minutes before four, but neither was Judge Root. He was in a hearing on another matter, and she was ushered in to await him. Meredith and Davis Shelton joined her after a few minutes. "Hello," Laura said, cordially.

Davis said nothing, as usual. "Hello, yourself," Meredith said, flinging herself into a chair."How long are we going to have to wait? I'm up to my ass in alligators; let's get this over with." Then turning back to Laura, she laughed. "You've gone and done it this time, you know—you've got everyone's jocks in knots. Charlie Sisson is beside himself; he's got reporters over there begging for details on the 'police corruption scandal.' "

Laura laughed. "Should I say I'm sorry? Because I'm not. Where's the Fraser investigation, anyway?"

"Barely underway, but there are a couple of things that checked out. She *was* involved in the Toys for Guns program from the get-go, and she did request the transfer to Public Affairs two years ago. So the circumstantial evidence bears out your theory, anyway."

"What about Tony Harrell? Did he volunteer for the program before he died?"

"Oddly, he did not, so the connection between Corey, and Fraser, and the guns is more tenuous. It's still feasible, though." Meredith chewed a thumbnail thoughtfully.

"But I take it, from your tone, that you believe that Fraser may have been the killer."

"Let's say I'm getting there. I want to see this kid, the one who you say will testify he bought a gun from Corey. Not to mention, of course, the gun itself."

"I can produce both. You can appreciate why I'm not naming the kid now."

"The judge can make you."

"Yes, he can, but I'm hoping he'll dismiss the charges against Jeff first. At the very least, I need a guarantee of immunity for the kid who bought the gun—I'm not looking to give him a criminal record, not at his age."

"Understood. But you won't get a dismissal from Root, at least not until some more questions about Fraser are answered."

Laura frowned. "You can't keep two suspects on the line for the same crime. Has Fraser been questioned?"

"Not as far as I know; she's off Sundays and Mondays, so she's at home, I assume. Internal Affairs is probably on their way over there now."

"Think she may bolt?"

Meredith shrugged. "It's possible, but she won't get far."

They fell silent, reflecting on Jennifer Fraser—had she seen the news? If she had, even though her name hadn't been mentioned, she must be expecting to be questioned. Laura managed to feel a little bit sorry for her. She remembered the bitten nails, and the lank hair, carelessly arranged. Someone that young should not look so *tired,* she thought; drugs were probably at the heart of it. Cops were notoriously vulnerable to drugs. Maybe this whole thing had started as Jennifer's bid to raise a little extra cash to support a habit. Maybe Tony Harrell hadn't been involved at all; Laura hoped not, for Mrs. Bledsoe's sake. Jennifer could have met Corey through Tony, and hooked up with him as a likely partner in her budding scam—a confluence of weaknesses. Maybe, maybe, maybe; she was beginning to want something more solid herself. At ten minutes past four, the door opened and Jeff was admitted.

"You're late," Laura said, accusingly.

"Got stuck in traffic," he said. He had been drinking, but not to excess. He pulled a chair from the far side of the room, and sat beside her.

"Don't say anything unless the judge asks you a direct question, understand?" Laura hissed to him.

"Okay. They arrested Fraser yet?"

"No. They're not going to arrest anybody while the charges are still pending against you; one step at a time."

They settled in to wait in an atmosphere of heightened tension, the friendly, professional conversation between Laura and Meredith ended by Jeff's arrival. Jeff passed the time by humming under his breath, and tapping a rhythm on his knee; Meredith seemed oblivious to his orchestration, but Davis Shelton glared at Jeff savagely. *Oh, Davis, lighten up,* Laura thought. She couldn't stand *fussy* men; crude as Jeff was, and as little as she liked his style, she would have chosen to be stuck on a desert island with him before she would a self-righteous little weenie-boy like Davis. She wondered how Meredith stood it; Davis seemed to her to be a simmering cauldron of resentment, a classic passive-aggressive case. Laura straightened up in her chair at the thought—could it have been Davis who was leaking reports about the case? It certainly fit: a powerless little weenie-boy, trying to puff up his importance, not to mention that he was probably one of those little nut-jobs who secretly hated working for a woman. When the whole thing was over, Laura decided, she would bring it up with Meredith, over a nice friendly lunch. No need to allow her to continue to nurse a viper in her bosom.

It was almost four-thirty before the door opened, and a harried Judge Root appeared. "I hate Mondays," he announced, to everyone and no one in particular. "Monday is the day all the lawyers go nuts. I have a theory that they go home over the weekend, and instead of spending time with their families, or working in the yard, like decent people do, lawyers sit around and draft motions. Motions to suppress perfectly legal testimony, based on some ancient precedent that nobody's ever heard of. Motions to dismiss charges—" he stopped and glared directly at Laura "—based on harebrained, cockamamie theories of conspiracies. And then I come in, after a perfectly nice weekend, all relaxed, and get hit with a mountain of paper. In this case alone, I have two motions—one to suppress evidence from the defendant's personnel file, and another to dismiss the charges entirely. Ms. Chastain, what the hell are you up to?"

"Hello, Judge Root," Laura said. He was a blowhard, but she liked him. "Just defending my client, and helping the police do their job. Quite a few things were overlooked that I think you'll agree may be relevant."

"A mystery witness—a minor, to boot—says he bought a gun from the deceased. Said gun turns out to have been taken in by the police in exchange for a teddy bear—Ms. Chastain, are you trying to blow smoke up my robe?"

"Of course not, Your Honor. I just managed to find some exculpatory evidence that the police overlooked. As my motion shows, my client had no motive to see Corey Taylor dead—but whoever was smuggling those guns to him sure did."

Meredith interrupted. "It's not exculpatory; it only goes to motive—which is not an element of the crime."

"Thank you, Ms. Gaffney, for the law lesson," Judge Root said, clearly irritated. "However, as for this new development, I agree with you. I see nothing that indicates that Corey Taylor's selling stolen guns had a bearing on his death."

"For pity's sake, Your Honor," Laura interrupted. "The district attorney wants you to believe that my client was so stressed by the effort of arresting Corey Taylor that he became enraged and killed him—and yet they can't produce even one witness who'll say that Detective Williams so much as broke a sweat that night. Then, when we produce another, actually *credible* motive for the murder of Corey Taylor, you question whether it's relevant?"

Meredith chimed in. "Your Honor, Detective Williams's record shows that he had a great deal of difficulty in controlling his temper. In fact, he was on disciplinary probation for having let it get the better of him on at least one occasion."

"Entirely different circumstances, and irrelevant, to boot—which is why I've moved to suppress any evidence relating to the department's disciplinary actions against Detective Williams," Laura said.

"Find me one cop—Lieutenant Kowalski included—who will say that Jeff Williams was enraged on the night of Corey Taylor's death." The judge held up a hand, indicating that he wanted silence. "Ms. Chastain, your argument has merit. If these charges against Officer Fraser are substantiated—and that's a big 'if' in my book—I would agree with you that another member of the police force had a more compelling motive for wishing Mr. Taylor dead. And, if Officer Fraser had equal opportunity to kill the victim, I would have to say—with deference to Ms. Gaffney's argument that motive is not an element of the crime—that the case against Fraser, being the stronger, would tend to exculpate Williams." He turned to Meredith. "As for you, Ms. Gaffney, you have your work cut out for you: You must make your case against Detective Williams without reference to the sexual harassment charges against him. Those are unproven, hearsay, and irrelevant to the death of Corey Taylor; I am granting Ms. Chastain's motion to suppress. And I warn you—if you can't make a case without using the detective's personnel file, I will have no choice but to grant her motion to dismiss, as well. At the same time, Ms. Chastain," he said, turning back to her, face stern, "I don't see a compelling case against this Officer Fraser, so, for the time being, the motion to dismiss is denied. The hearing will take place as scheduled, on Friday, unless developments between now and then compel us to reopen the matter."

"Thank you, Your Honor," Laura and Meredith said, as one.

"And, ladies, thank you for at least providing me with some entertainment. I can't remember when I've seen a more bizarre set of allegations. If they're true, the Atlanta Police Department will have egg on its face for years."

Laura couldn't tell if Judge Root thought that would be a good thing or not; he had a reputation as an eccentric, and he tended to be tough on the rules of evidence, so maybe he was on her side—to the extent, of course, that judicial impartiality allowed. They all rose to leave, and, as they did, someone's beeper went off. Everyone— Laura, Meredith, Davis, and Jeff—moved to check theirs.

Meredith held her beeper up. "It's mine, Your Honor. May I use your phone? It could be a development in the case. I told them not to beep me on anything else."

"Certainly," the judge said, waving at his phone. "Should we wait?"

"Probably," she said, stabbing at the keypad with one of her lacquered nails. "You beeped? Uh-huh . . . yes . . . when? Shit! Are you sure? Damn! I'm in Judge Root's chambers now; Laura Chastain is here too. I'll tell them." She put down the phone and turned to Laura, pale-faced and solemn. "That was Chief Sisson; Internal Affairs just went over to Jennifer Fraser's place to question her, but they couldn't. She's dead."

18

"It's not your fault," Kenny said.

They were sitting in a poorly lit booth at Manuel's Tavern, a pitcher of beer, virtually untouched, resting between them. Bar noises, barks of laughter, and clinking glassware filled the long silences; neither of them had a lot to say. Neither of them *could* say a lot; they were still ignorant of most of the details of Jennifer Fraser's death. They were expecting Kowalski to arrive any time, to lighten their darkness, but until then, Laura had made up her mind that, without her call to Sally Rivers, they would not be here at all.

"Apparent suicide," Meredith had said; a single gunshot to the side of the head. Quick, and decisive; it must have happened not long after Sally Rivers had broken her innuendo-filled story of gun-pirating at the Atlanta Police Department on News at Noon. Laura pictured Fraser, at home, on her day off, flipping on the television to get caught up with the world, hearing the story—and the footsteps. How was Laura to have known that Fraser would take a revolver out to her car, and blow her brains out in the parking lot of her apartment complex? Who could have predicted that outcome? Laura should have; she had met the woman, and had suspected instability, drugs, any number of things. She thought of Jennifer's parents, probably in possession of the sad news by now. "Somebody's daughter"; that was what Tony Harrell had said when he and Jennifer had found the runaway's body in that vacant lot five years earlier. Jennifer Fraser, sad and alone in the end, had started as somebody's daughter, too.

"I'm going to the ladies room," Laura said, sliding out of the booth. "Back in a minute." Once there, she retreated into a stall and hid. She didn't cry; that would have been self-indulgent—it wasn't her grief, after all. Hers was the agony of responsibility, real or imagined; *why had she made that call to Sally Rivers?*

She had been so stupidly egotistical; what did it matter if Meredith, or Davis, or anyone, was tweaking her nose via the media? Why had she felt that she had so much at stake—that, if she hadn't made good on her threat to leak information on the case to the press, that her future negotiations with the district attorney would be compromised? It was the kind of thing a man would do, and Laura had always sworn to herself, that, come what may, she would not act like a man in a man's world. She had promised to be true to herself, to bring her own, feminine perspective to a tough job. But she had sold herself out, and postured just as much as any man would have. A man, of course, would probably not feel this kind of remorse, she realized, but count that among the many reasons she was glad not to be one.

She emerged from the stall, and stood at a sink next to a big-haired woman layering on mascara in a hopeful frenzy. Laura checked her own makeup; she looked pale, but she didn't do anything about it. She washed her hands, and returned to the booth. Kowalski had arrived; she slid in beside Kenny, facing Amos, so she could see his face, and feel the full measure of his contempt for her.

"Amos says they're about ready to wrap up at Fraser's," Kenny says. "He came on here, because he doesn't think they're going to find anything else important."

Laura nodded. "Did Kenny tell you it was me who told Sally Rivers about the guns?"

"Yes. And you're probably wallowing in guilt and self-pity, aren't you?" Kowalski said.

"What, and you wouldn't? You'd just say 'That's the breaks,' and move on?"

"No. I'd try and get to the bottom of it, and figure out why things turned out the way they did. Would you like to hear some of the details, some of what they found? It might make you feel a little better, unless you're just determined to be miserable."

She shrugged. "Go ahead."

"They found her in her car, in the driver's seat; one shot to the right temple. The bullet passed through her skull, and shattered the window. It was pretty messy; I'm surprised none of the neighbors found her before Internal Affairs got there. Of course, most of them were at work, and hadn't gotten home when the investigators arrived."

"Why in her car?" Laura asked. "Why not in the apartment—or, even if she had to do it in the car, why in the parking lot? Why not drive someplace isolated? Who wants to die in a parking lot, for God's sake?"

"Who knows? People are funny about those decisions."

"Maybe she was fastidious about her apartment, and didn't want to leave a mess," Kenny suggested. "The car would be the next best choice, in terms of privacy, I guess."

"Could be," Kowalski said, "but this was not a fastidious woman. Her apartment was a mess. It was full of old newspapers, and magazines, not to mention matchbooks from every restaurant she had ever been to. They're going to be combing through stuff for a while, but they did manage to find a couple of interesting items."

"Like?" Kenny prompted.

"Like a couple of grams of coke, and some pieces of foil, with what may be heroin residue on them," he said. "Looks like she might have had some expensive extracurricular activities."

"See, Laura?" Kenny said. "You suspected that she may have had a drug problem. She was probably having financial troubles, too; addicts usually do."

"It's too early to tell," Kowalski said, "they'll have to look into her bank records, and her credit history. You're probably right, though; I'm betting that she was deep in debt. The stuff she was playing around with wasn't cheap."

"That could certainly explain why she was in the gun business," Kenny added. "It may have started as a way to get some spending money, but she must have gotten pretty serious about it over time— maybe that's why she wanted to make the move into Public Affairs, so she could expand the scale of the operation."

Kowalski nodded in agreement. "Wouldn't surprise me a bit. Any of this getting through to you, Chastain? The woman was a wreck; she was teetering on the brink the whole time."

"Yeah, and I'm the one who pushed her over," Laura said. "All because I had to get into a *pissing contest* with Meredith Gaffney."

"And that's why this poor woman put a bullet in her head— because of you? Never mind the drugs, or the guns, or the debt; never mind the fact that all indications are that Jennifer Fraser had Corey Taylor's death on her conscience: This is all about Laura Chastain. I believe that's what they call *narcissism*, Laura."

Laura stiffened. "Don't be ridiculous; I'm not responsible for any of the stuff Fraser did—but you have to admit that, if I hadn't jumped out there with that leak, she might be alive now, down at the station house answering questions and facing the music on *our* terms."

Amos shrugged, and took a sip of beer. "Possibly. On the other hand, she might have gone nuts when the investigators knocked on her door, started shooting, taken hostages—look, none of us knew how bad off she was. Cut yourself some slack."

Laura didn't answer; he did have a point, but she wasn't in the mood to concede it to him.

"Anything else, Amos?" Kenny asked.

"Not really. Wait—how could I forget? The gun she used to kill herself was one that had been turned in for a toy."

"That's interesting," Kenny said. "What was it?"

"An old automatic—Colt .45, World War II vintage. In good shape, though; someone had kept it up over the years."

"Why wouldn't she have used her own gun—her Police Department weapon? Wouldn't it be more reliable?" Laura asked.

"Who knows?" Kowalski said, with a shrug. "Why did she do it in her car? We're never going to have answers to questions like those; might as well not bother asking them. Maybe she had too much respect for her department-issue weapon. Maybe she was sentimental about it."

"She wasn't sentimental about her nightstick—she used it to throttle Corey Taylor," Laura pointed out. She laughed, without humor. "You know, there is one funny thing—Jeff insisted that it had to be a uniformed officer who killed Taylor, because he was absolutely positive a nightstick had been used. I tried to explain to him that, in the first place, there was no way to say with any certainty that it had been a nightstick, and not something *like* a nightstick. And, in the second place, a nightstick in a police station is hardly a smoking gun—if you'll allow a mixed metaphor."

"Allowed," Kowalski said. "But I don't think Fraser was required to carry a nightstick—they're only used on patrol, and she was no longer a patrol officer."

"But she was a uniformed officer, so she would have had one issued to her. Right?"

"I'm not sure," Kowalski said. "Kenny, you remember the rule on that?"

Kenny shook his head. "Hell, no, but even if I did, they've probably changed it ten times since I left."

"It doesn't matter, anyway," Laura said. "Even if the medical examiner was willing to swear Taylor was murdered with a nightstick,

Fraser, or Williams—even *you,* Amos—could have gotten your hands on one, I'm sure, if you had wanted to."

"Of course," Amos said. "Her being in uniform is ultimately irrelevant. Her being a drug addict, however, is not. Now, let's get some dinner and talk about something else."

Laura looked at her watch; it was almost eight, "I need to make a phone call," she said. "I'll be right back." She returned to the rest rooms, where the pay phones were located; she dialed Tom's extension at the office, and got the after-hours switchboard operator. The firm was stubbornly resisting voice mail, preferring the old-fashioned charm of a bored-sounding human who had no idea where the called party was located, or when he would return. Laura hung up, and tried his home number; his answering machine picked up. She left a brief message, saying that she was out, and planned to return home in a hour or so. Almost as an afterthought, she left her beeper number, even though she knew that Tom would probably disdain use of it.

When she got back to the booth, Amos and Kenny were looking at the menus, for what it was worth; the food at Manuel's wasn't exactly legendary. The bar was best known as a political meeting place; its founder had been a prominent local politician, and many high-level meetings had been conducted in its booths and back rooms in its glory days. Over the years, though, it had been expanded into a cavernous beer mill, haunted by video games and the dreaded California Grilled Chicken Sandwich. They all ordered hamburgers, probably the safest choice on the menu, and Amos and Kenny got lost in some discussion about a football trade.

Laura half-listened, smiling where appropriate, her mind wandering continually back to Jennifer Fraser's chewed manicure and sloppy, unwashed hair. A drug addict, a cop on the take . . . a murderer. She would know more when Meredith called her, as she no doubt would, in the morning, but she assumed that, if she agreed to give them Antrus Caldwell and his gun, they would drop the charges against Jeff. The thought filled her with relief, despite her remorse over the suicide; of course, she hadn't expected to meet any saints in her line of work, but Jeff Williams had grown more and more repulsive to her—more repulsive, even, than Alex Hunicutt. Jeff's surly ill-temper, and his constant use of vulgar language, made him appear thuggish, whether he was innocent or not.

It occurred to Laura that she might have preferred Jennifer Fraser as a client. She played with that scenario for a few minutes; she could have constructed an admirable defense—diminished capacity, resulting from her drug use. Or self-defense—there was an idea: Maybe Jennifer had gotten to Taylor before he could get to her. Two scorpions in a bottle, trying to sting each other to death. It was no good, though; she had defended Williams, who, despite his innocence, was less attractive to her than even the obviously guilty Jennifer Fraser.

"What are you going to do about Jeff Williams?" she asked Amos abruptly, interrupting a debate over the merits of this receiver and that free safety.

"Huh? What am I going to do? What do you mean?" Kowalski said, distracted.

"I mean, are you going to keep him on your squad after the charges against him are dropped? Or is he going to be transferred?"

Kowalski shrugged. "It's not up to me. He's still on probation, no matter what the outcome of the Taylor case. Would I *like* to have him transferred? Heck, yes. I'd like to see him off the force—he's a fossil, twenty years behind the times, despite the fact that he's only thirty. He doesn't play well with others, and I hate to saddle a good cop, like Eleanor Haines, with a partner like Williams. But no one else is going to volunteer to take him, and I can't see him fitting into any of the usual elephant cemeteries in the department."

"There's an opening in Public Affairs," Kenny said.

Laura glared at him. "There's no need to be tacky. Besides, Jeff would be the last guy you'd want to see dealing with the public."

"Don't I know it," Kowalski said. "If a burnout like Fraser could come up with a scam like the one she was running in Public Affairs, I shudder to think what Jeff could do. Give him one thing: he's no moron. Actually, he's pretty smart. There should be some job where he doesn't have to come into contact with the law-abiding public, some place where they can use his street smarts. He should be among the criminals—maybe Narcotics. But, after all the press he's gotten, he's no good for undercover work."

"Can't the department just get rid of him?" Laura said. "If he really told your clerk what I think he did—and I for one believe he did—isn't that enough to get him fired?"

Kowalski laughed, and shook his head. "I wish it were so easy, but it ain't. I guess you know the whole story now, or Jeff's version of it, anyway. That poor girl came to me in tears; she had to tell me what had happened, but I don't think she had ever said that word in her life—in that context, anyway. She probably had to wash out her own mouth with soap afterwards. Of course, I stormed right on up to Human Resources and told them they were going to have to fire him. I thought my troubles were over, but apparently it's not so easy. The Taylor case has muddied the waters, too; they're not going to want Jeff to claim that the department is getting rid of him because of the adverse publicity surrounding it. Anyway, that's my problem, and the department's; by this time tomorrow, you should be done with him."

"And I'll be glad of it," Laura said. A beeper screeched. "I think that's me." She dug it out of her purse, and squinted at the display; she couldn't make it out in the dim light, but it had to be Tom. "I'll be right back," she said, and hurried to the phones. It was Tom, at home; she dialed him gratefully, and felt a knot in her stomach untie when he answered. "Hi," was all she could say.

"Where are you?" He said. "You never came back to the office; I've been trying you at home for the past couple of hours. Where have you been?"

"Haven't you seen the news? My whole case blew up this afternoon—God has punished the guilty, and my client will probably be free to go on his way, bullying and insulting people, by tomorrow afternoon." She tried to make light, but her voice ended on an unmistakable sob.

"And yet, you don't sound happy," he commented.

"Oh, Tom, I'm not. Can I come over there?"

"Of course you can, sweetheart. Have you had dinner?"

"Yes. No, not really; I'm with Kenny and Kowalski. I ordered a hamburger, but it's disgusting, and I can't eat it."

"Why don't you come over here, then, and I'll fix you something that's not disgusting. You sound like you could use a bowl of soup and a cup of cocoa."

"All I want is to see you," she said.

"I'll heat the soup anyway," he replied.

She returned to the table, but didn't take her seat. "I'm pretty tired," she explained. "I'm going to head out." She didn't exactly say she was going home, but for some reason she was reluctant to tell Kenny and Kowalski that she was going to Tom Bailey's house.

"Just as long as you're not going to brood over Jennifer Fraser all night," Kenny said.

"Oh, no," she replied, as brightly as she could. "I'm really just exhausted, and tomorrow I'm going to move for the charges against Jeff to be dismissed. I'll have to be on my game, so I'll need a good night's sleep."

They wouldn't accept the money she offered for her uneaten hamburger, which made her feel guilty for having lied about the real reason for her departure. Once in the car, though, she forgot her guilt, glad that she could turn everything over to Tom. She was surprised at how eager she was to see him; the drive to his house seemed interminable. By the time she arrived, he was looking for her, flinging open the door as soon as he heard the crunch of her tires on the gravel drive. She parked her car, got out, and walked straight into his arms. "I cannot tell you how glad I am you're not in New York," she said, as he led her into his well-lit kitchen.

"That goes double for me; I've hated not being here, with you involved in this case. Although," he added hastily, "you seem to have handled it beautifully without me."

"Have I?" she said, accepting the glass of wine he poured for her, and following him into the den, where she collapsed on the leather couch. "I've followed Kenny's leads, and my nose, and we got to the truth. But it's all so messy."

"I know; it's shocking that she would commit suicide rather than face charges."

"I guess I can understand her killing herself—just not the way she did it. In her car? In a parking lot? With a gun? If I were ever in extremis, and felt that my only option was to kill myself, I'd like to think I would do it in a more private way, quietly."

"Most of us would choose a less dramatic ending, I think, but she must have been unbalanced. Look at her record, after all."

She nodded. "I guess she wasn't what you'd call normal. Whatever that is." She sipped her wine, and thought for a moment. "Tom, do you ever feel triumphant?"

He looked puzzled. "What do you mean?"

"When you win a big case, or get a new client—is it still a thrill?"

He was quiet for a moment before he answered. "No. It hasn't been a thrill for a long time. Most of the time, I find that I do what's expedient. But why are we having this discussion? Ninety-nine percent of the adults in the world have the same dilemma: youthful ideals discarded in favor of paying the bills. We do what we have to, Laura, even when it's not pleasant, and sometimes even when we have doubts about whether it's the right thing. But those bills have to get paid somehow."

She looked at him sharply; Tom had never needed to worry about paying bills; *expediency* should have been absent from his vocabulary. She made no comment, however, and he returned to the kitchen to get dinner ready, occasionally directing an innocuous remark as he pottered at the stove. She swirled the wine—a nice California Merlot—in her glass, and wondered. Why did Tom work at all, let alone in the flinty fields of the law? Why did he associate his Auden-quoting, Mahler-loving self with clients like the Hunicutts? They must disgust him as much as they did her, if not more so. He couldn't even claim that his association with the Hunicutts had expanded legal horizons—often as not, cases involving them and their firms were settled out of court, with no precedent-setting rulings emerging from his expert representation. What satisfaction could he take in a relationship with such repellent characters? She certainly wasn't fulfilled by getting Jeff Williams off the hook, not at the cost of Jennifer Fraser's life.

Jeff. Thank God she wouldn't have to deal with him much longer; his crude language and hotheaded demeanor had made her uneasy from the start. The case had been fun, exciting, up to a point, but she hadn't ever been able to escape the feeling that she was walking on the wrong side of the street. Kowalski, Eleanor Haines, and Meredith Gaffney had all disliked Jeff, and Laura had begun to feel isolated from people she respected, even though she, and Jeff, had been vindicated by the outcome. And there was a reason that they had all suspected Jeff, however unjustly, of killing Corey Taylor: Jeff was capable of using violence to solve a problem, and everyone knew it—just as Alex Hunicutt was capable of forcing a woman to have sex with him, or his father was of resorting to unsavory business practices. And she and Tom stood ready to defend them.

You're just tired, she told herself; *it was an ugly case. They're not all going to be like this. Besides, you were just doing your job. . . .*

No, that wasn't true. She had *chosen* the job; she could easily have said no to Jeff Williams, or even, with Tom's support, to Alex Hunicutt. She had embraced both cases, eagerly, and now she was paying for it with a painful moral hangover. She finished off the wine in her glass, and went to the kitchen seeking a refill. Tom smiled at her as he poured, and she smiled back. Tonight she was, with Tom's help, going to forget Jeff Williams, and Corey Taylor, and Jennifer Fraser. Especially Jennifer Fraser.

19

"The charges in this matter are dismissed. Detective Williams, you are free to go." Judge Root's gavel cracked decisively down, and Laura turned her head to avoid being kissed on the mouth by her client.

"We did it!" he crowed, triumphant.

"We didn't have that much to do with it, in the final analysis," she commented. "Jennifer Fraser did the hard work for us." She closed her briefcase, eager to get away from him. "We'll send you a bill; you can talk to our accounting department about working out a payment plan if you don't want to pay it all at once. Good-bye, Jeff, and good luck."

"Aw, c'mon, at least let me buy you lunch," he said.

"I'm sorry, I can't; I'm swamped at the office. But you should go out and celebrate; have a nice time. Excuse me; I have to say something to Meredith." She left Jeff, and hurried to catch the assistant district attorney before she left the courtroom. "Meredith! Wait a second!"

Meredith turned. "Hey, Laura. I'm rushing back to the office to stomp out another fire. What do you need?"

"Look, I wanted to say that I'm sorry about the way things turned out. I never wanted to fight this one in the media."

"Neither did I—but, unlike you, I *didn't*."

"Come on, Meredith; those leaks had to come from your office, even if not from you. What about Davis? Did it occur to you that he might be making a bid for independence?"

Meredith snorted a laugh. "Davis? Independent? That'll be the day. He sticks his head in my office to let me know when he's going to the men's room. Laura, buy a vowel—haven't you figured out that it was Fraser doing the leaking?"

Meredith's words hit Laura like an avalanche: heavy, wet, cold—

and suffocating. No, it had not occurred to her; she had been so sure that the leaks sprang from the district attorney's office that she hadn't stopped to think who else might have a motive for making Jeff look bad, and the means of doing it. But of course it had been Jennifer; Laura had been boxing against the wrong shadow the whole time. Jennifer would have been privy to the details of the case; how easy it would have been for her to make a few calls to the press, tipping them off that the rogue cop was being brought in at such and such a time—come one, come all, to the big-top media circus! Then, as public opinion threatened to turn sympathetic to Jeff Williams, it must have seemed a simple thing to drop a few character-damaging nuggets from his confidential file into the journalistic maw. Laura stopped herself there: Would Fraser have had access to the information from Jeff's personnel files? Not necessarily.

Meredith was looking at her, head cocked to one side. "You really didn't know, did you? Come on, Laura; I told you, over and over, that it wasn't us. It had to be someone in the Police Department. It was only a matter of time before the leaks were traced to her, anyway. All roads led to Jennifer Fraser; we would have busted her one way or another, in time. Your way was faster than ours, that's all. Don't be so hard on yourself, Laura—Amos says you're wallowing in guilt. Cut it out. She was a killer, Laura, and she saved the taxpayers some money by putting that bullet in her head. You did your job, and you did it well. Go buy yourself a new pair of shoes or something; you've earned them. Now, I really do have to get back and face my next crisis. We'll have lunch next week," she called over her shoulder, as she pushed through the door and clattered down the hall.

Laura followed, slowly, her mind still on Jennifer Fraser. What must her last days have been like? Desperate hours, trying to cover her tracks and throw suspicion onto Williams . . . a scorpion in a bottle will sting anything it comes into contact with; it will even sting itself to death. She was on the point of pushing open the glass doors that led outside, when she spotted a pay phone. She became decisive, and walked to it. She called information, got the number she needed, and dialed it. "Sally Rivers, please. Tell her it's Laura Chastain."

It took a surprisingly short time for Sally to come to the phone. "Hi, Laura. This has to be quick; we go on News at Noon in fifteen minutes. You got something for me?"

"No. I just have a question for you: You were there, when Jeff Williams was arrested. How did you know when he would be brought in?"

"We got a call, an anonymous call."

"Did you take it yourself?"

"Yeah, they asked for me. Why do you need to know?"

"Was it a man or a woman?" Laura persisted.

"Woman. Regular voice, no weird accent or anything. I assumed it was someone from the district attorney's office."

"So did I. What about the leak from Williams's file? That was your exclusive, right?"

"Yep. Another woman."

"Same voice?" Laura asked.

"Who knows? But the third thing, the sexual harassment thing, she leaked to someone else—Scott Ressler. Pissed me off; why did she all of a sudden have to go to the talk radio guys? Okay, so we're only on three times a day, but we do updates all day long, and we reach a much larger audience, not just a bunch of truck-driving pinheads. I treat my sources right, and I don't like it when they screw me. Look, I gotta go; I've got this stupid bump in my hair, and I can't go on camera looking like this. Later, okay? Call anytime!" She hung up, to deal with her hairdo crisis; you never saw Peter Jennings with a bump in his hair, after all.

Laura lingered by the phone for a moment, then pulled a business card from her wallet. She needed to be sure. She dialed the number, expecting to get a secretary; it was a surprise when he answered himself, tersely: "Kowalski."

"Amos? It's Laura Chastain."

"Hello. Got your man off scot-free, I hear; now he's my problem again."

"Sorry. I need to ask you a question, Amos; it's about Jennifer."

"Let it go, Laura. You didn't kill her."

"Just answer my question: Did Jennifer have access to the information from Jeff's personnel file—the fact that he was on probation, and the reason why?"

"Yes, she did. It wasn't an issue in the Taylor case, but when the complaint was first made against Jeff, I reported it upstairs, and there were a couple of damage-control sessions—me, the attorneys, and the public relations people—just in case the woman sued the department. Jennifer was there, at least at one of those meetings."

"So she could have made the leaks to the press?"

"Could have, and did. It was under our noses all along. Stop torturing yourself. Where are you, anyway?"

"Still at the Municipal Courts building," Laura answered.

"Let me buy you lunch, since you're in the neighborhood."

"No, I should get back to the office. I've let the rest of my work slide this past week. And I'm not really hungry, anyway," she added. The thought of food made her sick, in fact.

"Okay, but, remember, you promised we could get together—as friends."

"We will. Let's plan on next week; things are still pretty busy at work for me, and I'm kind of tired."

"I'll hold you to it. Promise me that you'll stop worrying about Jennifer Fraser. It wasn't your fault."

"I promise—I'm letting it go right now. See you soon, Amos."

She didn't let it go, though; she couldn't. She was distracted at the office; when she sat in on a deposition with Libby and one of her divorcing couples, their bickering barely penetrated her consciousness.

Back in her office, there was a message from the managing partner—had she sold her tickets to the Yule Log? No, she hadn't, and the stupid thing was next week. How could Laura ask someone to pay $200 to attend a party she would have given a kidney to avoid herself? She had been hoping that Jeff's case would drag out long enough for her to avoid the whole mess. She slumped into her chair, and worked on filling out her time sheets, which she had neglected for a few days. They should have warned us about these in law school, she thought, as a headache settled in behind her eyes.

She hadn't eaten lunch, but she wasn't hungry; she was only aware of the throbbing in her temples. *I should go home,* she thought; *I'll feel better if I take a nap.* She gathered her things, put on her coat, and walked out, stopping at Cecelia's desk. "I'm going home. I don't feel so great; tell anyone who's interested that I'll be in tomorrow morning." She stopped by Tom's office; he was out, so she left the same message with his secretary that she had with Cecelia. "And tell him I remember about the Hunicutt meeting tomorrow morning; he can call me at home if he needs to go over any details." She drove home, trudged upstairs, and changed into a worn T-shirt and a pair of disreputable sweatpants; she collapsed on her bed, and, in minutes, she was sound asleep.

When the phone woke her, the room was dark, and the glowing face of the clock told her it was six-thirty. "Hello?" she mumbled.

"Laura? Are you alright?"

"Tom. I didn't feel so great; I think I was just tired out from all the activity these past few days."

"Are you sure you're not sick?"

"Pretty sure. I tried to find you before I left."

"I got your message. You don't sound good. Are you up for some company?"

"Sure. I don't feel like going out, but we can watch TV, or something."

"I'm leaving the office now; I'm going to stop off at my house and pick up a few things. Do you need anything?"

"Not really. I'll see you in a while."

She moved downstairs to wait for him, flipping on the television. Jeff's story was getting its last coverage on the news; she saw him giving a statement to a group of reporters gathered on his lawn. "I'm just sorry that Jennifer Fraser didn't have the courage to face the charges against her. I think she should have—I didn't run away, or put a gun to my head, when I was accused of killing Corey Taylor. But I guess that's the difference in being innocent, and being guilty." It was as graceless a performance as she would have expected from Jeff; thank God he wasn't her client anymore. Poor Kowalski—what an albatross to have around his neck.

Tom showed up after about an hour, with an overnight bag, groceries, and flowers. He fixed dinner, and she even managed to eat a little. He watched her closely, and frowned when he cleared away her nearly full plate. "I'm not that bad a cook, Laura," he commented.

"No, it was wonderful. I'm just not hungry, that's all."

"Are you sure you're not getting sick? You're pale as a sheet, and you have dark circles under your eyes. I think you should see a doctor tomorrow."

She shook her head. "It's just this case; I can't get it off my mind. Why did Jennifer Fraser have to kill herself? My God, she would have been a more easily defensible client that Jeff Williams—juries hate to convict women. I could have used her drug problem, and her mental state, to show that she was in extremis. And it looks like Corey may have been blackmailing her, anyway; his ex-girlfriend says that he knew something about someone in the police department that would set him up for life. That would have made Corey look all the more despicable to a jury—what if he were *forcing* her to take those guns? Maybe she had a drug problem, okay; so what? I could have defended her; she wouldn't have done a lot of time—less than Jeff would have if he had taken Meredith's plea. . . ."

Tom led her to the sofa, and sat down beside her; he pulled her legs across his lap, and rubbed her feet while he answered all her wild speculation. "You have to let go, sweetheart. That woman had messed up her life long before her path crossed yours. I know what's going on here; you're second-guessing yourself. Stop it, right now. Jennifer Fraser wasn't your client; Jeff Williams was, and you did what any good attorney would do—you defended him, aggressively and thoroughly. And ethically, I might add. I would have done exactly what you did, including making judicious leaks to the press. This Jennifer Fraser was playing above her level, pure and simple; she lost control of the situation long before you came along. My God, Laura, she killed a man in cold blood! I think that you probably could have defended her, had she survived to face charges, but the fact remains that she walked into that room and choked a helpless man to death with her nightstick. Please, don't waste time pitying her."

"But what if Corey were blackmailing her? What if she had to kill him, or face losing everything? What would it take to force *you* to kill, Tom?"

"A great deal, I suspect. Fortunately, I don't put myself in a lot of 'kill or be killed' situations, unless we're speaking metaphorically. I have also never taken drugs, or sold guns to minors—I think that gives me a moral leg up on Jennifer Fraser and Corey Taylor. Forgive me for speaking ill of the dead, but they seem to have deserved each other."

"Two scorpions in a bottle," Laura said, softly. "I still feel sorry for her."

"Don't. Not every victim is a martyr, and sometimes even the martyrs make very poor saints."

"Who said that?"

"I did. I'm not all quotations, you know; I do have some original thoughts. What I mean by it is that you should stop being a moral relativist. You were hired to defend Jeff Williams, and you did. The fact that you began to find him repellent after a while—and sometimes, I grant you, we do defend bad guys—has no bearing on Jennifer Fraser's character. You've convinced yourself that she was somehow *better* than Jeff. If you had known her, you might have found that she was equally disgusting. In fact, I have the feeling that she was— a drug addict, a liar, a murderess. It's okay to feel superior to her, Laura. And to Jeff Williams, and Alex Hunicutt, and all the rest of them."

Laura looked at him carefully; he was speaking with more passion than he normally did. "Do you feel superior to your clients? What about Mr. Hunicutt?"

Tom looked into space for a moment before he answered her. "Alexander Hunicutt is a bad man. He has no ethics to speak of, and very poor taste. In a way, a lawyer is like a priest—without the power to grant absolution, of course. Like priests, we have to know the worst about our clients in order to save them; we can't reject them because they're flawed—if they were perfect, after all, they wouldn't need us. But it's our knowledge of their weaknesses that, ultimately, helps us do the best job for the clients. Take this case that we'll be discussing with Hunicutt tomorrow: It appears that a subsidiary of Hunicutt and Company, a recycling company, is being accused of unfair trade practices—paying kickbacks to win contracts, in short. Hunicutt will bluster, and curse, and fire a bunch of middle managers, but you and I will know that it was he who put the whole thing in motion, if not by direct order, then by creating a dog-eat-dog, winner-take-all atmosphere at his companies. The managers who offered the bribes, the ones who are about to lose their jobs, probably *thought* that they were following orders. Knowing that, I won't waste any time trying to convince a jury that our client wasn't involved. I'll do my best to keep this away from a jury, in fact; I'll spend my time and energy convincing Hunicutt that we have to do damage control—pay the fines, clean up the mess, promise to do better in the future. I'm under no illusions about him."

Laura had never heard Tom speak so directly of his dislike for Hunicutt; of course, she had suspected his feelings. She shifted her position on the sofa, and put her arms around him. "Why do you keep doing it, Tom? You don't have to; God knows you've proved yourself at Prendergrast and Crawley. You can tell Hunicutt to take a hike any time you like. You bring in enough business without him, like this thing in New York. Wouldn't it be nice to tell Hunicutt not to let the door hit him in the butt on the way out of P&C?"

Tom laughed, his face returning to its usual sardonic set. "It would be lovely. A nice dream. Speaking of nice dreams, I have your ticket for New York with me. My flight leaves tomorrow at 2 P.M. I booked you on the same flight for Friday; no one will care if you leave the office a little early. We are going to forget about Jeff Williams, and Jennifer Fraser, the Hunicutts, and the horses they rode in on. This weekend will be about how perfect and adorable you are. You will be worshiped as a goddess, and I will have roses strewn in your path."

"I can't wait," she said. "Worship is exactly what I need. You are exactly what I need." She kissed him gratefully, then pulled away a little and looked at him. "Some day, I'm going to tell everyone what a big gooey mess the dreaded Tom Bailey is. I'll ruin your fierce reputation; no associate will ever tremble at the sight of you again."

"You wouldn't dare," he said.

"Try me," she answered.

20

Hunicutt and Company had its headquarters in one of the tall, anonymous, steel-and-glass towers that freckled the northern suburbs of Atlanta, rising out of what had been, twenty years earlier, fields and pastures. In its haste to grow, the city had foolishly centrifuged its businesses out to the perimeter highway that ringed it, while the huge interstate highway, the coupled I-75 and I-85, sliced longitudinally through the city, acting as a sluice that drained people and life from the downtown area each evening. Most residents lived and worked outside of the city proper, in developments and office towers built by men like Alexander Hunicutt, who had grown tired of the picky concerns of urban planners—things like density, public transportation, and congestion. As a result of their unbridled building, the area around the perimeter highway suffered worse traffic problems than downtown Atlanta ever did. Belatedly, the city had extended a train line out to the perimeter, but the sprawl was so vast that a car was needed just to navigate from one office park to the next, so most workers continued to drive, one per car. Tellingly, the average temperature in Atlanta had risen almost five degrees in twenty years, a direct result of traffic and development. Did anyone care? If they did, their objections were drowned out by the honking horns and revving engines.

Tom and Laura arrived at a good time, midmorning, after most of the workers had settled in behind their desks, and before they piled back into their cars for the half-mile trip to the fern bar or mall where they would have lunch. Tom steered the Bentley, which looked extraordinarily out of place in these surroundings, into the parking lot of the Olympic Towers, Hunicutt's crown jewel, a pair of black towers topped by weird, postmodern, ziggurat crowns.

They went inside, and announced their arrival to the receptionist.

Hunicutt's waxy yet lifelike secretary came out and escorted them to a conference room to await the Big Man, offering them coffee to pass the time. Laura accepted a cup, which she had nearly finished by the time he joined them, offering insincere apologies for keeping them waiting—which, of course, they all knew he had planned to do anyway, a demonstration of his power. Alex Junior trailed him, a dog who might turn on his master at any moment, followed by Hunicutt and Company's in-house counsel. That was surely a thankless job; Laura knew that it had been offered to Tom many times, but Tom always refused, knowing that a prophet was indeed without honor in Hunicutt-land; the big cases were always turned over to outside counsel anyway.

The meeting got underway; Laura, after her conversation with Tom the previous night, watched carefully as he first listened to Hunicutt's blustery insistence on his innocence, and his demand for vindication. Then Tom asked the in-house counsel a few questions, and looked carefully at the subpoena that the company had received only that morning from the State Attorney General's office. Then, with a few well-placed questions, Tom proceeded to kick the props out from under Hunicutt's self-righteousness. In no time, they were talking about the potential size of the settlement, and Tom was promising to spearhead the negotiations. After a surprisingly short meeting—less than an hour—they were wrapping up, and Hunicutt was congratulating himself on his savvy maneuvering in heading off a prolonged investigation with an offer of settlement. What a stupid, stupid man, Laura thought; he should get on his knees and give thanks that Tom bothers with him. She was more than ever convinced that Tom should kick the Hunicutts out of the firm. P&C, and Tom, could do better.

They headed off an invitation for lunch, and returned to the lobby. To Laura's surprise, as she exited the elevator, she almost bumped into Jeff Williams. "What are you doing here?" she said; her question, unadorned by any greeting, sounded rude and abrupt, but she was as startled to see him here as she would have been to run into him at the symphony, or in church.

"Hi, Laura; nice to see you," he said, rebuking her by his cordiality. "I do some security work for Hunicutt and Company. Kowalski gave me a couple of days off, so I thought I'd get around and see some of my clients. You know, let them know that the whole Corey Taylor thing is over, and that I'm available for work again."

"That sounds like a good idea. Jeff, have you met Tom Bailey? He's one of the partners at P&C. Tom, this is Jeff Williams."

The two men shook hands, a collision of worlds. "Nice to meet you," Jeff said. "So you're her boss, huh?"

"In a manner of speaking," Tom said. "She really doesn't need much supervision."

"She sure did a good job for me. I bet you'll be working for her one of these days."

"It wouldn't surprise me in the least," Tom said, with a sidelong glance at Laura.

"We have to be going," Laura said, eager to end the weird encounter. "Good luck, Jeff. Call me if you need anything."

She felt him looking after them as they crossed the lobby and left the building. Back in the car, as he pulled out of the parking space, Tom laughed. "What's so funny?" Laura asked.

"It figures that your unattractive client would be in cahoots with my unattractive client. You know, there are no coincidences."

"Only unpleasant ones," she corrected. "I wonder what he does for Hunicutt, anyway?"

"Probably patrols construction sites, making sure that materials aren't pilfered. I don't imagine he's been hired for his razor-sharp mind," Tom said, accelerating and merging into the highway traffic.

"You got that part right," she said. "At least I'm rid of *my* nasty client."

"And I'm still saddled with mine," he said. "Maybe you're right—maybe I will tell him to go pound sand."

"Let me be there when you do," Laura said.

"If it means that much to you," he replied, taking her hand.

She didn't see Tom again after they returned to the office, but she had her ticket to New York in her briefcase, and she comforted herself with the knowledge that she would have him all to herself, Hunicutt-free, for forty-eight hours in the greatest city in the world. Her general outlook, in fact, was much more cheerful than she would have believed possible just a day before; news coverage of the Fraser suicide had subsided to a few column inches in that morning's paper, and Tom's remarks last night had carried a lot of weight with her. Then the documents arrived from the district attorney's office and the Police Department.

A subpoena is like a missile: Once fired, there's no stopping it from completing its course. Despite the fact that the charges against

Jeff had been dismissed, the Police Department had still been obligated to turn over the documents Laura had subpoenaed the previous week. There, neatly packaged and indexed, were the time sheets for all the duty officers for the night Corey Taylor was killed, as well as sign-in sheets for visitors. There were also complete records of the Toys for Guns program, from its inception. The district attorney, acting reflexively under the rules of discovery, had sent along all the exculpatory evidence that the investigation of Fraser and her suicide had turned up. If Laura had listened to her head—or to Tom's voice in her head—she would have walked the whole mess down to the file room, and had the clerk put it in Jeff's file—and mark the whole thing "Inactive." But Laura didn't; she closed the door to her office, and looked through the documents.

First, the Police Department package. She scanned the time sheets; names jumped out at her from the computerized printout—Williams, Haines, Kowalski, Fraser. All there, all with the opportunity to kill Corey Taylor, but only one with a real motive. The documents on the gun exchange were more interesting. They fell into two categories: internal memos and notes on the organization of the program— solicitations for volunteers, estimates of costs, records of donors, and collection sites. The other records were more impressive and official— the actual logs of the collected weapons, and the records of their destruction. Laura laughed when she saw the name of the company that had disposed of the weapons: Hunicutt Recycling—the very same company that now stood accused of unfair trade practices. Only unpleasant coincidences. It made sense, anyway, that the Police Department would have used them; Mr. Hunicutt's name also appeared on the list of donors, and he had donated the services of the scrap yard as well. Knowing, as she did, that the recycling company operated in an atmosphere of casual illegality, it didn't surprise her that Fraser had succeeded in bribing someone to sign off on a manifest for guns that hadn't actually been destroyed. She thought for a moment, and dialed Meredith's number.

"What can I do for you, Laura—in fifteen seconds or less? I have a meeting."

"I won't keep you, but I was just wondering if you and the police are going to continue the investigation of the gun-pirating?"

"No, in a word. It seems to have been limited to Taylor and Fraser, both of whom are no longer with us."

"What about whoever was doctoring the records at the scrap yard?

Fraser must have been bribing someone there, at least in the past couple of years, when she was running the whole program."

"It crossed our minds, but the decision was made at a higher level. We understand that there's a state investigation of unfair trade practices at Hunicutt recycling, so the guilty will probably suffer anyway."

"I guess so."

"Laura, you are planning to get on with your life one of these days, aren't you?"

"I'll drop it; it just looked like a loose end, that's all."

"There are always loose ends in real life—you've been watching too much TV, kid. Gotta go; how's next week look for lunch?"

"Any day is good for me; call me when you know what your schedule looks like. Good-bye—and, Meredith, thanks."

Laura set aside the Police Department files, and turned to the envelope from the district attorney marked "Fraser, J—Deceased." She opened it slowly. There wasn't much in it; the police report on the death scene—including a couple of photographs Laura could have lived without seeing—and a long list of the property that had been seized as evidence. Everything from the major (2.15 grams of suspected cocaine, the suicide weapon) to the minor (hairs from Fraser's hairbrush, to aid in identifying the body) was listed and cosigned. There was also some evidence that had been obtained after the fact: phone records, credit reports, and bank statements.

Laura looked at the financial reports; as they had expected, Jennifer was overextended, and barely a step ahead of her creditors. Her bank account was a crazy quilt of deposits, followed by withdrawals and bounced checks. Laura flipped through the stack; they went back a year. As she did, she noticed something: Once a month, Jennifer would make a large deposit—large, anyway, in comparison to her paycheck, which showed up as an automatic credit twice each month. The past month, when Laura would have expected to see a fairly large amount of cash from the gun scam, there was no variation—the paychecks, plus a $3000 deposit, just like every other month. Okay, maybe she kept the proceeds of the gun sales in cash, and never ran them through the bank. But the cops hadn't found any cash at her apartment. She could have spent it all, especially on drugs; two grams of must coke cost a decent amount of money. But where did the $3000 deposit come from? Trust fund? She hardly seemed the type. Laura picked up the phone again, and dialed Kenny's cellular phone.

"Hey, Ken; it's Laura. What's up?"

"Not me—I'm sitting in the truck, waiting for a wallpaper guy to come out of a big ol' two-point-five-million-dollar Habersham Road mansion. The owner has a theory that his wife is boinking the tradespeople. She's had her kitchen renovated twice in the past five years; it seems like kind of a bass-ackwards way to get laid, if you ask me."

"Maybe she's just in love with love."

"You should see this woman; there's not a soft spot in her heart. So tell me you have something better for me to be doing."

"Not really; I just wanted to run something past you. It's Jennifer Fraser, Kenny; I got a load of documents from the cops and the district attorney, and something's bugging me. I talked to Meredith, but it sounds like, from her point of view, the case is closed."

"Can you blame them? The cops are going to be living this one down for a long time—a corrupt cop selling guns to the kids. They want the whole thing buried with Jennifer Fraser."

"But I'm not sure that it stops there, Kenny. Jennifer was making large, regular deposits to her bank account—outside of her paycheck. Not just while the gun program was running; I would have expected her to be putting a little cash in the kitty in December, but there was nothing in this month's bank statement. Always, though, $3000 a month, like clockwork."

"And you're thinking blackmail?"

"Are you?" Laura said.

"Could be. But who would she be blackmailing?"

"Maybe she wasn't really the one boosting the guns—maybe there's a Mr. X in the Police Department. Maybe she was onto him, and had her hooks in him."

"For three grand a month? That's got to be more than those guns were worth to anyone."

"So what could it be?"

Kenny was silent for a moment. "I don't know. Let me think about it—get me copies of everything you have, and I'll chew on it while Hotpants here boffs the cabinetmaker."

"I'd appreciate it."

"No problem. I'll drop by and pick up the documents tomorrow morning."

"Thanks. You're a prince; I'll talk to you when I get back from New York."

Welcome back to the Scott Ressler show, folks. We got 'em this time, didn't we, Sidekick Mel? The liberals don't know who to point the finger at this time. Get this, folks—get THIS: after all this hoo-ha about racist cops, police brutality, and sexual harassment, it turns out that it was a WOMAN who killed the suspect in custody. Yes, a chick did it, and all the liberal hand-wringing was just a big waste of time. Of course, we know that it's always a waste of time, but they don't have anyone to point the finger at now.

That's right, Scott—they're being suspiciously silent now.

Isn't anybody going to jump up and talk about this problem we've got with violent women cops? Those meter maids—man, they're out of control. Better look out, Atlanta—that crossing guard might just beat the crap out of you if you look at her the wrong way. We have a caller. Earl from Conyers, testify—what's on your mind?

Yeah, how're you doing, Scott? I want to talk about the knuckleheads in the Braves front office who made that trade.

Tell me about it. . . .

21

It's too pat to say, of New York, that "you either love it or hate it." It's probably more accurate to say that you're a New Yorker—or a potential New Yorker—or you're not. A real New Yorker enjoys the drive in from the airport, past all the dull-brick piles of the hospital on Ward's Island, as much as that first glimpse of the Chrysler Building. Laura was one of those whose heart beat faster on the FDR Drive; she didn't need the more obvious seductions of Central Park, or Saks, to set her off. Of course, the knowledge that Tom was waiting at the end of the cab ride made it that much sweeter. When she arrived at the hotel, the newly renovated St. Regis, she was deprived of her bag by a quietly professional bellman, and ushered inside. At the desk, she introduced herself as Mr. Bailey's guest. The clerk not only knew Laura's name, she also told Laura that Tom had been delayed in a meeting, but that he expected to be there shortly. She was given a key, and a second bellman showed her the way.

An old-style New York hotel, unlike the towering glass edifices that define Atlanta, has no need to lift its head above its milieu; it is very much on a level with, and a part of, the city it serves. The room that Laura was escorted to was on the fifth floor, and faced out over the relatively narrow side street, which meant that the view was primarily of the windows of the building across the street. The point was this: If you want to see New York, get the hell outside and look at it. The hotel is not your destination. Still, as hotel rooms went, this one was as inviting as Laura had ever seen. She tipped the bellman, and took a quick tour. A large bed, a sitting area with a couch and chairs, a television discreetly hidden in a cabinet, and a bathroom that could house a family of four. Laura unzipped her bag, and shook out her clothes; she went to the closet to hang them, and saw Tom's suits already there. She went weak at the sight of his ties, neatly draped over a hanger, and the white shirts lined up like soldiers. She made room for her things beside his, an almost marital arrangement.

She looked at her watch; it was about four-thirty. The clerk hadn't had a clear idea of when she could expect Tom, so Laura decided to take a shower. Afterwards, she wrapped herself in one of the hotel's fluffy robes, dried her hair, and laid down on the bed, with the intention of resting, just for a few minutes. She was awakened, disoriented, by the sound of a key turning in the door; the room was darkening, and she couldn't see a clock. "Laura?" she heard him call, softly.

"Here I am," she said, pulling herself into a sitting position.

He came in, and shut the door behind him; she could make him out on the dim light, shrugging off his coat and pulling off gloves. "I'm sorry I kept you waiting, sweetheart; they would have gone all night if I hadn't just up and left. Nothing important happens on a Friday afternoon, anyway." He crossed to the bed, and sat down beside her. "Was your trip okay?"

"Fine," she said, reaching out and touching his face. "You're cold."

"I walked; it's only a few blocks, but the wind is kicking up. They say it might snow."

"Do they?" she asked, uninterested. She bent forward and kissed his chilled cheeks, and his lips. His mouth was warm; he moved it from hers after a few minutes, to her neck, and, pushing aside the robe, her shoulders. He untied the belt of the robe, and unwrapped her; he laid her back on the bed, and traveled the length of her body with his hands and lips. The only sounds were her soft cries, mingled with the occasional bleat of a horn from Fifth Avenue; she had to bite her lip to keep herself from saying "I love you," even though it was the truth. Laura suddenly saw that this affair which she had begun so thoughtlessly and carelessly was much more than that. It was terrifying and exhilarating; she lay in his arms in the half dark room, not speaking.

When they finally came back, a little, to the world, it was nearly nine, and neither of them had the energy to head out into the cold in search of dinner. They settled for room service and a movie, with a ridiculously overpriced bottle of wine. They could have done what they did—eat dinner, watch an old movie on the tube—anywhere in the world; to do it in an overpriced hotel room in the most exciting city in the world might have been a shame, but Laura didn't care. She wanted to stay in that cocoon a while longer, a world where only she and Tom had a right to existence, and everyone else was only a prop. They had the rest of the weekend, anyway.

They finally managed to propel themselves into the life of the city on Saturday; they wandered without a plan or a goal through the streets. Laura shopped, for herself, and for Tom; they drank wine and listened to music. They could have done anything, really, so long as they did it together. On Sunday afternoon, they walked to Central Park, and stopped to watch the skaters at Wollman Rink as fat snowflakes fell.

"Laura, there's something I want to tell you," Tom said.

"What is it? Is something wrong?" she asked, laying her hand on his arm.

"I don't think so. In fact, I think something's finally right. It has a lot to do with you, as a matter of fact; what's happened between us these past two weeks has made me think." He stopped, and turned his gaze back to the rink; they could hear the shouts of laughter from the skaters, and the strains of the waltz through the loudspeakers. "Laura, I'm leaving the firm."

"Why? Not because of me—Tom, I'll leave. You've spent so much more time there. But why should either of us go? We can be discreet . . ."

He shook his head. "It's not just our relationship, although that is a part of it. I want us to be a real couple, not just an 'affair', and as long as we're at the firm, we're obligated to keep our relationship secret. We have to play by their rules. As far as I'm concerned, the sooner we can drop the secrecy, the better. But there's something else, too, that's led me to this decision."

"What? Are you unhappy at the firm?"

"Not unhappy, just numb. It was something you said last weekend that brought it home to me. After we saw that movie, you accused me of trying to argue both sides of every issue—just like a lawyer. All of a sudden, I saw myself through your eyes, Laura, and I didn't like what I saw."

"But I like what I see, Tom; I don't want you to change!"

He smiled, but shook his head. "Thank you, sweetheart, but I think we both know I could use some improving. I want to drop my ironic detachment; I want to feel something again."

"What do you want to do, Tom?" she asked. "I'll back you up, whatever it is."

"Thank you. Did you know I inherited some money?" he asked. She nodded, and he continued. "A few years ago, for tax purposes,

I formed a foundation with some of my assets; my sister kicked some of hers in as well. It's significantly endowed. My sister has acted as the sole trustee for most of the last five years. You don't know her; she hates Atlanta, and never comes to town. She raises horses and exotic chickens—sorry, *hens*—up in the mountains. She's done a good job, but she's been complaining that I don't help enough. I agree. So, I'm leaving the firm to work full-time for the foundation. I'll tell the partners when I get back to Atlanta; I should be able to wind up my business with the firm in six months or so."

"I think that's wonderful, Tom. I want you to be happy."

"Oddly enough, that's what I want, too. And I'm not going to be happy if I continue to be the devil's advocate, dealing with people I despise, and trying to get the 'best outcome' for people who, frankly, deserve nothing but the worst. I'm looking forward to saying good-bye to Alexander Hunicutt most of all. That's why I've told you all along that you don't have to tolerate them, either. You can come with me, and work on the foundation, if you like."

"Thank you. It's too soon for me to make a decision, but I'm glad we'll be able to come out of the closet, anyway. You're extremely important to me, Tom; you were when you were my boss, and my friend, and now that we're . . . well, let's just say that I don't give a rat whether I make partner or not—as long as I can still wake up next to you."

"You'll always be able to do that, Grasshopper," he said, brushing melting snowflakes from her cheek.

She caught his hand, and looked up at him. "I love you," she said.

As soon as the words were out, she wished she hadn't said them. What if he felt trapped by her declaration, in the midst of these difficult decisions he was making? She started to say something to qualify the statement, but he hushed her. "And I love you, Laura."

And they kissed, right there in Central Park, in front of the skaters, and the mounted cops, and the pigeons. It was wonderful, cinematic, and then she got in a plane and came home, a thumping anticlimax.

She paid the cab driver at the door to her town house, and went inside, flipping on lights as she headed for the kitchen, where the answering machine blinked in two-four time. She punched the play button and half-listened to the messages while she hunted in the refrigerator for a beer. Her mother had called. A college friend wanted to "catch up"—that's going to take a while, Laura thought. Then Kenny's familiar voice, surprisingly serious.

"Hey, sugar, it's Sunday morning, and I know you're still out of town, but there's something real funny that I noticed. Well, it's not so much funny as . . . disturbing. I don't know what to make of it, but it's not good, no matter how I look at it. Call me when you get in—I'll be over at Amos's most of the afternoon. Cindy and the kids are going to a birthday party, so I thought I'd watch some football with Kowalski, and I want to talk to him about this thing, anyway. But I should be back home by six or seven tonight. Bye. Hope your weekend was good."

Laura straightened up. Disturbing? What could he have found? She started to the phone, to call him, but there was another message, a voice that it took her a moment to recognize—Amos Kowalski. "Laura, something's happened. It's Sunday, about six o'clock. Kenny's hurt. I'm down here at Northside Hospital, in the emergency room. I think you should come. Cindy's on her way." There was a pause. "It's not good, Laura."

It's not good. Kenny had said that, too. Laura scrambled to get her coat, and her car keys. She was out the door in a flash, in her car, gripping the wheel and praying.

The drive to Northside took about fifteen minutes in the light Sunday traffic; she parked and ran to the ER. It took her a moment to spot Kowalski, sitting with a woman Laura recognized as Cindy Newton. She had only met Kenny's wife a few times; she had always been smiling and laughing on those occasions—the perfect female cognate for her husband, easygoing and happy. She wasn't, now; she had aged ten years. Kowalski had his arm around her, but neither was talking. Another woman sat beside her, a friend, or neighbor, Laura guessed. The children were nowhere to be seen.

Laura slowed her steps as she approached; Kowalski saw her and stood. She clutched his arm when he reached her side. "Tell me . . ." she said.

He led her a little ways off. "It was a car accident, a hit and run. He left my place about five, to go home; he was on that stretch of North Druid Hills where it's two lanes, as it approaches Peachtree. There was no other traffic; someone heard the noise, and came outside and found him. His truck was sideswiped; it looks like it was run off the road. It rolled over; they had a helluva time getting him out of the cab."

"How is he?"

"Too soon to tell; he's still in surgery. He's pretty banged up. His leg is broken, badly, and there were internal injuries. It's going to be touch and go for a while."

Laura brushed away the tears that were falling down her cheeks. "Oh, Kenny. . . ." She looked up at Kowalski, realization dawning. "It wasn't an accident, was it?"

He shrugged. "The roads weren't wet, or icy, and there's good visibility on that stretch of road. The cops are all over it; Kenny has a lot of friends. Whoever did this left something behind—paint, tire tracks, something. They're going to move heaven and earth to find him. If they have to stake out every body shop in North Georgia, they'll do it. It might have been some drunk."

Laura tried to take it all in. "Or it might have been deliberate. It's my fault, Amos—it was the Jennifer Fraser thing. I put him up to it; it was all my idea. What was it that he had found, Amos? He told me it was something 'disturbing.' What did he mean?"

"I don't know." Kowalski straightened, and looked down at her. "He didn't say anything to me."

"But he said he was going to talk to you about it. He left me a message before he went to your place."

He met her gaze levelly, but his face was impassive. "He didn't say anything to me, but there were other people there, so I guess he decided it wasn't the time or place. What makes you think it was about Fraser, anyway? I thought that was all over."

She shook her head. "It was, but there was something I noticed, something in the stuff I got from the district attorney. I asked Kenny to look at it—if this is my fault, I'll never get over it."

"Don't get all dramatic; now's not the time. Tell me what it was that you saw." He grasped her shoulders, forcing her to look at him. His face was no longer a blank; he was verging on impatience. She had never seen him abandon his equilibrium to this extent.

"It was something in her bank statements. You must have noticed it, too."

"It wasn't my investigation; I never saw her bank records."

"Oh. Well, I noticed that she was getting money from some-where—several thousand dollars, outside of her paycheck, every month for at least the past year. I assumed it was blackmail, and Kenny did too. When I got his message, I thought he must have found out who was paying her. He *must* have. He said it was 'not good'; he said it was 'disturbing'. But that's all he said. Maybe he figured out who she had been blackmailing, and confronted him. Or her."

Kowalski took out his unlit cigarette, and fiddled with it, while he pondered what she had said. "Kenny's not enough of a numbnuts to have taken this on alone; he would have talked to me, or you. He knows better than to go into a situation like that without backup."

"Maybe it had something to do with you, Amos—maybe it was someone on your squad, or in the Department. Maybe this thing *didn't* end with Jennifer Fraser and Corey Taylor."

"Who else could it have been, besides Williams? Or me? Certainly not Eleanor; the idea is ridiculous. And my other detectives—no way. Only Little and Stevens were on duty, with Williams and Haines, that night—and both of them are new to the squad, and the department. They don't go back long enough to know Harrell, or Fraser."

"I don't know, Amos, I just don't know. If I knew what Kenny had been doing while I was away—the last time I talked to him was when he stopped by my office on Thursday to pick up copies of Fraser's bank statements."

"Can you get me copies? I could go to Meredith, but if you could get them tonight, maybe I could start to make some headway."

She nodded. "They're in my briefcase, in the car. I can get them now."

"Not now; let's go sit with Cindy. She needs us."

"No, she'll hate me . . . I should go."

"Don't be an idiot."

He put his strong arm around her, and propelled her back to where Cindy was sitting, pale but dry-eyed. She welcomed Laura warmly, and they settled in to wait, miserable, coffee-driven wraiths, each praying for Kenny's deliverance, each making separate promises to God. At ten o'clock, a door swung open, and an exhausted-looking doctor emerged. "Mrs. Newton?"

Cindy stood. "Yes?" she said, reaching for Amos's hand.

"He made it through the surgery. There was a lot of damage; he lost his spleen, and the liver was badly lacerated. We put some screws in the leg, but it's going to be a while before we can tell if the surgery was a success. It's going to be a long night; I don't want to lie to you. He's a fighter, though; a lot of people wouldn't have made it this far." Cindy nodded, mute. "I can give you something to calm your nerves, Mrs. Newton, make you sleep."

"No," she said, fiercely. "When can I see him?"

"He's in Recovery; I'll take you there now."

Cindy left to see her husband. When she returned fifteen minutes later, she managed a small smile. "I think he's going to be okay," she said. "I just looked at him, and had this feeling. I told him he better not die, anyway, because he didn't take the trash out to the curb like I told him to before he left for your place, Amos. I want to chew him out for that, so he has to get better."

Amos put his arms around her and laughed. "I'm sure he'll be telling you how sorry he is in another day or two."

It was good to have the tension relieved a little; a nurse came out and offered to find a bed for Cindy, so that she could get some rest; her neighbor allowed as how she'd return home and let the kids know their dad was getting better. Amos pulled Laura aside. "Let's go somewhere and take a look at those papers."

She nodded. "Okay. Oh, God—I just remembered something. I didn't call my . . . friend. I told him I would let him know I had gotten home safely. He must be frantic. Give me a minute." She dashed to a phone, and called the St. Regis. Tom answered, abrupt and worried-sounding. "Tom? It's me. I forgot to call you. . . ."

"Where in hell have you been? I called the airline, to make sure you got on the plane—I was on the point of calling the cops and sending them over to your place."

She told him where she was, and what had happened. He was silent. "Someone did this, Tom, and I don't know why. I'm going out with Amos now to look at everything again. Maybe a fresh perspective . . ."

"Laura, I don't like this, any of it. How much do you know about Kowalski? He was there the night Taylor was killed, Kenny was hurt coming home from his place . . ."

"There's no way Amos would have done this to Kenny. They're friends—good friends. I was the first one to drag up Amos's name in connection with Taylor's death, but it just doesn't add up. He wasn't even in Atlanta when the gun-pirating started."

Tom was silent for a minute. "I wish I were there with you. You be careful, Laura, and if you uncover something, keep it to yourself until you get in touch with me—don't go to anyone, not even Kowalski."

"Yes, Tom," she said. "I wish you were here, too."

"I'll call you first thing tomorrow morning," he said.

"Okay. Goodnight, Tom," she answered, starting to hang up.

"Laura?" he called. "I love you."

"I love you, too," she said, acutely aware of Kowalski, hovering, almost in earshot. She hung up the phone, and joined him. Wordlessly, he took her arm and led her to the parking lot. They were parked near each other, so they decided to drive, in separate cars, to a Waffle

House, the only place open this late on a Sunday night. Once there, they ordered coffee, and Laura handed the fat "Jennifer Fraser" file over to Kowalski. He read it, without speaking, for a long time, while she shifted restlessly, trying to get comfortable on the hard seat of the booth. She read the place mat-cum-menu, over and over again, reciting the Waffle House hash brown mantra to herself: *Scattered, smothered, covered; chunked, diced, topped. . . .*

Kowalski closed the folder, and looked at Laura, shaking his head. "She was blackmailing someone," he said. "But I can't see anything else in this file that would lead me to even try to guess who it was. Kenny must have found something somewhere else."

"I have no idea what he was looking at," Laura said. "It could have been anything. He could have spent the last three days questioning Jennifer's neighbors, for all I know—maybe there was someone who visited her at home."

"So, we ask ourselves: Who—and what—would Fraser have been in a position to know, that was worth money?"

"She would have known which cops had drug problems, I assume. Maybe someone in the department was dealing, and she knew about it."

"And you think she bought drugs from him *and* blackmailed him? That would make for a very unusual relationship."

"Maybe it was sex, then. I mean, what else do people get blackmailed over, if not personal vices? Someone was gay, someone was into children—have you thought about that? Corey Taylor might have known a fellow pedophile in the department. He and Fraser might have teamed on that *and* the guns."

"Who, someone he met at the Child Molesters' Guild? They're not social people, Chastain."

"I'm just thinking aloud, for pity's sake—you needn't be so disdainful of my ideas."

"Sorry. But I have the feeling this is simpler than we think."

"Kenny's been working some other cases—maybe he uncovered something by coincidence."

"I hope not, because we can't hope to duplicate a coincidence." He fell silent again, and Laura watched him. She could almost see him thinking, stern and serious. "I don't know how much time I'm going to have for this, Chastain—there's a new case I'm going to be spending a lot of time on. We've had two rapes that I think were committed by the same guy; I've called the FBI in to help in profiling him, and in looking through offender records. There's going to be a big hue and cry over this one. As callous as it may sound, I'm going to have to put Kenny on the back burner; we'd probably be just spinning our wheels, anyway, until we can talk to him."

Laura nodded. Of course Kowalski would have to spend time on other cases—for that matter, she would, too. Life was going on all around them, and Kenny's injury was not being treated as a crime—not yet, anyway, not *officially*. She looked at Kowalski, still frowning over Fraser's bank statement. What did she know about him, anyway, other than that he was a friend of Kenny's? "I want to talk to Amos about this," Kenny had said, in the message he left on her answering machine. An ambiguous statement; maybe Kenny had found evidence that Kowalski was involved with Fraser. Would Kowalski pay that much money to cover up an affair, if Fraser threatened him with sexual harassment charges? Had Kenny confronted him with it, and paid the price? No way. No way Kowalski would, in the first place, be hooked up with a skank like Fraser. Everything about Kowalski's physical appearance—strong, healthy, clear-eyed—and his orderly existence argued against involvement with drugs, or people who used them. Plus, Laura had a feeling that Jennifer wasn't his type, that Kowalski would prefer a woman of more substance. Besides, Amos couldn't afford to pay Jennifer three grand a month to keep her quiet, and even if he had been sleeping with her, so what? They were both single adults, free to do as they chose. She rebuked herself for vaulting paranoia.

"Are you hungry?" he asked, interrupting her reflections.

She hadn't eaten dinner. "I guess so," she said. "What time is it, anyway?"

"Nearly midnight. I think I'll order something, then call it a night. I'm going to call and check on Kenny first, though." He did, and when he returned, he was smiling. "He's doing much better; they're beginning to detect liver function. That's good, apparently. He's still unconscious, but that's to be expected. They might even keep him in a drug-induced coma, Cindy says, to give him a chance to recover." His face was relaxed for the first time that night, and he smiled with relief.

Laura smiled back at him. They ordered waffles, because it was the *Waffle* House, and talked about nothing for a while. Then Kowalski looked at her, a smile haunting his lips. "So, who's the guy? Kenny tells me you're shrouding your romance in mystery."

"Just someone I've known for a while," she said.

"I told Ken it had to be someone you work with. You're not in a job that lets you get out a lot, and besides, why be so hush-hush about it, unless you're breaking some rule?"

"Oh, my, you really are a detective, aren't you?"

He shrugged. "I just hope he's a nice guy."

"Thanks for your concern; he is." She fiddled, self-consciously, with the necklace Tom had given her. She looked at him, quizzically, and tried some detective work of her own. "What about you, Kowalski—what kind of women do you date?"

"Anyone who'll have me. It's a small, but eclectic group. I even dated a lawyer once, an assistant district attorney in Chicago. She got a kick out of slumming with a cop."

"I'd hardly call dating you slumming, Kowalski. Jeff Williams—now, that would be a walk on the wrong side of the tracks, but you're practically a yuppie."

"Oh, thanks. I feel much better. Well, you know where to find me if this guy doesn't work out."

He insisted on paying the check. When they left the restaurant, the wind was kicking up, and a chill rain was beginning to fall. Their cars were parked side by side; Laura's keys jangled as she fished them from her purse, but she didn't unlock her car door right away. She was reluctant to go home. "I think I'll go to the hospital in the morning," she said. "They won't miss me at work for a couple of hours."

"I have to go in . . . this new case is getting a lot of attention, and they would miss me. You'll call me, though, if anything happens . . . if he wakes up?"

She nodded vigorously. "Of course." They stood, awkwardly silent, for another minute; Laura's body was tired, but the two cups of coffee had stirred her mind, and she could easily have talked all night. "He's going to be okay. I know he is."

Kowalski reached out, and put a hand on her shoulder. "He is. He's too tough to let something like this stop him." She found herself sobbing, her arms around him. Exhaustion, worry, and fear had mingled to break down her reserve. He said nothing, just patted her gently until she could breathe evenly again. "I'm sorry," she said, averting her face, embarrassed at her weakness.

"Don't worry about it; that's what I'm here for. But you should go home and get to bed, Laura. Where do you live?" She told him. "It's on my way; I'll follow you there," he announced.

"You don't have to do that," she protested, blowing her nose on a tatty tissue dredged from her purse.

"Yes, I do," he said grimly. "If I'd followed Ken, we might not be here now." He shepherded her into her car, and got into his own. The streets were almost deserted; as she drove the short distance home, she looked back frequently, but the glare of the streetlights on his windshield prevented her from seeing his face.

22

All over Atlanta, Christmas decorations had sprouted. The malls, epicenter of life for the centerless, blared carols over their PA systems, nearly drowning the shrieks of toddlers forced, against their strong young wills, to sit on the laps of strange, red-suited fat men. The festivity felt forced, and false, under the dripping gray clouds that showed no inclination to move on. It was the rainiest December in memory. The weathermen grinned and joked, but the pall remained, day after day, damping Christmas spirits and sales. Laura didn't care; she welcomed the rain, embraced it; it fitted her mood, as she moved between her silent house, her office, and the hospital where Kenny lay.

They said he was improving, when she stopped in on Monday morning, but they were keeping him under, so drugged that he couldn't so much as squeeze a visitor's hand. They had moved him to a private room, at least, out of the intensive care unit. The kids were there, unusually somber; Laura sat in the waiting room with baby Emily and her older sister Sarah while Danny, the oldest, visited with his Dad. Sarah, as wise as any four-year-old, looked up at Laura, and asked, "Will Christmas come if Daddy's still sick?"

"Of course it will, sweetheart," Laura said, tears rushing to her eyes. "Your Daddy wants you to have Christmas just like always."

"So he'll come home?" she asked, unblinking.

"I don't know about that, but Santa will come."

"Will he come see Daddy in the hospital?"

"Sure; Santa always goes to the hospitals first thing."

Satisfied, Sarah nodded. Laura wished it were as easy to reassure herself. Of course, Amos could have reassured her, but he was preoccupied, according to the newspapers, with his new case; the papers had published some details of the two rapes, and the public outcry was just beginning, the radio talk shows lines jammed with second-guessers and instant experts. Laura didn't expect to see Kowalski for a while.

Back in the office, James Scarborough nagged Laura about her failure to sell her Yule Log tickets, prompting her to write a check for four hundred dollars, the price of two tickets, and thrust it into his hand. "Take it! Just leave me alone. I don't even want to go to the stupid thing."

"This is not the attitude to take, Laura," he said. "This is an important event for the firm, and you're expected to represent us with some *enthusiasm*. If Tom can't make it back from New York, in fact, you'll have to take his place and host the Hunicutt table."

"What do you mean, if Tom doesn't come back? He'll be here."

"What if he can't break away from his business in New York? What if the airport is closed because of this weather? You have to be prepared, Laura. I suggest you do a little attitude adjustment between now and Wednesday night."

Laura was not prepared to face the possibility that Tom wasn't coming home; her whole psyche was focused on having him there. Her internal clock was set to go off at four o'clock Wednesday, in fact, the scheduled landing time for his flight from La Guardia. Any alteration in the timetable was going to make her scream out loud—if she didn't break down before then, and scream at Libby, who was even more disorganized than usual, heading into a custody hearing without a hint of a clue.

Laura tried to be patient as Libby went over and over the same, irrelevant point. Finally, she snapped. "No, for the tenth time, it's *not* relevant—and the last time you tried to bring up the mother's boyfriend, the judge sustained her attorney's objection. Dammit, this is your case; you should have a grasp of these details."

Libby rose from her chair, enraged. "How dare you talk to me like that? Your attitude has gotten out of hand; I'm taking this to James, this afternoon. Just because Tom Bailey thinks you hung the moon doesn't mean that you can be rude to the other partners of this firm, young lady—and Tom Bailey can't make you a partner all by himself, no matter what he might have been telling you. There are a lot of us who think you're a little high-handed lately; you should never have been allowed to take on your own cases . . . where do you think you're going?"

Laura had risen to her feet, and started to leave Libby's office. "If you're through abusing me, I thought I'd go take care of some business back in my office. That'll give you a chance to call James Scarborough, anyway, and tell him all about my bad attitude. But you'll have to take a number, I'm afraid."

She left without looking back, ignoring Libby's demands that she return. She closed the door of her office, put her face in her hands, and sobbed. *I hate this job,* she thought; *I hate working with these people—it's only Tom that makes it bearable, and he's leaving. I'll quit, too, as soon as he does. I can find something else to do; somebody will take me on.* She put her head on the desk, and sighed. She stayed in that posture until Cecelia rang through to tell her Meredith Gaffney was on the line.

Laura blew her nose and took the call. "Meredith? What's up?"

"Nothing, really; I'm calling to check on Kenny, and see if you're free for lunch Wednesday."

"Thank God; I wasn't in the mood for a business call. Kenny's better, I guess; they say he has nearly full liver function. They're talking about waking him up, but probably not for a day or two. And I'd love to have lunch on Wednesday."

"Good; there's something I want to discuss with you."

"Care to give me a hint?"

"Nope. You'll have to stew. Let's say noon, at Dailey's. I'll make the reservation."

"See you then." What could Meredith have to say to her, in private? She didn't have time to speculate; Cecelia reappeared to tell her that James Scarborough wanted her in his office, on the double.

She presented herself for a tag-team reaming, Libby and Scarborough going at her from both sides. She said nothing in her defense, which infuriated them. They expected humility, and they weren't going to get it. Scarborough was an old maid, a fussbudget, and Libby was a hack lawyer, a genteel ambulance-chaser. Let them fire her. They were interrupted by a knock on the door; it was Cecelia. "Excuse me, Laura, but Tom Bailey's on the phone, and he says it's important. Can you take it?"

"Send the call in here," Scarborough said. "I think Tom should hear this."

Scarborough intercepted Tom's call, and unloaded all his and Libby's complaints about Laura. He then handed the phone to Laura. "He wants to talk to you."

Laura took the phone, and said hello, her voice barely under control.

"Hello, Grasshopper. Is there anything you want to tell me?" he asked.

"Yes. I quit."

"Now, sweetheart, that's not what I meant. I think this whole discussion should be tabled until I come back."

"Fine," Laura said, "but I doubt I'll feel any differently by that time."

"Why don't you take tomorrow off?" Tom suggested. "You've been under a lot of stress. I'll see you Wednesday night, and then we can all get together first thing Thursday morning, and talk about this calmly."

"Okay," Laura said.

"Let me talk to James again," he said.

"Okay," she replied. "Bye, Tom." She handed the phone back to Scarborough, and left the room.

Back in her office, with the door closed, Laura stared into space. *Did I just quit?* she wondered. *What is going on with me?* Cecelia tapped on the door, and stuck her head in, looking concerned. The secretaries always knew when something was going on. "Laura? Tom's on the line again."

Laura nodded, and picked up. "Yeah?"

"Want to tell me what that was all about?"

"If I could, I would. Something's screwy, Tom. Did you ever get the feeling that what we do may be . . . wrong? That we're not on the right side? Here I am, a decent person, defending Alex Hunicutt, who is guilty as he can be—of something, anyway, even if it's not exactly what he was charged with. And even the innocent one—Jeff Williams—makes my skin crawl. Should I be feeling this way, Tom?"

There was a long pause. "Yes. Living in a gray area shouldn't be comfortable, which is why I've made up my mind to leave. I'm hardly in a position to try to convince you to stay, Laura, but you're awfully close to partnership—lifetime financial security. Turning your back on that is a decision that shouldn't be made on the spur of the moment."

"I know. Thanks for buying me some time back there—although I'm not sure I'll feel differently when I've calmed down. My friend is in the hospital, and it may be because of something I set in motion. I don't think I should be able to sweep that under the rug, Tom."

"No. I don't expect you to, but there's no need to do anything precipitate, although you know you'll always have a place with me, if you're serious about resigning."

"I am serious about resigning, but I don't know what I want to do. I want you here, that's one thing I'm sure of."

"Forty-eight more hours. Now, go home, and I'll call you tonight."

She didn't do as she was told. She went, instead, to the Lexis terminal, on a sudden whim; Lexis was twinned with a powerful news database, Nexis; if anyone, anywhere, had gotten his name in the paper, it would be in there. She typed in a search string: *Kowalski, Amos.* It was a unique name—how many could there be? The screen asked for her patience while its benign demon darted through the data, looking for the man in question. In a surprisingly short time, it produced a list of citations. Laura pulled them up, one by one, and Amos Kowalski's career in Chicago took shape on the screen of her computer: Patrolman Kowalski, cited for valor in a hostage-taking incident by his then boss, Lieutenant Charles Sisson. Detective Kowalski, looking for a serial rapist. Detective Kowalski, again, tight-lipped after the kidnapping, rape, and murder of a young girl. Lieutenant Kowalski serving on a blue-ribbon panel, headed by Captain of Detectives Charles Sisson, to review procedures for the handling of sex and domestic abuse cases. Lieutenant Kowalski, defending the Chicago Police Department against charges of foot-dragging in a race-charged sexual abuse incident. More cheerfully, Lieutenant Kowalski joining in a program to exchange guns for toys and tickets to Bulls games, the brainchild of Captain Sisson, head of Public Relations.

Laura sat back. What had Amos said about the gun-exchange program? *Self-congratulatory. Useless.* So why had he participated in such an exercise in futility in Chicago? He hadn't in Atlanta; the records were clear on that point. She printed out the series of articles, and looked at them again. The frequency with which Sisson's name appeared struck her forcibly; he seemed to have been present at every key turning of Kowalski's career.

Laura entered a new search string: *Sisson, Charles.* The list of articles that appeared was far too long—of course, as head of Public Relations for police departments in two major cities, his name would be attached to virtually every newsworthy case in both. She narrowed the search by joining Sisson's name with another: *Fraser, Jennifer.* A handful of articles were returned by the dutiful machine; Laura read them. The first was five years old, an article about Sisson's inauguration of a gun exchange in Atlanta. Laura scrambled for the Fraser file, for her notes of her conversation with the dead woman— had Jennifer told her that it was the chief who started the program? No, she hadn't; in response to Laura's question, she had only said that the gun exchange was started in response to similar programs in other cities. No mention of Charles Sisson at all—a deliberate omission? If so, why bother? His involvement was a matter of public record. Laura turned back to the computer screen. Sisson had rolled out the program with fanfare; Fraser, then a patrol officer, had been asked for her take on the initiative. "I think it's great, you know, that we're doing this. I think the kids would rather have toys any day, than guns." Not entirely grammatical, but innocuous. The other citations linking Fraser with her boss were more recent, dating from an item marking Jennifer's transfer to Public Affairs; Sisson had commented warmly on the officer's abilities and his high expectations for the job Officer Fraser would do. There were a couple of high-profile cases on which both Fraser and Sisson had been quoted, but none seemed relevant. Laura searched on Fraser's name, without Sisson's; a slate of unrelated articles popped up, most bland comments on cases not important enough to merit the attention of the chief. There was the article about Fraser and Harrell discovering the body in the vacant lot that Laura had first seen in Mrs. Bledsoe's scrapbook; Laura printed it, along with the others. She reflected while the printer spit them out.

If I were of a mind, she thought, I could see a pattern here: Sisson initiates gun-exchange programs, and involves a loyal officer in them—first Kowalski, then Fraser. But why would an ambitious, *successful* man like Sisson involve himself in gun-pirating—on a penny-ante level, at that? If he had, it would make him pathological. Not that it was inconceivable; cops lived on the edge of right and wrong, and some were bound to go over to the dark side, eventually. And maybe the guns were picayune, small change, but what if Sisson were running similar scams in other areas—vice cops taking kickbacks from hookers, narcotics shaking down dealers for cash and drugs, all sharing the proceeds with the boss? It could amount to a significant business, and it would be almost undetectable, if conducted on a small enough scale. But if it were true, it would mean the Atlanta Police Department was rotten from the top down. Down to Kowalski?

No. There was nothing, beyond proximity to Sisson, to suggest that Amos had participated in anything illegal—not to mention that there was nothing to prove that Sisson himself was crooked. Laura recalled her meeting with Fraser, the meeting which had been joined by Sisson. His interest in the interview had seemed unusual to her at the time, as had Fraser's reaction to her boss's entrance. At the time, Laura had written it off to the chief's bullying, imperial management style, but could it have been something else—could Sisson had been involved with Fraser romantically? That would explain how she had gotten the transfer to Public Affairs in the first place, and why she was given carte blanche, despite her inexperience, in the administration of the gun-exchange program. An affair between Fraser and the boss would explain a lot—including the large sums of money in her account. Had she been blackmailing him?

Instincts warred in Laura's mind: Should she call Amos, and confront him with her suspicions, or wait until Kenny was able to talk? Prudence dictated the latter course; maybe she should stop in at the hospital and see how Kenny was getting along. She logged off, and took copies of the articles she had printed out. She told Cecelia she was leaving, and headed for the hospital.

She was met outside Kenny's room by a beaming Cindy Newton, who reported that her husband was doing much better—still not awake, but the doctors felt that he had turned the corner. "Can I see him?" Laura asked.

"Sure," Cindy said, "just don't upset him. In fact, if you don't mind, I think I'll take advantage of your visit to sneak off and get some lunch."

"Don't hurry; I'll stay here until you get back," Laura replied, glad to give Cindy a break. She went into the room. Technically, Kenny may have been improving, but he still looked like hell; one leg, in a cast, was suspended above the bed, and machines surrounded him, beeping and clicking. "Hey, Ken," she said, with forced cheerfulness. His eyelids may have fluttered, but she couldn't say for sure. "I'm going to find out who did this to you. I've been looking at Charlie Sisson—he was the one who put Fraser in a position to get her hands on the guns. I think he may have been crooked from Jump Street, way back in Chicago. He controls promotions and transfers—he could put his guys in every department. And he could afford to pay Fraser off—someone was. Maybe it was her cut, or maybe she was blackmailing him. But, Kenny, where does Amos fit in? Is that what you found out? God, I wish you could talk."

She sat in silence for a while, holding his hand. She looked up when she heard a tap at the door, and saw Kowalski himself enter the room. She jumped, startled; she felt vaguely guilty, as if he might be able to read her thoughts.

"Hello, Chastain. What's got into you? You look like you just swallowed your tongue."

"You scared me, that's all. I thought you were working on a big case."

"I am, but I wanted to see him. Where's Cindy?"

Laura had difficulty meeting his eyes. "She went down to the cafeteria; she needed a break. She says he's getting better."

Kowalski looked at his friend. "Can't tell it by me. Is he waking up?"

She shook her head. "Not yet. Soon, though." She watched Kowalski watching Kenny, speculating what Kenny's waking, and finding his voice, might mean to him. "Have you had a chance to think about Fraser's records any more?"

"No. I barely have time to eat or sleep."

"I looked Fraser up on Nexis," Laura ventured, wondering where she was going to take this line, even as she opened it up.

"What the hell's Nexis?"

"A news database; most law firms have it."

He shrugged. "Technology—I've had about enough of that for one day, with the FBI all over this case. Those guys take their computers when they go to the can. So what did you find?"

"Nothing. A couple of quotes from Chief Sisson." She watched his face carefully; it betrayed nothing.

"No surprise there; where there's a reporter, you'll find Charlie. I don't think you're going to find anything on your database, anyway; Fraser wouldn't exactly have announced her intentions to the press."

"No, but don't you think it's interesting that the chief took such a personal interest in her career?"

"Not really—except to the extent that it was one of Charlie's rare screwups; he's usually a better judge of character. He took a shine to Fraser, for some reason. You'd think, by now, that he'd be able to spot a bad cop. But Fraser fooled a lot of people. Chances are she was involved in something outside the department, anyway; I suspect she was shaking down a dealer."

"Have you talked to the narcotics guys?"

He shrugged. "Yeah, but they're busy, too. And, if she had a regular dealer, she was very discreet about it."

How convenient, Laura thought, that the drug cops were busy—and that Amos himself was "too busy" to look into things! She leaned over and adjusted Kenny's pillow, so that she wouldn't have to meet Kowalski's eyes. She wished Cindy would come back; she didn't want to stay with Amos, but she certainly didn't want to leave him alone with Ken. "Tell me about this new case of yours," she said, changing the subject. "I saw the papers this morning."

He shook his head. "It's pretty horrible; the press is all over it."

"Yes, the paper seemed to have a lot of details. Is that wise, to publish so much? Won't that encourage the man—or even copycats?"

"It's a risk we took; we thought it was important for the public to know something about the way he stalks his victims. He targets women leaving work late, alone; both of the women have worked at Buckhead office complexes. I think he parks near a car, after hours, and, if a woman comes out and gets in it, he follows her, then he forces his way into her house when she opens her door. We wanted people to be on the alert. His last victim ended up in the hospital; his next one may wind up in the morgue."

His face was impassive, but his tone chilled Laura. "How horrible!" she exclaimed.

"Yes. It is. You should be careful, too, Chastain, even though you're in midtown; we've got patrols all over the uptown parking lots, so he may relocate. Don't work late, and if you do, don't leave alone."

"I won't."

"That's right—you've got the boyfriend to take care of you."

Except that he's in New York, Laura thought. "I hope you catch him soon."

"Ditto." He looked at his watch. "I had hoped to see Cindy, but I can't wait any longer. Tell her I came by, okay? I'll call her later."

"Okay," she said.

He leaned over, and kissed her on the cheek; Laura cringed at his touch. "See you soon," she managed to say, but she was relieved when the door shut behind him. "Kenny," she said, turning to the inert form beside her, "I sure wish you could talk."

23

Laura awoke Wednesday only half-rested, but relieved: only a few hours until Tom returned. She was wise enough, at least, to be amused at her own simple faith that his mere presence would set things to rights. She dressed, and put her dress for the Yule Log, a slink of midnight-blue crushed velvet, into a garment bag; she planned to change at the office. The dress was too racy, really, for a corporate function, but since Laura officially no longer gave a damn about the opinion of the partners of P&C—with one exception—the point was moot.

At the office, Laura resolutely went to work on her time sheets, and research for another of Tom's simmering cases. She closed the door to her office, to discourage casual visitors, and the more determined depredations of Libby and James Scarborough—she didn't want to face them again until she had Tom in her corner. Thankfully, it was the day of her lunch date with Meredith; it gave her an excuse to disappear, and head downtown.

Dailey's was located in an old warehouse, hollowed out to make a restaurant; it was one of the few decent places to eat downtown, near the convention hotels, which meant that it was always crowded and noisy at lunchtime—not the ideal location for an intimate chat. They managed, nevertheless, to get a reasonably private table; they had hardly put napkins in laps when Meredith launched into her topic. "So, Laura, you've been a thorn in my side twice this month—first, Alex Hunicutt, then Williams. I know when I'm beat, and if I can't beat 'em, I ask them to join me. Laura, how would you like to take a pay cut, give up your attractive office and your generous expense account, and come work for me?"

Laura laughed. "Gee, you make it sound so tempting. Are you serious?"

"Absolutely. Davis is leaving—I'm pushing him out of the nest, to tell you the truth; he isn't cut out for the work. I found him a spot with the city attorney's office; he'll do a fine job closing down unlicensed strip joints. You, however, are perfect for criminal prosecution—you know where the jugular is, and you won't hesitate to go for it. I know that you're Tom Bailey's protégée, which means that you're probably a shoo-in for partnership at P&C; I can never match the money you would make there. All I can offer is the satisfaction of long hours, low pay, and the knowledge that you're doing the right thing."

"Meredith, I have no illusions about the prosecutorial discipline— I know how many times you have to cut corners, and compromise. You can't tell me you go home every night satisfied that you really *have* done the right thing."

"Maybe not always, but I can say that I think I've done the *best* thing. I protect us from ourselves, as I see it. Maybe the courts are revolving doors, but at least I can make sure they keep turning, and that the bad guys are shoved through them on a regular basis. It's a calling, Laura, and I think you have it."

Laura crumbled a roll on her butter plate, and looked down at the table. "You're hitting me at a good time, Meredith; I'll be honest with you—the Williams case shook me a little bit. I still think there are tons of loose ends out there, and it's bringing me down. Kenny's accident . . . it was no accident. I did my job, sure; I got my client off, but I don't have the power, or the authority, to punish the guilty— and the guilty didn't end with that bullet in Fraser's head, count on it. But can you honestly tell me that I'll feel better working with you? You've closed the file on Corey Taylor's death, haven't you, because it was convenient?"

Meredith raised a hand. "I'll reopen it in a heartbeat if you give me a compelling reason. Look, Laura, it's an imperfect world. Just think about what I'm asking, okay? No rush; it's going be a while before the door whacks Davis in the butt. Just think about it, that's all I ask."

"I will." They talked about other things for the remainder of their lunch, lapsing into girl-talk. Laura came as close as she had yet to confiding in someone about Tom; part of her needed to share her joy with another person, and Meredith was discreet. She stopped herself; she realized that she really didn't want to let a third party into her private world with Tom. They would be out of the closet soon enough, anyway, with the whole world at their feet.

As soon as she returned to the office, Laura put the Delta Airlines flight information number on her speed dialer, so that she could check on Tom's flight. To her dismay, the clouds that were blanketing Atlanta extended northward, all the way to New York; there were delays on the ground at La Guardia, as well as at Hartsfield. Tom's four o'clock arrival was in grievous doubt. At four, in fact, his plane was still on the ground, although the weather up there was rumored to be lightening. Finally, just after five, came the word that Flight 452 was on its way. That would put him into the airport just after seven; he'd have to come straight to the Cherokee Club to make the opening bell of the Yule Log at eight, but he would be there. Thank God.

At six-thirty, Laura began to get dressed for the party, turning her normally orderly office into a shambles of makeup and discarded clothing. As she struggled with her zipper, there was a knock at the door. "Who is it?" Laura called.

"It's Ray Norton, from accounting. I have a question for you; it'll just take a minute."

"Oh, for the love of God. . . ." Laura opened the door, and let him in. She didn't know him well; he was a quiet guy, an accountant in a law firm, who receded like a dull-gray pigeon in a flock of screeching blue jays. "What's up?" she asked, noting his discomfiture at the bra that dangled over a chair back.

"Uhh, nothing, really; I just need someone to check out this payment plan I worked out with your client, Williams."

"Ugh," Laura said. "Let me take a look at what you have."

He handed her a sheaf of papers. "See, he's got most of his assets tied up in stocks; if he sold some, to pay the bill all at once, he says the capital gains would kill him. So I worked out a plan that would match up well with his cash flow—which is pretty good. He doesn't have any debt, other than his mortgage, and one note he apparently pays off a few thousand a month. He's offered to secure the note with a pledge of some of his stocks. I personally don't think that's necessary, given his income, but if you think so. . . ."

"Income? He's a cop, for God's sake—the only reason he could afford us is that he inherited some money. His income is a cop's salary." Laura flipped through the pages Norton had given her. Her own cursory review of Jeff's financial condition had been limited to looking at his balance sheet, not his income. Now, she looked at the records of debits and credits to the cash management account, and her eyes widened. "Holy smokes . . . what the hell?" Jeff may have inherited money, but he also had a considerable income stream—much more than he would earn as a cop, or even from moonlighting as a security guard. His statement showed large monthly deposits, far larger than any Police Department paycheck. There were also large payments going back out—to "Cash": Three thousand a month.

Laura stood, frozen, as the truth hit her, like a mackerel across her face. "Kenny had copies of these statements. This is what he saw ... Norton, leave these with me. I'll get back to you." She dismissed the baffled accountant, and stumbled to her chair.

Jeff Williams was taking in bags of money from somewhere, probably an illegal source, and he had been paying out *three thousand dollars a month*, the same amount that Fraser had been taking in. But why? Obviously, there was a connection between Jeff and Jennifer; whatever it was, Jeff was willing to pay big to keep it between the two of them. She could guess all night what secret two crooked cops might share—the possibilities were legion—but the origin of the bond between them was less important, at the moment, than its implications: Jeff had a motive to kill Jennifer Fraser. As they closed in on Jennifer, Jeff's own activities were imperiled; she would have rolled over on him, surely, to save her own skin. Her suicide must have been faked. By Jeff Williams.

Laura thought back to all the hints Jeff had given her, pushing her in Jennifer's direction: his insistence that a nightstick was the weapon used on Corey Taylor, and that a uniformed officer must have killed him, was a clumsy attempt to point her to Jennifer. And the press leaks—the first two, to Sally Rivers, from an unknown woman, must have come from Jennifer. But the third one, to Scott Ressler, must have been made by Jeff himself, who knew that Laura would make good her threat to expose Jennifer in the press. And that, of course, set up her "suicide." And where had Jeff been the afternoon of Jennifer's death? Laura remembered calling him, needing him to be present at the meeting in Judge Root's chambers, and finding that he was out—and he showed up late. He had plenty of time to dispose of Jennifer, then go get a drink to provide himself with an alibi.

She wasn't absolutely sure she had the whole story—there was a big blank, for one thing, in the link between Jeff and Jennifer. How far back did it go, and what had started it—the guns? And which one of them had actually killed Corey Taylor? Both had motives, if Jeff was in on the gun pirating. And he most likely was; he had a connection to the scrap yard, through his "security" work for Hunicutt and Company. She groaned at the memory of seeing him at Hunicutt headquarters. That should have warned her that something was afoot; anything involving the Hunicutts should be automatically suspect. She gasped, and covered her mouth with her hand, at the thought that jumped into her brain: *Had she been set up, all along?* Had Jeff really chosen her because he had seen her on television, and heard Kowalski complain about her? Or had Mr. Hunicutt recommended her for the job? *And what did Tom know?*

She refused to believe that Tom was in this; she could readily accept Alexander Hunicutt's relationship with Jeff—they were two of a kind—down to the gun-pirating from the Hunicutt scrap yard. But the idea that Tom had led her into this maze was intolerable; he would not do that to her. He loved her. And he hated the Hunicutts; he was leaving the firm to get away from them. No, it couldn't be, and Tom himself would tell her so, in just a short while.

Meanwhile, she had to try to make sense of what she knew, but there were big blank places. She needed help. Kowalski, she thought. Amos can put it all together, of course. She was suddenly flooded with joy at knowing that Amos wasn't crooked after all. He hadn't hurt Kenny, and he wasn't sitting, with Charles Sisson, at the top of some huge pyramid of police corruption. She could almost laugh at her suspicions, now; she would tell Amos all about it, and he would laugh, too. But first she had to call him. She looked up the number, and dialed.

She got his voice mail. "Press zero for assistance," the soothing female voice that followed his terse message said. Laura pressed zero as it had never been pressed before. A click, then another bout of ringing, which finally ended in when a real human answered. "I need to talk to Lieutenant Kowalski; it's urgent."

"He's in a meeting, and can't be disturbed," the woman said, prissily. Laura wondered if this was the same civilian employee Jeff had harassed.

"Just tell him Laura Chastain is on the line," she urged. "He'll want to talk to me."

"I'm sorry, I have instructions not to disturb him. I can take a message, or give you his voice mail."

"Give me his voice mail," Laura snapped, not trusting this flunky to convey the urgency of her message. More clicking, and ringing, before Amos's recorded voice came back on the line. "Kowalski, it's Laura Chastain. I think I found something here, but I'm not sure what it is. It's like Kenny said, though—disturbing. Call me here, at the office, or beep me; I have to go to this stupid black tie thing tonight, but call me." She left her office number, her beeper number, and, for good measure, her home number. She hung up, frustrated.

Why hadn't she believed Kowalski, and Eleanor Haines? They were so positive that Jeff had done it, because they knew him; they knew that he was capable of murder. Still, Jeff had done a good job; even Amos thought Jennifer had killed Taylor, then herself. Poor Jennifer; those nails, that hair . . . she was guilty of something, but that didn't make Laura feel better. Of course she was no saint; she had a drug problem, and she was a blackmailer, but she hadn't deserved the death she had gotten, at Jeff's hands. No one did.

"Come on, Kowalski, call me back," she said, slapping the phone impatiently, as if that would cause Amos to dial her number, but, at seven-fifteen, he still had not called, and she could no longer delay her departure for the Yule Log. Laura called Kowalski one more time, and left a message that she would be at the Cherokee Club. She also called Delta; Tom and his plane were still circling somewhere above the city, in sight, but out of reach.

24

Laura drove north, in the light rain; at a stoplight, she peered into the sky. She couldn't see any stars, let alone one circling jetliner. She arrived at the Cherokee Club, and pulled into the porte-cochère at the side of the building, where the valet relieved her of her car. She checked her coat, and hurried upstairs to the rooms where the Yule Log was to be held. The rest of her coworkers were gathered there already, cooling their heels at Scarborough's command, eyeing the bar, which was off-limits before the guests arrived. Scarborough glared at Laura, and made a show of looking at his watch, making it clear to her that she was still not forgiven for her outburst in Libby's office on Monday. She knew that she was expected to be on her best behavior; she was the Prodigal Associate, her readmission to the bosom of the firm conditional on meek obeisance. She knew at that moment that, no matter what else happened, she would be leaving Prendergrast and Crawley.

The Cherokee Club was housed in a huge old mansion on West Paces Ferry Road; its rooms were furnished in the luxe style of the pre-Crash '20s, with thick rugs, dark paneling, and portraits of buck-toothed patricians staring down from the walls. The Yule Log was held in one of the larger banquet rooms; the bar was set up in an anteroom, where the members of the firm would meet, greet, and ply the guests with booze before they went in for the actual dinner and the speeches. There would be dancing, too: a couple hundred white folks hopping around to Motown covers. Oh, the horror, the horror!

The whole thing was absurd; Laura found herself suppressing giggles when she saw that Scarborough had actually adopted a theme for the festivities: Dickens's *A Christmas Carol*. In the anteroom where they waited, he had set up three displays: Christmas Past,

Christmas Present, and Christmas Future. "Past" was a display of photos from Logs of yore; "Present" was a television, set up with a live feed from the as-yet-empty dining room and dance floor—later, it would be broadcasting the revels *as they actually happened*. "Christmas Future" was the funniest: a computer, wreathed with holly, flashing greetings. It was all benignly, hilariously cheesy.

The bar was not yet open, because Scarborough didn't want the help getting sauced before the clients arrived. Laura wished he'd let them at it; she'd paid for three tickets, and she planned to drink her share of the bar she was helping to finance—and if Tom didn't show, she'd drink for him, too. It occurred to her that she should check on his plane while she had the chance; she scooted out, and down a hall, where she found a pay phone. "Cleared for landing," they said. Allowing for time to taxi to the gate, and the trip back to the terminal, getting to his car, and driving, that would put Tom here in about an hour. For good measure, she tried Kowalski again, and got the voice mail. She didn't bother leaving another message. She returned to the anteroom, where the guests were beginning to arrive; a knot of people surrounded the bar. Laura elbowed her way in, and ordered a red wine; she took it and retreated to a quiet corner. Not quiet enough; Alexander Hunicutt had arrived, and he sought her out.

"Laura, how are you?" he asked. Then, not pausing for her reply, "Where's Tom?"

"On his way in from the airport; his plane was delayed by the weather." Alex joined them, a hefty glass of booze in his hand, and a lopsided grin on his face. "Hello, Alex."

"Hey, Laura. Man, I hope this thing isn't as boring as it was last year."

"Oh, no," Laura assured him. "James has gone out of his way to make everything special this year. I believe there's going to be a human sacrifice between the salad and the main course." The Hunicutts looked at her, bafflement on their thick faces, strangers to hyperbole. Despite her rudeness, they stuck to her like gum to a theater seat. Laura drank two glasses of wine in an effort to calm herself, smiling broadly as Hunicutt talked, and not hearing a word he said. Eventually, they got the word that it was time to go in for dinner; Laura took her place at the table, across from Tom's conspicuously empty seat. Several more Hunicutt executives, and two associates from the firm, bluff, good-natured, golf-playing guys, joined them, and relieved her of some of the conversational burden.

The atmosphere, despite the inclusion of women, was oppressively male; the only women there, in fact, were firm employees and a few female clients. None of the men seemed to have brought a wife, or a date. *They might as well have kept it stag,* Laura thought; *we'd all have more fun that way: They could tell dirty jokes, and I could watch TV.* When the waiter came by and asked if she'd like more wine, Laura nodded. She was getting buzzed; Tom had never seen her like this. Oops. Maybe that would teach him not to leave her alone. While the men ate their salads, and talked about golf, Laura excused herself, and returned to the anteroom.

The bartender smiled at her; she smiled back, wanly. She went to the ladies room, splashed water on her face, and drank a couple of glasses, hoping to undo the effects of the wine. She sat down on the sofa across from the sink, and looked at herself in the mirror. She was pale, but with two spots of high color in her cheeks, feverish-looking. Her heart was thudding heavily; she closed her eyes, and leaned back against the soft cushions. In a few minutes, she felt calm enough to return to the table. She braced herself by stopping again in the anteroom, pretending an interest in the "Christmas Past" display.

The Yule Log went back twenty-five years; in the pictures, she recognized younger, prebald versions of several of the partners, smiling and holding cigars, or drinks, or both. The pictures were all dated: 1972—bad hair year; 1980—had anyone ever really thought that plaid cummerbunds were a good idea? One picture especially caught her eye, and made her heart soften. Dated exactly five years earlier, to the day, it showed Tom—less gray in his hair, the planes of his face smoother—standing between Alexander Hunicutt and James Scarborough. He was looking straight into the camera, smiling without even a hint of his usual sardonic detachment. It was a different Tom. Laura had joined the firm a few months later, but in her time there, she had never seen Tom looking so soft, so happy—even when he was looking at her. Maybe it was just a trick of the camera, she thought, moving in closer, and peering at the photo.

The three men were standing at the edge of the dance floor; in the background, she could see couples frozen in motion. Couples—women? But, she thought, the Yule Log was all-male until the year Laura had joined P&C. What gives? She tried to make out the faces of the two women who were facing the camera; they were young, and flashily dressed—not clients, certainly not wives. Oh, no, she thought—*hostesses?* Would they have dared, as recently as five years ago, to hire call girls to entertain the guests? Apparently so. She stepped back, disgusted.

Then, something hit her like a tsunami—the date underneath the picture. *December 11.* What had happened on December 11, five years earlier? She saw the date, glowing on a computer screen, on a printout of an old newspaper article lying on top of a pile of papers in her briefcase. December 11 was the day a young girl's body was found dumped in a vacant lot, after an anonymous phone call. Found by Tony Harrell and Jennifer Fraser. Such a coincidence. She stepped back again, and rubbed her temples. Too much wine.

"Laura?" The familiar voice behind her nearly buckled her knees.

She turned, and saw him standing at the edge of the room. They were alone; the bartender had left. He hadn't changed into black-tie; he was still wearing his ordinary business suit, and one of the ties they had bought in New York the previous weekend. He looked so . . . *Tom.* He came closer to her, and looked at her, frowning. "What's the matter? Are you feeling alright? You don't look so good."

"Tom . . . you're here. There's something I want to talk to you about. . . ." She trailed off, not sure where to start.

"Yes? I'm here, angel; tell me what's on your mind."

"This picture," she said, pointing. "Why are there women in it?"

He looked where she was pointing. "That idiot Scarborough; he shouldn't have had a camera there."

"They were hookers, weren't they?"

"Call girls, please; it made them all feel so much better about it if they didn't refer to them as "hookers." I never touched them, Laura; most of us didn't. I was glad when we were able to invite real women, when we could move the dinner here, and not have it in some tacky convention hotel."

"One of those girls died that night, didn't she?"

He raised his eyebrows. "What on earth makes you say that?"

"A body of a young girl was found dead, the next day, in a vacant lot."

He shrugged. "So you assume she died at the Yule Log—why?"

"Because I know what happened next. Jennifer Fraser was a patrol officer back then; she and her partner found the body. They must have also found out who put it there, and where it had come from. Now, Jennifer Fraser and her partner are both dead. And guess who Jennifer's partner was? Tony Harrell, half-brother of Corey Taylor, the man Jeff Williams was accused of killing. That's too many coincidences for me—especially since Jeff does "security work" for one of this firm's largest clients. I think Jeff got rid of the body, for someone connected with P&C."

"You're making a huge leap in logic, Laura. Yes, I admit that the firm hired call girls to entertain the guests. Those were bad old days. But as for murdering them and dumping their bodies. . . ." He laughed again, and put up his hands in a gesture of mock horror.

"Of course it's a leap; I don't have all the facts yet—but it makes sense. All along, I've had the feeling that I was missing a few pieces. When Jennifer Fraser killed herself, it was all too neat. Did you know that she was blackmailing someone—or that she was on someone's payroll? She was getting a substantial amount of money every month, more than her cop's salary."

"And?" He shrugged. "Can you connect those payments to the dumping of the body?"

Suddenly, he wasn't laughing, or trying to cajole her back to "reason." He wasn't Tom Bailey, her supportive boss, or even her lover; he was now the Tom Bailey she knew from the courtroom: cool, detached, weighing the opposition's case and pinpointing the weaknesses in it.

She shook her head, and looked at him defiantly. "No, I can't," she said. "But I will. Someone knows something, and they'll tell me, eventually. There were a lot of people at that party, and I'll find one with a troubled conscience."

"And what will you do then?"

"Give it all to Meredith Gaffney, and make sure that justice is done."

"Justice! Good Lord, Laura, you sound like a first-year law student! What's justice, anyway? Is Meredith Gaffney going to raise the dead? Make restitution to the bereaved?"

"Of course not. She'll punish the guilty. Does that alarm you, Tom?"

"No, not especially. You're talking about something that happened five years ago, something that may not even *be* a crime."

Laura shook her head, grimly. "I'm not talking only about the dead hooker the firm hired; I'm talking about the bodies that have been piling up since then. I think that Jennifer Fraser, and Tony Harrell, and Corey Taylor were all murdered because they knew who dumped the body—and why. Kenny must have figured it out, too, and confronted whoever it was. And now I think I know what Kenny knew—it was your pal, Jeff Williams."

"Jeff Williams? He's *your* client."

"Not anymore, thank God. And I think he was really your client all along, anyway."

"Why do you say that?"

It was her turn to laugh. "Oh, come on, Tom—I know that Williams works for Hunicutt. Jeff's smart, he's a cop, and he's not too honest—a perfect combination. Who else would Hunicutt have called when his cocaine killed a teenage hooker? And when Williams got in trouble, who better to get him off the hook than Tom Bailey, Alexander Hunicutt's personal attorney? After all, it was in the Hunicutts' best interests to keep Jeff out of jail; Lord knows what he might have told the DA to get off the hook. But you didn't want to take the case yourself; too many moral conflicts. I, on the other hand, had none—that I knew of, anyway—and I was always bugging you to let me take on more criminal work. You handed it to me, and let me follow my nose—to the wrong conclusion, at first."

Tom shook his head in frustration. "Laura, you have no proof of any of this. It's ridiculous—not only are you accusing your own client of murder, you also seem to think that Alexander Hunicutt and I have masterminded an elaborate cover-up. Can you really believe that I would do that?"

She shook her head. "Consciously? No. But once you were half pregnant, so to speak, what choice did you have? You couldn't turn in Hunicutt for giving that girl cocaine, not without violating privilege and risking disbarment. But you *could* turn a blind eye to what Jeff Williams did; he wasn't your client. You could guess what was going on, but as long as nobody told you, you were in the clear. God, you disgust me; you've split more hairs than Delilah. And you're still doing it, and you're lying to me. Well, no more. I'm not listening to any more of your lies and excuses." Without looking at him, she walked past him, to the exit. He stopped her, and she turned to face him again. "No more lies, Tom," she said.

His face was solemn; he was no longer the lawyer, weighing skimpy evidence and dismissing it arrogantly. His voice broke when he spoke. "It was an accident, Laura, I swear to you; that girl—the one who died at the party—she was drinking far too much, and then she did some coke. God knows what else she had been doing; the girl was a wreck."

"Who brought the coke, Tom?" He didn't answer. "It was Alexander Hunicutt, wasn't it?"

"They came to me after it happened, Laura. The party was held in a hotel that year, and Hunicutt had booked a suite for the night. They had taken her up there when the party started winding down, but I never set foot in that room, do you hear me? I was ready to leave when one of Hunicutt's executives came and found me, and told me what had happened. I tried to get Alexander to call the police. Her death was an accident. No one forced her to take the drugs."

"But they didn't call the cops, did they? Hunicutt didn't want to have to explain where she got the coke. But he called *a* cop—Jeff Williams, his 'security consultant.'"

"I left, Laura; I honestly don't know what happened."

"You didn't want to know, I believe that. So let me tell you what happened, if you haven't already put the pieces together: Jeff Williams came, took the body away, and dumped it in a vacant lot. Then *he* called the cops—anonymously, of course. A patrol car was sent to the scene. Tony Harrell and Jennifer Fraser took the call, and found that poor girl."

"Who is Tony Harrell?" Tom seemed genuinely puzzled.

"Who *was* Tony Harrell, you mean—he was Fraser's partner, and, not least importantly, Corey Taylor's brother. He died, mysteriously, just after he found that girl's body. All night I've been racking my brain, trying to figure out the connection between Jeff Williams and Jennifer Fraser, and now I know: Jennifer and Tony figured out, somehow, that Jeff disposed of that girl's body. Poor, naive, Tony; he probably worried himself sick about what he should do. He must have talked about it with his wife, and maybe even his sweet little brother Corey, before he went to Williams and confronted him. Poor, naive, *dead* Tony—how easy do you think it is to fiddle with a furnace, so that the carbon monoxide doesn't vent properly? My God, Jeff killed a perfectly decent young man, and his wife—and broke an old lady's heart. But Jennifer was a different story. *She* didn't threaten to turn Jeff in; she asked for a piece of his action. And Corey, seeing a good opportunity, asked Jennifer for his own cut. Jeff must have helped Jennifer funnel the guns to Corey; Jeff could have easily arranged it with the scrap yard—the *Hunicutts'* scrap yard. It was all going along beautifully, until Corey got himself arrested. Jeff must have known he would do anything to get his sentence reduced—including turning in Jeff and Jennifer. Jeff was pushing me toward Jennifer all along; he told me it had to have been a uniformed officer who killed Corey. If Kenny hadn't found out about the gun pirating, I'm sure Jeff would have found a way to let us know about it. My God, he was good; he framed Jennifer perfectly."

"Maybe not; maybe Jennifer Fraser did kill Corey—you told me yourself that she had the opportunity. And, if what you say is right, she had as much of a motive as Williams did."

"Yes, she was there that night, but she didn't have as good an opportunity as Jeff had. Besides, Jennifer's dead, and that tells me all I need to know—Jeff arranged her 'suicide.' He was late to our conference with the judge the afternoon she died, and he wasn't at home, either; I tried to call him. He killed her; I'm sure of it."

"Laura, you can't prove any of this. A jury would see these as a series of suspicious, but not necessarily connected, events. In any case, if I had thought for one moment that this kind of thing was going on, do you believe I would have continued to represent the Hunicutts?" His voice was pained, and sincere. If she hadn't been so sure of herself, she might almost have believed him.

"Of course, you wouldn't have *knowingly* participated in any of this, Tom, but there were certain things you made sure you didn't know. Your ignorance was mighty convenient. Still, you could have guessed some of it. Why did you let me take Williams's case?"

"Williams had done some security work for Hunicutt's construction firm: Alexander asked me if I thought you could handle the case. I told him you could. Do you believe that I was part of a conspiracy? Of course I wasn't! I knew you loved doing criminal work; I thought it was a great opportunity for you to stretch your legs a little. You can't believe that I knew Williams was guilty all along—if he is."

He was still hedging, not admitting anything. She looked at him for a long moment, trying to judge whether he had known Williams was guilty when he let her take the case. "No, I don't think you did. I think you should have, but you put on the blinders the day Hunicutt and Company put you on retainer. Poor Tom; you thought you would give little Grasshopper something interesting to keep her happy— and you ended up ruining everything." She felt genuine pity for him.

Hurt creased his face, but he stood his ground. "Laura, please, you've been drinking. Let's go home, and talk about this when you're calm."

"I don't see calm in my future, Tom. I was set up; you can't expect me to do nothing—even if *you* did nothing all this time."

Tom was pale and serious. "What did you want me to do, Laura? I couldn't do anything that night, when the girl died, as much as I wanted to. Hunicutt was my client; I would have been disbarred if I had told the police what he told me in confidence. I advised him to go to the authorities, but he ignored my advice, so I left."

"Privilege doesn't apply to the planning or execution of crimes."

"There was no crime committed that night—that I knew of, anyway."

"Because you made sure you wouldn't know. You turned a blind eye to the drugs, and to the dead body. . . ."

"I advised Alexander to call the police, and I left. Privilege *did* apply to the discussion we had; if Alexander chose to disregard my advice . . ."

She stopped him before he could finish his sentence. "Don't give me the *law*, Tom—this is me you're talking to; I want to hear you talk about right and wrong, not *legality*. Look at what you did: You continued to act as Hunicutt's attorney all these years; you even dragged me in. You know what you are, Tom? You're a vampire. You had this lonely little secret all to yourself all these years, before you mixed me up in it. Now I'm a vampire, too, tainted with privilege, because Hunicutt is my client, as well as yours. You know what, though? Screw privilege! I'm going to Kowalski, and Meredith. I don't care if they do disbar me; I'd rather be able to look myself in the mirror—unlike you, apparently."

"Laura, that's unfair. I love you; I always have. There is no way I would have done anything to hurt you. And I'm leaving the firm; it's over now. Hunicutt can keep his secrets by himself from here on out. We can put this behind us, Laura; I promise you, we can work it out." He stepped toward her, arms outstretched.

She took a step backward, and held up her hand to stop him. "Listen to what you're saying, Tom; you're asking me to turn my back on five bodies—that girl, Harrell and his wife, Corey, and Jennifer—not to mention Kenny, over there in the hospital, alive just because he's lucky. I'm supposed to go off and be happy with you, knowing you helped cause all this pain? I don't think so."

"Fine; we can get Williams, at least for Jennifer's murder. I'll even give them Hunicutt, if that's what you want—that way, I'm the only one who'll face disbarment."

"Who's getting disbarred?" They turned, and saw Alexander Hunicutt, glass of bourbon in hand, crossing the room toward them, smiling as he came. "Where'd you go, Laura? I thought you went to the ladies room—I was going to check and see if you'd fallen in. But I see that Bailey's here now. You must be having some serious discussion, if you're talking about disbarment."

Tom didn't answer him; he only looked at Laura. Laura looked at Hunicutt, and spoke to him, her voice like a whip. "Yes, we are, as a matter of fact. We're having a very serious discussion—all about dead teenage hookers, and cocaine, and blowhards like you who think they're above the law. I know everything about your big night out, Mr. Hunicutt—and don't look at Tom; I figured it out all by myself. Pretty good for a girl, huh? And I guess I need to thank you for the client referral, too; you take care of your people, don't you, down to getting them the best legal advice they can't afford—if it'll keep your sorry ass out of trouble. Isn't it funny, though, that I got your son and Jeff Williams off scot-free, but I'm going to send *you* to jail?"

Hunicutt was livid; he pointed a shaking finger at Laura, and blustered. "What the hell are you saying? You're on my payroll, Laura, and you better not forget it. I will have you disbarred, godammit!"

Laura laughed contemptuously. "I don't care what you do; I'm calling the cops. This whole thing is coming out. I don't know what they'll be able to charge you with at this point; the chain of evidence is pretty well destroyed. I figure you're good for a few months for conspiracy, anyway, for trying to get rid of the girl's body. I think they can establish that much. Maybe accessory to murder, if Jeff cooperates to lower his sentence."

Hunicutt clenched his fists and stepped toward her. "Godammit, Bailey, get her under control. Tell her what's going to happen to her if she goes ahead with this."

Tom shrugged. "She knows, and she doesn't care. Meet your first honest attorney, Hunicutt."

Laura looked at Tom. He was smiling at her, a sad, tender smile. The strange thing was that she didn't love him one bit less at that moment—maybe she even loved him more for knowing him completely. But she would never be his Grasshopper again, and no matter what the outcome, they would never be together again. It wasn't Hunicutt's fault; as much as she would have liked to blame him, he had nothing to do with it. Tom had made the decision that led to all this suffering.

As she and Tom looked at each other, wordlessly, Hunicutt continued to fume and rant. Finally, she had seen enough; she walked past Hunicutt, without looking at him, past Tom, and out of the room.

25

The answering machine was blinking; she looked at it, uninterested. An hour earlier, a message from Kowalski would have been the most important thing in the world; now, she had to force herself to play it back. He was sorry they kept missing each other; he wanted to talk to her, but he was tied up in meetings on this new case. She should call him as soon as she could, and ask for Eleanor—she could pull him out of the conference room, so that he could take her call. Mechanically, Laura dialed his number. She bypassed the voice mail, and got a human, a grumpy desk sergeant. "Eleanor Haines, please," she said.

Eleanor picked up after a moment. "Haines," she said, brusque.

"Detective? It's Laura Chastain. Amos said I should call you; I really need to speak to him."

"He told me. He's still tied up. It's this new serial rapist; the FBI is down here, going over all our old files looking for anyone who fits the profile. Where are you now?"

"At home."

"Let me go pull him out; it'll probably take a minute. Do you mind holding?"

"No. Hang on, it sounds like someone's at the door." It had to be one of her neighbors; no one else could get in from the street without ringing from the security phone at the gate. The postman got the mail mixed up again, probably. "Just get the lieutenant to call me back right away, here at home; I'm not going anywhere."

She hung up, walked into the front hall, preparing to smile and be friendly. Please, let it not be Mrs. Davies, she prayed. Mrs. Davies, the autocratic president of the condo association, was always complaining about Laura's car being parked outside of the garage, or her flower beds not being sufficiently well groomed. Mrs. Davies didn't approve of renters, especially single female ones. *I can't deal with her tonight,* Laura thought. *Not tonight. . . .*

As she neared the door, she heard strange sounds. Metal on wood, metal on metal . . . someone was forcing the lock. She froze, just for a second, before turning back to the kitchen. Get to the phone. Get a knife. Just *don't panic.* Too late. She wasn't even halfway down the hall before she felt the cold air as the door swung open.

"Hello, Counselor," Jeff said, walking in and closing the door behind him, as if he were an invited guest. "You need a better security system; I followed another car right through that gate."

"What are you doing here, Jeff? Let me guess: Mr. Hunicutt called you. So, you must know that I managed to figure out what really happened."

"No flies on you, Laura. But, really, you just got lucky."

"I'm guessing you're here to try to convince me not to go to the cops. You're too late; I've already called Amos. He's on his way over here," she lied.

Jeff shook his head. "No, he's not; he's up to his ass in FBI agents. He's not leaving the office tonight. It's just you and me, baby."

"So what's your plan, Jeff? Are you going to kill me, too? You won't get away with it—I've told too many people. Tom Bailey, for one."

"I'll have to take care of him separately."

"Get real. You can't kill me, right here in my house, then kill Tom, and expect to get away with it. Your luck's out. For one thing, Kenny's going to make it—and he'll tell what he knows, just as soon as he can. Just give up. You can get some slack if you give up Hunicutt, especially if you can tell them where he and little Alex get their coke."

"Do you think I'm that disloyal? Hunicutt's been good to me; I've been on his payroll for seven years, almost as long as I've been on the force. He's been like a father to me—helped keep Jennifer off my back, and helped keep Corey, that little idiot, quiet. He even got you to represent me when I got into trouble. I'm loyal, Laura, to the people who help me."

"Up to a point, Jeff—I helped you, too, if you remember. I got you off scot-free for murdering Corey Taylor when he became a problem for you. What did Corey know, Jeff? Humor me; fill in the gaps for me." They were still standing in the hall; to Laura's right was the living room. Jeff was blocking the front door, and the stairway, but, if she caught him off-guard, she might make it to the kitchen and out the back door to the deck. He had never been there before;

that was her advantage—he wouldn't know where the back door was. For the moment, she stood her ground. Any movement would alarm him. She needed to get him talking, thinking about something other than her. "Tell me about Corey."

He shrugged. "Corey wasn't my problem—Jennifer was. Corey was *her* problem. Jennifer knew about the body I helped Mr. Hunicutt get rid of, because Tony Harrell had found some wino who saw me that night."

"I thought so. Why did Tony come to you, though?"

"Tony was a serious guy—he approached me 'as a fellow officer,' asked if I wanted to come clean. He thought I'd feel much better if I came forward with it. So I got all choked up, and told him I needed the weekend to think about it. Idiot; I went to his house, fucked up his furnace, and no more problem for me. Until Jennifer came after me—but she was a different matter. I took one look at her little red eyes and the runny nose, and I knew how to take care of her. Mr. Hunicutt gave me the money. He never once complained, you know that? He's a great guy; just put me on his payroll, and said, 'Jeff, I take care of my own.' And you think I'm going to give him up? Dream on."

Keep him talking, Laura told herself. Buy time. She searched for a question. "So what did Corey have on Jennifer? Did he know about the body—about your killing Tony?"

Jeff shook his head. "No. All Corey knew was that Jen had boosted a couple of guns from the toy exchange; he sold them for her, when she was short of cash. He had no idea about me. So, I helped ol' Jen solve her problem—she threw a few crap guns Corey's way once a year, and he was happy. He was a punk. I never met the asshole until I arrested him, but I took one look at him, and I knew he'd roll over on Jen, and that she'd roll over on me . . . I did what I had to do. No one was going to shed any tears for him."

Now Laura was genuinely puzzled; Corey had been Jennifer's problem, not Jeff's. Why had Jeff killed him? It would seem simpler to let Jennifer take the fall for the gun piracy; surely Hunicutt would have compensated her for her silence. The answer to her own question came to her with painful clarity: Jeff would always solve problems with force when he could.

She noticed that Jeff was looking pleased with himself. Laura sensed that she could keep him talking, basking in his own cleverness. "So Corey Taylor wasn't your problem—he was Jennifer's. Why did you kill him? Why not let him roll over on Jennifer, and convince her to take the fall—surely she would have, if you and Hunicutt had offered her the right incentive.''

He threw up his hands. ''She knew too much about me, and she was getting out of control. I was tired of it. She begged me to help her with Corey; she knew that he was gonna give her up. I agreed, because I saw that it was a way to take care of her at the same time. If I could just point someone to her relationship with Corey, they would nail *her* for killing him. Worked out just like I planned it, too.''

Sickened by his grin, but encouraged by his volubility, Laura fished in her mind for another question. ''Why then? Why decide to get rid of her after almost *five years*—why did you let it go on so long? Three thousand a month is a lot of money, Jeff!''

Something like pain crossed Jeff's face. ''Jen wasn't a bad girl. She was fun.''

''You were lovers?''

He nodded. ''Yeah. We had kinda drifted apart, but it was good, for a while. Then she started up with the heroin, and it got kinda hard to reach her. She didn't want sex, after that. On weekends, she'd just smoke that shit, or snort it, and stare into space.''

Laura tried to seem sympathetic, to encourage him in this mellower mood. ''It must have been hard for you to see her like that.'' Without losing eye contact with him, she began weighing escape routes and potential weapons. Except for the umbrellas in the stand, there was nothing that she could use to attack him in the hall. She would have to get him into the kitchen . . . she pulled herself back to their ''conversation.'' ''You must have been pretty broken up when she started using the drugs.''

He shrugged, his momentary nostalgia gone. ''I missed the company, but she was never a real great lay. I started seeing someone else a few months ago. It got so that it was a drag when Jen would call, you know?''

Laura found that remark as chilling as anything else he had said or done—he killed his lover, because she was a danger to him, sure, but also because she was a ''drag.'' Still, better that he stay in this contemplative mood as long as possible. *Think, Laura; think. Keep him talking.* ''So you saw her at the station when you brought Corey in that night.''

''Yeah. She was in a panic. She knew we were bringing him in; that's why she was there—to be at the press conference where the chief announced the arrest. She came to me while they were fingerprinting

Taylor, and begged me to do something. The whole plan came to me on the spot."

"So you took Corey to the interrogation room, and you killed him then?" Just as everyone—Kowalski, Eleanor Haines, Meredith—had said he had done.

He grinned. "It was like shooting fish in a barrel; he had no clue I was hooked up with Jen. Just sat there and talked about his 'rights,' and how he wanted an attorney. I picked up a nightstick that one of the uniforms had left in there, and did him, boom. Walked right out like nothing was wrong. I was terrified that Kowalski would go in there for some reason, but he didn't. No one did, until the lawyer got there—which was more than a half hour later."

"And that was long enough to confuse the issue."

"Oh, yeah. A hundred people could have walked past the room in that time. And they would have no forensic evidence—of course, fibers from my jacket would be on the body. I had arrested the sonofabitch. It was a beautiful setup."

Yes, Laura thought, if you want to kill someone, a police station is a fine place to do it. Her hands were shaking, and her stomach was tossing around the wine she had so unwisely drunk. *I can't keep this up,* she thought; *I can't keep talking to him, hoping that Amos is going to get my message. I'll have to try to get away.* Think. "Did you and Jennifer talk, afterwards?"

"Sure. She was even more wacked than usual. I tried to tell her it would be okay, but she panicked when they arrested me—she thought I was gonna give her up."

"That's when she started leaking to the press, trying to make you look bad, right?"

He nodded. "She wasn't the sharpest tool in the shed; her thinking wasn't too clear. So she started all that leaking shit, trying to get me to the point where things would look so bad for me that I'd take a plea. I knew it was her, all along. At first, I was going to point you to her, but you and Newton did such a good job, I didn't have to. Then, when you got all mad, and said you were gonna go to the reporters with the leak about Jen and the guns, I got the idea."

"The idea to go to Scott Ressler and leak her name, you mean." Could she hit him with the coatrack? Not unless she got between it and him, and she didn't want to make any sudden moves.

"Yeah. I knew I had to get rid of her, or she was going to blow it for me. I had thought about making it look like a drug deal gone bad, but the suicide thing was so much better, so I called Ressler.

When the story broke, I knew it would look like she was despondent, or whatever they call it, knowing that she was probably gonna get arrested. So, after the story broke, I went over to her place, hid beside her car, and waited for her to come out. When she got in, I popped up and shot her. Grabbed her hand, and held it on the gun, so she even had traces of powder on her—smart, huh? It was perfect; she never knew what hit her." He said that almost tenderly.

Laura shifted on her feet, edging imperceptibly—she hoped— toward the entrance to the living room. She kept a letter opener on her writing desk; if she could get to that. . . . "What about Kenny? How did you know he knew something?"

Jeff laughed. "That was the big disadvantage of hiring a good lawyer and a good PI—you two were bound to see when things didn't add up. But, after the charges were dismissed, I thought I was in the clear. It was really a coincidence, finding out that he was still looking into things."

"How did you know he was?" she asked, genuinely curious this time.

"See, I was real pissed at Kowalski. I was supposed to go back to work on Monday, but he called me Sunday and told me not to come in, until they decided what to do about a disciplinary hearing. That twat still had her bullshit harassment complaint in. I rode over to Kowalski's house; I wanted to talk to him about it. I thought he should back me up—like he would ever back up one of his people, that dickless . . . anyway, I was there when Newton showed up. He looked real surprised to see me. He had some papers on him, my bank statements—I recognized them when I saw them sticking out of his pocket. I hung out, didn't give him a chance to talk to Amos alone. Finally, he left, so I followed him. Ran him off the road as soon as I got a chance. I didn't have time to plan it real good, so I wasn't surprised that it didn't kill him. I thought maybe it would turn him into some kinda vegetable, though, you know—knock some of his memory out."

"But it didn't; there was no head injury. He's already waking up, and beginning to talk a little. As soon as he starts to make sense, you're cooked."

"Yeah, but I figure I got a couple of days to put my life in order. Look, I know that they're going to get onto me eventually—especially after I do you and your boss, but it'll buy me day or two, and that'll give me time to get out of the country. My money's already there; I realized I was going to have to book when Newton didn't die. I didn't expect you to catch on, too; thank God Mr. Hunicutt called me."

Laura's heart sank; he could kill her, and Tom, and be on his way, out of the reach of extradition treaties, by the time Amos put things together. Jeff was no idiot. There was a moment of silence; he took a step toward her, and she braced herself to make a desperate run for the kitchen. Then, the phone rang. Both of them jumped.

Laura pivoted, and ducked through the doorway behind her, heading for the phone. It had to be Amos; if she could just scream, once, into the receiver, he would come for her.

Jeff was caught off-balance, but he was quick; he was after her in a second. Laura had kicked off her shoes as soon as she came inside; when her stockinged feet hit the hardwood floor, she slipped. He grabbed her legs in a flying tackle; they fell to the ground together.

The phone continued to ring, until the answering machine cut it off. Laura struggled, kicking at Jeff's face, as he tried to perfect his grip on her. She heard her own cheerful message, and the beep. Amos called out her name to the air. *Please, Kowalski, be suspicious— wonder, for Christ's sake, why I don't come to the phone.* It was her only hope, that he would sense something amiss, and send someone over, or come himself. But she would be dead by that time. She pounded her fists on the floor and screamed in rage and frustration; Jeff clambered up her back, and clamped a hand over her mouth. She bit him, and tasted his blood. He kept his hand in place, and jerked her to her feet, his other arm around her waist, lifting her off the ground. He carried her, cursing her, into the living room.

He took his hand off her mouth briefly, and she screamed again. "Shut *up,* you stupid twat," he snarled, putting an arm across her throat, and choking her into silence. "No one can hear you, anyway. We can make this as quick as you like; I'm not gonna waste a lot of time on you. What a coincidence, Laura," he said, releasing the pressure on her neck, and letting her gasp for air, "while they're down there profiling this guy who's been raping women in Buckhead, he's broken into your house! Imagine that! What a sad, sad coincidence. Oh, and he's a sick bastard, too; you wouldn't believe the things he does to women, Laura—I didn't, when Kowalski told me about them. You know," he threw her into a chair, and stood over her, preventing her from rising, "I've been on sex crimes for four years, since I made detective, and I never got used to it. I mean, the women who get raped—old ladies! Kids! Ugly women, fat women!"

He shook his head. "Me, I couldn't rape an ugly girl. Fortunately, we don't have that problem tonight."

Laura, still gasping for air, managed to speak. "The DNA won't match. They'll know right away it's a copycat."

"Like I said, I don't care; I'll be gone. But even if I did, this guy's a New Age rapist—uses a condom. How 'bout that?" He produced a condom from his pocket, and grinned. "Laura, this is going to hurt you *much* more than it's going to hurt me—hell, I might even enjoy it." He jerked her to her feet again, and began pushing her toward the couch.

"Let her go."

Laura couldn't see the speaker, but she recognized the voice. "Tom," she said, softly.

Jeff wheeled around, keeping his grip on her. Tom was standing in the doorway, looking as calm as he ever did. "Bailey. Fuck, this is inconvenient. You're fucking up my whole plan, man."

"I said, let her go." Tom took a step toward them. "It's over, Williams; I've called the police."

"Bullshit. Well, at least I have the two of you in one place. So now it's a lover's quarrel—you guys are fucking each other, am I right? So, you're going to kill her in a fit of rage. Saves me the trouble of raping her, at least—not that it was any trouble. Then you're going to kill yourself. With a knife; it'll be a big mess. I happen to have one here," he said, producing an ugly, single-bladed hunting knife, and passed it in front of Laura's face. She twisted in his arms, and tried to kick him.

"You're not killing anyone," Tom said, shaking his head. "It's over, Jeff. I just resigned from the firm, and told the managing partner the whole story. He knows about Hunicutt, and the dead girl, and about Corey Taylor, and Jennifer Fraser, and Newton. You're not getting away with anything."

"As I've been telling Laura here, I know that. I'm on a plane as soon as I get rid of you two. So you've even saved me some time, Bailey. Thanks. I guess you get to go first."

He threw Laura aside, and advanced on Tom, knife in hand. Laura fell heavily to the floor, banging her head sharply. When she looked up, she saw that she had fallen beneath her saddle; she saw the silver gleam of the stirrups swinging to and fro just above her head. Laura was an athletic rider; she liked a heavy, utilitarian stirrup. The things must have weighed a half-pound each, pure tempered steel. She slid her hand under the flap, and pulled the stirrup leather from its hook, and struggled to her feet.

"No!" she screamed, as she saw Jeff fall on Tom.

In one step, she was across the floor, swinging the stirrup in her hand. It made contact with the back of Jeff's head with a sickening crunch, splitting the scalp and baring bone. He howled, and struggled to regain his balance. She swung again, this time aiming for the thinner bone at the side of his head. The metal bit deep into his skull, splitting it; pinkish matter flew out, splattering on the floor and on her dress. He sank to the floor, his mouth open in a silent question, and toppled forward, dead.

Laura dropped the stirrup, and looked at Tom. He had staggered backward, and was leaning against the wall, one hand on his midriff, barely covering a spreading stain. "Tom," she cried, stepping over Jeff and going to him. "You're hurt."

She eased him down into a sitting position, and peeled his hand away from his wound. There was less blood than she expected, but she had a feeling that most of the damage was inside. She reached into his jacket pocket, took out his cell phone, and dialed 911. She heard herself, surprisingly calm, giving her own address, requesting an ambulance, and asking that Lieutenant Kowalski be informed. Then, reaching into a chair for a cushion, she laid Tom down, and stroked his hair. "You're going to be okay, sweetheart; they're on their way."

He smiled at her. "Laura."

"I'm here, Tom; I'm here. Just be quiet."

"I love you, Laura."

"I love you too, Tom. I didn't mean any of what I said—you're not a vampire. I was just upset. We can go away. Let's leave Atlanta, and the stupid firm, and Hunicutt."

"It was always you. When I interviewed you . . . I said, she's the one. Little Grasshopper."

"Shh, don't talk." She unbuttoned his shirt, and flinched at the sight of the wound. Jeff had twisted the knife, opened a huge gash; the pain must have been unbearable. Where was that ambulance? Laura took another cushion, and used it to stanch the bleeding. Tom's lips were moving, but she couldn't make out what he was saying. "What? I can't hear you. Just be still." She could hear sirens, and prayed that they were coming here.

"Laura," he said, faintly, and the blue eyes darkened.

"Tom, no, don't go," she said. "No . . ."

There were noises at the door; footsteps in the hall. The cops were finally there. She didn't even look up, just sat there and rocked him in her arms, saying "No," over and over. They tried to make her move, but she pushed them away. Finally, a familiar voice spoke in her ear. "Laura, let him go." It was Amos, putting an arm around her shoulders, wrapping her in a blanket. "He's gone; you have to come with me."

"No, he's okay. He's okay," she said, even though she knew he wasn't. So still, so pale.

"Shh," he said, lifting her in his arms. "Come with me, sweetheart; I'll take care of you." He carried her out the door, into the night. She felt the cold drops of rain of her face, and they reminded her how to cry.

Welcome back to the Scott Ressler show. You know what I think?

I didn't know you did think.

Ha-ha. Remember, Mel, it says in the contract that I'm the funny one. No, I think this woman—this Laura Chastain—is HOT. Unbelievably hot.

Why is that, Scott?

Well, just look at the facts: She gets a guilty guy off a murder charge, and then, when she finds out he did it, she offs him. Boom, just like that; no questions asked. Didn't even collect on her bill! I find that amazing. And arousing—she killed him with a stirrup! That's kind of kinky, don't you think? That's a leather thing, right? Hey, Laura, if you're listening, give me a call; I've been a very baaaad boy.

I don't think you're her type, Scott.

What makes you say that? Chicks dig me! And I've dated lawyers before.

Getting bailed out is NOT a date, Scott.

Tell that to my lawyer. No, back to this Laura Chastain—you know, we got a tip from that guy Williams. We can say that now, can't we? I hope so, because I just did. Anyway, I think she wants me. Yeah, I could tell when I saw her on the news last night. Her boyfriend's dead, right? So she needs a man, and I got a . . .

Shut up, Scott.

What? You're telling ME to shut up? That's definitely not in the contract.

Just shut up. That woman went through something terrible, and I don't think that even you can make it funny, OK?

Whoa, the troops are revolting! What bug got up your rear? She knows I'm just kidding—don't you, Laura?

I'm not kidding; let's talk about something else.

Fine. Did you hear that the mayor is taking a trip to the Caymans? That's right, at your expense, Atlanta. Give us a call and tell us what you think. . . .

26

The sun was out, but the effects of the recent rain were still evident; she could hear her shoes squishing as she walked, and water was already beginning to dampen her socks. She tried not to crush the delicate, light-green blades of grass that had just begun growing again after the dormant winter, but there was no pathway. She thought she was heading in the right direction, but she had only been here once, on a gray December day—and then, there had been crowds of people marking her destination. Today, there was nothing but grave markers, hundreds of them, spreading in all directions; she might walk for days without finding the one she wanted. To her surprise, though, as she crested a hill, she recognized the place. It helped that the ground was still churned and exposed where the new stone had been recently placed. She stopped, and looked at it from a distance, reluctant to come upon it too quickly. When she started walking again, her steps were slow and measured. Finally, she was standing above the flat slab of black granite. The inscription was pure Tom:

> *O remember the great dead,*
> *And honour the fate you are,*
> *Traveling and tormented,*
> *Dialectic and bizarre.*

"Oh, Tom, not even a major work!" she said, laughing as she dashed away the tears that were coursing down her face. Of course, he would want W. H. Auden to keep him company, but he had chosen a passage from a poem that went unhonored itself, ignored by the critics and scholars. But Tom had loved "Atlantis," and Laura admitted that it was, somehow, right. She bent down and ran her fingers over the sharp edges of the freshly carved letters, tracing his name and the span of his life.

"I'm okay," she told him; why she felt she had to speak aloud, she couldn't say. If he was out there, he would know her thoughts, unspoken. "It's been hard, and I miss you every day. Every second," she amended. "Did you realize how much time we used to spend together—even before we were lovers? I bet there are people who're married for twenty years who haven't seen as much of each other. I keep on looking for you, Tom; every time something happens to me, I turn around to tell you about it. But of course, you're not there."

She stopped, and looked up at the sky. A few clouds marred the clear blue; the trees, a little ways off, were beginning to green up. A pretty place. "I left the firm. Technically, I'm on a leave of absence, but it's understood I'm not coming back. I don't know what I'll do; Meredith is holding a job for me. I should take it, I guess; she can't keep the door open for me forever, but I don't know if I'm ready to jump back into a courtroom. Everyone is very *kind* to me; they talk to me as if I have some huge disfigurement that they have to go out of their way to ignore. Everyone except Amos, of course." She stopped again, thinking about Amos. "I wish you had known him, Tom; you would have liked him. He has such a *moral* viewpoint on everything, and, of course, you were so good at seeing every side of an issue. I would like to have seen the two of you go at it. He's smart. We spend a lot of time together. But we're not lovers," she added. They weren't, although an awful lot of people assumed they were; she spent many nights at his house, in his spare room, and it was a foregone conclusion, when the weekend rolled around, that they would be spending it together—like this one. From the first, when she had awakened in a dark, strange hospital room, crying for Tom, and had heard Amos say "I'm here," she had clung to him. "I should let him go; he deserves a real relationship," she said, feeling guilty at her selfishness. "I can't give him what he needs. The man needs to get laid, for one thing, but I'm always around."

She fell silent again, and listened to the wind. If she'd had a little more imagination, maybe, she could have heard a reply from Tom, but all she heard was wind. She sat on the edge of the marker, and rubbed off a couple of splotches of mud. "The district attorney charged Hunicutt with second-degree murder for what Jeff did to you, Tom. It was Meredith's idea, I think; she got a record of the phone call he made to Jeff, and, with that and my testimony to the Grand Jury, she got an indictment. Libby is representing Hunicutt;

it's been a comedy. You would appreciate it. Libby tried to plea-bargain with Meredith. I wasn't there, of course, but I heard about it. She walked in and said he'd plead to conspiracy. Libby's an idiot, of course; Meredith had no incentive to negotiate, although she did offer to knock two years off Hunicutt's sentence if he pleaded and saved the taxpayers the expense of a trial. Anyway, Libby's bombarding the judge with her usual half-witted motions to dismiss, and to suppress evidence. She tried to have my testimony suppressed; she said that anything Jeff said about Hunicutt to me that night was hearsay, and that I was an unreliable witness because of my relationship with you. With Libby in his corner, it looks like Hunicutt will be doing twenty to life. I can't wait for Libby to cross-examine me; it's going to be a hoot. I wish you could be there." But she always wished he could be there, every day, every minute.

She changed the subject. "Kenny's better; he walks with a cane, and he's in physical therapy, but he's still Ken. Oh, and your sister Emily has been wonderful; she put me on the board of the foundation. I haven't done much of anything yet, other than go to a couple of meetings, but she's encouraging me to get more involved. I will, I think; with that kind of money, you can really shake things up. I think that's what you would have wanted—to shake things up."

She didn't speak again, but she continued to sit on the stone for a while. She felt oddly comforted, as if he really were there, and telling her that he was alright, and that she would be, too. Finally, she rose, and reached into her pocket. "I didn't bring flowers, Tom; they'd only die. I thought you might like this better." She wound up the metal grasshopper toy she had found at a flea market, and placed it on the stone. "Goodbye, Tom; I'll visit you again." She turned and walked away, while the grasshopper still whirred and hopped frantically on his grave. As she came back over the hill, she spotted Kowalski, leaning against his black Jeep, twiddling an unlit cigarette, anxious, waiting for her. He looked up, saw her, and waved. She waved back.